THE BEAST WITHIN

Between 2016 and 2018, Rudraneil Sengupta embedded with the Delhi Police for a series of investigative reports for a national broadsheet. This is his first novel. He is also the author of *Enter the Dangal: Travels through India's Wrestling Landscape*.

THE BEAST WITHIN

RUDRANEIL SENGUPTA

context

cntxt

Published by Context, an imprint of Westland Books, a division of Nasadiya Technologies Private Limited, in 2025

No. 269/2B, First Floor, 'Irai Arul', Vimalraj Street, Nethaji Nagar, Alapakkam Main Road, Maduravoyal, Chennai 600095

ISBN: 9789360450472

10 9 8 7 6 5 4 3 2 1

This is a work of fiction. Names, characters, organisations, places, events and incidents are either products of the author's imagination or used fictitiously.

Typeset by Jojy Philip
Printed at Thomson Press (India) Ltd

A WORD ON DELHI POLICE

Unlike in other Indian states, Delhi Police does not come under the state government, but reports directly to the Union government's Ministry of Home Affairs. As a result, Delhi Police ranks are slightly different from police ranks in the rest of the country. The Commissioner of Police (CP) heads the force, under whom are Special Commissioners (Special CPs) who head the major divisions—Law & Order, Traffic, Operations, Security, etc. Below the Special CPs there are Joint Commissioners (Joint CPs), but the operational role of heading various divisions and police districts falls to the Deputy Commissioners (DCPs), who report to the Joint CPs. Assistant Commissioners (ACPs) report to the DCPs and head sub-divisions. Officers who come through the Indian Police Service system enter the force as ACPs.

The actual groundwork of policing, including investigations, is done by teams headed by an Inspector, who reports to the ACP of that particular division.

As is expected for a large force, Delhi Police has numerous departments (some listed above, plus the police districts—North, South, South-West, etc.—along with a host of other departments, including Passport Services, Airports, Railways, Narcotics, Cyber

Crime, etc), each headed by a DCP. However, in this top-heavy, bureaucratic world, Delhi Police is perhaps unique in that it does not have a separate department for murder. Depending on the profile of the murder, the case may land up with the Crime Branch, a department that investigates incidents that require special attention, which may be armed robbery or murder or a big scam, or anything really that is deemed fit for dedicated deployment of force and resources. The local police force of each district works under a strictly defined jurisdiction and is burdened with any case that comes its way, whether it's murder or domestic quarrels. The Crime Branch, on the other hand, has fluid jurisdiction throughout Delhi, a lot more resources and the ability to deploy its units to one case at a time. Our protagonist, an Inspector, heads a Crime Branch unit.

I

BAWANA

1

This is where they throw all that needs to go. Like a crushed Coke can flung from a car window without a thought. All day long, the monstrous garbage trucks groan up towards crumbling landfill mountains, leaking sludge, showering polythene confetti, like wounded pigs trailing blood and pus.

When the wind picks up, the dirt cuts through skin, the smell is chemical. Plastic, so much plastic that the ground is thick, shifting under the feet. The carcasses of cars, whole trucks brought to rust. People? People too. Yanked away from other places, from railway stations and demolished slums, displaced by fire or flood or hunger, disgorged on their promised land. People who turn into bodies that turn big, blue and bloated. The one fished from the canal that he had poked and prodded the other day, trying to make sense of who it was, man or woman, old or young. A crowd had gathered, taking photos with their phones. What would they do with those photos? Who would they show them to?

It was different when he was a boy straddling his father's broad shoulders, clutching at his thinning hair as they made their way through the throng to watch the great wrestlers in action. Bawana was a village then. Old houses with old walls, and doorways painted blue. Peepul trees with enormous trunks soaring to the sky, the branches bursting forth with tiny, soft green leaves. Fields that shone with the bright yellow of mustard. Ponds with shimmering, cool water and frolicking dragonflies.

No dragonflies anymore. Only fat flies the colour of gun metal. One day soon, Bawana would be sucked under the garbage and forgotten.

Huh.

Good that on this cold, wet night, he could see nothing of the place. Could not see, for example, the soot-covered bare-brick building that advertised Industrial Cutting Tools from a billboard hung askew, threatening to crash down on the addicts passed out below in the bitter cold. Or the charred hulk of the freakish miniature fort with turrets. The burnt-out transformer with cables erupting out of it like decapitated snakes fleeing a hole. A week had not passed since the fire in that unlicensed death trap making rubber parts for air-conditioning units. Four sleeping labourers dead. The homeless, the addicts, they couldn't use it as a shelter, not yet.

It could be, if he was in the right frame of mind, the Bawana of his childhood. The winters when, wrapped in two hefty shawls, he would sit on the terrace of their house in the dense fog and imagine himself an explorer of lost worlds.

He was not in the right frame of mind.

In the ashen blindness, he could barely breathe, the grey miasma beating at his windows.

Inspector Kumar focused on his breathing: I know when I'm breathing in, I know when I'm breathing out.

The car smelled of acid, raw onions, rotting food and bleach. Nobody's fault but his.

The frame of his small grey Wagon R shuddered as another vehicle sped by, a reckless moron driving blind in the fog. Inspector Kumar considered calling the men at the roadblock: stop the speeding car and throw the keys into the canal.

Next to him, Sub-Inspector Das muttered an expletive and readjusted himself in his seat for what seemed like the thousandth time.

Kumar felt a sharp thrust of violence rise in him. If he could slap Das right now, he would do it, and enjoy it too. Take a man away from his phone, this is what happens, he thought. Fucking junkies.

For a brief second, the smog shifted on a dim view of the wide, straight street. Tension made his shoulders twitch. If only it were Colonel next to him. Bullet to the leg, his dear friend. So many years on the force and now he gets shot.

'Colonel will be very pleased if we get this motherfucker,' he said aloud.

SI Das started at his inspector's voice. It had been more than an hour since the last word was spoken. He was ready to die from a mix of restlessness, fear and bad smells. His knees throbbed. If he shifted his weight, his back spasmed. He wanted a cigarette. He had scratched the dry skin on his calves bloody. His eyes ached from fighting pointlessly against the fog. They might as well have been sitting at the bottom of the filthy canal. What are we doing here? he wanted to ask.

'I've been meaning to ask, sir,' he said, 'is Colonel really his name?'

'Oh yes. His father was in the army.'

It dawned on Kumar that his answer was vague. He made a mental note to ask Colonel the next time they met. Odd that he had not already. Did that mean he did not really care about his friend? Probably. A self-centred man. An empty man. That's all I am, he thought. It was not a new thought for him.

'Sir, what do you think of BCG coming in?' Das asked, glad to have a conversation going.

'What's BCG?' Kumar shot a sideways glance at the young policeman.

The rookie shifted uncomfortably in his seat. How could his inspector not know? Idiot constables, barely literate and straight from the hinterland, knew.

'Uh … BCG is Boston Consulting Group,' he said. 'It's a very big company, a big American company that other companies hire when they want to start getting rid of people. BCG does a survey to decide who they should fire.'

Das watched, faintly disgusted, as Kumar picked his nose while pretending to smooth out his moustache.

He had believed his luck had changed when he was posted from Traffic straight to a Special Cell unit, but this man, his boss, primitive, lethargic, boring, ignorant! Whose son, brother, uncle or nephew was he to be heading a Special Cell unit? Here they were, sitting in the impenetrable night in a car on a highway, waiting to be killed by Bawaniya, so paranoid that he did not sleep at the same location two nights in a row, even slept on pavements like a homeless man. Here, right now, the icy gloom offered the policemen a chance to remain in the shadows as they hunted. What a small hope to hang their lives on.

'Everyone knows about them, you know,' he said.

'Delhi Police is not a private company that you can fire people when you want.' Kumar fell silent. The fog shifted.

'They want to modernise the police force, get rid of the flab …' Das felt forced to continue talking.

A wave of exhaustion swept over Kumar. Delhi Police was short in every single department. Every station needed more officers. Every year the department lowered the bar for recruits. He sighed and peered down his moustache at his belly.

'I am growing fat,' he said.

Das was hit by a fresh bout of nausea. 'You never know, fitness may be a BCG criterion for retaining people,' he shot back.

Nine days since Das had been posted to Kumar's Special Cell unit. Nine unhappy days. When the paperwork was dumped on him, his spirit sank under its weight. Sitting in Kumar's room, poring over forms, requisitions, memos, court orders and FIRs, observing his boss scrolling listlessly on the phone, it began to dawn on him that the Special Cell, for all its resources and 'super cops', was little more than a glorified extension of the Anti Auto Theft Squad. Terrorism was a distant concern, its prevention dependent largely on tips from informants with day jobs in the gun- and drug-running, alcohol-smuggling gangs. A deal had been struck a long time ago: the gangs were left alone to do what they did in exchange for the intelligence they promised to provide, and did provide, if they sniffed any terror-related stuff going down. Gangsters did not like terrorists. A terror attack resulted in a sweeping, indiscriminate crackdown. It was bad for business.

Last week, Das had been out of the office only thrice: once to the Tis Hazari courts to depose in a Traffic case, and twice to catch bike thieves.

The exception to Special Cell's delicate handling of gangsters occurred when a gang member murdered someone from the police. This is why they were here this appalling night, hunting Vijay Bawaniya, the young leader of the gang that controlled the vast badlands of Outer Delhi. Bawaniya had killed not one but two policemen. He shot them in broad daylight, though his real target was a gang member, Mona, who had eloped with his sister. Mona had surrendered soon after the elopement, and was being produced at Tis Hazari. Bawaniya and two accomplices rode up on motorcycles as the vehicle carrying their target stopped at Gate 4 for checking. They emptied their pistols into the car. Eleven bullets. Three dead. Mona, and the two constables guarding him. Colonel, who was waiting for his favourite mango shake at the juice shop right outside the gate, caught a stray one in his leg.

Bawaniya had removed his helmet as the bike came up to the car, perhaps to let Mona know, in his dying moments, who has shot at him. The CCTV cameras had a lovely, clear grab of his face as he fired. Earned him a place on the Special Cell whiteboard that lists police killers. 'Blackshirt', what he was wearing.

Blackshirt. Blackshirt. Madarchod. Fuck your mother. Fuck your whole family and entire generations of it. Kumar's thoughts moved like sludge.

He glanced at the car's clock: 3:02 a.m. Biting cold outside, clammy and stifling inside … except for the tips of his fingers, which felt frozen. The slow, familiar dread of sitting silently in a car, hoping for your prey to show up.

Just twelve hours earlier, a bank official was explaining the reason he could not offer Kumar a loan for the house he wanted to build, when the inspector received a message from an informant: 28.7455247, 77.1022530. Then, another message on his other phone: '*Bacche ko bhej dena, saadhe teen litre doodh ke saath.*'

A location. A time. He stared at the phones, breathing hard. He smiled at the bank man and told him to leave.

A message from a man who would not lie to him.

The first thing to do was to send the lone member of his team who was from Bawana—big, brawny, soft-spoken Sushil, a constable who kept to himself and never stepped outside the boundaries of an order—away on a different assignment. Out of the city. No reason to distrust Sushil, but Bawana was essentially a village.

That meant sacrificing one more constable to partner Sushil, which was always going to be Parveen, a man Kumar did not trust in the best of circumstances.

Not much choice but to put the newest member of his team, SI Das, in the lead car with him.

Once he was reasonably prepared with the plan, he went to his DCP. Time was of the essence. He needed everything in place at the location on the Bawana highway, near an abandoned factory three kilometres down from the Yellow Line terminus at Badli.

Kumar did not like the DCP of the Special Cell, but then, he did not like most people he took orders from. What he could count on was that the DCP was a bloodthirsty man whose eyes lit up every time someone said the word 'raid'. As he heard Kumar out, the DCP's pasty complexion turned red. Needlessly, since they were the only two people in the room, he began to whisper details: Kumar's unit, a second Special Cell unit, ACP in the control vehicle, the DCP himself at Special Cell HQ, liaising with the local stations and 100 PCR to set up roadblocks along the highway. No one needed to know why. Special Cell privileges.

But even those privileges had their limits. The soul-crushing process when it came to the requisitioning of official vehicles at short notice, for example. Kumar needed half a dozen, but could only count on two—his own, and Head Constable Hari Singh's. For the rest, gritting his teeth, he wrote a request letter he had written hundreds of times, got his ACP's signature, his DCP's signature, wrote URGENT in big bold letters in red and found a PHQ-bound person who could hand it in to the office of the DCP, Ops.

Kumar knew it was pointless.

By the time the vehicle request crawled through its chain of signatures, it would be another forty-eight hours. But it was necessary—without the requisition on record, he would not be able to claim reimbursements for fuel or the insurance money in case of damage to a vehicle in the line of duty.

Then there was the matter of guns. They had their Glocks on them but needed MP5s. There were none at the station.

'How is it possible that they have all been taken?' the DCP bellowed at his assistant. 'Are we at war? Why would anyone need so many sub-machine guns? Are they planning a massacre? Get me the register, I want to see who has taken them and for what fucking reason.'

Kumar was even more anxious about the BVs. There weren't enough of those either. Presumably, the war effort needed both guns and bulletproof vests.

With Hari Singh beside him, he sorted through the pile of BVs they had collected, picked the best one for Constable Zeeshan, the man in the most forward position, wrote a small z with a black marker on the collar. Away from Hari Singh's scrutiny, he had kept the worst vest for himself.

Das was fiddling with the clasps on his BV when a sickly yellow glow appeared out of nowhere and coasted to a stop outside the factory gate. A chill ran through the car. Kumar felt the sudden urge to pee. His phone vibrated. It was Zeeshan, the only man on foot, hiding as close to the gates of the factory as possible. Kumar had agonised over the position he was putting Zeeshan in, but it had to be done.

'Two people in lone vehicle, Scorpio,' Zeeshan said in a low voice.

Kumar signalled with his fingers. Das, ignoring the stab of pain in his lower back, quietly contorted his way to the back seat.

'Profile match?' Kumar spoke in the soft, distinct, flat voice he reserved for radio communication during raids. It had the quality of being both nearly inaudible and perfectly clear.

'Visual is poor,' Zeeshan replied.

Kumar relayed the message on radio—via the ACP in the control vehicle fitted with comms and GPS screens to the DCP sitting in his office at Special Cell HQ.

He glanced at the clock on the dashboard—3:29 a.m. He waited. The feeling of wanting to pee had gone and he felt calm and alert.

Das was finding it hard to swallow. His mouth was so dry his lips were glued shut. He slowly wound the window down—a hard shiver went through him as cold air flooded the car. At least he could breathe. His gun was out. He gripped it tightly with both hands.

3:33 a.m. The DCP's voice on the radio. 'Proceed.'

Zeeshan still on the line. 'Stay behind the wall. Zeeshan, don't engage,' Kumar said, 'we'll shoot blind.'

The fog swirled around the smudged headlights. A minute passed. Two. Three. Zeeshan's voice on the phone was a tight whisper: 'Something is wrong. Engine still running. No one's coming out.'

Kumar felt a tingling sensation in his arms. 3:37 a.m.

He reached for the ignition. The Scorpio roared to life. A shot went off, hollow, muffled—Zeeshan?—a small flash of lightning swallowed by a gigantic black cloud.

The Scorpio was making a frantic U-turn. Kumar hurtled forward, angling right, aiming to hit it, missing narrowly. He swerved hard to bring the car back in line behind the Scorpio.

Blinded by the beam of his own headlights reflected by the fog, he could just about make out the mass of the car ahead. Bawaniya was headed back up the highway. Kumar floored the accelerator. The engine rocked violently.

A shot exploded past Kumar's ear, setting off a long, high-pitched whine inside his head. Then a second shot. Das. Kumar swallowed hard, ignored his throbbing eardrums. He gripped the steering wheel. Dim red and blue flashes in his rear-view mirror. Backup.

The Scorpio was still ahead of him, popping in and out of the fog like a ghost. Another 800 metres, he calculated, and the men at the Western Yamuna Canal crossing would block the bastard.

Das took another shot. The car disappeared, trailing wisps of dirty air. They had switched off their lights.

A sense of utter confusion billowed through Kumar, as if he had plunged off a cliff but did not know it. His heart constricted into a tight little ball. He was afraid. The car rattled and groaned as he kept the pedal floored. Only a couple of minutes since the chase started, but Kumar was sure he could not do it a second longer.

'You are going to kill us,' Das said.

'Can you see anything?' Kumar said in a shaky whisper. Before Das could reply, they saw the red glow of brake lights come on ahead.

'Right, right, they are going right!' Das shouted.

Kumar swerved, following the lights. The car bumped brutally onto a cratered field. Kumar felt the air go out of him again, as if he had been kicked in the chest. Das hit his head on the top of the window frame. The pit of his outstretched gun arm smacked into the bottom of the frame. He moaned as the pain shot through him, blinked his unseeing eyes to get the focus back.

'There's the motherfucker,' Kumar said, as the SUV's brake lights flashed again. It seemed an arm's length away. Kumar was not afraid anymore. He offered a silent, feverish prayer: don't stall my car, I am close.

The two policemen could see the Scorpio clearly, bucking up and down like a maddened bull. This is going to end now, Kumar thought.

'Get your hand in,' he yelled at Das. He yanked viciously at the steering wheel. Das did not have the time to let out a scream as he saw the black SUV loom up. His body went cold. The two cars collided with a sickening crunch. The Scorpio left the ground and tipped to its right. Kumar's hatchback swung in a tight arc from right to left and jolted to a stop as the rear end of the car hit a ditch.

Kumar felt his pants go warm and wet. He ignored it. He breathed. He was still breathing. In, out.

'You alright?' he asked.

'Yes.'

'Get out, go.'

Das tumbled out, followed by Kumar. They stayed low on the ground. A shot blasted out from the Scorpio.

'Stop shooting, you fucking idiot,' Kumar shouted. 'Do you want us to kill you? You won't last a minute. There are at least fifty men coming at you. Can't you see?' Another shot rang out. Das extended both arms, fired three shots. Kumar frantically patted him on the shoulder to stop.

'Look outside, motherfucker,' Kumar shouted again. 'You'll be shot so many times no one will recognise you.'

It was not a bluff. At least six pairs of headlights and a whole lot of torch beams could be seen approaching the two cars.

'Oye, Bawaniya? It's you, right?' Kumar made a last attempt. 'You are a man with brains, a leader. Give up. What's the point of dying here?'

Kumar felt frozen and breathless. He opened his palm to gesture to Das to stay put. The sirens closed in. There were no other sounds to be heard.

Kumar touched Das's shoulder: Go.

Das crawled for a couple of feet until he found himself within touching distance of the Scorpio's undercarriage. He could smell the diesel. He glanced left, saw that Kumar had broken cover too.

'I surrender.' A faint voice rang out. 'Surrender. Don't shoot.'

Kumar raised himself to a crouched position. His head spun. His right shoulder felt like it had popped out of its socket. Currents of sharp pain flowed through his neck. His wet pants were ice.

He turned his radio on. 'Don't shoot, he has surrendered!' He spoke loudly, so Bawaniya could hear him. 'Stay where you are, don't move, don't try to come out.'

A swarm of policemen and a blinding array of lights surrounded the two wrecked cars. Kumar walked unsteadily towards the front of the Scorpio. He peered at the spidery windshield. The lights made his head hurt. He could see two men huddled awkwardly on top of each other. The man on top was Vijay Bawaniya, blood running down his face, a halo of light around wet, shiny hair. The other man was slumped under him, unconscious. One of his arms was bent under the steering wheel in a way that was only possible, Kumar noted, if he had broken it. The angle of his neck did not look good either. A shard of glass sticking out from near the lower ribs caught the light and glinted like a jewel.

Kumar's ears began to ring. He began roaring for Zeeshan. He began to scream at the policemen to get the men out of the car. He didn't care who heard him shout. He didn't care that they were dragging him away from the scene.

He had to save that man in the car.

It was past six when he climbed the dank stairs to his home on the first floor of the police housing society building. The sun had yet to rise. The dim light from the single, naked bulb on the stairwell cast tremulous shadows. He had bathed and changed at the hospital. The doctor had given him a shot of Voveran and a clean chit. A police car had dropped him home. Unsteady from the Diclofenac, Kumar still remembered to open the door with both hands—one to softly pull it inwards, the other to turn the key. This way, it opened without a click.

Five calculated steps in the dark, and he slumped onto the sofa. He took off his shoes, kept his thick socks on and lay down in his puffy jacket. His legs did not fit, but he was beyond caring.

As he drifted into sleep, he heard his wife's voice.

'Where were you?'

He opened his eyes. She was standing near him but he could not see her. His heart pounded.

'At the office,' he mumbled.

'That's what you always say.' Her voice was hot with fury. Kumar felt something slithering in his chest, something wet and heavy.

'Were you drinking?'

'No,' he slurred.

'Whoring then?'

'Ahh, you know that's over, it's long in the past.' He found it difficult to breathe. He kept his eyes shut.

'That's what you always say, but you are a liar.'

Kumar thought he was going to kick out in the dark, catch her hard wherever his foot landed, but no, not really. She was not at fault. He was the guilty one, his was the shame. She was right to be angry. He did not understand what he could do about it. He never did.

'Someday, you will realise you threw away the living for the dead, but it will be too late,' his wife said. The anger was gone. She sounded sad.

The dead grip the living, Kumar thought, and the old feeling of grief and loneliness swept over him. He was falling, falling a long way down, it was dark, he had no way to arrest his fall.

2

There it was. The trembling of the walls, the rattling of the windows—the northbound train on the Violet Line headed to Kashmiri Gate. Constable Zeeshan checked his watch to see if it was 7 a.m. already. He closed the notebook in which he was making a list of Inspector Kumar's court dates in his meticulous handwriting, leaned back in his chair and scanned the room.

The big glass-topped desk had been cleared of its usual load of files and papers. The two framed citations were gone. The messy stack of sports magazines and old newspapers had been removed from the corner where they usually lay. The tea kettle, the electric plate, the shoe rack, the tiny Indian flag on a paperweight, the sorry mass of bulletproof vests that were always heaped under the window, the newspaper clipping with a photo of Kumar, Zeeshan, Colonel and the rest—3 May 2016—the day they had caught the DTC bus-driver killer—all gone.

The only thing that remained—Zeeshan had made sure of it, as a totem for the next occupants—was the whiteboard that bore the names of the unit's targets, and their status.

The last of those entries: Vijay Solanki aka Vijay Bawaniya aka Blackshirt, Notorious Criminal & Bad Character, PS

Bawana. Leader of gang involved in extortion, bootlegging, contract killing, carjacking. Recently committed a sensational murder case of police officers on duty (vide FIR No604/2018 u/s 302/307/34 IPC & 25/54/59 Arms Act, PS Tis Hazari).

Status: Apprehended

Zeeshan felt lonely. Five years in this room at the Special Cell HQ, and now it was time to leave. At least he was still attached to Inspector Kumar's unit. A relief. Zeeshan considered himself an outsider in the force, a mild-mannered man with an appetite for paperwork. He was neither old nor new to the profession—apart from the five-year stint with Kumar, he had spent two years as PA to DCP North and another two in Central, a time he had used to befriend numerous government officers and clerks in countless departments. Zeeshan was not a particularly gregarious person, but he networked with passion. He remembered the names and details of everyone he met and people found him easy to talk to. He was effortlessly helpful—if anyone told him about a difficulty, Zeeshan knew a person who knew a person who could possibly do something about it. He would make the introductions.

In Kumar, Zeeshan had found a mentor, a man towards whom, without really knowing why, he felt a fierce kind of loyalty. When the time for a transfer came, Zeeshan decided, he would go begging on his hands and knees to stop it. He went back to his notebook.

The door creaked open. Head Constable Parveen walked in.

'Where's the inspector, Zeeshan bhai?'

In this morning hour, in the bare room, Parveen's voice sounded louder and more grating than usual.

'PHQ,' Zeeshan muttered, without looking up. His geniality did not extend to Parveen.

'Why?'

'Today's the ceremony, don't you know? For the raid.'

Parveen sat down on the inspector's oversized black chair, put his gun on the table. He laughed loudly.

'Behenchod, how much will he get? Will he give us some? Madarchod sent me away on a stupid case and bagged the big one himself, eh? Did not even have the balls to kill the vermin. Who was in the car with him? You? That would explain why Bawaniya got away. Neither of you have any … look here!'

Zeeshan looked up instinctively, though he should have known better. Parveen cupped his crotch and leered at him.

The door creaked again. SI Das.

'Ready to leave?' he asked Zeeshan, glancing around at the empty room. 'What are you laughing about?'

'Just that our sweet-as-rose-water friend and his lover boy the weeping inspector do not have …'

'Don't you have any work to do, Parveen?' Zeeshan said.

'No, Mr Biryani, I don't, I am here to give you company while you polish the inspector's shoes.'

Das settled himself in a corner. He was unsure whether he felt pleased or upset about the way Parveen treated Zeeshan. Certainly, he was envious of the swagger with which Parveen carried himself. He found Zeeshan likeable but slavish, and wanted to occasionally torment Kumar's little sidekick too, but refrained, fearing retaliation. Fucking North Indians and their machismo.

He busied himself looking at profiles of women on Facebook.

Zeeshan, normally good at ignoring Parveen, walked to the whiteboard and jabbed his finger at the red line cutting across Vijay Bawaniya's name. His nails made a revolting sound against the plastic.

'You see that? That's our inspector who did that, okay? Number one gangster in the city, down. When will you do something like that? You are lucky to work under him.'

Parveen smiled sweetly and put a heavy hand on Zeeshan's shoulder. 'It's okay, boss, it's okay, no need to get so angry,' he said. 'Give me a kiss.'

Zeeshan brushed his hand off.

'Will you eat lunch? I'll buy, come,' the big policeman said. 'One would think that you and the inspector have been married for twenty years!'

'Actually, Zeeshan and I had plans to go to Nazir for kebabs,' Das said without looking up from his phone. 'Will you come?'

Parveen screwed up his face in disgust. 'Absolutely not. Meat eating is not for me. Can't even stand to watch it. You go have your fun.'

Parveen took the stairs one floor up to the Narcotics Department. He too had a final ritual to take care of before he left the building. He walked down the narrow corridor to the corner room, the malkhana. Constable Kapil was on duty. Parveen broke into a smile.

'My man!' he said, pulling out the wooden chair. He put his forearms on the table between them and grinned ear to ear. 'Janab, how are you today?'

Kapil looked at Parveen from behind heavy-lidded eyes. Wearily, he swung the register open—unfurled, it took up most of the table. Parveen peered down the corridor. It was empty. He looked back to see Kapil shutting the register with a thump.

'What?'

Kapil shook his head.

'Nothing?' Parveen's smile pinched into a scowl and his nostrils flared.

'No,' Kapil said coolly. 'A lot of the old stuff was disposed of two weeks back. Didn't you see? The DCP came with a magistrate. There was a ruckus. I got indigestion. Fuckers. What we have now, all of it will come up for evidence in the next three months.'

'So?' Parveen tapped a finger on the register. 'Pick a lot and do what you always do, say "rats ate the drugs" in your deposition.'

'Fuck no, you idiot. Don't you read the newspapers? Look!' Kapil turned with some difficulty to point at a clipping stuck on the noticeboard behind him.

Parveen leaned forward to read it. The headline said, 'Supreme Court pulls up Delhi Police for missing evidence.' Below, it read: 'SC today pulled up Delhi Police for "pitiable conditions" at malkhanas or evidence rooms in police stations. In narcotics cases, police often tell the court that "rats ate the seized drugs in the malkhana". SC pointed out that the statement has been used 37 times in the last three months and reprimanded the police ...'

'Next thing you know, BCG will be here and I'll be out on the street with a begging bowl,' Kapil said.

Constable Zeeshan and SI Das were lost in the fragrance of kebabs hot off the charcoal. To not be able to walk out of office, go a few steps and end up at Nazir was going to be a tragedy, Das thought, as he tore a chunk off the sweet, buttery khameeri roti. He brought the bread to his nose and inhaled deeply—fennel, ghee, smoke—before wrapping it around a slice of tomato and a bit of the glistening kebab. Zeeshan was busy squeezing half a lemon's worth of juice on his onion rings.

Das waited for Zeeshan to fully sink into the pleasures of the food—leaning over his plate, both elbows on the table—before he asked him again about the informer.

Zeeshan gave him a sheepish look, shrugged and continued to chew.

'Oh, come on, brother, tell me already!' Das said. 'I saw how Inspector Kumar reacted. You know I love the man as much as you do. To see him like that, to see him lose control like that …

'I mean, I had a hand in that, right? I was the one firing, not the inspector. I want to know too, for myself.'

'I don't know anything, really, bhaijaan, believe me,' Zeeshan said. 'This is inspector saab's … you know … personal stuff, Allah keep him.'

They went back to eating in silence and were soon absorbed in the splendour of the meal.

Outside, Zeeshan lit Das's cigarette, then his own and sat down under a looming peepul whose roots were breaking through the road as well as the decrepit building next to it.

'This guy …' Zeeshan took a deep drag and blew out slowly. 'Three years ago, he saved our lives, I mean sir's and mine. We were walking into a trap. He warned us off, took a big risk to do it, Allah be praised. Don't ask me more, bhaijaan. Stuff about informers is always very sensitive, you will see.'

'That's why sir got so desperate to save him?'

A call to prayer caught Zeeshan by surprise. He looked at his watch. Other voices joined in—three, then four—till the calls weaved into each other and blended with the sound of traffic.

Zeeshan stubbed out his cigarette carefully so he could reuse it, closed his eyes and waited for the azan to end.

Das smoked, his eyes narrowed on Zeeshan.

'Inspector sir has a death wish, I think,' Das said. 'That raid was reckless. I don't know how I am alive. Is it going to be like this here?'

Inspector Kumar stopped for a moment as he crossed the driveway to look up at the massive mural of Gandhi that occupied a section of PHQ. A thing of beauty that injected life into a dreary place.

'Yes? Are you lost or what?'

Kumar had reached the metal detectors without realising it. The constable at the gate had an arm extended to stop him from walking through. For a moment, Kumar was resentful. White Bombay Cotton shirt, blue jeans, moustache, the beginnings of a belly on a tall, wide frame, polished brown leather shoes—everything about him said 'officer'. Fucking low-rank pest, speaking to him in that tone.

'Sorry,' he said and produced his ID.

He walked past the ATM next to the reception and wondered if he should pick up some money. There was a crowd at the machine. It could wait. He skipped the lift and went up the stairs. It smelled of stale piss. On the fourth floor, he entered the area marked 'Delhi Police 100 PCR', and was greeted with an indignant shriek from the grey-and-white cat that habitually hung out there. He poked his head into the PA's cramped room and said to no one in particular, 'Is DCP sir in?'

Two men cradling phones glanced up but ignored him. A scowling woman turned in her chair to look him up and down. She broke into a smile.

'Inspector Kumar, Prashant Kumar? I remember you from a case, five or six years back. A missing child in Rohini, you remember?'

'Yes. Kidnapped by the neighbours. Found her in the trunk of their car. Miracle she was still alive.'

She was heavyset, possibly in her late forties, beads of sweat marking out a faint moustache. Kumar did not remember her.

'I was PA to DCP West then,' she said.

'Nice to meet you, madam. They are treating you well in PHQ?'

'Oh yes, yes,' she smiled. 'I'll tell DCP sir you are here.'

'Thank you, madam.'

A few minutes later, she took him past the long line of policemen, some in uniform, some not, clutching folders erupting with sheets of paper, down the narrow corridor outside the office of the DCP 100 PCR. Kumar felt mildly guilty.

DCP Ranjit Khandekar was bent over a stack of papers, signing one page after another. A man stood by the edge of the table pointing out what to sign next. Another man—obese, blue turban—sat in a visitor's chair with a smirk on his face. A young, thin boy, the DCP's runner, stood at the entrance of a small recessed space in the office which had a microwave, a fridge and crockery. Kumar stood respectfully at the door. Khandekar looked up with a grimace and motioned for him to come in. He signed a few more pages, slammed the folder shut and handed it to the standing man. He picked up another folder, leafed through the sheets, signed where he needed to and dropped it on the floor next to him. After going through the same sequence four or five times, he pointed at the mess of folders on the floor—'Joint CP's office,' he told his runner, 'and tell Sarvesh two teas and biscuits, quick.'

Khandekar turned to the man in the turban. 'Yes, Inspector Singh, as for your problem, first you need to get me the report on the streetlights, no? Identify the dark stretches, note down where there are lights that are not working, where there are no lights at all. We'll take the report to MCD, DDA, PWD, whoever, and then we can discuss the app. Okay?'

'Sir, sir,' the turbaned man nodded. 'I'll take your leave, sir. Jai Hind.'

'Well, well, if it isn't the hero of the day!' Khandekar turned to Kumar with a smile. 'How are you, Prashant? You're getting fat.'

Kumar reflexively sucked in his stomach.

'I am well, sir, how about you?'

'They put me in this awful place, I sign papers all day long, my wrist will break off one day.'

The bureaucracy trap, thought Kumar. If you have the gall to do your job well, we know how to put you in your place.

'How much longer?'

'I have at least a year more of this hell. But tell me, what's happening with you? Bawaniya was a big, big strike. Wonderful work!'

Tea was brought in. Kumar followed the boy with his eyes as he put the cups down and left the room. He stared at the closed door for a moment.

'You can tell me, Prashant,' Khandekar said. 'An asshole gossiped to me about how you lost it during the raid.'

Kumar leaned forward in his chair. There was only one senior officer in the force that he trusted, right from his days as a sub-inspector posted at a district thana when Khandekar was the ACP there.

'The man who was with Vijay in the car, sir, he was my informant, he gave me the location,' he said in a low voice.

'Is he alive?'

'Yes, but paralysed from the waist down, multiple surgeries. And here I am, getting rewarded for it … for destroying the life of someone who was trying to help. Man's never going to walk again.'

'But he is alive,' Khandekar said. He put a cube of sugar in his tea and stirred it. 'That's good, isn't it? I mean, look, informers are getting killed all the time. What's so special about this one?'

'He is my nephew.'

'Oh. Now I see.'

No, you don't really, Kumar thought. His father's death was my fault. I could not keep him away from a life of crime. You have no idea what that guilt feels like.

There was a knock on the door. The lady PA peeped in, looking hassled. 'Sir, those two constables are here.'

The DCP's face twisted into a furious sneer. Two uniformed men entered the room, snapped to attention with exaggerated precision. Stretched to breaking point by his belly, a button tore off the shirt of the one whose badge said Ct Kant. It ricocheted off the edge of Khandekar's table and landed on the floor. The DCP followed the button's trajectory, as did Kant, who made a quick move to try and retrieve it before stopping in his tracks when Khandekar bellowed, 'Stay where you are.' Kant snapped back to attention so hard his whole body quivered.

Constable Ajay Kant was tall, overweight, balding, close to tears. He was in his late forties but looked older. Constable Ram Kishore beside him was of average height, had a bushy moustache dyed henna orange, paan-stained teeth and dark, liquid eyes which stared vacantly at the book-lined wall behind the DCP.

'What am I going to do with you?'

An uncomfortable minute passed in silence. Ram Kishore said, 'Sir, what happened was, Sipahi Kant was thirsty—'

'Shut up!' Khandekar snapped. 'I did not ask you a question.'

Ram Kishore's face took on a deeply baffled look. Khandekar smiled with malice. His voice softened into a lilt. 'But really, what happened? How did you manage to get everything stolen from your vehicle? What did you lose? The radio set? First-aid box? Stretchers? Torches? The fucking logbook? All of it. We had to change our codes overnight.'

Kumar, who had spent most of this time staring at the table in front of him, turned in his chair to get a better look at the two PCR van operators.

'It's a real miracle that your guns were on you, only god could have saved you if—'

'Yes, sir.' Kant found the courage to interrupt Khandekar. 'We are very careful with our guns, most careful, in fact, it's always—'

'But he is at fault, sir,' Ram Kishore spoke up. 'I had to pee, I was looking for a place, I had left the car with him, he—'

'How dare you, janab?' Kant drew up to his full height to face Ram Kishore. 'I had been telling you I was thirsty for a long time, you said you'll just take a piss and you were gone for fifteen minutes—'

'Wait a minute, are you drunk right now?' Khandekar barked. 'Were you drunk that night? Are you, in fact, alcoholics?'

'No, sir, it was a Tuesday, we never drink on Tuesdays,' Kant said.

'Nor do we eat meat,' Ram Kishore added.

'Technically, it was not Tuesday, it was 1:30 a.m., so it was Wednesday,' Kant observed.

'On Wednesdays, I never get haircuts,' Ram Kishore said.

'You are not supposed to get haircuts on Fridays, idiot,' Kant retorted.

'No, Wednesdays, my father told me—'

Khandekar slammed his fist on the table so hard it made everyone jump.

'Out! Out! Both of you!' he shouted. 'Nonsense! Out! You will both be suspended for a long, long time. Bloody fools!'

The two constables hurried out looking stricken. Khandekar took a deep breath.

'There's Delhi Police for you. They left their PCR van, did not even bother to lock it—it was the middle of the night—on a lane in Shahdara. The car was stripped clean.'

'I've worked in Shahdara. I remember the time a man set fire to his own home after murdering his wife. He thought all the evidence would be destroyed. You know how the houses there are, all joined to each other; the fire spread quickly, house to house.' Kumar drew a grid with his fingers to indicate how cramped the area was. 'You won't believe it, even as the firemen were hosing the street, a gang was going into the burning houses and grabbing whatever they could. We nabbed three young men with TVs, money, cellphones. End of the day, one police car radio had been stolen and the fire brigade lost a dozen brass couplers and a few oxygen cylinders.'

'Are you defending those two buffaloes?'

Kumar could not help it. He started laughing. Khandekar joined in.

'Go on, Prashant, it's almost time,' Khandekar said, 'but first tell me, what's the new posting?'

'South District, sir. Hauz Khas thana.'

'What? You got a district posting? Are they punishing you like they are punishing me?'

Khandekar held Kumar in high regard as a cop, a man with great instincts and a single-mindedness that had not yet been dulled by his superiors. But the higher-ups disliked effective policemen and women who didn't stop when told to stop. A district posting ensured that Kumar would lose the autonomy he had in Special Cell and become a worker ant toiling at whatever weary little thing his ACP or DCP ordered him to do.

Kumar allowed the gloomy silence to linger. 'No, sir,' he finally said. 'I'll be heading a Crime Branch Special Investigation Unit.'

'That's a great posting. Why do you look gloomy then?'

'It sounds good in name, but I have a feeling I'll spend my days being servile to businessmen who live in mansions surrounded by barbed wire and go looking for missing Mercedes Benzes as if it's the biggest emergency in the world.'

'You are being cynical,' Khandekar said. 'You would rather be hunted down in Outer by the Bawaniya clan? You'd be most unproductive if you were dead.'

Kumar considered that for a moment and then asked the question he had been meaning to ask.

'Why is it that we don't have a murder squad?'

'You know why. It's not a priority and it never will be. We are in the capital. Our priority will remain security. We are a glorified security company. If a clever commissioner of police decides to shake things up and create divisions that make sense, what do you think our dear home ministry will do to him?'

'All the same, sir, it's a horrid system. One day we're in a gunfight with gangsters, the next day we're rounding up bike thieves and the day after that we're called in for a triple homicide. The rest of the time, we're growing old waiting in courts. The only reason I can think of for not having a murder squad is that we don't care enough about people dying.'

'It's what it is, Prashant. Live with it.'

Kumar rose from his chair.

'Oh, I had another question too. What is this I am hearing about an American company called BCG whom we are paying to help us get people out of the force?'

Khandekar peered at Kumar from over his glasses. 'It's illiterate sipahi nonsense, Prashant. You should know better. We are in government service. We cannot be fired. Now go.'

Kumar walked out. Being at PHQ made him feel mildly nauseous.

II

SOUTH DELHI

3

'Do you know what I hear when I sit in my room with eyes closed at night?'

'What?'

'Nothing. Absolutely nothing.'

'I don't understand.'

'You won't.'

'Help me understand.'

'Inside here, and here,' she pointed at her head and chest. 'It's empty.'

She laughed but her eyes were filled to the brim with tears.

He felt deliriously in love. Her wild tangle of hair, the sorrow in her eyes, those downturned lips like a lotus bud—his heart beat like a hammer. The next moment he was gripped with a strange fear that made his blood cold.

'Don't cry,' he said. 'People will see you.'

She looked down the path. With a shock she realised that there were indeed a man and a woman walking towards them whom she recognised, and who, in turn, would recognise her. She drew her knees up to her chest and buried her face in them.

He slid a couple of inches away from her and looked in the other direction.

Men were playing volleyball a few feet away, arguing loudly. Children ran past with a football, their shrieks filling the air. The park was filling up. A dog came and sniffed his feet, gave him a questioning look.

'Not now,' he whispered. 'I'm busy.'

He wanted to reach out and hold her, tell her that everything would be alright, but he could not find the courage.

'I don't have anything to live for,' she said.

'No! Don't talk like that. You have me!'

'You?' She looked at him as if she were looking at someone she had never seen before. He couldn't bear it. He jumped to his feet and kicked the gravel.

'Why would you want anything to do with me? I'm fifteen and already a whore.'

'No!' His eyes flashed, his voice hardened. 'You are saying whatever's coming to your head. It's not you. It's him. I'll find a way to stop him. I will.'

He realised that he was being loud. People were looking at him.

'We have to go, come on.'

She got up without a word and followed him. They walked down the red gravel path. When they passed the crematorium, she asked, 'Where are we going?'

'To a place without so many people.'

'I have to be back soon, otherwise they'll know I went out and I'll be treated like a mangy dog.'

'Don't worry, we're almost there.'

When they reached the mohalla clinic by the water tower, he pointed to a fenced-off part of the park. 'Have you ever been in there?'

She looked through the bars at overgrown wild grass and a thicket of flowering plants. The wall of an ancient rampart ran like a spine through the middle of the park.

She shook her head.

'How do you get in?'

He led her to a towering black gate, chained and padlocked. There was a grille missing on the gate. He pointed at it.

'We'll slip through,' he smiled. 'We are thin enough.'

They went past a group of young men sitting in a circle, playing cards and smoking. The men stared at them in a way that scared her but she kept her head down, kept walking. Soon they were directly behind the crematorium, where a sea of thorny vines had almost swallowed the path.

'Here,' he said, sitting down on a wide, flattish stone projecting out of the ruins of the old wall.

'You remember what we talked about earlier?'

She nodded without looking at him and chewed on her lip.

'We'll do it right now. There's no one around. No one will see us or hear us.'

'How will it help? Will people believe me?'

'I'll take it to a friend who knows about these things. He'll take it to the police. You'll see. Everything will be alright. That monster will rot in jail.'

She swept her hair back and tied it deftly with a band that she was wearing around her wrist. She took a deep breath and looked up at him.

'I'm ready.'

Head Constable Parveen Tomar looked at his reflection with a happy spark in his eyes. He felt well-slept. Two months had passed in a tranquil lull. He leaned in towards the mirror, ran a finger over his moustache, rubbed his jaw to feel the smoothness of the shave. Straightening up to his full six feet and one inch, he loosely coiled his chequered keffiyeh around his neck. He looked good. His arms looked big. His white cotton shirt was spotless. His bright pink pants were tight, his pistol bulged out of the waistband.

A red silk cord, with one of its ends attached to the butt of the gun, the other end clipped to his belt, added another dash of colour.

'Arrey, sir, you look just like Singham,' said the rotund barber, beaming at the mirror. 'Should I get you tea? Momos?'

'I thought you would be closed today,' Parveen said. 'Aren't you closed on Fridays?'

'Yes, but I wished to see your handsome face today.'

'Your wish has been fulfilled … that's me, fulfilling wishes,' Parveen said, leering. He moved closer to the barber, put a hefty hand on the back of his neck. He looked at the only other person in the shop, a young apprentice watching a movie on his phone, snapped his fingers to get his attention, gestured for him to get out. He looked the fat barber in the eyes and grinned again.

'Listen to me, Anwar,' he said, bringing his face to within an inch of the short, sweating man's. 'Have you memorised my number?'

Anwar made slight, reluctant movements with his head.

'Why not? Repeat after me, 8816767819.'

'8816767819.' Anwar giggled nervously.

'A magic chant, an incantation,' Parveen said. 'When you are in trouble, when your fat nose is being smashed to the ground, who will you call?'

'You …'

'Yes, that's exactly right. Now give me my gift.'

'Wha …'

'The fucking charas, you motherfucker. Either you reach under that shelf there and bring it out yourself, or I start breaking stuff. Don't act dumb. It's insulting to me. I get hurt quickly. I get angry when I get hurt. You are my Musalman brother. What are you?'

'Your Musalman brother.'

Parveen let him loose. Anwar shuffled down the narrow length of his small shop and reached up to the top shelf.

'Yes. I'll come to your house for Eid and you'll treat me to paneer biryani. What will you feed me?'

'Paneer biryani.'

'When I come to your house, I'll say hello to your brother. What's his name?'

'Uhh …' Trying not to look at himself or at the reflection of the policeman in the wall-length mirror, Anwar strained on tiptoe to bring out a rectangular plastic box.

'His name is Danish. You should try to remember your brother's name. I know that you are an honest barber, a good man. You do your namaz, you take care of your old mother. You sell charas on the side, no one fucking cares about that shit. But Danish is another story, isn't he? A bit crazy, headstrong?'

'Yes, headstrong.' Anwar opened the box, took out a disc of shiny black charas, a tolah's worth, wrapped in clingfilm.

'He makes a lot of money selling all kinds of drugs. But I'm a kind man, I'm good to my friends, so I'll let you two be. In return, all you have to do is give me information when I need it. Burglaries. Car theft. Organised motherfuckers, not small-time shit like you and Danish. Anyone hoarding or moving large sums of money. Anyone planning to kill anyone, you get a whiff of it, you call me. Okay?'

'Okay.' Anwar handed the disc over, finally looking Parveen in the eye. The policeman scratched at the plastic, brought the disc to his nose and inhaled deeply.

'Ahh,' he sighed. 'The good stuff. Thank you, you didn't have to do this.

'What I'm telling you, it's for your own good, you understand? A chance to be of use to your country, show patriotism. You clearly eat well, now you will sleep well.'

Parveen exited the shop smiling to himself. He looked left and right down the narrow lane, eyed a young girl passing by, wondered if he had the time to smoke a joint. It was a bit early in the day, but this was South Delhi, they had so little to do anyway.

Parveen's phone rang.

'Are you close by?' It was SI Das.

'Yes.'

'Caught one of the motorbike thieves from that gang we were tracking. Come down to the station?'

'Five minutes.'

Parveen got on his motorcycle, adjusted his gun, admired himself in the rear-view mirror and rode away at a reckless speed through the narrow lanes with his thumb pressed down on his horn.

Inspector Kumar and Constable Zeeshan pored over the shiny prospectus forms from Chaudhary Charan Singh University in their room at Hauz Khas police station.

'CCS,' Kumar muttered under his breath, peering at the prospectus through the little reading glasses perched on his nose. 'There's Café Coffee Day, CCD, and then there's CCS.'

'My university is called Bra,' Zeeshan said. 'Bhimrao Ambedkar.'

The inspector looked up and smiled. This posting was not going badly. He would go so far as to say that it had been a bit of a vacation. Every day, as he drove to work, Kishore or Rafi on the stereo, sometimes punctuated by Nusrat, he felt grateful for having time on his hands. He did not miss the murder and mayhem of Outer, the endless flow of shootings, stabbings, rape, robbery, drugs and bodies fished out of canals as much as he had thought he would. He had even stopped scrolling through the murder photos that swarmed the police WhatsApp groups. He had his moments of boredom, yes, but he had found one good case to keep him busy, and found the desire to get a law degree, long on the shelf, return.

Zeeshan read the application letter he had typed out and handed it to Kumar.

'Who does it go to?' Zeeshan asked.

'DCP Crime Branch will clear it, doesn't have to go beyond that.'

'What about our DCP South?'

'We'll send him a copy once we get clearances. But first go tell ACP madam that we are sending this request to the boss. Go now. She should be in the loop.'

'You're in a real hurry, sir.'

'What's the point in waiting? It has to be done anyway.'

Kumar squinted at the application letter, holding the paper at arm's length. He patted his pocket for a pen, took it out, signed the letter.

'The LLB, Allah keep you, will really help.' Zeeshan felt proud of his boss. 'BCG will not be able to touch you.'

'There's no point worrying about BCG, it's not in our hands, although I've been told that news is untrue.'

'If they come, you'll have to save me, sir.'

Kumar made no comment. After a while he said, 'What we need is Evidence Act, CrPC, Criminal Law … but LLB courses begin with Torts.'

'Tarts?'

'Torts … Law of Contracts … stuff about when companies or factories fuck over their workers, you know.'

'What will we do with that?'

'Yeah. We don't get to the criminal stuff till the second year. Anyway …' Kumar handed Zeeshan the prospectus. 'Call that number, ask when the classes begin. Oh, and don't forget to say we're from Delhi Police, they have a separate system for us.'

Constable Hari Singh knocked on the door and let himself in. He was a heavy man, but he moved easily. He wore small reading glasses on his hawkish nose, exactly like the ones Kumar was wearing. He was leading a team in making the chargesheet for the case that Kumar and his unit had taken up when they moved here, a cheating scam for a government recruitment exam called the SSC, or Staff Selection Commission.

'I am absolutely drowning in this case,' Hari Singh spat his words out, like he did when he was stressed. 'There's no bottom to this well. We can't do this on time.'

'Why? How far have you got?' asked Kumar. 'We only have eight more days.'

'We have sixty or seventy thousand pages to go through. Forensics says they can't give us the report on the hard drives for another two weeks, so that means they won't send it for a month. We have eleven accused. Eleven! Each one needs a separate chargesheet. I can't see how we'll make it in time.'

Kumar stared at Hari Singh and chewed his lower lip. 'Can we add Section 409? Go to court tomorrow, make the appeal, see if they will give us ninety days.'

Hari Singh looked down at his fingers and thought for a moment, looking miserable. He should have been a farmer. His father was a farmer, so was his grandfather, half a dozen of his uncles and two of his four brothers. They had their struggles, but they also spent most of the year sleeping two hours in the afternoon after an enormous lunch. Hari Singh popped acid blockers every morning and ate boiled food. He was going to turn fifty in a couple of months, two years older than Kumar. His doctor's advice to him was to reduce the stress in his life. Hari Singh laughed out loud at the thought. Kumar frowned at him.

'Okay,' Hari Singh said, 'they were acting as a well-oiled team, maybe we won't chargesheet all eleven separately. But who do we name as the ringleader?'

'That's up to you,' Kumar said. 'What about that guy Gurvinder? Best educated of the lot, speaks good English, knows his software, he's a likely candidate.'

'But his father is in UP Police, no? He came to meet you that day, remember?'

'So what? Don't worry about that. If you think the judge will be convinced, make him your main accused. We can change it as we get deeper into the case. Give him an alias to make it sound more authentic. Gurvinder alias ... Guru! I'll take care of the rest.'

'Okay, sir.'

'Where is Sushil?' Kumar asked. 'Still in Sonepat? If he hasn't caught his man yet, tell him to come back tonight and help you. Zeeshan and I will go to court tomorrow to file the 409.'

Hari Singh left the room.

The door that doesn't creak, Kumar thought. Strange, the things you miss.

SI Das came in holding a thin young boy of about eighteen by the scruff of the neck.

'Caught this one with a stolen motorbike, sir.'

Kumar looked up at the boy over his reading glasses.

'You've got the bike?'

'Sir, Yamaha FZ.'

'Checked the registration with Auto Theft?'

'Stolen.'

'This one's comrades?'

'He was with one other boy who got away.'

Kumar looked the boy up and down. Dressed in frayed jeans, an old, tattered shirt too large for him, seriously underfed, or more likely, a junkie. Eyes trained on his feet. Hands clasped together in front of his crotch as if he expected to be hit there.

Kumar took off his glasses and leaned back in his chair.

'Will you speak or do we have to beat you up?'

The boy began to cry.

'Sir, I don't know anything … some boys gave me the bike …'

'Why did they give it to you?'

'Said, get the bike sold …'

'To you? Why? Do you sell bikes? Is that your business?'

'Not to me, to this other boy, they gave it to him.'

'How did it come to you?'

'Sir, I was with him, I know him …'

'Where is the other boy now?'

'I don't know, sir, he told me to wait with the bike and disappeared.'

'You don't know where he is or where he lives?'

'No, sir.'

'You are not making sense, you know that? What do you do for a living?'

'I used to work in a factory making toys for babies.'

'Now?'

'Now, nothing. I am looking for a job.'

'Are you married?'

'No, sir.'

'How old are you?'

'Twenty … no, twenty-two.'

Parveen walked into the room, strode straight up to the boy and grabbed his thin neck in a vicious grip. 'This guy won't talk,' he said.

The boy folded his hands together and whimpered.

'Speak properly,' Parveen bellowed. 'What's your name?'

'Arun.'

Parveen slapped him in the face. He stopped crying.

'Arun, listen,' he said. 'This work is mainly done by Muslims. You are a Hindu, why are you involved in stealing bikes? Don't let this get worse for you. Cooperate. You can't move up in life if you are not nice to the police.'

'No, sir, I have nothing to do with …'

Parveen slapped him again.

'So, you will get beaten up, you will talk eventually, unnecessarily you will harm your body.'

'Let's make him talk,' Das said.

Parveen, with a gleam in his eyes, propelled the boy by his neck out of the room. Das was following them when Kumar called him back.

'Das, you are sure he was stealing?'

'The bike is stolen for sure. He was on it with the other boy, he's not lying about that. I was watching them. The other boy walked away before I reached them. So, it's either him or the other guy, or most likely both, who do the stealing. Of course, someone else controls them.'

'Okay, get names. But be careful. Keep it under control. The boy is weak, he won't be able to take too much.'

'Yes, sir.' Das went off grinning.

Kumar sent Zeeshan away. He wanted to be alone. There was a time when he saw these beatings as simply a part of his work, no different from attending meetings or making phone calls.

Now Kumar felt a revulsion for the work he did, for having to provoke betrayal. He felt … he was not sure what he felt.

The rough hands taught to slap and punch, the boots meant to deliver kicks, the stick, the gun, a voice trained for threats and insults. He was tired of it.

4

All in all, reflected Ct Kant, they had got off easy. He smiled to himself and massaged his neck. He wanted to reward himself with something. But what? It was four in the morning. He could barely keep awake. He nudged Ct Kishore, who was snoring with his mouth open in the driver's seat. It had no effect. Kant opened the door of the car gently and stepped outside. He leaned against the side, lit a beedi.

It was their second day back at work after two months' suspension. They had expected to be shunted to guard duty. Instead, because of a severe shortage of staff, they found themselves back behind the wheel of a PCR van.

Kant and Kishore had been policemen for twenty-seven years and spent the last nine of those inside a PCR van. They loved everything about it. The crackle of the radio, the banter that went on through the shift, the way they could sink into the comfortable seats of the Toyota Innova. Or, their favourite, sounding the siren for no reason but to feel like they owned the street. Sometimes they flicked it on in quiet lanes, late at night, PA cranked to full, just for laughs.

Kishore loved to drive and especially liked the patrol protocol of cruising, very slowly, in second gear. When he did that, he imagined the car had a life of its own, it was driving itself, and he spoke to the car under his breath.

Kant had his own love—filling the call ledger with his fastidious handwriting. For as long as he could remember, he had been fascinated by penmanship. His grandfather used to be a scribe back in the day, writing letters for those who were illiterate or not literate enough.

Kant and Kishore loved night shifts and could not understand why so many of their colleagues did not. Most nights passed without incident. What they loved most was finding the perfect spot to park and kill time. In this, they were aesthetes of the highest order. Put them in any zone in the city, they could lead you to an old tree with a generous canopy, an ancient ruin with cold stones or a narrow lane off an overcrowded, unruly road where the city and its sounds abruptly ceased to exist.

They would park their car, sit back, smoke a beedi, talk of old times. Or simply go to sleep.

They were at such a place right now. Their vehicle stood next to the remains of a thirteenth-century wall. The drooping leaves of an enormous neem caressed the roof of the car.

Behind them was Shahpur Jat, a small 'urban village', thin, meandering lanes squeezed by stolid, chaotic houses that ran wall-to-wall. The buildings were granted life by the bewildering variety of small shops that they hosted at the street level. Kant and Kishore loved these villages that dotted the city—there was hardly one where they did not have a close friend or family member. Indeed, both of them lived in such neighbourhoods—Kant in Khirki, Kishore in Mahipalpur. They had witnessed the transformation of their old agricultural lands. Wheat and sugarcane fields swallowed by roads and highways; hotels, apartment complexes and city parks where their cattle once grazed.

To their right and ahead lay Panchsheel, a neighbourhood of sprawling houses with pretty gardens, wide, well-spaced roads and shady trees. Kant and Kishore found no joy in places like that.

In the dim glow of a streetlight, Kant could see fruit bats flying in and out of the canopy of a gnarly pilkhan a few metres ahead. He wondered if bats really did drink blood. They always seemed to be eating fruit.

Kant felt hungry.

He was startled by the radio coming to life.

'Leo three-two, Leo three-two.'

Kant slipped back into his seat and picked up the set. He looked at Kishore and gave him a hard shove.

Kishore spluttered awake.

'Leo one, Leo three-two, carry on, janab,' Kant said.

'Leo three-two, report of a dead body at house number 327, Block C, Panchsheel Park. Caller is saying the body is on top of a wall. Please get there immediately.'

'Roger, janab. Please repeat the house number?'

'327, Leo three-two.'

'And the block?'

'Block C.'

'You are sure it's Panchsheel Park and not Panchsheel something else? There are these different places here … Panchsheel Enclave, Panchsheel Colony, Panchsheel Vihar.'

'Leo three-two, why don't I come over, we can get chai, look at a map and discuss exactly where this house is?'

'Roger, janab.'

'Just start moving, Leo three-two. Where are you? Is your zone location not Panchsheel P4?'

'Yes, yes, janab, moving.' Kant noted the call time in the register. It was 4:27 a.m., 3 April.

Kishore started the car as the radio continued to issue instructions—the report of a dead body was no small matter. More PCR vehicles were directed to the scene. Local police was informed.

'Left?' he asked.

'No, right, the one up ahead. 327 should be really close. Right, then immediately left, I think.' Kant had a photographic memory of street layouts and house numbers.

'Yes, look, it's 319 right here, take the left,' Kant said. 'What do we do if there really is a dead body?'

Kishore, who was still feeling the effects of being rudely awoken, was jittery.

'We do nothing, of course!' Kishore said. 'We do what we always do: report back, sit tight, wait for LP to arrive.'

'And what do they mean the body is on a wall?' Kant said.

Kishore spotted the house they were looking for. It was hard not to. Despite the ungodly hour, there were people gathered around it, phone torches drifting like fireflies against the yellow gloom of the streetlights. There was no doubt about it.

Kant checked the time again. 4:31 a.m.

'Behenchod,' he said, looking at the crowd with a sinking feeling.

As the PCR vehicle rolled to a stop, a few people came running towards them.

'This way, this way,' they said, as Kant stepped out of the car. He followed them on foot, struggling to keep pace with his heavy shuffle, already feeling out of breath. He followed the men along the high boundary wall of a house, turned a corner, walked further along the wall, went past impressively tall gates, turned again. They were in a narrow lane, less than six feet wide, flanked on both sides by walls that rose ten feet up.

'There,' one of the men pointed. Kant switched on his Eveready torch and flung the beam where he was shown. At first, the light simply bounced off the whitewashed wall. Then it caught a hand, hanging limply. Kant moved his beam along the line of the arm. His head spun. He took a few unsteady steps towards the wall, rested against it to stop himself from falling.

He forced himself to look again. Above the wall rose long, slender rods that tapered to sharp, deadly spikes spaced evenly along the perimeter. Spreadeagled on these spikes was a young girl. She faced the sky, her hands and legs dangling off the wall. At least one spike had gone straight through her and jutted out above her stomach.

'Bhaisaab …' Kant croaked for his colleague, fumbling for his phone. Kishore had followed in the van and parked at the mouth of the lane. When Kant's torchlight found the body, he had seen it too. He clicked the radio on.

'Leo one, Leo one, Leo three-two.'

'Carry on, Leo three-two.'

'Body is confirmed. One dead. We need an ambulance here, more vehicles. How far is LP?'

'Local police will reach any time now. What's happening there?'

'There are crowds, this could be bad. Please notify DCP South. There's a girl lying on top of the wall, and there are these spikes … and … she … the spikes … have gone through her. Her body is stuck on the spikes. The locals are trying to reach her.'

'Is she alive?'

'Alive? No, no, I'm sure she is not alive.'

'Secure the area, Leo three-two, don't let anyone near the body, you understand? LP will reach any minute, hold the civilians off.'

'Yes, yes, janab, noted.'

Kishore was not about to do any of that. As far as he was concerned, their duty was done. Two patrolmen, a crowd of people, a dead body—Kant and Kishore had enough experience not to try to interfere. There was nothing more unpredictable than the wrath of a crowd.

Inspector Kumar rocked gently on his heels, staring up. The girl was on her back, impaled on the spike drilling through the middle of her stomach. Another spike jammed into her shoulder. Fifteen? Sixteen? No more than seventeen, Kumar concluded.

He noted the time on his phone—8:19 a.m. It was April, but already the sun was high up and hot. He stood straight, lifted his chest, lifted his chin. Methodically, he imprinted the scene in his head, moving his gaze along the girl's toes. Her feet were bare, no nail polish. Her legs dangled on either side of the spikes. The pelvis curved down. The rod that went through the stomach looked, at first glance, like the cause of death. Her clothes were soaked in blood, so her heart was still pumping when she fell. Part of her intestine hung in a bloody loop. The next spike had smashed into her right shoulder, but meeting bone there, had not quite managed to pierce through. The upper part of her body was held up higher. Her neck and head were flung back, tilted towards the left. Her mouth was open. Her eyes were closed.

Kumar felt strange, weightless. He heard no sounds, saw nothing but the girl. *The sound of your inhalation is hong, the sound when you exhale is sau.* He could hear his own breathing, the hong and the sau. She looked like …

His ears filled with a hum, a flash of a vision like a hard blow to the head with a blunt object. His right eye closed from the pain and he put his palm on his eye. His hands trembled. That's her. It's happening again. He can't move. His legs are too heavy. No, she is alive, what are they doing to her? He hasn't yet said goodbye! He had not called! He was drunk! A monster!

It's okay, child, it's okay, there's no more pain.

A shower of fiery sparks engulfed the body. Kumar brought his attention back to his breath. Process. Training. One step at a time.

The gas-cutters were here. They were burning through the metal spikes. Kumar felt himself slowly being pulled back into the chaos. The forensic team had finished photographing the scene and collecting on-site samples: blood swabs, fingerprints, shoe prints, hair and cloth. The men and one woman—the police doctor—had climbed off the makeshift scaffolding. They stood huddled with the imperious figure of the DCP of South District, the diminutive Crime Branch ACP Sofia Ahmed and a few other senior officers.

There seemed to be fifty people inside the compound. The forensic team, six senior officers, twelve uniformed policemen and women, the five hired hands who had put up the scaffolding and were now using the gas-cutters, the district magistrate and two of his officers. There were others whom Kumar could not quite place—family, house staff or curious civilians who had slipped past the tape.

Beyond the walls, on the other side of the yellow tape, a crowd seethed, jeered, filmed on their phones. TV cameras too. Uniformed constables standing behind the sagging tape were yelling at everyone to stay back.

A broken brick arced up from the other side of the wall and descended towards the senior officers where they stood conferring. The DCP jumped as the missile hit his shoulder. He howled, lost his balance and clattered into ACP Ahmed. The officers went down in a heap. The collective attention inside the compound shifted. Kumar turned away and strode towards the house, dialling Zeeshan. He spoke over the noise of people and police sirens, asked his constable to meet him at the glass windows that overlooked the front porch. Zeeshan got there gasping for breath, his shirt wet with sweat and clinging to his chest, untucked, missing a button.

'Crowds got to you?'

'Motherfuckers!' Zeeshan wheezed. 'Sorry, sir. I didn't mean to say that ... I got shoved by a constable because I was in plainclothes. When I got my ID out, I got shoved by the crowd. Almost ripped my shirt off.'

'The crime scene is being treated like a public urinal. Nothing here for the techies,' Kumar said.

'What's new?' Zeeshan spat, wiped his mouth with his hand and checked for blood.

'Right, now you go quickly up to the terrace from where the girl fell, scan, take photos. If anyone stops you, tell them Madam Ahmed sent you. Take Waseem's name if you need to. He is here, heading the forensic team. Okay?'

'We'll take the case?'

'Yes. I am riding with the girl. I need to get Dr Kharb to do the autopsy. If I don't go, she'll be dumped in the morgue and her autopsy will go the way of our crime scene.'

'Okay, sir.'

'Anyone from the unit here, do you know?'

'I saw Parveen thrashing someone to get them off the property.'

'Good, call him, take him with you.'

An ambulance had entered the driveway with difficulty. Kumar made his way towards it. He heard glass shatter. More stones came sailing over. Only a matter of time before the uniformed men charged with lathis. He strode towards the ambulance, which was inching through the crowd. Kumar banged on the driver's door with his ID out. He made his way to the back where the paramedic opened the door for him. He got in, sat next to the body. He was already exhausted. He called Dr Kharb en route. When it rang out, he dialled again and did not stop till the doctor picked up.

'Yes, Prashant? Is it an emergency?' Dr Kharb sounded weary, far off.

'Sir, sir, yes, of course this is an emergency, I wouldn't do this if it wasn't. I am coming in with a body, I want you to do the autopsy, not one of your cleaning staff,' Kumar said.

'That can't be done. I have a body open in front of me. My whole team is on the Sharma case, there's no time.'

'Sir, please, you know I would never ask if I did not think it was absolutely critical. You are not just the best forensic doctor in Delhi, you are the best in the country.'

'You don't have to tell me that, Inspector, why do you think I am so busy?'

'Sir, you know it says in my will that I want you to do the autopsy on me if I die an unnatural death.'

'Yes, you've told me that before. So, are you dead?'

A joke, good. This would go his way.

'I wish, sir. But I have the body of a young girl with me, the kind no one will look at twice. If you don't do the autopsy, I won't have a case.'

A few seconds of silence. Kumar held his breath.

'Okay. How far are you?'

'Close, passing Yusuf Sarai market, let's say ten minutes?'

'I'll have Dr Basu receive you, take the body in. I'll join you in an hour. But you do know that you are not supposed to call me at all, right? Please don't put me in this position again.'

'I never called you, sir,' Kumar said.

'And I hope I don't see the day when I have to cut you open, Inspector.'

5

ACP Sofia Ahmed sat hunched on one of the uncomfortable wooden chairs arranged in a row facing the DCP's long table, waiting for her boss to put down the phone. She gripped the armrests, forced her spine straight and scanned the bookshelf that lined the wall behind the DCP's hulking figure. *The Culture of Terrorism*, Noam Chomsky; *Meditations*, Marcus Aurelius; *The Art of War*, Sun Tzu; *Beyond Good and Evil*, Frederic Nietzsche; *A History of Western Philosophy*, Bertrand Russell.

She was sure the man sitting across from her, cooing on the phone with a superior at PHQ, had never read a single one of these books.

Fucking pretender, she thought. Was her contempt showing on her face? She lowered her gaze to her phone, scrolled aimlessly.

'Sir, yes, sir. Sir. I understand, sir,' the DCP droned on. 'No one better than me, sir, you can rest easy. I've done it many times before, it's nothing for me … sir, yes, sir.'

Sofia's eyes went back to the bookshelf. *The Myth of Sisyphus* by Albert Camus, a book she loved. A row of holy books: the Bhagwad Gita, the Holy Quran, the Holy Bible, the Tibetan Book of the Dead.

Comprehensive, Sofia thought, but what about the Jews? What's the holy book of the Jews? Did the Old Testament cover it? And what about the Talmud? It struck Sofia that she had never seen a copy of the Talmud.

There are six hundred and thirteen commandments in the Torah, she thought. She knew because she had just finished reading a book called *The Rabbi's Cat*.

'Right! Ready, everyone?' The DCP's booming voice crashed her thoughts. Realising that she had slid down on the chair again, she straightened herself. While she had been daydreaming about books, the room had filled. Both Crime Branch inspectors attached to Hauz Khas police station were present, along with half a dozen men from their teams. There was the lady officer from the Women & Children unit, the Hauz Khas SHO and assistant SHO, and the DCP's assistant.

A proper turnout for a meaningless meeting. What had to be done had already been done. Sofia was convinced that she had done the right thing. She considered herself far above the average intelligence and intellect of the force, despite her inexperience. Bullshit book displays notwithstanding. It had taken her very little time to figure that out.

'A simple, simple case,' DCP Ashish Singh said, sweeping his gaze left to right to take in everyone present in the room. He paused for effect and said, drawing out the first syllable, *suicide*. 'Yet, for some reason, our Crime Branch SIU has shown a lot of interest in this case. So much interest that I just got off the phone with the Special CP Crime, who felt it necessary to personally call and ask me to give the case to SIU.' Ashish Singh glared at Sofia.

'Why, Madam ACP, could you not ask me directly? Am I such a difficult person that you could not come to me with a simple request?'

Sofia averted her gaze, wondering for a moment if he really expected her to answer that. He did not.

'Anyway,' DCP Singh continued, 'it seems that our Crime Branch people have plenty of time to kill. So much so that yesterday a notice came to me that Inspector Kumar has applied for a law programme. So, perhaps you are looking for easy cases to notch up rewards, eh?' He looked at Sofia again, but she had her head turned towards Kumar, who was busy picking his nose, lost in his own world, as if he were alone in the room.

Disgusting, thought Sofia.

This morning, when Kumar had called her frantically, asking for the case, Sofia had wondered why he wanted it so badly. A servant found dead in a house, with no clear signs that she had been murdered—it was not easy for Sofia to take a case with such a low profile off the local police. She knew that she could only do it because of the weight of her father's name in the department and that made her uncomfortable. She had taken an instant dislike to Kumar. Prone to daydreaming and picking his nose. Likely an ill-educated misogynist. She would like to put him in his place when the time came.

Yet, there was his case history. The Balihar gang encounter. A fifteen-year-old boy who had been strangled by a classmate and his father and dumped in a drain. Most IOs would have closed the case immediately, without even trying to identify the body, but not Kumar. The little girl kidnapped in Rohini, sedated and hidden in the trunk of a car. And the case that caught Sofia's fancy, of the DTC bus driver who had run over and killed twelve people over five years. No one had suspected that these were murders, no one except Kumar. He had gone against his superiors, against the department, made an absolute mess by leaking evidence to a journalist, forcing the police to go back on their public stance … a real talent for creating trouble.

Sofia found it hard to reconcile this deflated-looking man and his work, but she agreed to his request, made the necessary calls. The case was going to be his.

'A case on a platter!' said DCP Singh. 'I have already done more work in the last two hours than all of you in this room, and that is a shame, considering I am your commanding officer.' He paused again. A fat diary fell from the hands of a policewoman with a loud thump. DCP Singh's nostrils flared.

'What have I done?' he soldiered on. 'I have interviewed the family. I have all the facts of the case.'

'You found the girl's family?' Sofia said.

'What? No! The girl has no family, don't you know? Clearly you don't know much, so I'll brief you, then SIU can take over. Who will be the IO?'

Sofia glanced at Kumar to check if he was still picking his nose and said, 'Inspector Kumar.'

'Okay, IO sir,' DCP Singh said with a sneer, 'I have done most of your work, and even though it's a clear case of suicide, I have personally asked Dr Kharb at AIIMS to do the autopsy. He is a good friend of mine and, as you know, the best forensic doctor in the country.'

If Kumar was surprised at this blatant lie, he did not show it.

'Second, the facts of the case: the girl who is dead, her name is Jyoti something, a tribal girl, lived as a servant in the house belonging to Mr Tarun Srivastava. Everyone knows him. He is a businessman, a good one. He is into plastics, with manufacturing units in Meerut, Bareilly, Bawana. He lives with his wife.'

DCP Singh broke off to consult a sheet of paper, holding it close to his nose. 'Yes, wife, Mrs Neha, and one daughter, who is twelve, her name is Astha. Small family. Mr Srivastava's uncle from his father's side is the MLA from Sardhana in Meerut.'

DCP Singh paused to let that sink in, but there was, yet again, a disruption. Head Constable Tomar had pushed his chair back with a screeching noise and excused himself loudly. He had to use the toilet. DCP Singh watched him go, his mouth a thin line, his eyes narrowed.

'Other people in the house,' he continued. 'Two drivers. One Kuldeep, who is at the station right now. A young boy called Rajesh Mondal, recently employed, is missing, along with one of the cars.

'The boy is our main point of interest. There are two guards, Ram Charan and Bir Singh. Ram Charan was on night duty and did not see or hear anything. Presumably, he was asleep. There is a cleaner, Laxman, who lives in the house. Both are here at the station. The two drivers don't live in the house. There is also a woman servant, Usmana. She comes early in the morning and leaves late, but does not live in the house.'

'Sir, what is the full name of our victim? What's her age?' Sofia asked. DCP Singh began leafing through his papers.

'Dhurwa,' Kumar said from his corner. 'Jyoti Dhurwa. She is fourteen or fifteen. An orphan from Chhattisgarh. She has been working at the house for a little less than a year.'

'A bit young to be working full-time in a house,' Sofia said.

'Not really,' DCP Singh snapped, trying to take back control. 'You should know your laws better, ACP Ahmed. Fourteen is legal age.'

'Yes, but not for working after 7 p.m.,' Sofia said. 'She was a live-in employee, so I assume she was working at night as well.'

'Take it up with the Women and Child Welfare commissioner,' DCP Singh said, pointing at the door. 'She is right outside the thana, keeping my constables busy, working up the crowd, talking to the reporters and threatening a hunger strike or whatever they do to waste time. You can join her if you like. What relevance does it have to the case? It's a goddamn suicide.'

'We don't know that yet, sir,' Kumar said, more to himself than to anyone else, but he was heard.

'Maybe you don't know it, but I do,' DCP Singh said. 'I have much more experience, a better education, a more logical mind.' He slapped his palms on the table and stood up.

'Let me tell you why, and then I am done and you can do what you want. The girl, like so many stupid teenagers, was in a relationship with this young driver … what's his name? Yes, Rajesh Mondal. Fellow started working at the house about three months back. Mr Srivastava told me himself that he came in and started causing trouble immediately, going after the poor girl. God knows what he did. Probably got her into bed promising marriage. After having extramarital sexual relations, the girl must have been putting pressure on him to marry her. The boy is twenty-one or twenty-two, obvious bad character, good-for-nothing troublemaker. Of course, he had no intention of marrying her. Tarun-ji … I mean Mr Srivastava … told me that he thinks he was beating up the girl. He had made up his mind to ask the poor girl about it, get rid of the driver, but tragedy struck before he could get around to it. Unfortunately, he made the mistake of not registering his servants with us.'

DCP Singh directed his furious gaze at his SHO, who had not expected to be involved and was busy scrolling on his phone. 'You, Inspector Panwar, I am looking at you.'

The phone almost slipped out of Panwar's fingers. He straightened up and said a crisp 'sir'.

'This is why I tell you, Inspector Panwar, to make sure that every household under your jurisdiction has their servants registered. Why were the girl and the boy not registered? That is your fault. Start a drive immediately. I want a file with details of every servant working in the area within a week. Today a girl has jumped off a terrace, created trouble for all of us. Tomorrow someone will steal. Or there will be a murder and robbery, and what will you tell me then? That the servant was not registered?

'Anyway, today has been terrible. This driver has run away with a Maruti Alto; I have put out a QST for the vehicle. We have not had a hit yet.

'So, you see, Inspector Kumar, the case is clear like water. Boy and girl have sex. Girl jumps to death, boy runs away. Get the boy. Book him for abetment. A simple manhunt should be easy for you with your resources. Make it quick. The poor family is under great pressure. People have vandalised their home. Bricks were thrown. I was hit by one. Bloody villagers! I have recommended to the Resident Welfare Association that they put up more walls, more barbed wires and more CCTVs to keep the villagers in check. We will help them with that. Absolute nuisance in a good neighbourhood. You have family in Shahpur Jat village, don't you, Inspector Panwar?'

The SHO of Hauz Khas, who was still sitting scrunched up with tension, muttered a meek assent.

'A bloody village, backward in every respect, everyone always looking for a fight. No respect!'

'Yes, sir.' SHO Panwar put some energy behind it. 'They have no work but lots of money from the rent. They do tend to like fighting.'

'They have destroyed anything the forensics team may have hoped to find,' DCP Singh said. 'Trampled over everything. Scared the poor little Srivastava girl so badly that she had to be sent to her uncle's place in Meerut. CFSL has put us on nine months waiting, but I expect the case to be solved in two days anyway. Dismissed.'

The guard Ram Charan, driver Kuldeep and house staff Laxman were the only people the police could bring down to the station for questioning. Kumar would have liked that the cook Usmana be brought down too, but they would need a woman officer to ask the questions, and none was available. What he would have really liked was to have the Srivastava family here, each in a different room—yes, even the girl—and put them through two or three hours of questioning.

'How old are you?' Kumar asked the driver. Zeeshan was in the room to take notes.

'Fifty-one.' Kuldeep had close-cropped hair and a stubble with more grey in it than black. He was big, with large muscles bunched around his shoulders and arms, a well-rounded belly, and the slouched posture of a man used to sitting for long hours behind the steering wheel of a car.

'How long have you been working for the Srivastavas?'

'Fifteen or sixteen years.'

'Is it fifteen or sixteen?'

Kuldeep began counting silently on his fingers.

'Sixteen, sir.'

'Do you drive Mr Srivastava or Mrs Srivastava, or both?'

'I drive Sir. If I'm free, and Madam needs to go somewhere ...'

'Where were you after midnight, the night the girl died?'

Kuldeep looked taken aback.

'I was at home, sleeping,' he said, his right hand on his chest.

'Who was at home with you?'

'My wife, my daughter, my mother, my son.'

'Who was sleeping in the room with you?'

'My wife and my mother, sir.'

'And where do you live?'

'Chhatarpur village, Tyagi mohalla.'

'Your own house?'

'Yes, sir.'

'What can you tell me about the night the girl died? What time did you leave the house?'

'I think it must have been around ten o'clock, I'm not sure. It was definitely after nine. At nine, I went into the house to ask if I could leave for the day. Garg sir said no, we may need you, stay a little longer.'

'Who is Garg?'

'He handles saab's work. You haven't met him yet?'

'No. Then? Did you have to drive them somewhere?'

'No, I called home to say I might be late, waited for a bit, but Garg sir called and said I could go, so I left.'

'Where were you waiting?'

'Outside, in the guardroom.'

'What else can you tell me?'

'Garg sir had got a new driver, Rajesh. You must know that he's missing?'

'Yes.'

'The girl and Rajesh were, you know, like …'

'Don't be shy.'

'They were, ah, like …'

'Fucking?'

'No, no, sir, I don't know about that.' Kuldeep squirmed in the chair with a look of alarm. 'But they had some kind of a friendship.'

'How do you know?'

'I could see it in the way they spoke to each other. Anyway, that girl was very arrogant, you know how young girls are …'

'No, I don't,' Kumar said. His eyes narrowed. 'I don't have a daughter. But you should know, you have one.'

Kuldeep squirmed again. He vigorously shook his head.

'No, no, sir, my daughter is nothing like this girl. She was an orphan, came from a village … nothing like us, nothing like us at all, you don't know these tribal girls, Inspector saab, they are dangerous.'

'I am not an inspector, but if you had Inspector saab here … you haven't seen rage if you haven't seen his temper. You don't want him asking you questions, believe me. You get the time five minutes wrong, he will have your pants down inside a lock-up howling for help.' Kumar chuckled. He enjoyed telling these lies. 'So, you better tell me everything, leave nothing out, leave no reason for me to ask the inspector to come talk to you.'

'Sir, yes, sir, everything, sir. The truth is, I had nothing to do with it. I was nowhere near the house. I am a simple man, sir, I've been a driver all my life. My son is studying to be an engineer. He is in college, sir, a good boy. I am a proud father. I have nothing to do with this. The new driver, Rajesh, he is the one you want. Hundred per cent he had a scene going on. As I told you, the girl was aloof, did not talk to any of us. Always sulked. Did not even look us in the eye if she came to give us water. But she talked to Rajesh. They think no one saw them, but one time it was a Sunday afternoon, everyone in the house was asleep. I saw the girl leaving. Five minutes later, I saw Rajesh leaving. They went in opposite directions. A few minutes later, I was going to get myself a paan, and I saw them sitting together near the main road, laughing and talking.'

'You followed them?'

'No, sir, I was going to get myself a paan.'

'You are lying,' Kumar said. 'But leave that aside. Where was Rajesh when you left the house that night?'

'He was still there, he stays late usually, he was in the guardroom.'

'What kind of a person is he?'

'Seemed OK to me, a good driver, polite, friendly, but you know what young men are like. Who knows what demon was lurking inside him?'

'Where can we find him?'

'I don't know, sir.'

'You don't know where he lives? You never asked?'

'I did ask him, but back then he said he was looking for a place to stay.'

'And? Did he find one?'

'I don't know. I didn't ask again.'

'What are the Srivastavas like?'

'Oh! Wonderful people, sir. Very nice people. Both of them. Their daughter too. Well educated. He is a big businessman. I drive him from meeting to meeting, to his factories … what can I say? I am lucky that I work for them.'

'You can go. Tell Ram Charan to come in.'

Ram Charan entered the room. He sat on the chair and began to cry.

'What's this? Pull yourself together,' Zeeshan said.

'It's my fault, sir,' Ram Charan said through his tears. He was a short, chubby man with thick glasses and a moustache shaped like two crescent moons joined together. He looked like a guard in caricature.

'*You* killed the girl?' Kumar said.

Ram Charan jerked his head up like a fish caught on a line.

'Oh no, no!' His eyes darted from Kumar to Zeeshan and back again. 'I thought the girl killed herself?'

'Then what is your fault?' Kumar said.

'I was asleep, sir. I did not hear or see anything. I should have been awake, but, but … you will not arrest me, will you?'

'When did you wake up?'

'When the guard from the next house starting banging on the gate.'

'Then?'

'I opened the gate and came out, I was very scared, I followed him. He showed me with his torch. I thought I would die. I thought it was a witch come to get us. Then I realised it was the girl who worked in the house. I came back to my room, called the house on the intercom.'

'Did you notice what time it was?'

'No, sir.'

'What happened next?'

'Srivastava-ji came out to see.'

'How quickly did he come?'

'Must have been ten minutes? Maybe five.'

'Do you remember anything correctly?'

'I was scared, it was confusing. By the time Sir came out, the other guard had already called the police. People were gathering.'

'Where was Rajesh?'

'He had gone out on an errand late at night.'

'What time?'

'Must have been around one, I don't exactly remember. I opened the gate for him to take the car out, Saab had already told me to allow him.'

'Where was Rajesh before that?'

'With me, sir, in the guardroom. He was watching a movie on his phone.'

'What time did you get to the house?'

'Five minutes to nine. My shift starts at nine.'

'Where was Rajesh?'

'He was outside the house, talking to Bir Singh.'

'The day guard?'

'Yes. A few minutes after Bir Singh left, Rajesh told me he was going out for dinner and he left too.'

'When did he come back?'

'An hour later, more or less.'

'He stayed in the room till he had to leave for the errand?'

'Yes, sir. I mean, he went out once to smoke or something. Five or ten minutes. Then he came back in.'

'The next time he left was with the car?'

'Yes.'

'What time did you say that was?'

'Around one.'

'So between ten and one, Rajesh was with you in the room, except when he went out for ten minutes?'

'Yes.'

'You were awake the whole time?'

'Yes.'

'Does he often go out on late-night errands?'

'Yes, yes, I mean …'

There was a loud thud that reverberated through the room, followed by distant, angry shouting. Ram Charan jumped up from his chair.

'Sit down,' Kumar barked. Ram Charan flopped back down like dead weight. The chair wobbled. Kumar gestured to Zeeshan, who left the room.

'Now listen,' Kumar sneered, 'if you lie about anything, you'll be in so much trouble you won't know your ass from your face. That was the sound of my team thrashing a suspect. I sent bhaijaan to check if the poor fellow is still alive.'

Ram Charan quivered in his chair. He folded his hands and said, 'I swear I'm not going to lie about anything.'

'I'll ask you again. Is it normal for Rajesh or any other driver to run late-night errands?'

'Sometimes Saab comes home late, sometimes Madam comes back late.'

'But do the drivers go out by themselves that late?'

'No, that's rare. I think it's happened before. It's definitely happened before, though not recently.'

'Are you always on the night shift?'

'Yes.'

Zeeshan entered the room.

'Is he alive?' Kumar asked.

'He'll live,' Zeeshan said, without missing a beat.

'I'll ask you again,' Kumar said, fixing his gaze on Ram Charan. 'Were you awake the whole time between ten and one, when you claim Rajesh was with you?'

Ram Charan looked down at his feet and shook his head. 'No.'

'And you don't know where Rajesh lives, or where we can find him?'

'No.'

'You can leave.'

Kumar watched Ram Charan shuffle out.

'What happened?' he asked Zeeshan, who broke into a smile.

'That idiot tow-truck driver rammed a car into the wall again while trying to park it.'

'I thought as much.'

In the other room, Hari Singh was making progress with Laxman.

'You clean all day long?'

'Yes, sir. Everything has to be clean. There's a lot of white stuff in the house, it takes time, sir. I also do the laundry, fold clothes. I go to the market. Yes, sir, that's it, sir.'

Laxman was about five foot eight, but looked taller because he was so thin.

'Do you have a disease?'

Laxman laughed shyly. 'No, sir, my health is good. I don't know why I am so thin. I eat enough. My grandfather remained thin all his life.'

Ten minutes into the conversation, Hari Singh decided that he would be very surprised indeed if Laxman was involved. The man was too easy to read. An earnest, happy soul. Perhaps a bit simple. Hari Singh could not remember the last time he had a person answering questions in this room with as much ease and trust.

'What was Jyoti like?'

'A good girl, sir. Quiet. Hard-working. She could work a lot. Like me. She used to tell me, Laxman bhai, do you eat enough?'

'Why would she take her own life?'

'I don't know, sir.' Laxman shook his head slowly from side to side. 'She had no family, no one to call her own, but she had found at least a roof over her head. I wish she had not done it.'

As for the night of the incident, Laxman had neither seen nor heard anything—he had slept like a dead man himself, cocooned in his small outhouse at the back of the compound, the doors and windows closed, and a standing fan that drowned out all other noise running the whole time. He always slept by eleven, was always up by five. He had woken up to the commotion, seen the body and nearly fainted.

'How can you be so close and not hear anything? You were twenty feet away!'

'Sir, believe me, I didn't hear anything.'

'Do you have family?'

'Yes, sir, a mother, wife, a son. They live in the village, in Banota, Rajasthan.'

'If you did hear something, now is the time to say it and we will protect you. If I find out later that you were lying, it's not just you but your family who will suffer for it. Think about that.'

'I am telling you nothing but the truth, sir.'

'Anyone in the house had reason to kill her?'

'Oh no, sir!' Laxman made a theatrical sweep with his arms, his eyes wide with surprise—even that reaction, Hari Singh noted glumly, felt authentic.

'Not at all, sir. People in the house are refined people, sir.'

'Why, nice people don't kill or what?'

'No, sir, how can you be a good person and kill?'

Hari Singh sighed.

'What about Rajesh? Why did he run away?'

'I don't know, sir, I don't know him. Whatever little I saw of him, he seemed nice. When I would go out to feed the birds—I feed the birds every day in the park near the house, I put out fresh water for them—he would smile at me, tell me that I was doing good.'

'Did anyone scold the girl on the day she died? Or the few days before that?'

Laxman thought for a while. 'That is possible.'

'Who?'

'That's hard to say. Everyone gets scolded in the house some time or the other, what else will they do if you make an error? It's only natural.'

'What do you mean by error?'

'Like, if you don't clean properly, or you put things in the wrong place or maybe you broke a plate …'

'Did she break something?'

Laxman paused to think. 'No, sir.'

'So, who scolds her?'

'It could be Usmana didi, who does the cooking, or Madam.'

'What about your saab?'

'It's possible, but he keeps away from matters of the house.'

'Is it possible that someone hit her in anger?' Hari Singh had years of experience in noticing split-second pauses, and he saw one now.

'Just tell me, Laxman Singh, who hit her?'

'No one, sir, I swear, no one hit her. She was OK. It's a rich person's home, sir, a city home. They don't do things like beatings.'

'You are so full of what people do or don't do,' Hari Singh snapped. 'Are you slow?'

'No, sir.'

'So, who hit her? Forget that, tell me about any incident of one person hitting another person in the house that you've seen or heard of. Do you understand my question?'

Laxman lowered his eyes and nodded. After a moment, he said, 'Baby, the little girl, she once hit Jyoti. It was just a childish thing. No harm done. Madam can get very angry, but she has never touched anyone. Saab once beat up a fellow, a long time ago, a gardener who could not maintain the grass on the lawn properly. He left the job.'

'What about your madam and saab? Do they get along? Hit each other ever?'

Laxman folded his hands in prayer and said, 'What kind of question are you asking me, who am I to talk about Saab and Madam?'

'It's not that hard a question. Someone has died in your house. The questions could get much harder.'

Laxman looked gloomy. He scratched the back of his ear and looked down at the floor.

'Saab and Madam are good people, they have no problems, sir.'

Kumar checked the time on his phone. Still half an hour to go till the briefing with ACP Sofia. He had released Srivastava's staff after the preliminary questioning. Now he was hungry. His left shoulder was frozen in an excruciating knot. There was a throbbing ball of pain in his lower back. He reached over and across with his right hand, slapped down on his shoulder to create some heat, dug his fingers into the muscles till the pain spluttered into sparks of pleasure. Then he straightened up and walked out of the station. 7:45 p.m. The TV crews had thinned. A riot van was packing up.

Kumar turned left, walked briskly past the parked cars, the TV vans, the milling reporters and camera people, the taxi garage and the garbage dump till he reached the crossing at Hauz Khas market. He turned left, slowing down to appreciate the neat rows of vegetables laid out at the shop on the pavement. Tomorrow, maybe, I'll have the time to buy little red radishes to take them home for dinner, he thought.

He reached his favourite tea shop and immediately started feeling better. The aroma of eggs frying in butter embraced him. He sat down on a stone on the side of the pavement and smiled at Sharma-ji, who smiled back toothlessly from under his faded red baseball cap and poured Kumar a paper cup of tea without being asked.

It was a quiet, pretty spot, set back a little from the road, hidden by the overgrown bushes and trees spilling over from the bordering park. But the important thing for Kumar was that the man made an excellent bread-omelette. He asked for one. He watched the tea-seller at work and drifted into a lingering daydream: he had quit the force, left his family, lived alone and now ran a tea-and-omelette shop. There was nothing in his world that caused pain. His mind was blank, immersed entirely in simple, repetitive tasks. Boil milk. Bash spices. Chop onions. Crack eggs. No worries, no violence, no desires.

Kumar watched as the small man with white hair and a wiry, white beard broke two eggs into a steel tumbler, added a pinch of salt, a pinch of pepper, a spoonful of finely chopped onions, a half-spoon of chopped coriander leaves and green chillies and—his own little touch—the tiniest bit of chopped ginger. In went a generous block of butter into the bent, old pan. As the butter foamed, the man poured the beaten eggs in a stream, swirling the pan in small circles.

This, Kumar thought, was the meditative life, the life of counting beads, the life of god holding you in a warm embrace. The freedom to not have to intervene in the lives of others, the freedom to not speak.

Smoke rose from the pan. The man jabbed at the bread with his spatula to cut it into smaller squares, flipped them neatly on to a sheet of newsprint and handed it over. Kumar helped himself to a spoonful of fiery green chutney. Zeeshan called to say that it was time.

With a last gulp of the hot tea, he hurriedly shoved money into the tea-seller's hand, grabbed his bread-omelette and broke into something between a brisk walk and a run through the diesel fumes and blasting horns of the angry traffic.

He would have to be convincing with ACP Sofia. She was kind to him, but what was he going to tell her? He could not tell her the truth, because that had nothing to do with the case. It helped, he thought, that so many journalists had come to report the story. Crime Branch liked the attention.

This work will kill me, he thought.

'So …' Sofia said, peering over the just-arrived crime scene photographs. 'Any reason to think it's not a simple suicide? I am inclined to believe DCP Singh's theory, which he has proclaimed to every journalist in the city.'

Kumar looked at the photos slowly, and felt an odd sensation that they showed something different from what he had seen this morning, something that had happened a long time ago.

'I don't know … it's … she is young, and such a horrible way to die,' Kumar said, running his fingers uneasily, aimlessly through the stack of photographs. 'If I wanted to jump off a building to kill myself, I don't know, it's hard to think like someone who wants to die, but I don't think even in that condition I would want to jump onto metal spikes. I mean, what would be the thought behind it? That the height isn't good enough? The fall alone won't kill me?'

Sofia picked up one of the photos, taken after the girl had been removed from the wall. Her eyes were closed, she looked peaceful. Her mouth was twisted slightly downwards. She noticed that her T-shirt had a faded print of Mickey Mouse on the front, barely visible through the bloodstain. She was a child.

'Her age bothers me too,' Sofia said, placing the photo carefully on top of the stack. 'What else are you working on?'

'The SSC case, but I don't have much to do with it, except go to court tomorrow.'

'Good. What's the plan?'

Kumar outlined it for her. He and Zeeshan to lead the questioning of the household. HC Tomar to lead the team questioning everyone else in the neighbourhood. SI Das and a couple of constables to handle the documents and liaison: photographs and reports from the Mobile Crime Team, CFSL, autopsy, Auto Theft, phone records, CCTV. Top priority for all teams, of course, was tracing the driver. He would be sending in the Call Data Record request for the driver's phone first thing in the morning, as well as a request to put interception on the number. Subsequently, any number that seemed relevant from the CDR.

Sofia herself would have the all-consuming job of filing reports to Crime Branch DCP at PHQ, liaise with the DM and follow up on the permissions for data and interceptions.

'Right. Let's wrap it up quickly and cleanly,' Sofia said. Not convinced that it sounded emphatic enough, she added a shade of harshness to her voice: 'No mess, no wasting time. I know about your fuck-ups. If I get even a hint that this is going to be another one of those, I'll take the case away from you as easily as I got it for you. Do you understand?'

'Yes, sir, madam, I do,' Kumar said, stacking and rearranging the photos as if they were a deck of cards. To Sofia, he seemed distant and lost.

'One more thing, madam, you know we have an SI, his name is Colonel, who is out of duty recuperating from a gunshot wound. We are really in need of an SI. I have been sending in requests for months.'

'Oh yes, I followed up already. It seems there isn't anyone you can get right now,' Sofia said.

Kumar pushed his chair back and stood up with drooping shoulders, straightening himself vertebra by vertebra for the salute.

'Hold on.' Sofia opened her top drawer, took out a sheet of paper and glanced at it. 'I have an SI who has been assigned to me as a PA. I'll attach her with you for this case.'

She gave Kumar the sheet of paper.

Walking out, Kumar felt more miserable than before.

6

SI Meera, who went by one name, adding a 'Kumari' only if necessary for official reasons, smiled widely. It felt a little stupid, but could not help it. She was nervous. And she smiled a lot when she got nervous. She shifted her weight on the balls of her feet, slapped her butt with the hollow of her palm, as she always did before a fight, exhaled forcefully from the diaphragm, knocked on the door and pushed it open without waiting for an invitation.

Inspector Kumar was looking through the file on the missing driver. HC Tomar was carefully inscribing the 'Om' sign on the top edge of the whiteboard with a red marker to bless the day with an auspicious beginning.

SI Meera snapped to attention, eyes twitching as she tried to control her smile reflex. Kumar had no such inhibition. He grinned warmly. He had made a small adjustment in his attitude since last night.

'Come, we have been waiting for you. At ease.'

Meera smiled till her face hurt. She looked around the room. The men stared back. Tomar looked her up and down. In a less conspicuous way, Das checked her out. She had small but full lips, slightly slanted eyes, high cheekbones, a fine, strong nose that was broad and long. Her hair was cut short, falling in jagged strands around her ears, which caught the attention of the men in the room because they were a mass of mangled tissue.

Through the uniform, which clung tightly to her, it was apparent she was built like a bodybuilder. Das got up smiling and pulled up a chair for her. Meera smiled back at him but remained standing.

'We have a celebrity on our team,' Kumar said. 'SI Meera Kumari, for those of you who don't follow wrestling, is a true champion. She has had the national flag raised in her honour at international tournaments. I remember sitting in my office and watching her win gold at the Commonwealth Games.

'You remember, Zeeshan? In the old office? That obese lawyer, what's his name, he had come down to speak to us about the DTC case. The national anthem began to play and we jumped to attention to fuck with him. Remember how much time it took for the corrupt, self-righteous bastard to get to his feet?'

Zeeshan laughed, failing to take his eyes off her muscles.

'Madam, welcome. I am a big fan of wrestling. I may be your boss for the moment, but I am also your fan,' Kumar said.

There was a round of muted applause from the men.

'You are from Rohtak, right? Are you a Phogat?' asked Parveen. 'I am Head Constable Parveen Tomar, from Hisar. I was a wrestler too. Tried boxing as well. Too much work for me!'

'Yes, I am from Rohtak, from Jai Veer Akhada,' Meera said, noticing that Parveen's ears—small for his big head, and rounded—were perfectly fine. People who saw Meera for the first time almost always tended to see her ears first, 'cauliflower ears', as they were commonly known, the result of repeated blows to the head that caused blood vessels in the ears to rupture. On her part, like many wrestlers, Meera almost unconsciously scanned a person's ears. Her world divided neatly into two categories: wrestler/non-wrestler.

Parveen was not a wrestler. Neither was anyone else in the room for that matter.

'I am not a Phogat,' she laughed. 'I get asked that a lot because the Phogat sisters are everywhere in wrestling. There are so many of them too! I have lived and trained with them at their village in Balali. Such a pretty place. Far from here, forested, a small village, you should see the akhada their father built for them. Wow! I don't know if anyone will remember, but I got silver at the Asian Championship in 2014 in 54 kg. That time, the older sister, Geeta, she was on the team for 60 kg, she got gold and …'

Meera stopped. She smiled, bit her lip and looked at her shoes. They were black, shiny, heavy. She had a feeling she was speaking too much. People always told her that. She wanted a new beginning for herself, to make a different kind of impression.

Kumar picked up the thread.

'SI Samiran Das, our Bangali babu. Like you, he is new to the unit, but he can show you some of the things we are doing and how we do them. Constable Zeeshan Qureshi and Head Constable Hari Singh, veterans, should have retired, but clinging on.' Zeeshan and Hari Singh smiled sheepishly at their boss's attempt at a joke.

'Feel free to ask them anything if you have doubts,' Kumar continued. 'They know the CrPC, IPC and Delhi Police manuals like a priest in Banaras knows the Hanuman Chalisa.' He was on a roll.

'Parveen introduced himself, and this is Constable Sushil Kumar, whose muscles are big but whom you would probably floor in a second. Unlike his more famous namesake, he is no wrestler.'

Everyone laughed. Meera laughed so hard she snorted through her nose. She stopped abruptly. She felt that everyone was looking at her.

'You've been briefed by Madam ACP, I believe,' Kumar said, 'so, let's get straight to work. You have joined the team at the frontline on the first day of attack, so you can think of it as bad luck, or you can think of it as auspicious.'

'Certainly auspicious, sir,' Meera said. 'Always ready for battle, sir.'

Kumar took off his sandals, put on his sharply polished brown leather shoes. He picked up a black bag with the HP logo on it, the kind of backpack distributed in their hundreds at conferences, and a thick notebook with a maroon cover.

'Right. Join me and Zeeshan, we'll go over to the house. Scene of crime. Your first.'

The house loomed imposingly, soaring walls bleached a blinding white in the bright sunlight. The first- and second-floor windows, visible above the boundary wall, were set deep. Barbed wire, heavy iron spikes, CCTV, a towering gate—it reminded Meera of prison. She had done a tour of Tihar during training.

Following a couple of steps behind Kumar and Zeeshan, she said, 'Seriously secure house, isn't it? Is there a threat to their life? Or are they paranoid?'

Kumar ignored her. Zeeshan half turned and brought his finger to his lips. Meera smiled—she understood.

But Kumar had heard her. This girl is not from Delhi, he thought. The security measures here were nothing special. Colonies behind giant gates, houses behind walls and concertina wire, people behind bolts and shutters, deadlocks and barred windows in a city nursing anger, anxiety, fear and loathing. An irony that most murders are committed by people known to the victims. Was that what happened here? Was Jyoti killed? If she was, then certainly someone in the house was involved. He thought of the things that had happened immediately after the discovery of the body. A hoard of locals from the village, along with an assorted crowd of domestic workers, construction labourers and drivers stormed the house, broke windows, declared the girl had been killed, her employers were responsible, that the police would be bribed to look the other way. In a retaliatory fit, the rich and influential residents of the posh colony called their friends in high places to demand enhanced security. DCP Singh's phone rang as incessantly as the honking of cars in peak-hour traffic and he almost collapsed in a grovelling frenzy. The DCP had spent most of yesterday and today ensuring there were manned nakabandis on each of the major roads going through the colony, that police were going house-to-house registering servants and drivers—a mobilisation of resources on a massive scale. The DCP personally attended a meeting with the Resident Welfare Association where he signed a document pledging that Delhi Police would offer their technical expertise as well as supervise the building of new boundary walls with concertina wire, new gates where the temporary roadblocks had been set up and install CCTVs at all kinds of 'critical' points.

What this meant in the context of the case Kumar could not quite understand. A girl had fallen to her death from her room on the terrace. Later, everyone got together to build walls.

Kumar found himself at the place in the wall where the body had fallen. He began to scan methodically for CCTVs. He asked Zeeshan and Meera to fan out and do the same.

It was a narrow, blind lane of solid back walls. There was nothing pointed at it. The lane itself had been combed by the Crime Team in the hope of finding the girl's phone, without luck. If this was a movie, Kumar thought, something would glint in that patch of weeds, I would bend down to find the one clue that would illuminate the whole case. He turned on his heels and walked briskly towards the front. The guard and the constable stood up as he strode in through the main gate. He stopped when he saw his reflection in the glass facade. The front door was open. A man blocked it. Kumar looked at him and said, 'Inspector Kumar, Crime Branch.'

'Yes, sir, I know.' The man had a soft, pleasant voice. 'Please come in. Sir will join you in five minutes.'

'You are?'

'Shri Umesh Garg. I am the manager.'

'Managing what?'

'Sir's manager, ah, I mean, I am Mr Srivastava's personal assistant, looking after his businesses. Why don't you come inside?'

Umesh Garg was a tall, broad-shouldered man with close-cropped hair that was mostly white, a neatly trimmed moustache that was perfectly black, a wide forehead, a strong, heavy jaw. He reminded Kumar of his grandfather, who was in the army and maintained his tight-lipped, rigid bearing all the way to his deathbed. Garg was dressed simply but neatly in a well-pressed and spotless white kurta-pajama. He pointed to a spread of sofas.

'Tea? Coffee?'

Kumar sat down on the edge of a white sofa that could swallow ten people. He dared not put his whole weight on it and clung on to the armrest with one hand. Meera considered whether it would be rude to speak, but could not help herself. She asked for a black coffee. 'I like coffee,' she said, smiling nervously at Kumar, who asked for tea. Garg picked up a phone and spoke to the kitchen.

Meera looked around the house. What looked like a prison from the outside was glass and shiny metal on the inside. In the far corner there was a steel sculpture of a tree, a champa without leaves, that gleamed and caught her eye. Her spirits sank a little. On the wall was a massive rectangle of marble—white, with veins of grey—housed in a golden frame. It confused Meera. Why would you frame a sheet of stone? The other side of the room was raised by a step. Meera could glimpse the kitchen through a door, a dining table that may have been ten feet long, an even longer cabinet along the wall behind, a staircase going up to the second floor. The cabinet held a variety of colourful objects, of which Meera only recognised a sizeable Ganesh decked with flowers. The ceiling featured an intricate, gilt-edged chandelier and concealed lights running end-to-end along the periphery.

Under her feet was a thick, soft carpet with geometric blocks of pale ivory, grey and brown, that was easily thirty feet long and equally wide. Visible at the margins of the carpet was the parquetry underneath. She pressed down on the carpet and thought it was cushioned enough to practise on.

What struck Meera most was the whiteness of the room. Apart from the carpet, the gold accents and a few objects on top of the cabinet at the far end, everything was white: sofas, curtains, cupboards, shelves, the identical lamps dotting the room, the bookcase, tables, cushions. Light streamed in through the glass wall. The whole place glowed. How did they keep all the white so white, so clean? If this house was in her village, the white would disappear under cow dung and mud.

Meera felt anxious that her shoes were leaving dirt on the carpets.

Only Zeeshan unselfconsciously walked around, picking up things to inspect them. Garg followed him with his eyes.

'Do you live here?' Kumar asked the manager.

'Oh no,' Garg said, taking his eyes off Zeeshan. 'Sir maintains an office in the house, so I am often here.'

'Were you here on the night the girl died?'

'Yes, in fact, Sir and I were finalising a new project so I stayed till about nine, which is as late as I ever get. Then I left, went home.'

'Did you notice anything odd?'

'No. Everything seemed perfectly normal, though I'm not the best person to ask since I was inside the office.'

'Where is home?'

'Rohini.'

'That's far. Address?'

Garg gave his address and phone number. Zeeshan wrote them down in his notebook.

A short, heavy woman in a tightly fitted salwar-kameez, a hairnet covering her head, came out of the kitchen with a tray bearing three white cups and three glasses of water. She made no eye contact, put the tray down on the glass-topped table between Kumar and Garg, left. Meera picked up her cup and took a sip. It was instant coffee mixed with hot water. She looked at the cup—a cheap, thick variety that streetside tea stalls used before plastic and paper took over—it was chipped. She put the cup back on the tray.

Kumar eyed his weak tea and said, 'Can we see the girl's room first?'

'Yes, of course, please follow me,' Garg said.

Kumar rose carefully from the sofa, digging his toes into his shoes. They were led outside the house and around to the back, where there was another, smaller lawn, beside which, from a square of stone paving, a narrow spiral staircase rose steeply.

The expanse of the terrace was covered with potted plants in bloom. Where the stairs had brought them up, there was a small room. On the other side from the room were solar panels, a series of water tanks and a solar water heater.

'CCTVs?' Kumar asked, looking around.

'None on the terrace,' Garg said. 'Yesterday we submitted our footage to you people.'

Zeeshan took out a paper cutter from his backpack and cut the yellow police tape stuck in the shape of an X across the door. Meera entered.

'What is it? About ten feet by six feet?' she said.

'Yes, about that,' Garg said, standing outside.

'No windows,' Meera thought aloud. 'I wouldn't be able to sleep in here.'

A flimsy box bed had been stripped of its mattress and sheets by forensics. The only other things in the room were an empty but newish-looking aluminium trunk, an earthen pitcher of water and a palm-sized, frameless mirror on the wall. The room led to an untiled toilet barely large enough for one person to stand in. There was a plastic bucket and a mug. Sachets of shampoo and conditioner garlanded the water pipe. There was a bottle of coconut oil and a piece of soap melting in its tub on top of the flush.

Kumar sat on the bed. He looked up at the ceiling. Not high enough for a fan. Young girls usually hang themselves from ceiling fans when they want to end things. Maybe she jumped because she had no other way.

He got up, lifted the flimsy plywood cover and peered into an empty box. Zeeshan got on his knees to scan the floor. Kumar stepped outside and spoke to Meera.

'Check the side with the solar panels. Move things around if you need to. Use your phone torch. Look carefully.'

'What am I looking for, sir?'

'Anything. Anything missed by forensics. A button. Hair. A piece of cloth.'

Kumar stood with his back to the room. On his right was the crowded street that carved its way through Shahpur Jat and emerged onto Outer Ring Road. On his left was where Jyoti had fallen. Counting his steps, he walked till he reached the exact spot. He knelt to examine the wall and the floor.

When he stood up, the wall came below his waist. He leaned forward. The drop seemed a long way down. He thought, what would it feel like? He looked at the spears, almost directly below him, and was filled with dread. The two awkward gaps where the cutters had done their work interrupted the symmetrical march of the spikes. It made Kumar dizzy, so he forced himself to look away. His gaze settled on the terrace of another house, a smaller house, one floor lower. It looked disused and full of junk: old air-conditioning units, a broken washing machine on its side, the fragment of a kite, a few dead potted plants, smashed flowerpots. Beyond was the Outer Ring Road. Kumar stared for a moment at the pedestrian overbridge across it. No one was using it except for a young couple standing midway, looking down at the heavy traffic.

'The manager says his sir is waiting,' Meera said. Kumar turned and walked to where Garg was standing, at the mouth of the spiral staircase.

'Take us down through the other way,' Kumar said in a flat tone that did not sound like a request. 'The stairs from inside the house.'

'It's locked.' Garg's tone was unfriendly.

'Call and get it opened.'

Kumar kept Garg locked in his gaze till it was done.

'Ah, Inspector, I've been waiting.'

Tarun Srivastava was a tall man with big, slightly protruding eyes, a clean-shaven face and thinning hair. He could pass for a white person, thought Meera. He wore a powder blue shirt and khaki pants.

'Let's start, though really, I don't have much to say. I'm not at home most of the time, don't get involved in the running of the house.'

He strode rapidly through his home. In the living room, the air conditioning had been switched on. He lowered himself next to a woman, and leaned back into the sofa. Mrs Srivastava.

Looking at Meera, Kumar nodded in the direction of the kitchen. She turned on her heels and headed off.

'Tell me how and when you came to know Jyoti had died,' Kumar began.

'I was sleeping when the bell rang. I checked the time. It was around four. I knew something was wrong immediately. I rushed downstairs and our guard told me about it. He looked agitated. I saw her body. Man, I thought I was going to have a heart attack. Nasty business. There was a crowd, though it was still dark outside. Somebody had called you fellows already because the police car came around soon after. I tried to speak to the cop, but he ignored me.'

'Do you remember the exact time?'

'No. Would you if your life was suddenly turned upside down and vandals came to attack you and your family in your own house?' Tarun Srivastava's voice rose a notch.

'And you, Madam? Did you wake up with him?'

Neha Srivastava, like her husband, was pale-complexioned, but in a way that looked like the blood had been drained from her. She kept her hands clutched together to stop them from shaking. The veins on her hands were faint blue etchings. She was wearing a white T-shirt that strained against her breasts—the word 'Balenciaga' was printed on it. Kumar, for no reason he could think of, scribbled the word in his notebook. She had paired it with neon pink track pants and a good amount of make-up. Her long black hair was shiny and straight.

'No,' she said, as if startled awake, 'I have difficulty sleeping, so I take pills. I had no idea till Tarun woke me up …' She dragged her words, devoid of inflections.

'What time was that?'

'Around six,' Tarun Srivastava interjected.

Kumar got the feeling the two of them didn't sleep in the same room.

'Your daughter? Where was she?'

'She was in her room, sleeping,' Tarun Srivastava answered for his wife again. 'Look, I don't understand what you are trying to do. I already spoke to your DCP. The girl killed herself over a stupid fucking affair. Son of a whore! Ran away with our car! I'll kill him with my bare hands unless you catch him first. He knows exactly what happened. He is the reason the poor girl killed herself. Why are you wasting our time and your time sitting here?' Tarun Srivastava was half a turn away from shouting. His wife stared blankly at him.

'Sir, a suicide, like murder, is an unnatural death, which means we investigate following certain protocols, that's all,' Kumar said. 'It will be over soon. Just a few questions, so we have a better understanding of what happened.'

Tarun Srivastava scowled. 'You won't understand anything by talking to us. We were asleep till the guard rang the bell.'

'What about your daughter?'

'She was sleeping in her room.'

'You saw she was sleeping? Or that her bedroom door was closed?'

'I saw she was sleeping.'

'Is she here?'

'Oh, Tarun!' Neha Srivastava woke up.

'No, she's not. Why do you need to speak to her? She is twelve years old. I don't think you should be allowed to speak to her.'

'Legally, we are okay as long as it's a policewoman speaking to her. If you want, we could have a magistrate present for the interview. Where is your daughter?'

'She is with my parents in Meerut. I really do think you are crossing a line, Inspector … what's your name again?'

'Kumar, Prashant Kumar.'

'Kumar? What caste?'

'Is that important? Respectfully, you are wasting time yourself. Please answer our questions the best you can.'

'Listen, whoever you think you are, even the DCP doesn't speak to me like this, you understand?' Tarun Srivastava rose from his seat.

Kumar was unperturbed. He clutched the side of the sofa and twisted from the waist to ease his back. 'Have we got her elimination prints? Your daughter's? It's okay, when she is here, we'll take her prints.' He fidgeted some more and faced Tarun Srivastava.

'We need the prints to check if there was someone else in the house or the terrace apart from the family.' He smiled amiably. 'Do you go up to the terrace?'

'Rarely,' Tarun Srivastava said.

'Did you go up yesterday?'

'Yes.'

'For what?'

'It's my house, why do I need to tell you why I went to the terrace?' Tarun Srivastava glanced at his wife. 'I went up to smoke. My wife doesn't like me smoking where Astha can see me.'

'Does Astha go up to the terrace?'

'Listen, Inspector, I told you already, it's our house, we go where we want. We all go to the terrace some time or the other.'

'Does Garg go up? Or the drivers?'

'No.'

Kumar turned to the wife. 'Did you go up yesterday?' Neha Srivastava shook her head.

'If I knew you meant to treat us like this, I would have called my lawyer,' Tarun Srivastava said. 'I thought you wanted to talk to us about the damage done to our house by the mob. I spoke to the commissioner. Your DCP was here when the crazy crowd started throwing stones.'

'You could call your lawyer, we can wait,' Kumar said.

Tarun Srivastava sat up, his eyes bulging, about to lash out. He decided against it, looked at his wristwatch, ran his hand through his fine hair and said, 'You've got ten minutes.'

'What did you do after you discovered the body?'

'I called Garg. He sent a car and security staff from one of my factories. I woke up my wife and daughter and sent them to my father's place in Meerut. I called my father.'

'Your call data would back this up?'

'Yes.'

'What I don't understand, help me ... a girl falls from your terrace, gets impaled on your wall, dies. None of you hears anything?'

'Of course. If this girl decided to jump, she is not going to scream while she is falling, is she?' Tarun Srivastava had his hands stretched out in front of him, palms up, his eyes fixed on Kumar. 'Yes, Inspector Prashant? Would she scream?'

Kumar offered no reply.

'Also, our doors and windows were closed, curtains drawn, air conditioners on. The house is virtually soundproof. How else can you live with the sound of traffic? Or the bloody dogs howling at night?' Tarun Srivastava pointed at the glass facade behind Kumar. 'Everything is double-glazed, extra thick, 8 mm, with weather proofing. Can you hear any outside noises right now?'

'When did you last see Jyoti?'

'Around nine-thirty. She served us at dinner.'

'Madam? When did you last see her?'

Again, that spooked look of a woman who is elsewhere in her head. 'Yes?' She unclasped her hands.

'Madam, when did you last see Jyoti that day?'

'Last, well, maybe around ten-thirty,' she said in her distant voice. 'I was in my room … no … in Astha's room, upstairs.' She bent her head in that direction.

'Alone?'

'No!' Her eyes widened. 'I was with Astha … my … my daughter. Upstairs.'

Kumar noticed Mr Srivastava squeezing his wife's hand, his eyes on her, his mouth tightened in a thin smile.

'Jyoti came up to the room?'

'No, she called from the kitchen.'

'On the intercom?'

'Yes.'

'How do you know the time?'

Neha Srivastava looked up, her eyes wet, confused.

'You said it was ten-thirty when you last spoke to her.' Kumar's voice was gentle, as if he were speaking to a child. 'How do you know what time it was?'

'Oh.' Neha Srivastava looked at Kumar brightly. 'It's the time I take Astha's phone away so she can sleep.'

'Where were you at that time?' Kumar asked Srivastava.

'I was in my office.'

'Is that usual? Work after dinner, I mean.'

'I don't see that's any of your concern, Inspector, but yes, I like to do a bit of work after dinner,' Srivastava grimaced.

'You were alone downstairs? Apart from Jyoti, I mean.'

'Yes. I had locked the main door before going into the office.'

'Was it possible for Jyoti to open the door if she wanted to?'

'No. Only I, my wife, my daughter and Garg know the codes.'

'How does she go up to her room?'

'Using that staircase,' Srivastava said, pointing at it. 'Once she closes the terrace door behind her, she can't open it again. It only opens from the outside if you disable the lock. The lock was not disabled. I checked after the body was found.'

'How long were you in your office?'

'Till around one. I had music on.'

'Is there a camera inside the house?'

'Like CCTV?'

'Yes.'

'No. Anyway, your forensic guys, or crime team, or whatever you call them, already asked me this. We have no cameras inside the house.'

'So, nothing strange or suspicious on the night and neither of you thought something was out of place with Jyoti?'

'No.'

'Madam?'

Neha Srivastava nodded absent-mindedly, brushing a stray lock of hair back and fixing it behind her ear.

'Right, we need to ask this question of your daughter, and then we'll be done.'

Tarun Srivastava leapt to his feet. 'Good,' he said. 'And Inspector … umm … Prashant, right? I was curt with you before. I'm sure you can understand how stressed I am about the whole thing.' He flashed a warm smile.

Kumar looked at him blankly, turned again to his wife. 'One more thing. About the last conversation you had with Jyoti, do you remember it?'

Neha Srivastava began to cry. Tarun Srivastava towered over her, the smile replaced by a sneer.

'Can you stop these questions?'

'I'm sure you understand the seriousness of the situation. A young girl has died in your house. You want us to do a watertight job so no one can raise questions later and cause trouble.'

Tarun looked at Neha and reached his hand out to touch her. He thought better of it and sat back down.

'At around 10:30, she called to ask if I needed anything more,' Neha said, plucking a piece of tissue paper from a box on the table to dab her eyes.

Kumar noticed, with a flash of despair, that instead of feeling empathy for the lady, his attention was on her breasts as they rose and fell with her laboured breathing.

'I said no … that the work is … it's done ... she should switch off the lights, go up to her room. She always forgot to switch off lights.'

Mrs Srivastava hurriedly reached for the box of tissues and put it on her lap.

'Before that I had spoken to her right after dinner, told her to wash the spinach, peel garlic and … and I don't remember, a bunch of other small things to do … kitchen things for the next day.'

'Did she get a scolding from you that day?'

'No, no,' she stammered. 'I mean, I may have corrected her for some mistake or the other, but that happens every day, it's nothing bad.'

'Nothing she did that made you angry in, say, the last few weeks?'

Mrs Srivastava gave a brief shake of the head. No.

Kumar allowed for a pause, keeping his eyes on her.

'Mr Srivastava, was Mr Garg in the house that night?'

'Yes, he was here till around eight-thirty, maybe nine, working with me.'

'What kind of work was it?'

Tarun Srivastava pushed out his lower lip and shrugged.

'Work, you know. This project, that project. This payment, that payment. One factory has a broken machine, another has a new order.'

'Mr Garg looks at all these aspects? Accounts and day-to-day running?'

'Well, I have teams for everything. What I have is a big operation, dear inspector. It makes millions. Garg is very important to me, he is my single point of liaison with all these other departments.'

'When did any of you last see Rajesh?'

Tarun Srivastava uncrossed and re-crossed his legs. He looked up at the ceiling.

'Well, Garg called him into the office before he left, so again, around eight. He came into the office, Garg spoke to him about a job. That was that.'

'I had sent him to the market at around seven, for groceries,' Mrs Srivastava added.

'What kind of job?' Kumar asked the man.

'You have to ask Garg.'

'You don't know?'

'Garg knows better.'

'Alright,' Kumar sighed. His back hurt trying to balance on the sofa, but he still had questions. He liked to spread them out, toggle back and forth between strands. He found it threw people off.

'Time of death …' he began.

There was a sharp intake of breath from Neha Srivastava. Kumar looked up, impassive, trained his eyes on Mr Srivastava. 'What we have here is between one and three. Where were you around that time?'

'I was in my office, working, till around one. Then I went up to sleep.'

'Are you sure you didn't hear anything? Think about it. You were possibly awake when she fell.'

'I already told you I didn't hear a thing. I'm not senile. It wouldn't make much difference anyway. I told you already, thick glass, blackout curtains, air conditioners.'

'Do you usually sleep late?'

'Yes.'

'What about you, Madam?'

'I … I was asleep long before that. Astha doesn't sleep if I don't sleep.' Neha Srivastava toyed with the box of tissues, then threw it on the floor.

'Listen, she was like a daughter to us,' she said forcefully. Her eyes widened and the whites shone. 'She was an orphan. We took her in. Is that our sin? She came from a jungle. We wanted her to go to school, get a chance at life. She had more than she could ever hope for. You are talking to us like we are common criminals. Do you know who my husband is?'

Kumar nodded. He did know, but he had the feeling she was going to tell him anyway. When she didn't, he said, 'I am sorry for your loss. How did she come to work in your house? Through an agency?'

'No. Her aunt works for a relative of ours in Lucknow. She brought her to us.'

'Where is the aunt? Has she been told?'

'Yes,' Tarun Srivastava said. 'Yes, of course. She is not here. She is only a distant aunt. They were not close or anything. She helped her when she needed help, that's all. Do you have any more questions, Inspector?'

'We will need her name and phone number.'

'Garg will give you the details.'

'How much did she get paid?'

'Garg has the details.'

'What were her responsibilities in the house?'

Mr Srivastava looked at his wife and sighed.

'Not much, a little bit of everything. She helped me around the house, cooking, cleaning, washing small clothes, folding laundry, that kind of thing. She helped my daughter if she needed anything, like a big sister. Light work. I was looking for a school for her.'

'Did you find one?'

'No, not yet,' she said fretfully.

Kumar waited for her to gather herself.

'How long did she work for you?'

'A year, no, a little longer.' She looked at her husband for confirmation. He ignored her.

'She was about fourteen when she came?'

Neha Srivastava shrugged.

'How long since Rajesh joined you?'

'About six months,' Tarun Srivastava said.

'Where does he come from?'

'You have to ask Garg. Do you think I have the time to deal with such things?'

'Was Rajesh involved with Jyoti?'

'Garg told me a few days ago, that the other driver had talked to him about it.'

'I was told that Rajesh was up to no good,' Neha Srivastava said. 'Our cook … but she didn't say much … "Ma'am, you should be careful about Rajesh, he is getting very friendly with Jyoti." I asked her what she meant, but she did not want to say, just said she was worried because Jyoti was so young … "

'That was a few days back, a week at the most,' she added. 'I had not even had time to think about it.'

'You did not personally see them together inside the house?'

A spark flared in Neha Srivastava's eyes. 'Absolutely not! They would not dare!' She looked at her husband and said angrily, 'But I want these drivers of yours not to come inside the house at all.'

'And I kept telling you not to let the girl go out of the house on her own,' Tarun Srivastava retorted.

'Is it possible that Jyoti and Rajesh were seeing each other outside?' Kumar said.

'Of course,' he replied. 'This is not a prison. She was free to come and go as she pleased. But maybe she should not have been, because of her age. Who knows who she met or did what with.'

The interview came to an end. Kumar relocated. Zeeshan joined him in the office with Umesh Garg.

The cook was bustling around in the kitchen and looked disapprovingly at Meera when she entered her space. Then she smiled, displaying perfect white teeth, her face creasing into deep lines. She tucked a hennaed strand back inside the hairnet and said, 'You want something?'

'I have to ask you a few questions,' Meera smiled. 'What a great kitchen!'

'I keep it clean,' Usmana said. As if to prove her point, she began to vigorously rub the counter with a towel. 'I have a lot of work to do, you know.'

'Please, go on,' Meera said, as she leaned against the counter with her arms folded across her chest. The kitchen was a long, narrow space with two enormous refrigerators facing each other like sentinels at the door. One was infested with magnets, the other bare. Two counters ran parallel to each other for almost the entire length of the kitchen. One was interrupted by a gas system with six burners and a spacious oven underneath it. The other featured a sink about four feet wide, divided into three sections. Rows of cabinets advanced above and below the counters. Usmana opened a cabinet to bring out a bowl. The door shut itself with a soft swoosh. There was a Nespresso machine with a stack of pods arranged neatly next to it.

'That fancy thing makes coffee,' Usmana said, following Meera's gaze.

'I know, I love it.'

With a paring knife, Usmana began to peel garlic. She had five full heads to get through. She dropped the peeled pods into the glass bowl.

'Are you new?' she asked shrewdly, keeping her eyes on the garlic.

'What do you mean?'

'Like, new to your job.'

'Yes, how did you know?'

'You are the only one who smiles.'

Meera's smile got wider.

'Do women need a body like yours to join the force?'

'No, aunty.'

'Are you married?'

'No, aunty.'

'You'll find it difficult to marry with a body like that. You are pretty, but you are built like a man.'

'We'll see, aunty, no hurry. Jyoti worked by your side?'

The cook's eyes filled with scorn. 'I never thought I would see anything like it. I was walking here when I saw those people outside the gate and my heart sank.' She wiped her face with her sleeve. 'I thought maybe there had been a fire, or an accident, I was sure someone had died. At first, I thought it was Baby …'

'Who's that?'

'Oh, Madam's daughter. I saw *her*, impaled on the wall. God save me!' Usmana swallowed hard.

Meera waited till Usmana went back to the garlic again. 'Did Jyoti say anything to you?'

'Not to me. She gave me no importance. I don't want to speak badly about a girl who has died, but I found her behaviour odd.'

'Odd? Like how?'

'What can I tell you, I am a mother, I can only imagine what it's like to grow up without a mother or a father … but she had a bad attitude, you know? She hardly spoke, she was always withdrawn, always a tortured look on her. But everyone was nice to her. She found a home here. I'm a mother,' she said again, looking up plaintively at Meera. 'I could have helped her, but no, she did not want my help.'

'Help in what way? What was she troubled by?'

Usmana put the paring knife down, washed her hands, picked up a steel tumbler from the counter, filled it with water from the dispenser attached to the fridge. She drank it in one go. 'I see things, you know.'

'Like what?'

'Like the way she used to look at that new driver Brajesh.'

'Rajesh?'

'Yes, him, the one who has run away. When you get him, you should thrash him to within an inch of his life. Swear to god you will do it?'

'You saw them together?'

'I don't want to talk about such things.'

'It's alright, aunty, you should tell me. If anyone is to blame for the girl's death, we should know. Only then can we take action.'

'Blame? Who is to blame except the girl herself? She was too proud of her beauty, you know? God be kind to her in heaven, but at her age … the way she would look at Brajesh …'

'But you never saw them together?'

'No, but people would tell me, you know. They would say, "Usmana, you are a mother, teach the girl right from wrong, put her on the right path." But she gave me no respect. She did not even behave well with Madam, do you know? Madam is a kind and generous person, but would this girl ever even smile at her? No! How can that be good for the atmosphere of the house? Especially since she was supposed to keep our Baby company?'

'Who would tell you about them?'

'Huh?'

'You said, people would tell you to talk to Jyoti …'

'People in the neighbourhood.'

'Give me a name?'

'Like the guard outside.'

'Would it be possible for Rajesh to go up to Jyoti's room without being noticed?'

'Maybe at night, yes. I'm sure they were up to no good. But most of the day, I'm in the kitchen. See that window?' Usmana pointed at one, at the far end, with a view of the back garden. 'I would be able to see him if he went up.'

'Are you here most of the day?'

'Yes, I come at six-thirty in the morning. I stay till seven in the evening.'

'What about your kids?'

'What about them? I have two boys. They both work outside Delhi. Their father died a long time ago. I raised them all by myself.'

'Okay. Next time I come to the house, make me one of those.' Meera pointed to the Nespresso machine and winked.

'Where were you between one and three that night?' Kumar asked, feeling far more comfortable in a chair. Umesh Garg sat across the desk from him. The desk was made of dark wood that had been polished with care. Unlike the glacial living room, the office was warm and compact. The chairs were of leather, a deep tan. Heavy curtains of brown velvet. One wall had a TV, with the only sofa in the room, a black single-seater, facing it. A framed poster of *Mother India* dominated another wall.

'I was home, like I told you earlier,' Garg said.

'Right, in Rohini,' Zeeshan said, looking at his notebook.

'Yes.'

'There are people in your house who can vouch for this?'

Garg laughed. 'You are not serious. Has there been a murder I don't know about? Am I a suspect?' He put his elbows on the table and frowned at Kumar. A laptop, two iPads, a telephone and a few files lay in front of him.

'Till we are able to determine the manner of death, nothing is ruled out,' Kumar said. 'Who else is at home? Who can vouch for you?'

'My wife. My youngest son. I have three. The other two live and work abroad. My mother. We have a live-in servant. She was in the house too.'

'I don't suppose you saw or heard anything to indicate Jyoti might take her own life?'

'No. But she was a sullen kid, moody at the best of times.'

'I have a feeling nothing happens in this house without you knowing about it.'

'When I'm in the house, I'm cooped up here. So, no, that's not true.'

'Did Jyoti's employment happen through you?'

'No.'

'How much did she get paid?'

'She got a stipend, 2,500 rupees a month.'

'2,500?'

'She had a room to stay in for free, water, electricity … all free. No bills to pay, even got food from the house and Astha Baby-ji's clothes. Twenty-five hundred is generous, no?'

'You said you spoke to Rajesh once that evening, for work. What work?'

'He had to go to one of our factories for a delivery.'

'Which one? The one in Bawana?'

'Yes.'

'What kind of delivery?'

Garg fiddled with the stuff on the desk. He shifted one iPad from left to right, aligned it with the other one. He fixed Kumar with a conspiratorial look. Cleared his throat.

'Well, I'm not sure I should be telling you this, but the fucker has run away, the girl has died, we are in this terrible situation, so …'

Kumar waited without a word. He began to inspect something under his left thumbnail with great care. He yawned and made a half-hearted attempt at stifling it. Zeeshan knew the signs. This was the interview that really interested him.

Garg leaned forward, as if to whisper.

'I had to rush money—cash—for one of the Bawana gangs. A payment was due, I had forgotten, I received a threat. Do you have knowledge of the Bawana gangs?'

Kumar shook his head, almost imperceptibly. 'No,' he lied. 'How much cash?'

'You will need a court order for that answer,' Garg said with no malice. 'It was quite a lot.' Garg interlaced his fingers and cracked them all in one motion. He untwined them and pointed the index finger of his right hand at Kumar.

'Here's what I think happened. Rajesh had something going on with Jyoti. Maybe he raped her. I hate saying things like this, but it's possible. Maybe she was threatening to tell on him. When I gave him the money, he hatched a devious plan—to get rid of Jyoti and disappear with the cash. Or, another possibility. He got her into bed promising marriage. Then he decided he wanted to steal and run, forget about her. He called her after getting away, told her he was not coming back. She killed herself out of shame.'

Kumar closed his eyes, rubbed his nose with his palm. 'You've put a lot of thought into this,' he mumbled.

'I've thought of nothing else since the tragedy happened.' Garg sat back in his reclining chair, clasped his hands behind his head. Outside the room, Zeeshan heard footsteps, the muffled thud of a heavy object being put down.

'So, when Rajesh took the car, he left on your instructions?'

'Yes, of course, how else would he have been allowed out of the gate?'

'Mr Srivastava knew about it?'

'Yes, though he may not necessarily remember. He has a lot on his mind. I only mentioned it in passing before I left. And I only told him because the delivery was going to happen late at night.'

'What time?'

'The handover was to happen at two-thirty in the morning.'

'Where?'

'Outside our factory.'

'Do these things usually happen like this? With barely any notice?'

Garg sat up straight, eyes on Kumar.

'I always assumed you people knew how these things happened and were in on it.'

Kumar smiled his stupid smile. 'Not me,' he said. 'I've no experience with gangs.'

'Yes, that is how it always happens. Sudden, quick. I guess it has to do with avoiding traps. Anyway, like I told you, we really cannot talk about it. If this goes to court, I will deny I said any of these things.'

'The money was not handed over?'

'No.'

'Rajesh did not make it to the meeting?'

'No.'

'Were you in touch with him?'

'Yes, he called me when he left. He was supposed to call me when the handover was done. He didn't. I waited for ten minutes, called him, but his phone was off.'

'Your call data will support this?'

'Yes.'

'What did you do then?'

'I panicked. It had never happened before.'

'Did you call Mr Srivastava?'

'No, I was trying to sort things in my head, figure out what went wrong. The next thing I knew, Mr Srivastava was calling to tell me about the girl.'

'A sleepless night.'

'Very much so.'

'Rajesh joined you around six months back, right?'

'Yes.'

'Yet you trusted him enough to send a large amount of cash for a crucial handover in the middle of the night? Why not send your old driver? He was here that night too.'

'Rajesh had done it before with no problem. The cash was packed in a cardboard box with an industrial goods label, wrapped in plastic, sealed. He should not have known there was money in it, just a thing to drop off at the factory. As for the other driver, Kuldeep, I thought I should spare him on account of his age. He has a family to go back to. I was being considerate.'

'That does not sound right, does it, Zeeshan?'

Zeeshan, who had sat through many such interviews with his boss, was adept at being a shadow, silent and insubstantial. He did not say anything.

'You are more considerate about your old driver than concerned about a massive sum of money and a notorious gang?'

'You really are inexperienced in these matters, aren't you?' Garg laughed. 'Look, we are a big operation. Lots of factories, offices, employees, all of that. Things are always happening. People are always coming and going. It's not a big deal. Money has been dropped off for the gangs by all kinds of employees, at all hours. We operate on a basic level of trust. Our employees know we are not to be fucked with. You don't reach where we are by getting fucked, you know? This is the first time anything like this has happened in all my years here. Perhaps you are right. Perhaps we got complacent, we slipped. It won't happen again.'

'Was Rajesh supposed to do the handover himself?'

'That's a good question, Inspector, you are catching on. We wouldn't trust a rookie with a handover. He was supposed to give the package to the guard at the factory, who has worked with us for over a decade. The guard is from Sir's village, in fact.'

'What time did you speak to Rajesh last?'

'Like I told you, when he left the house. Around one.'

'How was he hired?'

'Through our transport agency.'

'The agency can give us more details about him?'

Garg opened a drawer and took out a black organiser. He shuffled through it and produced a card. 'Here,' he said, handing it to Kumar. 'This man can give you the background on the driver.'

'Where does Rajesh live?'

'I don't know.'

'No?'

'No. When he was on night duty, he slept in the guardroom outside. Otherwise, I don't know, never asked. You will catch him, won't you? He needs to be caught and punished.'

There was an urgency in Garg's voice. He pushed his chair back and stood up. 'Inspector, I have work to do. *Mehnat hi jeevan hai, kadi mehnat mera hathiyar hai.*'

Kumar ignored Garg's attempt at ending the questioning. 'Jyoti and Rajesh were both newly employed at the house. Who used to work in their positions before them?'

Garg uttered a disapproving click with his tongue.

'The previous driver's name was Ujwal. He used to work for Mr Srivastava's father. He was needed back in Sardhana, so he went back there. We work with a large pool of drivers.'

'And Jyoti's predecessor?'

'Was a nanny from a service provider.' Garg took his phone out and found a number. 'Here is the company. Girl called Sangeeta worked here for four or five years.'

Zeeshan took the phone and jotted the number down.

Kumar took a final look around the room. His eyes rested on a large portrait of a man who bore an unmistakable resemblance to Tarun Srivastava. The same protruding eyes, imposing physique, the nose a straight line—it was an older version of the same man, with a walrus moustache thrown in.

'And that?' Kumar asked.

Garg turned to look at the portrait—oil on canvas, the half-lit brown and dark tones found in old-fashioned portraits of Indian royalty—and smiled. 'That is Tarun-ji's father, Narender-ji. He built this business empire from the ground up. It's all his. The factories, the houses … A great man who came from humble beginnings and served the nation with his blood and sweat. He changed the face of Sardhana, bringing employment and riches. A lion.'

7

Parveen whistled tunelessly as he and Sushil moved through the neighbourhood asking questions. They were both big and brawny, and Parveen delighted in the effect they had on people, the eagerness with which most people seemed to want to share information with them, the relief on their faces when they were done.

It meant nothing to Sushil, who found police work boring. He followed orders, and that was that. Sushil went through life with quiet apathy. The only time he came out of his shell was when he lifted weights, twice a day, no matter what. He ate simply, for nutrition: a lot of dal, boiled food, very little salt, thick rotis drenched in ghee. He was enormously powerful but, unlike Parveen, he detested fights, even confrontations.

The man they were questioning was getting on Parveen's nerves. He was the guard in the house next to the Srivastavas'. The one who had discovered the body.

He could be seen on CCTV pacing up and down the short stretch of pavement between the two houses almost the entirety of the night the girl died. As he told it, he had heard a dog howling and wanted to shut it up. He thought maybe the dog was in the alley between the two houses. He had shone his torch into the alley, moved the beam around. That's when the body caught his eye. CCTV footage showed him standing at the mouth of the alley with his torch, methodically moving it side to side, before turning in haste and running towards the Srivastavas' gates. The time was 3:58 a.m.

Yet, he had heard nothing unusual. For most of the time that he was pacing, he had earphones on. Devotional music. His father was a priest. He was too, but fallen on hard times in this dark age.

'Why were you pacing like a madman?' Parveen asked him with a grin.

'Madman? What do you mean, sir? I am the only guard here who does his duty,' the man replied, his face pinched into a scowl. 'Everyone else sleeps through the night. Ram Charan was snoring. I had to bang on the gate to wake him up. You call them guards? My father taught me the importance of duty. I walk to stay alert, it's good exercise. I listen to bhajans the whole time, so it's spiritual exercise as well. Mind, body, duty!'

The guard, who was a small man, stood very straight. He wore a thick red tika on his forehead.

'How can it be that such a terrible thing happens not twenty feet from where you are, and you hear nothing?' Sushil asked in his serene voice.

'How many times will you ask me that? This is why people don't want to call the police. I heard nothing. I had my earphones on, I was listening to music. What else can I say? I don't lie, I am a priest, I have honour.'

Parveen wanted to take the man down to the station, slap him around for fun.

'Okay, fine, so help us by telling us something else, will you?' he said, scratching his moustache. 'Since you stay alert and all that, you must be seeing a lot of things other people don't see, right?'

'Absolutely!'

'People have told us the girl was going around with a new driver at the Srivastava house.'

'Rajesh.'

'Yes, Rajesh. What can you tell us about that?'

'It's true, they were up to something. I saw the two of them together, talking in whispers outside the house. Shameless. At least twice I saw them coming back together from the park over there. Can you imagine? A young girl like that! I told Rajesh one day, "What are you doing? How were you brought up by your parents? Did they not teach you a bit of decency?" He dismissed me rudely, told me not to talk about things I didn't understand. Now tell me, what is there to understand? I tell you, Inspector sahib, what are you police doing? You should be raiding the park every night. You will see what terrible things go on there.'

'Did you see Rajesh and the girl together on the day, or the night, she died?'

'No. I saw a car leave their house late, after one in the night, and I assumed it was Rajesh driving, but I did not see anything else.'

'How well do you know Rajesh?'

'Not well. But he was always hanging around, so I did speak to him, the troublemaker.'

'What do you mean?'

'From the day he came, he started feeding stray dogs, even stray cats. Created a mess! The dogs started following him around, wanted to bite other people. Some of the people who live here told him not to do it. You think a young nobody like him would show respect to his elders and betters. But no! He kept doing it. Like I said, a shameless type.'

'The girl? Did you know her?'

'Girls today, sir, what can you say? They are asking for trouble. You know what I mean, I'm sure. Especially tribal girls like this one. Their parents sell them off when they are young, they know nothing about decency. Northeastern girls too, there's a lot of them here. A bad influence.' The guard spat on the street. 'One needs to close one's eyes and pray to the mother goddess when one sees them. Signs of the Kal Yug.'

'It sounds like you look at the girls a lot, Mr Priest?' Parveen flashed him a big smile.

The guard turned a bright shade of red.

'Look at you,' Parveen said, 'your face looks like a ripe tomato. I asked you about that girl,' Parveen pointed at the lane where the body was found. 'Not the girls you stare at while listening to bhajans.'

'I have nothing to say to you.'

'I'll slap your face so hard you'll have a lot to say to me afterwards,' Parveen said with a snarl, squeezing the guard's shoulder, two fingers jammed into the collarbone. 'Ever seen a tomato getting squashed under a boot? How the skin splits and the red juices burst out?'

Sushil put a hand on Parveen's arm. 'We are going, but first you tell us what you know about Rajesh's friends. Who are the people he spoke to apart from those at the house?'

'People like him always keep bad company,' the guard said under his breath, still red in the face; he was not going to back down, he was not afraid of a lowly policeman. 'There's an MCD sweeper here who thinks he's an important person.' He spat with renewed venom. 'Important person! You should see him moving around like he owns the place. He has a bike like yours. Talk to him. Both he and Rajesh ran after those dirty strays. I don't know his name, but you can ask at the garbage dump, they'll tell you. He is the only one with a fancy bike.'

Parveen and Sushil did not have to work hard. They walked for seven minutes down the leafy Panchsheel lane till a medieval wall came into view. Across the street, where Panchsheel ended and the village of Shahpur Jat began, was the municipal dump. The man they were looking for was sitting on his bike and chatting with other sanitation workers.

Sushil took an immediate liking to the young man—he had a splendid physique, beautifully developed muscles, a showily upturned moustache, close-cropped hair, a thick gold ring in one ear.

'A Bhim Army type, eh?' Parveen said under his breath. 'Must be a troublemaker. Look at the moustache. In our village, a man from his caste with a moustache like that? We would have burned his house down.'

'He's done well with his body,' Sushil said. 'Excellent muscle definition, well balanced.'

The man, whose name was Deepak, was sullen and evasive. He was not the least bit intimidated by the two policemen and gave them next to nothing, except that he knew Rajesh and was friendly with him because they both fed strays in the neighbourhood. Nothing about Rajesh's family or where he lived, who his other friends were. He could not, or would not, tell them anything about where Rajesh may be or if he was in a relationship with the minor girl. Deepak did not know the girl. He was the area supervisor, his job was to visit the garbage dumps under his jurisdiction, check if the sorting work was going alright, if the workers who collected the waste were doing fine.

Parveen was polite and careful with him. He kept his tone in check.

The worker who collected the garbage from the Srivastava household was present too. He said he knew both Rajesh and the girl, but could not recall if he'd ever seen them together.

Parveen and Sushil took everyone's phone numbers.

Kumar, Meera and Zeeshan left the house and walked at a rapid clip towards the Panchsheel Park Residents Welfare Association office. They had a little less than a kilometre to walk. It seemed to Kumar that Meera spoke the entire time without pausing for breath. He marvelled at his new SI's lung power. After all, she was an international athlete.

The RWA office was a small, low building at the corner of a park, its roof ablaze with a profusion of pink bougainvillea.

At the office—furnished with computer tables, chairs, a small sofa and a poster celebrating a streetlight initiative by the local MLA—the association president introduced himself as 'Captain Kapoor'. He was in his late sixties, with a thick army moustache dyed the darkest shade of black. He stood around with his chest puffed out, wearing a pair of oversized sunglasses that made him look blind and some kind of a showy hat.

'My father was a captain in the army too, sir,' Kumar said as he shook the man's hand.

'Oh, I was not in the army,' Captain Kapoor said, 'I was in the merchant navy.'

Kumar wondered if civilians could use rank once they retired. He dismissed the thought and got to the point. 'You said on the phone you have information for us?'

'Yes, you see, the driver you are looking for, I know something about him,' Captain Kapoor said. 'He is of a criminal mind, a born crook.'

'What did he do?' Kumar asked.

'He made trouble all the time. When servants don't know their place, it leads to nothing but trouble, don't you think? You can't trust them. They come here, settle into servants quarters. Then they feel they own the place. Next thing you know, they've robbed you and disappeared.'

'Did that happen to you?'

'No, thank god. But, listen, our ladies don't feel safe inside the colony. The servants are always loitering, staring at them. They are sitting around in our parks. You go now, you'll find them, as if they have no work to do, as if we are paying them for doing nothing. Our children can't play in the parks because of them. We distributed a circular banning the use of parks by anyone but house owners, but they still do it. Can't you stop them? I complained once and they sent a constable, but he told me he couldn't do anything since it's a public park. Public? The RWA maintains these parks, it's our money! Look at how they live, go to the servants' quarters. Filth everywhere, throwing garbage wherever they feel like ...'

'Hold on, wait. Tell me about this driver Rajesh. You said he was a troublemaker. Why?'

Captain Kapoor leaned forward, as if to get a closer look at Kumar.

'What did you say your name is?'

'Inspector Prashant Kumar. You were saying you have information on Rajesh Mondal. Can you tell me what it is?'

'Ah, wait, let me introduce you to two of our most respected residents,' the captain said, looking over Kumar's shoulders and breaking into a smile. Kumar turned to see a young couple striding towards them. The three shook hands with enthusiasm.

'The youngest members of our association,' Kapoor said. 'Mr Ganguly, our secretary, his wife Mrs Tanya Singh, our vice-president. Mr Ganguly is with the Boston Consulting Group. Missus is a partner at Shah and Shroff. Very decent people.'

An alarm bell went off in Kumar's head. BCG! DCP Khandekar had said there was nothing to it. Even so, dare he ask?

Kumar was aware that he felt a little intimidated by the young couple. Their clothes must have cost a fortune, and they looked like they had stepped out of a movie. They spoke with an easy charm. They were delighted to meet a lady officer. Kumar thought about telling them Meera was a decorated athlete, but refrained. They went on and on. How honoured they were to assist the police in their noble work, really, how hard and thankless police work was.

'You have information about our case?' Kumar spoke in Hindi, getting a curious look from Meera.

'Oh yes, I am not sure how it will help your investigations,' Mr Ganguly said, in English, 'but we can vouch that the poor girl who died was involved with the driver.'

'Why do you say that?'

'We run in the green belt over there. We've seen them together, walking in the park—really close,' said Tanya Singh, gesturing with her long, elegant fingers. She wore rings on each hand and a sleek smart watch on her left wrist. How mellow and measured her voice was, soft, cool and warm at the same time. A movie voice.

'One time, we saw them arguing, furiously arguing. Another time, we saw her crying, sitting alone on a bench. A few days back, she looked like she was crying again.'

'Did you hear them, speak to her?'

'No!'

'Look, we don't believe in caste and class and things like that,' Ganguly said. 'My wife is a celebrated human rights lawyer. We donate to several charities for the upliftment of the poor, but the truth is, at the end of the day, you have to see things in a practical way. These servants, they are not well educated like you or me, they are obviously desperate for money, so they do things you or I would not do. I think this is what has happened here.'

Kumar had no idea what he was talking about. What did they think had happened? He did not know if the case had to do with money.

'So, you work for BCG?' Kumar said.

'Yes, that's right, why?'

Kumar stared at the man for a moment. He noted the thin wire-framed glasses, the perfect shave, the haircut as neat as his freshly ironed shirt, shoes that may have been brand new—looked like a man who had been gift-wrapped.

'No, nothing,' Kumar said. 'You were telling us you have information on the driver that's relevant to our case.'

'That driver was quite an aggressive person, he umm, actually, he even misbehaved with my wife once.'

'What happened?' Kumar asked.

'Well, you see, we have a stray dog menace in our colony. We tried to start a drive to remove the dogs, but he came with another fellow on a bike, a dangerous-looking guy with an exaggerated moustache, shouted at my wife, actually dared to throw the law at her, the chump.'

'But the law does say you cannot remove dogs, you can only spay them,' Meera interjected. Her tone surprised Kumar. She spoke in Hindi, the accent on every word landing like a hard stop. 'And,' Meera added, 'the law protects those who feed stray animals.'

'That's right, darling,' Tanya Singh said. She took off her sunglasses, smiled at Meera. She had beautiful eyes, big and dark. 'We fully support that. We love animals. We go on wildlife safaris every year. Have you ever been on one? We have a dog ourselves. But you can't always blindly follow the law, can you? What happens when the dogs start biting children? What about the rights of our children? Our right to live safely, walk and play without fear?'

'Have there been cases here, of dogs biting children?' Meera said.

'We are not sure,' Ganguly said.

'How many cases do you know about?' Meera asked.

'Can't tell you about a specific case … but the other day …'

'So, you have no cases of dogs biting, you have nothing really to say to help our case, but you thought it would be a good idea to bring us here and waste our time? *Falana, dhimkana, kuch bhi* … Do we look like your servants?'

'How dare you speak to us like that?' Tanya Singh's voice was transformed, hoarse.

Kumar intervened. He raised a hand and said, 'That's it! We are done. Thank you for your time.'

At the station, he asked Zeeshan to leave the office. 'Get us tea.'

Meera stood with her head bowed. Zeeshan closed the door behind him.

'What the hell was that?'

'I am sorry, sir, I don't know what came over me,' Meera said. She looked up. 'Actually, I do know. I love dogs, sir. I feed strays myself. I've had nasty fights about it with people like those three.'

'You mean rich assholes?'

He wondered about the chances of coming across a BCG bigshot during the investigation and immediately making a bad impression on him. It could only happen to him. He imagined Mr Ganguly smiling, telling him in his crisp English that he was no longer needed on the police force.

'No … rich, not rich, English-type, Hindi-type, village, city … not those things, I mean people who don't like animals.' Meera was exasperated, annoyed that Kumar had not stood up for her. 'Do you like animals, sir?'

Kumar ignored the question. He kept his eyes on Meera.

'Also, they kept saying, servant, servant, servants' quarters … that was getting to me too.'

'I don't understand, is there a problem with the word?'

'My mother worked as a house help,' Meera said. 'When I was quite young, when I first moved to a sports hostel in a city, I was fourteen. My mother came with me, she needed to find a job to support my training. My father had fallen ill, lung cancer, we were in a bit of trouble for money. She worked as a cleaner in a big house, close to the sports authority centre.'

Meera rocked back and forth on her heels as she spoke. She did not think Kumar understood.

'Sir, I grew up in a village, a proper interior place, where we did our own cleaning, cooking, washing … no one called anyone else a servant there. Anyway, when I was eighteen, I moved to the US, I was there for three months.'

'Really? Where?' Kumar motioned for Meera to take a seat.

'Colorado, the US Olympic Training Centre. I stayed with a coach there. Thing is, sir, they don't have servants either. In fact, they treat the word like an insult. One time, there was this girl who I did not get along with, she was always trying to get under my skin. I knew her from my Lucknow camp, the sports authority hostel. We trained together at USOTC, though we did not live together, thank god. One time, the coach asked me to get her laptop from her office, and this girl, she said, in front of the coach, she said, "What are you, her servant? Like your mother used to be." I tell you, sir, coach was so angry, she was so angry, she made the girl run laps around the wrestling hall, gave us a lecture about words we cannot use, about dignity, said there are no servants except god's servants, we are free, we are equal.' Meera took in a lungful of air like a swimmer mid-stroke. 'We can be of service, service is a great thing, we can be good at our jobs. She had a saying: All work is good work, all work is hard, all work is easy.'

Kumar smiled. 'Listen, we are not in America; this is India. If you go off every time you hear the word servant, how will you be of any service?'

Amused by his own wordplay, he grinned widely at Meera and waited for a response. But Meera was still stewing in her sense of injustice.

'My mother used to tell me, *Chhori, is gam main rahna, cheenti kha gi hathni ne, haan ji haan kahna*, she said. If you want to live in this village, if someone tells you the ant ate the elephant, you say: yes sir, yes sir. Seems like I haven't left my village behind.'

'That kahawat can be applied to the whole world,' Kumar said. 'Anyway, on a case, you have to keep these things under control. If you need to speak your mind, come back and do it here, not in front of the subjects. There is now a clear line between you and the rest of the world, you understand? You are police, they are civilians. You are the investigator, they are subjects. Not people: civilians. Subjects. Right? End of the day, your job is to manipulate them. Can't do that if you let your emotions win. Same as in wrestling, I would think. Do you go into a fight full of emotion or do you go in calm, looking to find your opponent's weakness?'

He made sense.

'Calm, sir.'

'Right.'

'Right, sir.'

8

'You are either very brave or very foolish, Prashant.' Dr Kharb was a small man with a round face and curly hair. Every day, he power-walked through a sprawling park near his home with his dog, yet he never seemed to lose weight.

Dr Kharb had cleared the office, usually filled with subordinates and police, so only the two of them sat in the spacious room, across a wide table stacked with files, books and papers.

'Are you sure you are alright?'

'I am better than I have ever been, doctor saab,' Kumar said, 'but I fear that being better makes me a worse police officer.'

'You look good to me,' Kharb said. 'How's your wife, Prashant?'

'She's doing well,' he murmured.

'Still teaching?'

'Yes, she is.'

'Must be happy with her salary hike? Best thing this government has done in a long time. Pay the teachers well, you secure future generations.' Kharb opened the file with the autopsy report. 'I think you don't want to believe the girl killed herself,' he said.

'I'm not sure about it.'

Kharb leafed through the report.

'Well …' Kharb had to rise from his seat to hand the report over, across the desk. 'Certainly, she was not dead before she fell. The cause of death is the fall itself, there's no doubt about that. If she did not kill herself, she was pushed. There is no way to say for certain either way. The angle of the fall is such that she could have jumped or she could have been pushed. There is even the possibility that she fell accidentally.'

'Any evidence of violence on her?'

'Yes.'

Kumar's heart raced. Kharb pointed to the report. Kumar placed it on the table and began to read.

Report of post-mortem conducted on 03.04.2018

Place: All India Institute of Medical Sciences, New Delhi

Time: 11:35 a.m.–01:00 p.m.

Doctor(s): Dr Indrajit Kharb, Head, Department of Forensics, AIIMS. Dr Sujit Basu, AIIMS

General information: The victim Jyoti Dhurwa is a female around 14–15 years of age, in good health.

Height—5 feet. Weight—approximately 42 kg. Brought dead with two metal spikes in her body.

Description of clothes: Cotton T-shirt with print, cotton pajamas with print, heavily soaked with blood. Clothes perforated as corresponding to injuries described subsequently.

Description of injuries: There are two spikes in the body. One spike going from the back to the front of the body, entry from the lower border of the scapula, 2 cm x 2 cm in size, round in shape, with irregular and inverted margins, emerging from the anterior of the chest.

On subsequent dissection, the tract of the wound is going into the chest cavity, piercing the posterior wall of the left ventricle, then the anterior wall of the heart and exiting on the left side of the chest, fifth intercostal space, near the left nipple.

Second spike entry is from the back of the body, below the lower and lateral to T12 (thoracic vertebra), exiting from the front of the body, at the level of the umbilicus and slightly lateral to it. On subsequent dissection, the tract of the wound is lateral to the spine, piercing the back wall of the stomach, piercing the complete stomach, perforating the large intestine, exiting from the front wall of the stomach.

The margins of the wounds are reddish in colour and there is continuous bleeding from the injuries, which are ante-mortem in nature.

Other injuries: Restrain mark on left shoulder. Restrain mark on right upper arm. Injury is recent.

Four fingertips contusion on upper side of right arm, 1 fingertip contusion on the bottom side, greenish coloration, injury is 6–7 days old.

Two fingertips contusion on left buttock, greenish coloration. Injury is 6–7 days old.

4 fingertips contusions on the left side of the neck, 1 fingertip contusion on the right side of the neck. Injury is reddish in colour, recent.

3 crescenting abrasions in the antero-medial aspect of right arm around 6 cm above elbow joint. Injury is recent and reddish in colour.

Contusion measuring 4 m by 2 cm on the left side of the face on the cheekbone, reddish in colour. Petechial haemorrhages in the left eye. Injury is recent.

Kumar stopped reading.

'Going by the recent injuries,' Kumar said, 'someone held her by the throat, scratched her, slapped or punched her in the face?'

'Yes, someone strong, who intended to hurt,' Dr Kharb said. 'It could have happened at the time she fell, or jumped, or was pushed, or it could have happened two, three, up to five hours before that.'

Kumar pursed his lips and began to pick his nose. He realised what he was doing and began to rub the tip of his nose instead.

'She was beaten up before.'

'Or, at least, held forcefully.'

'What about sexual violence?'

'Apart from the injury on her buttocks, nothing else to indicate sexual violence.'

'Was she sexually active?'

'You know that question has been banned by the Supreme Court as irrelevant in an investigation, right? I will not answer it.'

'But no signs of rape?'

'No.'

Kumar read again: *No sign of asphyxia, no bluish discoloration of nails or lips, hyoid bone is intact.*

Cause of Death: Haemorrhage and shock due to penetrating injury to heart as a result of piercing by metal spikes.

Time since death: Post-mortem lividity is on the back of the body except at pressure points. Lividity is blanched and not fixed. Rigor Mortis is present all over the body except in fingers. No evidence of decomposition. Death was within 9 to 12 hours of post-mortem.

Stomach findings: Food particles in stomach are identifiable though they are semi-digested. Dal, rice and leafy greens are visible. Person died within 3 hours of eating last meal.

Blood collected for DNA and toxicological analysis.

Clothes collected and sent for DNA and other technical analysis.

'You think you will find DNA?'

'Unlikely,' Dr Kharb said. 'The body was handled poorly, I understand. Lots of people touched her. They even tried to pull her out, lacerated the injuries. I doubt we'll find anything through technical analysis. I can tell you right now that she was not poisoned and she had no alcohol in her system. Did your forensic team lift fingerprints from her body?'

'No,' Kumar said. 'They didn't even bother. Same reason. Too many people had touched her by the time they got there.'

Dr Kharb sighed. He wanted to say something nasty about the way the police worked, but refrained. Instead, he asked if the forensic team was likely to find anything at all.

'They will find nothing,' Kumar said in a low, faraway voice.

'Is anyone here to claim the body?' Dr Kharb asked.

'No,' Kumar said. 'We'll have to cremate her. I'll be the witness.'

Kumar hesitated before he said the next words: 'When I was a child, there used to be a magnificent peepul tree near our house. I used to imagine its canopy was a city unto itself. It was so huge, so spread out. In the evenings, when the birds came home, the noise was deafening. In summer afternoons, the silence under its shade was like god himself had hushed all life. I thought that tree could never die. That if the tree disappeared, the village would vanish with it. One day, the tree was cut down. The area had been marked for new apartment buildings …

'No one noticed, you know. The tree. No one missed it. It's like it wasn't even there, that I had imagined the whole thing. I would stare at the empty space where it once stood, and I would get confused. Was it really a dream?'

Dr Kharb got up from his seat and put on his coat. 'Come,' he said. 'I'll join you.'

They followed the hearse van through the distinctive entrance of Lodhi Crematorium—the roof slanted like a ramp, a series of hanging arches below—a stairway to heaven. The hearse came to a stop next to a sign that said CNG Crematorium. The assistant director was waiting for them. Kharb had called ahead. Kumar was glad of that.

The man shook hands with Dr Kharb. 'Good to see you,' he said. 'The arrangements are done. Do you want a frame?'

Kharb looked at Kumar, who nodded.

'Is he the mourner? Family of the deceased?' the man asked Kharb.

'No,' Kumar replied. 'This is an MLC death. I am the IO. She has no family. We'll need a mourner.'

'Got it,' the man said. 'You have the paperwork?'

'Of course,' Kharb said, handing him a folder.

The man asked them to wait and went to his office.

Kharb and Kumar sat on a bench under the shade of a sprawling neem. It was quiet. A slow day. They could have been sitting in a park if it wasn't for the tall, jagged chimneys that rose from the warehouse-like building in front of them. No smoke came out of them. No bodies inside.

The assistant director came out a few minutes later with three other people—the priest, a mourner, an operator. They carried a trolley with them, with a small bamboo frame on it, and the funereal objects—a jar of rice, another of ghee, an earthen pot.

Kumar touched Kharb on the shoulder. 'I'll pay,' he said.

'Not her employers?' Kharb said. He realised his mistake immediately. 'Of course,' he nodded.

The hearse driver helped unload the body, which was wrapped from head to toe in a white sheet. When they placed her on the bamboo frame, Kumar took a step forward and arranged the corpse so it lay on the centre of the frame. He took the opportunity to gently squeeze her arm once. He hoped no one noticed.

'I'll wait outside,' Kharb said.

The body was trolleyed into the electric crematorium. A row of eight steel ovens lined the room. The one that had '3' scribbled on its front wall was active.

The priest began his chant. The mourner cut the stitches on the white cloth near her head and revealed her face. He placed a few grains of rice in her mouth. He touched his index finger to the ghee and touched her face with it. He took the rest of the ghee and sprinkled it over the body. The operator entered his glass-enclosed booth. As the mourner circled the corpse holding the earthen pot of water, the operator remotely opened the oven door. Kumar flinched at the blast of hot air. He helped the mourner lift the frame and place it on the trolley attached to the oven. The mourner looked back at the glass booth and raised his hand. The trolley rolled into the oven. The door clanked shut.

9

The day's last call to prayer floated above the brutal sound of traffic. Isha, thought Zeeshan, and checked his watch. 8:07 p.m. He was noting down the day's events in his diary.

Kumar had bathed in the station toilet after the cremation and changed his clothes. He sat nursing a paper cup of tea.

Meera was walking rounds of the station, fulfilling two objectives at once: satiating her compulsion to keep moving and familiarising herself with the layout of her new workplace. On reaching the entrance, she turned smartly on her heel and stepped in. To her right, on a table with the dimensions of a king-size bed were two computers, a fat register and multiple phone lines manned by two constables, one male, one female—a police station's idea of a reception. To her left, a set of three sofas faced a wall-mounted screen split into four news channels. Straight ahead, a narrow corridor with office doors on either side widened into a broad staircase. As she walked towards it, she left behind the Women & Children's Cell, its doors closed, followed by the maintenance room, doors open, a technician working on an eviscerated CPU, a records room packed with filing cabinets, Auto Theft, Cyber Cell, Dispatch, Patrol, the toilets, and finally, an airy holding cell. Past the toilets, Meera took a left down a slim aisle to exit into the inner courtyard.

Delhi Police's South District HQ was a two-storey building that rose on three sides of the courtyard, the fourth side a low wall with a closed gate that led to the compound of the police housing society complex. It reminded Meera of a school. The ground-floor offices that opened to the courtyard included Inspector Kumar's room, where Meera could see Zeeshan and the boss talking, the unit's personnel room, which was empty, followed by the twin rooms of the second Crime Branch unit, and a pair of rooms for the Special Cell unit, culminating in the windowless room used for interrogations. Meera saw the door ajar and peeked in. Parveen was sleeping belly up on a bare wooden bed.

Across from where she stood, the inner offices included a large hall with a water dispenser where riot police gathered, and a canteen, where Meera could see Sushil eating by himself. The second-floor offices had windows overlooking the courtyard—DCP South District's was the largest, befitting his position. ACPs for South District, Crime Branch, Special Cell, Cyber Cell and Auto Theft were up there behind smaller panes. The second floor had the Control Room with its bank of screens, computers and mics, always kept at cold-storage temperatures. There was also a basement in the building, with an electronically controlled gate at the staircase to access it, that led to the malkhana—part evidence room, part weapons depot.

Next to the district HQ stood its smaller, more rundown version, the local police station of Hauz Khas, which also housed the South District Traffic room.

Meera retraced her steps till she had exited the district HQ compound. She found Das smoking outside. Das dropped the cigarette, ground it with his foot and gave Meera a sheepish look. They watched a busload of armed constables roll up. Hari Singh parked his small car next to the bus. Must have been a long, tiring drive, all the way from UP, Das thought. Hari Singh waved at him as he got out of the car, his phone pressed to his ear. Seconds later, Das took a call from Zeeshan asking him to report for the briefing.

It had been three days since the girl's death.

Kumar stood in front of a whiteboard with a marker in his hand and scanned the room—Sub-Inspectors Das and Meera, Head Constables Hari Singh and Parveen, and Constables Zeeshan and Sushil—the full suit.

'This,' he pointed at Meera with the marker, 'is where we talk freely. What have we observed in the last three days? What is on our minds? What is bothering us? What do we want to focus on? Meera, you start.'

'I felt claustrophobic in that house when we were doing the interviews, things felt off, but I could not understand what. I thought it's just that something awful had happened, so of course everyone would be awkward…'

'Zeeshan, why did SI Meera feel this way?'

'Because everyone in the house was lying about something or the other, or at least hiding things. She may have picked up on that.'

'I think she did, didn't you, SI Meera?' Kumar felt partial towards the young woman. 'Do we have any evidence of a lie?' This question was open to the house.

'Not yet,' Das said. 'Preliminary checks of phone records, CCTV and witness accounts corroborate that the neighbour's guard spotted the body, alerted the Srivastava guard, who woke up Mr Srivastava, who called Garg, then a driver came to pick up Mrs Srivastava and her daughter and drove them to Meerut. I spoke to the driver and saw his phone records. Rajesh left for an assignment late at night—CCTV confirms the time—and is untraced since.'

'Feels odd to me that Garg sent Rajesh with a big sum of money in the middle of the night to do a sensitive drop,' Zeeshan said. '*Businesswaala aisa chutiya hoga kya? Era gera ko bhej dega?*'

Like looking into a mirror, Kumar thought.

'Clear signs of assault, both older injuries as well as injuries close to the time of death,' Hari Singh said, waving the autopsy report.

'The most interesting thing so far,' Kumar said.

Parveen leaned back in his chair and raised his hand.

'Yes?'

'I hate to say it, but the motherfucker DCP and that sisterfucker Garg are right. Rajesh was taking advantage of the girl. Probably raped her. Maybe promised marriage backed out. Got all that cash and saw his chance to make a run for it. Girl confronted him and threatened to kill herself. He told her to fuck off. Slapped her around. She jumped. Perhaps in front of him. Perhaps after he left. That kind of stuff happens all the time, no? Daily, in fact.'

'Or he pushed her,' Zeeshan interjected.

'Any which way, he is guilty,' Parveen continued. 'Stole the money, stole the car, fucked off.'

'Hari Singh?'

'You can't deny that these things happen all the time.' Hari Singh took a bidi out of his pocket and dangled it from his lips without lighting it. 'Young boys and girls are a pain. We should focus on Rajesh.'

Kumar walked up to the whiteboard, wrote Rajesh Mondal on the top with a red marker.

'At the moment, we cannot eliminate Tarun Srivastava or Umesh Garg either,' Kumar said. He pursed his lips and squeezed his eyes shut, lost in thought. 'Or for that matter, Mrs Srivastava,' he continued. 'Meera, can you and Zeeshan work together to find the earlier nanny, Sangeeta?' He wrote the name on the board under Rajesh Mondal. 'Perhaps she has a story to tell about this household?

'Meanwhile, we have a manhunt. Let's grab our guy. He's young. As far as we can tell, has no criminal experience. Doesn't look like he planned much. He'll slip up soon. We have his phone under surveillance. At some point, he'll switch it on. There's a QST out on the car, so any toll he crosses, any nakabandi, we will know.'

Parveen slapped his hand on his thigh. 'We get him, case is over,' he smiled.

'It won't be hard, inshallah, it won't be hard,' Zeeshan said.

'The peculiar thing is, we don't know where Rajesh lives. He moved out of the address that is with the transport agency months ago, right?' Kumar asked.

Hari Singh, who had made the enquiries, nodded.

'For all we know, he could be sitting in his room wherever home is, watching TV, while we are tramping around like buffaloes in heat,' Meera said.

'His driver's licence is from UP, same address on his Aadhaar,' Hari Singh said. 'It's a one-room apartment in an old building in a village called Habibpur. Small village, paddy fields, surrounded by an industrial area. Anyway, he lived there on rent for three years, from 2014 to 2017. I met the landlord today. He didn't have much to say. Hundreds of people pass through that building, the landlord doesn't get involved unless renters don't pay up. The boy was regular with his rent. His phone number is linked to this address too. I checked with Surajpur police station, which is the closest one to the village. They have no records on anyone by the name of Rajesh Mondal either.'

'The guy has lived under the radar for the last year,' Sushil said. 'No one can tell us his address. When he lived in Habibpur, he worked in a printing press nearby as a driver. The press is owned by a relative of Tarun Srivastava. I spoke on the phone to the manager of the press, who remembered Rajesh. Said he kept a low profile, did not make any trouble during his time there.'

'Did this manager say anything about Rajesh being involved with a Muslim girl?' Hari Singh asked.

'No.'

'Well, the landlord said there were rumours that he was in a relationship with a Muslim girl, but he had certainly never brought her home, or else he would have been kicked out then and there.'

'There's a girl story wherever he goes, isn't there?' Parveen said.

'No social media?' Kumar asked Das, who had spent the day trawling through the internet to find any traces of an online life.

'No, sir, nothing.'

'Our luck we get the one person in Delhi who is not on social media.'

'I'm not on social media,' Hari Singh said.

'You have one foot through heaven's door anyway, why would you need social media?' Kumar said.

Hari Singh guffawed and slapped the table. 'My grandson made a Facebook page for me once. I hung him upside down till he deleted it.'

'Jyoti has no online presence either,' Zeeshan said earnestly. Kumar gave him a weary glance.

'At least we know what Rajesh looks like. You have his photograph from the Aadhaar and the DL?' Kumar said.

'Sir, I forwarded both on the group,' Zeeshan said.

The photos were almost identical: they showed a square-jawed young man, dark-skinned, clean-shaven, hair combed down flat on his scalp, sculpted eyebrows, piercing eyes and thick lips.

'According to his Aadhaar, he is twenty-three. The Aadhaar was made two years ago, so this photo is pretty much what we expect him to look like now, which the Srivastava household confirmed. Same hair, still shaves daily,' Kumar said.

'What about Rajesh's friend, Deepak?' Kumar said to Parveen. 'Why didn't you bring him in for questioning? He knows something; he did not give you a thing.'

Parveen shrugged. He was busy picking at something stuck between his teeth. His eyes wandered towards Meera, who was reading the post-mortem. He let his eyes linger. She is hardly a woman, he thought, with those ugly muscles. You can't tell her butt from her breasts from her biceps. She could have been beautiful if it wasn't for that. Still fuckable, though.

'Parveen?'

'Because,' Parveen said, inspecting the thing that had been stuck in his teeth. 'He is not an idiot you can rough up just like that. Motherfucker is an MCD Safai Karamchari Union leader. You try and get him here, see what happens. I'll meet him again tomorrow, follow him if necessary.'

Kumar looked at his watch. It was 9:12 p.m.

'What about the car?'

'No trace,' Das said. 'I went to PHQ, checked with Traffic, Auto Theft, PCR, border records. Nothing.'

Rajesh's CDR showed that he had made two calls to Jyoti that night, first at 10:22 p.m., a short call that lasted less than thirty seconds, and again at 11:37 p.m., when they spoke for ten minutes. Jyoti was, presumably, still alive. At 1:14 a.m., according to the CCTV at the Srivastavas' gate, Rajesh left in a Maruti Alto, the smallest car in the house, used only to run errands. At 1:15 a.m., according to his CDR, he called Garg's number. The call lasted forty-three seconds. His phone remained on for twenty more minutes after he left the house; the location pings showed him moving towards Bawana. SI Das had done well, Kumar thought, made the right moves in putting the information together in such a short time. The car had not passed through any of the toll plazas on the northwest border of the city. Das had managed to spot the car at two other locations. First at the traffic CCTV at Defence Colony crossing at 1:23 a.m. Then at the ITO crossing CCTV at 1:39 a.m. He was driving fast. Six minutes later, his phone was switched off.

'Who could have accessed the terrace that night?' Kumar said.

'Anyone inside the house,' Meera said. 'Astha, Neha Srivastava, Tarun Srivastava.'

'The outside stairs go straight up to the terrace with no doors or gates,' Zeeshan said. 'So, anyone within the gates of the house could go up as well. Rajesh. Ram Charan. No one else entered through the gate that night after Garg left, I checked the CCTV.'

'None of you think it's strange the girl fell to her death and no one heard anything?' Kumar said, his eyes closed. 'I know what they said, soundproofing in the house, ACs on, the guard was wearing earplugs … a girl jumping may not scream … but still. It seems impossible. Would the stray dogs not make a ruckus?'

Kumar opened his eyes. Everyone was looking at him.

'Do you want to do a reconstruction?' Hari Singh shifted uncomfortably in his chair. 'Do we have enough to convince the bosses?'

'We have the assault on the PM,' Kumar said, 'that should be enough. They will sign off on a deeper investigation.' He brightened. 'Okay, next steps: Hari Singh, take the arrest warrant and go to the branch where Rajesh has an account. We want an alert the moment his ATM card is used. Also, pull out his transaction details for the last six months. Zeeshan, you have Rajesh's CDR?'

'Sir.' Zeeshan rooted through his backpack, pulled out a sheaf of stapled papers.

'Excellent. You and Das start calling every number on the phone that does not belong to either Garg or the Srivastavas. Find out his connections, his friends, his family.

'Das, you speak Bangali?'

'Bangla, sir, or B*e*ngali,' Das corrected Kumar with a smile. 'Yes, I speak it.'

'Our good luck, then.'

About Jyoti Dhurwa, there was nothing. No parents. No friends. No photographs or addresses. Her phone was missing. Except for her employers and Rajesh, no one had called her. She called nobody. She did not have a bank account. There was no information about her past except the name and number of that one aunt as her 'guardian'. Kumar had called the woman, who lived in Lucknow and worked for another branch of the Srivastava family. She said she barely knew the girl. She knew people from Jyoti's village. When both her parents died—killed when a vehicle they were travelling in crashed into a truck on the highway—someone in the village had called her because she provided city jobs for people from her village. That's how Jyoti had found employment.

Even when she lived, she was like a ghost, Kumar thought.

For the next three days, the SIU headed by Inspector Kumar immersed itself in the search for the runaway. They went door to door speaking to cleaning staff, drivers, cooks, nannies, guards, gardeners.

Hari Singh drove to Surajpur to visit the local branch of the Punjab National Bank. He was made to wait for an hour, in which time he promptly fell asleep on an uncomfortable, scuffed sofa in the lulling heat. It took him a few seconds to realise where he was when the peon came to summon him. It took another fifteen minutes for the branch manager to print out the transactions from Rajesh's account for the past year, a time in which Hari Singh went around showing Rajesh's photo to the nine people who worked at the bank, asking if they knew anything.

Afterwards, he revisited the old house where Rajesh used to rent a room. Again, he showed the photograph to whoever he could find. A few people recognised the man, but no one had anything useful to say. Hari Singh pushed the girl angle. Everyone who knew Rajesh knew the rumour, but no one had any knowledge of who she was.

The policeman ate a late and spartan meal of chhole and rice at a roadside shack outside the massive walls of a Yamaha Motors factory before heading back.

Meera visited the agency from where the Srivastavas' nanny was hired, but Sangeeta had long left the company, and all they had on record was a phone number that did not work and a bank account that did not exist anymore. She went to the bank and was told to get an official letter if she needed personal information about a previous account holder. She called Zeeshan, who said it would take a couple of days to get the letter approved.

Zeeshan and Das cold-called the numbers on Rajesh's list. They reached an animal shelter. They reached the sanitation worker Deepak who said, 'At least you are working the case, that's something. One of your guys is following me, I think his name is Parveen. Tell him he can come talk to me.'

They reached a sex line. Das noted it down for his own use.

They discovered Rajesh had called nine different people in Haridwar and Rishikesh in the space of three days, looking for an apartment to rent. Zeeshan got excited. 'This is where we'll get him, bhaijaan, this is where he is!' When these people heard that Rajesh was married and planned to move in with his wife, he had been rejected. Young couples were untrustworthy, spelled trouble. Case in point, they were talking to the police right now!

Zeeshan called Kumar, who called a friend in Uttarakhand Police posted in Haridwar with a request to send teams to these houses for physical verification and go door to door with a photo of Rajesh.

Zeeshan's request to go to Haridwar was turned down.

Two of the numbers on the list turned out to be friends of Rajesh, but one worked at a call centre in Kota, Rajasthan, the other in a factory in Roorkee. Neither knew anything.

Less than an hour's drive from Haridwar, Roorkee was of prime interest. Kumar called his Uttarakhand colleague with the new information and a police team was sent to raid the friend's house even as Zeeshan called the man and kept him busy on the phone with an endless stream of questions.

Nothing came of it. Zeeshan once again put in a request to go to Roorkee and Haridwar and was turned down.

'First, we will do it the electronic way. Put that phone number on your trace list,' Kumar told him.

Parveen followed Deepak for a day, from one municipal dump to another, with stops at two different houses, before he disappeared inside the MCD office in Green Park. At exactly 5 p.m., Deepak left the office. Parveen kept on his tail, patiently staying behind the sanitation worker's hefty Enfield as they traversed the city south to north, past his old haunt, the Special Cell office at Kotwali-Daryaganj, past Rajghat and Shanti Van and the old iron bridge, across the Yamuna at Yudhisthir Bridge, where cars were crammed together like chicken in a poultry shed, before entering Welcome Colony.

When Deepak parked his bike outside a single-storey, whitewashed house, Parveen stood with his engine idling at the mouth of the thin, tree-less lane lit by dim yellow lights. To the policeman's alarm, Deepak swaggered over.

'I'm sure you want to see if Rajesh is hiding in my house?'

Parveen, who was readying for a verbal fight, was taken aback.

'It would help the case if you let me,' he murmured.

'Come.'

The house was battered and poorly built, but it had a coat of cement and paint on it, unlike the one across, which was just exposed bricks. Parveen felt queasy going in. It was one thing to enter low-caste homes when you were on a raid, another thing to be invited in. What if Deepak offered him something to eat or drink? He would refuse of course. He held his breath.

Deepak's wife opened the door and stared silently at the policeman for a couple of seconds before letting both men in.

'Would you like some water?' Deepak said.

'No,' Parveen replied curtly.

'Rooh Afza then? It was a long drive, you must be thirsty?'

'No. Let's finish this, I have to get back.'

Deepak looked Parveen in the eye and his lips curled viciously upwards, as if to say, I know what this is about, but I won't say anything because you are a guest in my home.

There was not much to see. The house had three small rooms, a kitchen and a toilet. It was neatly kept. The TV was a large new flatscreen. The fridge looked new too. In one room, a young girl, ten or twelve years old, was sitting on her bed doing her homework. When Deepak opened the door to her room, she smiled and said, 'Papa!' Her eyes widened when she saw Parveen. She swallowed whatever else she wanted to say, watched as Parveen glanced at her room, then got down on his knees and checked under the bed.

Finally, Deepak led Parveen up a rough, undulating set of steps to the terrace. It was empty.

'Happy?'

'Yes.'

The next day, Parveen and Sushil checked out the other two houses Deepak had visited when he was being followed. One was Deepak's brother's, the other belonged to a friend. People at both houses said they had never seen the person whose photo Parveen pulled up on his phone.

Every morning, the SIU met with Inspector Kumar and discussed their progress, which Kumar then recounted in his daily briefing for ACP Ahmed.

10

On 10 April, Kumar had both his wishes fulfilled. Astha Srivastava was available for an interview. The family agreed to thirty minutes, in the presence of her parents. ACP Ahmed called Kumar into her office and said she would do the interview herself, with Meera. She negotiated with the Srivastavas so only Astha and her mother would be present at the interview, not the father. Umesh Garg told her they could do the reconstruction the same evening. The Srivastavas would leave the house at 9 p.m., after the interview. The police needed to be gone by 11 p.m.

Kumar briefed his superior for Astha's questioning, handed her his notes on the interrogations done thus far. Sofia spent a couple of hours diligently reading every line, trying not to feel too bothered by the spelling and grammar.

At 8:15 p.m., Sofia and Meera sat across from Neha Srivastava and Astha in a living room ablaze with light. The chandelier, the concealed lights, the many table lamps—everything seemed to be on. Usmana came into the room, placed a tray with two glasses of water on the table, caught Meera's eye and gave her a withering look.

Sofia put on her best smile. 'Hi, Astha!'

The girl did not smile back. She stared at the two policewomen with blunt curiosity.

'Say hi, baby,' Neha said in her lazy drawl.

Astha looked like a smaller, slightly chubbier version of her mother. They wore their long, straight hair in identical fashion. They both had soft, downcast eyes. They held hands. Neha Srivastava sported a fitted gold silk shirt with a deep V and white pants. She looks much happier than when we met her last, Meera thought, more in control. Astha was in a summery, floral dress that came to her knees.

'If you are police, why are you not in uniform?' Astha asked.

'That's because we are not ordinary police,' Sofia said. She was wearing a powder blue shirt tucked into tailored khakis. 'We are special. We get to wear what we want.'

'Special in what way?'

Sofia hesitated. She did not want to say things like 'murder'. Neha Srivastava came to the rescue. 'Let them ask the questions, baby, we don't have too much time. Manu Uncle and the kids are waiting for us, no?'

'You are small and she is big.' Astha pointed at Sofia and Meera in turn.

'You know why we are here, Astha,' Sofia said. 'Can you tell us about Jyoti?'

'She was a strange girl,' Astha said, as if speaking about someone much younger than her. 'All the time sad. I didn't like her.'

'She was not your friend?'

'Friend?' Astha laughed as the twirled a strand of her hair. 'How could she be my friend?'

'We don't encourage friendship with the workers,' Neha Srivastava intervened. 'They become difficult to handle.'

'Why didn't you like her, Astha?'

'I told you, she was always sad. She was older than me but she couldn't count after ten. So stupid! Her English was so bad. She could not say omelette. She said mamlet.' Astha broke into peals of laughter.

Neha Srivastava gave her a disapproving, if half-hearted, nudge. 'Baby!'

Sofia waited for the merriment to die down.

'Do you remember what time you went to sleep that night, Astha?'

'Yes, I always sleep before eleven.'

'Were you disturbed?'

Her broad mouth pulled down. Meera was scared she would start crying. 'Papa told us, hurry up, get ready.'

'When?

'Early morning.'

'Did you hear anything or see anything that felt strange that day?'

Astha thought about it for a while, chewing her hair. Neha yanked the hair out of her mouth. Astha turned her head from side to side. 'No.'

'Did anyone behave badly with Jyoti? Did anyone hit her?'

The words had an effect on both daughter and mother. Their faces became withdrawn, sullen. They really do look remarkably alike, Sofia thought.

'So?' Sofia said. 'Who?'

'No one hits anyone in this house,' Neha Srivastava snapped. 'Be careful what you say. As it is, your circus is making our neighbours uncomfortable. God knows what they are thinking of us.'

'We found evidence that she was being beaten up,' Sofia said.

'So? It must have been that crook, Rajesh!' Neha Srivastava's voice was strained, compressed.

'Astha?' Sofia disregarded the mother, directed her question at the daughter.

Astha shook her head.

'If you have something to tell us, you should tell us,' Meera said. 'We are the good people. We are here to help you. Did Jyoti tell you she was in trouble?'

Neha Srivastava shot Meera a vicious look. She turned to Sofia. 'You have more questions? Why is that one talking? What is her rank that she can ask us questions? We are getting late.'

'Nothing strange?' Sofia asked Astha again. 'Did you hear anything when you were going to sleep?'

There was no reply from the girl. She stared at her feet, looking close to tears.

'Do you go up to the terrace, Astha?' Sofia said.

'No.'

'Okay, we are done.' Sofia flashed a smile at the girl. 'Astha, what a pretty name you have.'

To Neha Srivastava, she said, 'There is a fingerprint guy in the office with Mr Garg. Please get your daughter to give her prints on your way out.'

'She knows about the violence,' Sofia said. 'They both do. Maybe the girl spied on Rajesh and Jyoti? Told the mom?'

'Or maybe Neha Srivastava was beating her up, or her husband,' Kumar said, standing on the lawn. 'Maybe it's Neha Srivastava who gets beaten up by her husband.' A minute ago, they had watched the Srivastavas sail out of their house in a big white BMW driven by Kuldeep.

'We'll talk about it later, we've only got a couple of hours before these bastards start dancing on our heads,' Sofia said. 'Why don't you assign me a task? I'm here anyway.'

The forensic team handling the investigation walked into the compound with two men carrying a dummy—a hard plastic frame for skeletal structure, foam, sand and gravel for padding, sewed into a thick artificial leather casing to mimic skin, epidermis, dermis, hypodermis.

Sofia pointed at the dummy. 'Is that to size?'

'Yes, Ma'am,' Kumar said. 'Five foot, forty-three kilos. PM report said forty-two kilos, but she had lost blood and was unclothed for their measurements.'

They watched the forensics men go into the house, where they were met by Umesh Garg.

'Take Astha's room,' Kumar said to Sofia.

'Yeah, okay.'

'Ma'am, when you are there, look for a diary? Young girls like to keep diaries, no? If you find one, read as much as you can, take photos if there's something interesting.'

Sofia rolled her eyes and walked away.

'Pick up a radio from Zeeshan on your way up,' Kumar called out.

Meera was stationed in Neha Srivastava's room. She had taken the opportunity to saunter around the first floor—a small kitchen, four spacious bedrooms, each with a bathroom. Three of the bedrooms opened to balconies. One, the girl's, didn't.

Neha Srivastava's room only deepened Meera's cabin fever. The carpet, sofa, curtains, bed linen, they were all in subtle variations of beige. The cushions were covered with a heavy, rough, silk-like fabric in silver and gold. The mirror, easily six feet tall, was bordered by a wide frame of silver filigree. The lamps on each side of the king-sized bed were shaped like silver candlestands. A headboard ran halfway up to the ceiling, broad panels of bulging beige. No dirty laundry in the bathroom. Shampoo and conditioner in glossy plastic. Fluffy towels.

Gleaming chrome. Not a strand of hair, no discards. Nothing to suggest the room was occupied by a living, breathing human being. What was she to look for?

In the next room, Sofia locked the door. It was the smallest of the bedrooms. Out of twenty posters, the only two she recognised were of P.V. Sindhu and Justin Bieber.

Sofia dealt with the bed first, removing the baby pink sheets, the pillows, a Jaipuri duvet. The mattress was the size of a bouncy castle. Sofia struggled to get it up. Breathless and straining, she managed one corner at a time. Nothing. On the desk were a Mac and an iPad. Both were locked with passcodes. She opened the drawer. Notebooks. One by one, she leafed through them. School stuff. A sketchbook—pencil portraits, mom, dad, friends presumably. Astha was good. The room was tidy, apart from the profusion of shoes under the bed.

Sofia opened one of the wall cabinets and a cloudburst of clothes showered down on her. Her radio came to life.

'All stations, come in.'

'Bravo 2, ready,' she said weakly.

On the terrace, Waseem and Kumar weighed their options. Waseem balanced the dummy on the parapet. Kumar judged the distance and the angle, like a director deciding on a frame.

'Dropping in 3, 2, 1,' Kumar said on the radio. Waseem let go with a slight nudge. Zeeshan, standing next to him, let out a high-pitched scream, as he was supposed to. They watched one arm of the dummy hit a spike—a ripping sound—rotate and flop heavily inside of the boundary wall.

'Shit, missed it,' Waseem said.

'All stations, we'll do it again, give us ten minutes,' Kumar said.

Sofia rummaged quickly through the cupboard, looking for a diary. Nothing.

'Everything is done on electronic devices, Inspector Kumar, you old-timey moron,' she muttered under her breath, as she stepped out of the bundle of clothes.

Parveen was in Laxman's confined, bare room at the back of the house, the standing fan roaring away at full speed, doors closed. He could barely hear the radio. Fat chance he would hear anything happening outside, he thought.

Das was in Ram Charan's guardroom. Hari Singh sat in silence with Umesh Garg in the office room on the ground floor, doors and windows closed, air conditioner turned on and music on the speakers.

Sushil paced outside the house, wearing earbuds. Instead of devotional music, he was listening to a Sidhu Moosewala playlist, like he usually did at the gym. He saw his radio blip green and took off an earplug to listen.

'Dropping her,' Kumar's voice came on.

'It!' said Sofia to herself.

'In three, two, one …'

A moment later, the voice crackled again. 'All stations report to assembly point.'

The reports threw Kumar into a bleak mood.

Hari Singh had heard the scream. The thud of the body landing was fainter, but still audible. If he was asleep, as Ram Charan was, it would be easy to ignore both.

No one else had heard a thing.

11

12 April. ACP Sofia Ahmed was exhausted. It was a Friday, which meant a series of meetings—first with her immediate boss, DCP Crime Branch, then the big one with Crime Branch ACPs to compare case notes if anyone had overlaps or leads that could help another case, and finally, a review meeting with the Special CP of Crime. In the middle, she had made a dash for the Saket District Courts for an appearance before hurrying back to PHQ. She had not had time for lunch and thanked god her breakfast was so good—a thick slice of sourdough bread, a perfectly ripened avocado, two fried eggs, a handful of baby spinach briefly blanched and dressed with olive oil and sesame seeds, and a glass of juice from two Malta oranges.

She had her second meal of the day—a roast chicken salad she had packed from home—at 7 p.m., exactly twelve hours after breakfast, when she came back to the station.

Her PHQ commitments meant that she had missed her morning team briefing, so here she was, late in the evening, sitting in the SIU's office, surrounded by Kumar and his team.

'Rajesh's phone?' she said.

'Off,' Kumar replied.

'Whereabouts?'

'No idea.'

'QST on the car?'

'No hits, ma'am,' Das said.

'When Zeeshan and Das were calling the numbers on Rajesh's CDR, we stumbled on his mother,' Kumar said.

Zeeshan had made that call. A woman had answered in Bengali and he quicky handed over the phone to Das.

'He comes from a place called Prantik in West Bengal,' Das said. 'I tried speaking to the mother, but she would not answer my questions, kept asking why I was calling, if I was really police. When I told her Rajesh was missing and was a suspect in a murder, she began to rail at me. Then a man came on the line.

'This uncle said Rajesh was last in the village more than a year back, that he had not called home since dol, that is, Holi. They knew nothing about his life in the city, only that he sent money home regularly.'

'Anything else?'

'I got their address in the village. Hari Singh cross-checked with the bank. He did send money regularly to an account linked with that address. The account is in his mother's name.'

'What else do we have from the bank transactions?' Sofia turned to Hari Singh, who sat up, fixed his reading glasses and looked once at the sheaf of papers he was holding before speaking.

'Very little. No suspicious transactions at first glance. The only regular payments were to his mother. He has a little money in the account.'

'How much?'

Hari Singh checked the last sheet. '52,748 rupees.'

'The other thing I got was another account from where he's received money a couple of times,' he continued. 'I got a female, works as a saleswoman in a mall in Mumbai. His sister. Married. Husband is ground staff for Indigo Airlines. She confirmed they are three siblings, the youngest is in the village with their mother. The father left long ago, a drunkard and gambler. Rajesh left the village six years back, worked in a couple of factories in Haryana, at a call centre in Rajasthan, then steadily as a driver. She said they were close, so I scrutinised the transactions. She sent money for bhai dooj and his birthday. When she tried his number, it was switched off. She said that's rare. He had not told her about a girl, she was not aware of his relationships. When I finally told her, she broke down. She vehemently denied her brother could do such a thing.'

'They all say that,' Sofia said. 'No one's son or brother is ever capable of doing wrong.'

'Yes, ma'am.'

'We need to send a request to West Bengal Police, ask them to go over to his mother's house.'

'Absolutely,' Kumar said. 'These kinds of fugitives, without any history of crime, they usually run straight back home to their village. If he is there, they should have no trouble picking him up.'

Sofia spent the next hour sorting through the paperwork and permissions required for tracing more phones, and making official requests to the police in West Bengal.

At 10 p.m., Kumar and Zeeshan were the only ones left in the room. Kumar was bent over his big maroon notebook. Zeeshan rummaged through the call data yet again, looking for locations and cross-matching numbers.

'Sir, we should put Deepak's phone on trace as well, I think,' Zeeshan said aloud. 'We won't get into WhatsApp. Or do we need a bug on the phone?'

'Add it for trace. Go first thing to the Secretariat tomorrow and submit the list. It will take them two days to get permission.'

'Sir, for Rajesh's family, you have to give me a letter for the Home Ministry too, because they don't live in Delhi.'

'Oh yes, I'll do that right now.' Kumar made a face. 'Means at least four days before the permissions come through.'

He typed the letter out.

'Zeeshan, I want you to take SI Meera with you tomorrow, she needs to be quickly exposed to as many aspects of our work as possible.'

'Umm, sir, about that,' Zeeshan said, almost inaudibly.

'Yes?' Kumar looked up from his laptop.

'Can you pair her with someone else?'

'Why?'

'It's just that, she's a woman. It's …' Zeeshan hesitated. He did not like contradicting Kumar. 'It's not comfortable, to be alone with her all day, in the car, or eating together … I mean, how will I explain it to my wife?'

'What's there to explain? She is a policeman, you are a policeman, policemen always work in pairs. Why is it any different because she is a woman? Your boss, the ACP, is a woman too.'

'That's different, sir. I'm taking orders from her, not working in close contact with her or spending the day with her. I'll have to tell my wife. It won't be easy, it will lead to a misunderstanding.'

Kumar felt too tired to argue. He asked Zeeshan to leave the room. Better to be alone. He leaned back and closed his eyes. One by one, he began to organise everything he knew so far: Jyoti Dhurwa was last seen at around 10:30 p.m. on 3 April, when she retired to her tiny room on the terrace. At this point, the people left in the house were Tarun Srivastava, his wife and their daughter. Also, the night guard Ram Charan, the driver

Rajesh Mondal and the servant Laxman, who lived in a room at the back of the kitchen. None of them heard or saw anything out of the ordinary. No one saw the girl fall. If Jyoti had killed herself, what happened to her phone? Did it fall with her and get picked up by someone in the crowd when the body was found? Why did Rajesh run away with the money on the same night? How could it not be connected?

They had CDRs for Kuldeep, Ram Charan, Rajesh Mondal, Laxman and Jyoti. Laxman had made a call to his family in Banota, Rajasthan, around eleven, his location put him in the house for the rest of the time. Kuldeep made three calls on his way home: to his wife, to a friend, then to someone who owned a fleet of app-taxis—he was looking to leave this job, join the fleet. It checked out, as did his location. Ram Charan made no calls.

Zeeshan took off his reading glasses and rubbed his eyes. They were dry, his head hurt. 11:30 p.m., he'd had enough. He was not going to sleep at the station yet again. Zeeshan wanted to go home. He was hardly ever home. He had been married only two years and already he and his wife had drifted so far apart they found it uncomfortable to be in the same room. He had the feeling his wife was happier when he wasn't there, that she would not miss him if he stopped going home altogether. Restless and irritable, Zeeshan went over to Kumar's room. 'Sir, your wife called.'

Kumar, lost in his thoughts, was startled by Zeeshan's voice. He wished his door creaked like in the old office. 'Why are you still here?' he said. 'Go home.'

'Yes, sir. Your wife called, sir, she said she was trying to get through to you but couldn't. Wanted to know when you would be back home.' It was a lie, but it had happened so often, Zeeshan felt he could pull it off easily without Inspector Kumar or his wife being any wiser.

'Oh yes, yes, I am leaving, I was waiting for the traffic to die down a little.'

Kumar stuffed his notebook and laptop in his bag and left the office, forgetting to switch off the lights. He got into his car and sat there for a while, feeling exhausted. He was depressed about the state of his car, how dirty and unkempt it looked, its non-functioning AC, the noise it made. Kumar connected his phone to the car audio system, clicked on the playlist for the film *Anand*. He skipped the opening track, Lata Mangeshkar's rendition of *Kahin Door Jab*, and played Mukesh's version. The upbeat opening bars segued into three bare, melancholy notes. Mukesh's voice filled the car and Kumar felt tears well up. He closed his eyes and thought about Jyoti and felt an undercurrent of despair tug at him. Maybe she jumped, alone, unloved. She must have been so lonely and lost in that house. But she was also scared. Something was happening to her that still lay buried. Why the marks of a beating? Who?

By the time he got home, he felt less troubled. He was already thinking of the next day, the things that had to be done. And he had a feeling that Rajesh would be compelled to use his phone soon. Or use his ATM card. It was only a matter of time. He was desperate and on the run. He was going to make a mistake.

12

HC Parveen Tomar bellowed for tea and scanned his phone for updates. He rose from his bed and stared at himself in the small mirror on the wall, tensing his neck muscles and baring his teeth in a wolfish sneer. He watched with pleasure the veins on his neck swell up. Parveen could hear his son and his wife talking in the kitchen. He shouted for tea again, then called out to his son, who came bounding into the room. He was five years old. He stood there grinning at his father in his white-and-light blue school uniform. Parveen let out a low growl. His son squealed in delight and tried to run away. Parveen was quicker and swept him up in his arms, swung him upwards.

'Let's forget school today, go have fun, what do you say?' he said to his son, holding him aloft.

'Like what?'

'Like … like the water park we went to, you remember? With the big slide?'

'I was scared there.'

'Scared? But you didn't want to leave; I had to yank you out of the water, fool.'

Parveen sat down on the bed and placed his son on his knees.

'You are getting too heavy for me! Soon you'll be big, I'll be old and I won't be able to lift you at all.'

'When will that happen?'

'Tomorrow.'

'No!'

Parveen's wife came in with his tea and biscuits and set the plate on the table next to the bed.

'Okay, today you go to school, think about what you would like to do on Sunday, when you have a holiday, we'll do that, okay?' Parveen said.

'Yes, Papa!' He ran out holding his mother's hand.

It was 14 April. The mornings were losing their mildness at great speed. Parveen did not feel like going to work. He was yet to drink his tea when his wife came back in.

'Your tea?' she said.

Parveen reached out and held her hand. Her breasts swelled invitingly beneath her salwar-kameez. He put his other hand on her breast and squeezed. She flinched and went stiff.

'I feel like celebrating this morning, it's such a wonderful day, don't you think?' Parveen said, tightening his grip on her wrist.

'That hurts,' she said. 'And, and, I can't do it right now, it's that time of the month,' she stammered, looking down at her feet.

Parveen moved his hand away from her breast and she flinched again.

'Don't worry, I'm not going to hit you,' he said.

She smiled nervously, 'No, it's not that …'

He punched her once in the stomach, a quick, hard jab that came from nowhere. The breath went out of her. She doubled over in pain. He steadied her roughly by the hand that was still holding her wrist, steered her over to the bed.

'Here, sit down, it'll be alright, did that hurt?' He smiled, placing her hand on his crotch, forcibly moving it in a rubbing motion.

A call came on his phone. It was Anwar, the barber in Shahpur Jat. He felt a surge of excitement as he listened to what the barber had to say. He ended the call, threw his wife's hand away, picked up his tea and went to the bathroom.

Parveen's wife sat still for a few more minutes. Then she went to the kitchen and washed her face.

Constables Sushil Kumar and Hari Singh were in the office when they got the call from Parveen.

Sushil holstered his gun.

'Do you have yours?' he asked Hari Singh as they scrambled towards his car.

'No, it's in the malkhana, but we won't need it, let's go.'

Exiting, they saw SI Meera emerging into the courtyard.

'She'll insist on joining us,' Hari Singh said.

It was not possible to do real police work with a woman on the team.

'Let's go in there,' he said, pointing to the nearest door. Two men were already inside the waiting hall, drinking tea. The pair from the PCR unit.

Constables Kant and Kishore recognised Hari Singh and Sushil too; they prided themselves on never forgetting a face, or the name that went with it.

'Come, come, sit down,' Constable Kant said, 'join us for tea. Go, get tea for our guests, janab,' he said, gesturing expansively at Constable Kishore.

'We have to leave right away,' Hari Singh said, eyeing the two morons who had allowed the crowd to overrun the crime scene.

'Where are you gentlemen off to in such a hurry, how can we be of assistance?' Kant said.

Hari Singh looked at Sushil. If the driver was in the house and made a run for it …

He asked Kant and Kishore to join them. Hari Singh peered out to see if SI Meera was in sight. She was not. The four policemen bundled into Sushil's small car, drove the two kilometres from the station into the bowels of Shahpur Jat. They parked on the main road, next to a Pizza Hut and a row of designer clothes shops. The inner lanes were too narrow for a car. Kant and Kishore knew the building. They led the way down a winding alley lined with cave-like shops where men were dying fabric in bubbling vats.

'You see these men working?' Kant said. 'Illegal immigrants from Bangladesh. Destroying the village. This village! The village of Panwars. A great race of men. Warriors! You look like the perfect warrior to me, Sushil-ji, are you a Panwar?'

'No,' Sushil said. 'Walk quicker.'

'You have wonderful muscles,' Kishore said. 'A true warrior.'

'The Panwars are an old, venerated caste in our great country,' Kant continued breathlessly as they picked up the pace, avoiding pushcarts with vegetables and the occasional motorcycle wobbling through.

'Do you know Puru? Porus? The great warrior who stopped Sikander as he marched into India after conquering the world? The Panwars are descendants of Puru. Men who would choose death over dishonour. Had a great kingdom, ruling over Malwa and Ujjain, but then came the Muslim invasion, and the Panwars were never the same again. Look at them now, most of their village taken over by Muslims. The driver you are looking for, he is Muslim, no?'

'No,' Hari Singh said. 'Where is the house? How much farther?'

'We've reached.' Constable Kishore flopped down panting next to a sleeping dog, on the stone steps outside a long three-storey building. The dog woke up, stretched, left.

Sushil checked the narrow passageway between this building and the next. A few barred windows on the upper floors, not big enough for a child to squeeze through. Common walls with the building behind and the one on the other side. No exit route but the main door. You could possibly jump from one terrace to another in three different directions.

In one part of the ground floor, a man in a lace skullcap sat behind a counter. Behind him, glinting from floor to ceiling, small plastic jars of a dazzling variety of coloured sequins. Hari Singh showed him the photograph. The shopkeeper nodded slowly.

'Is he in there?'

'I don't know, saab.'

'When was the last time you saw him?'

'Can't remember, saab, but probably not in the last couple of days.'

'Where can I find the owner of the house?'

Hari Singh powered briskly down the alley following the shopkeeper's directions, took a left at a T-point, emerging into an open square, at one corner of which sat a few old men on plastic chairs, smoking hookahs.

'Sombir-ji?' Hari Singh enquired.

'Who's asking?' A heavyset man with close-cropped white hair and hooded, bloodshot eyes looked up.

'Hari Om,' Hari Singh said, handing the man his phone.

'Hari Om, Hari Om,' said the man, studying the photo. He asked Hari Singh to follow him. Kant, Kishore and Sushil were already standing outside the building.

Addressing them, Sombir-ji said, 'If you sisterfuckers do any damage to my house, I'll bring the whole village down to the police station and break your cars.' He pointed to the second floor. 'I can't go up the stairs, I'll wait here. Doesn't mean you don't behave yourselves. He lives in the third room on the right.'

The old man grabbed a plastic chair and sat down in the dim hallway.

Many eyes followed the two policemen as they made their way up the stairs, passing young men in various stages of undress. Along the corridor were doorways but no doors. For privacy, tattered bed sheets hung like curtains. The floor was dirty and wet. The smell of frying onions and garlic competed with the stink of urine. It reminded Hari Singh of a brothel. He made eye contact with the men standing in the aisle, put a finger on his lips.

They stared back blankly at the two men—who were not in uniform, but whom everyone recognised as policemen—as they walked on their toes towards the third room. A head popped out from behind the curtain, saying something. Sushil cut him short, throwing a reflexive punch. The head jerked and disappeared into the room with a howl of pain, followed by the two policemen. Hari Singh stood blocking the doorway. Sushil waved his gun around. The punched man held his hands to his face and lay groaning on the floor. There was no one else in the room. Sushil roughly pulled his hands apart to get a look at the face. It was bloody. It did not belong to Rajesh.

'Shut up, you, shut up, or I'll hit you again,' Sushil hissed. 'Where is Rajesh Mondal?'

Hari Singh turned back and spoke to the crowd of men standing outside, peering in to get a better look at the action.

'We are looking for Rajesh Mondal, who can tell us where he is? We'll give you good money.'

After a moment's silence, everyone began talking at once. When Sushil and Hari Singh managed to calm the crowd down, they learnt two things: that Rajesh had not been around to the house for several days now. Since that was not unusual, no one had bothered with it. But if there was someone who would know where Rajesh was, it was his roommate Mona. He was not around either. Sushil got Mona's number, passed it on to Das so he could put a trace on it. Then he called Kumar requesting forensics.

Kumar stood in the middle of the cramped room Rajesh shared with two others and watched the forensics team in action. There was no furniture, except two small plastic tables. One had a TV on it, the other an electric stove and some steel plates, glasses and bowls. Four single mattresses on the floor, a number of cheap duffel bags stacked in a corner. Barely any space left to stand. The forensics men were emptying the bags.

'Send this guy's clothes to the lab,' Kumar said pointlessly.

One of the forensic guys handed him two photographs. One showed Jyoti and Rajesh sitting next to each other, smiling at the camera. It was a selfie, printed poorly in colour on a sheet of A4 paper, cut to size and pasted on cardboard.

It was the first time Kumar was seeing what Jyoti had looked like when she was alive. They were both smiling. She was in a blue kurta. A lock of hair falling on her right eye. Hoops on her ears. Nose ring. Kumar did not remember her nose being pierced. Rajesh was in a black T-shirt, hair tousled. There seemed to be a lake in the backdrop but it was hard to be sure.

The other photo was a close-up of her face. Dark, shiny skin, thick lips, small but wide nose, no jewellery. She wasn't smiling.

Even in the cheap, hazy print, her eyes shimmered with a kind of wistfulness. A life with so much promise. Or was it? If she were still alive, what future did she have? She had no money and no family. The Srivastava girl had described her as dumb. 'Could not say omelette!'

Kumar realised he was in a reverie only when it was broken by the ring of someone's phone.

He stepped out of the room, saw Parveen, notebook in hand, questioning a bare-chested man in a lungi. Sushil stood a few feet away, talking to a short, well-built young man wearing a chequered shirt. Kumar took the stairs. In the corridor of the first floor, Hari Singh and a constable Kumar did not recognise were sitting on plastic chairs, addressing a crowd of young men seated on the floor.

'Forty-seven men live here, shouldn't house more than twenty, janab,' Hari Singh said to him.

'Where's Zeeshan?'

'Court date.'

'Das?'

'PHQ, I think.'

'Meera?'

Hari Singh shrugged. 'Probably at the station, sir.'

'None of you thought to call her? How will you get any work done?' Kumar stormed off.

At the station, he found Meera doing push-ups in a corner of his room. She did not hear him come in. He put his notebook on the table with a thump. She sprang straight up from the ground and stood at attention.

'I was wondering where everyone was,' she said. 'I called them but no one picked up.'

'We found the driver's address, right here, in Shahpur Jat. But he's not there. Hasn't been around for a few days. He has a close friend, a roommate. He was not there either. We'll be watching the house today.'

'That's great news, sir.'

'We found a photo of Jyoti among his belongings.' He gave her the photos.

'So, they were together,' she said softly. 'She is beautiful.'

The word hit Kumar hard. Beautiful. He had seen Jyoti's beauty, those sad eyes, the mouth of a child, and felt the awful pull of a love he had smothered ruthlessly a long time back. He felt its wild, enormous waves and feared for the dam he had built. He did not know Jyoti, but he knew she was a soul without blemish. Thrust into the world of savage men. Now dead, discarded, forgotten.

No. Not yet forgotten.

'Right. I'm going to relieve Hari Singh and Sushil. They have court dates. You and Das do the stakeout. He should be here soon. The man we are after, his name is Mona. Sells ganja. Parveen has WhatsApped a picture of him on the group.'

Das came in thirty-five minutes later, looking dejected. There was still no sign of the car. He could not understand it. Stolen cars were hard to find because there were organised groups behind the theft who specialised in avoiding detection, often by taking the car apart at a garage in the city. But this was a lone man on the run. The city had a hundred-and-twenty-two nakabandis on any given day. Thirty-eight major border checkpoints. The car should have been spotted by now.

Parveen was sitting inside a cheap eatery, next to the cashier, when they reached him.

'This guy knows Mona,' Parveen said. 'This is a Bengali restaurant.' He looked at Das and grinned. 'Bangali babu, stinks of fish. How do you eat that stuff? I can barely sit here without vomiting.'

'You don't think someone would have tipped him off?' Das said.

'Maybe, maybe not. He's new, not too many people know him, those who do seem not to like him very much. He's high most of the time.'

'Where are the two constables from the station?'

'Inside.' Parveen pointed at the building.

'Not in uniform, are they?'

'No.'

'Good. Stay here. Meera and I will wait outside.'

Parveen flashed his lewdest smile at Das. Outside, Das bought a cigarette. He walked a few steps away from Meera and leaned against a wall.

An hour passed. Das grew restless.

Meera seemed loose, relaxed, pacing a short section of the lane, smiling at passing women, often exchanging a few words.

It made Das jealous. In the land of Haryanvis, he would always be the outsider. Even if he wanted to, he would not be able to begin or join a conversation with such natural ease. He'd never be anything more than the stranger looking in, observing, sullen, keeping his thoughts to himself.

The evening deepened, the crowd grew. With the profusion of lights, people, smoke and sounds, Das grew anxious that they would fail to see their man. The photograph they had was not great. There had been at least twenty men in the last two hours who Das believed was their target. Many men had entered the building they were flanking, and many had left it. Das's jitters were punctuated by a sweet feeling of nostalgia. He had spent part of his childhood in Varanasi, and this narrow, winding lane with its bright evening lights and tightly squeezed shops, the sweet-sharp aroma of onions, garlic and chillies frying in oil, the fragrance of incense, a vegetable seller pushing a cart full of tomatoes and blocking the way for everyone, bikes trying to wedge through … all these people … then there was Meera, smiling, men looking at her as they passed by. He was looking at her too, and she looked back at him, a small pursing of the lips, a shine in her eyes. He needed another cigarette. She looked away, straining her neck to see something. He took it in, the powerful shoulders, her T-shirt stretched against the muscles of her back, thighs that looked like they had been hewed with hammer and chisel. Maybe, if he could just …

A scrawny, clean-shaven man in his twenties entered the building, his hands deep in his pockets, eyes down, chin to his chest. Meera and Das watched him go in. Parveen came out of the eatery in a rush, signalling to Das with a jerk of his head. Mona.

'Stay outside, madam, might get rough,' Parveen told Meera, sticking a hand out to stop her from following them. Meera wanted to grab the hand, twist it till she had broken a bone. She turned on her heels instead and took up a position a foot from the entrance.

Parveen and Das entered the building. Mona was climbing the stairs. As he reached the first landing, Mona saw one of the two local constables who had been stationed inside. Even in plainclothes, the man had all the markings of police—a hanging belly, moustache dyed orange, a shuffling gait with his hands clasped behind his back. While Mona considered the man coming down the stairs, Parveen crept up behind him. He clamped a hand down on Mona's shoulder.

'Mona,' he said, 'come with us.'

Mona flinched, looked back. He smashed his elbow into Parveen's face. Expecting no resistance, the policeman caught the full point of the elbow under the nose. He staggered, fell backwards, pulling Mona down in his grip, and crashed into Das.

The three men tumbled painfully down the narrow stairs. Das had just enough time to bring his arms up around his head to cushion it before he thudded on to the ground floor, landing with Parveen on top of him. Mona was the first to jump up. He sprinted for the exit. Meera was waiting for him, crouched low on the balls of her feet, legs and arms spread in a strong, defensive posture. Mona tried to dodge her, squeezing his thin body, catlike, to one side. He was almost through when she pivoted in a flash, flung herself at him, grabbing him by the waist and plunging her shoulder into the side of his stomach. The two flew out of the doorway together, brushing past an elderly lady in a sari carrying a shopping bag of vegetables—tomatoes, potatoes, onions and cauliflower scattered like shrapnel. They crashed into a man on a bicycle. Meera looked up to see that they were dangerously close to a pressure cooker on a gas stove that had been placed outside the eatery. She rolled away, maintaining her grip on a screaming Mona.

The whole street erupted. Parveen, holding his keffiyeh to his bleeding nose, raised his police ID with his other hand, shouting above the din to get people away from the scene. Das rushed to Meera. Constables Kishore and Kant emerged from the doorway, trying to pacify the crowd. Meera and Das dragged Mona down the lane towards the car, followed by Parveen in quick retreat.

An empty, airless room on the ground floor of Hauz Khas police station was used by both Crime Branch and Special Cell for interrogations. The local police steered clear. On a narrow bed of rough wood, the man called Mona had been stripped down to his underwear and laid out prone in the position the policemen called the 'helicopter'. Hari Singh held the suspect's ankles, knees bent at ninety degrees. Das had his hands pressed down on the suspect's back, and Zeeshan held the wrists so that the man's arms were fully extended.

Sushil started, 'Tell us where Rajesh is, tell us, tell us now, we'll break every bone in your body, you motherfucker, we'll set your cock on fire, we'll break your teeth, make you swallow them. Tell us where Rajesh is …'

He punctuated his questions with slaps on the face, hooking his fingers under the collarbone and pressing deep. Parveen was standing next to Hari Singh, holding a short, fat stick with which he beat the soles of Mona's feet in a fast, hard rhythm.

Mona was bawling freely, screaming over and over, 'I don't know, I don't know.'

Sushil was relentless. 'Tell us, tell us, tell us where he is, tell us, tell us, tell us where he is …'

After fifteen minutes of this, Sushil stepped back. The beating stopped. With his victim's fingers interlocked with his, Zeeshan pleaded in a sweet, placatory voice, 'Why don't you tell us, bhaijaan … tell us and this will stop, you can go home, we don't want anything to do with you, we want to know where Rajesh is, that's all.'

Sushil circled back, fuming, shoved Zeeshan aside and said, 'Motherfucker won't talk like this, he'll talk when he is passing blood through his cock and vomiting on himself. Move, let me at him.' He slapped Mona hard on the face.

'Rajesh is your friend, right?'

'Yes,' Mona whimpered.

'He was going around with that girl, Jyoti?'

'Yes.'

'He was fucking raping her, you son of a whore,' Sushil screamed, slapped Mona again. 'He fucking killed her.' Another slap. As if in the grip of a blind rage, Sushil held Mona's face in both hands, jerked it side to side.

'What did he tell you after he killed her?'

'I have not spoken to him since it happened, I have not heard from him,' Mona protested.

'Liar!' Sushil roared in Mona's face, punched him in the ear.

Hari Singh gestured to Sushil with his eyes to tone it down a bit. If they had to arrest the suspect and produce him in front of a magistrate, the beating had to be done without leaving too many marks.

Zeeshan took over, asking gently, 'When was the last time you spoke to Rajesh?'

'Two or three days before the girl died, that was the last time I saw him. After that, he was sleeping at his employer's house, doing night duty.'

'What did you talk about?'

'I don't remember ...' Mona hesitated. Sushil swooped in.

'I'll tell you, I'll tell you what I know!' Mona screamed in fear. 'I told Rajesh it was bad news, that he should not get involved with such a young girl, but he didn't listen. He said one day he would run away with the girl, she was in trouble ... I asked him what he meant. He said she was just a kid, but she was like a slave, he would free her, and I said what are you talking about, you sound mad. He said, no, you don't know, he had to do something about it. I said, what can you do, what do you mean? He was silent. This was a few days before he disappeared. I've known him for two years, he has never disappeared, I swear I don't know anything else, I swear.'

'You know where he is, you little piece of shit, you know where he is,' Sushil said. 'Give me the stick, I am going to break his head to find out.'

Inspector Kumar poked his head in to see how it was going. Sushil walked over to him.

'Anything?'

'He says he doesn't know where Rajesh is. But Rajesh had told him he was going to run away with her, the girl was a slave,' Sushil said, breathing hard.

'Okay, break for dinner, food's here. Tell Zeeshan to stand guard.'

The men gathered in Inspector Kumar's room and began to eat without ceremony. They were famished.

The news showed the chief minister of Delhi going on a hunger strike outside the secretariat, complaining about how the Central government was interfering with the state. He said to the camera: 'I'm a quarter chief minister of half a state.'

The men roared with laughter.

'Whatever you may say of him, he's got a way with words,' Kumar said.

'He's not wrong. If Delhi is a state, the police should be under the state government, not the Central government,' Hari Singh said, deftly making a pocket with a roti and dipping it in dal.

'What good would that do?' Kumar asked.

'At least most of the force won't be deployed as bodyguards for politicians.'

'Boss, you are being cynical. Tell me, if we worked for the Delhi government, we wouldn't be under the thumb of a vicious, bloodthirsty sarkar, would we?' Hari Singh spoke low, only for Kumar to hear. He feared the government's reach and vengefulness. For example, he did not trust Parveen. Most policemen were only too glad to play along with a brutal and repressive rule. It suited them just fine.

Unseen by the men, Meera entered the interrogation room. Zeeshan got up, startled.

'Leave the room,' she told him.

'But ma'am …'

'Step outside the room, constable,' Meera said. 'That's an order.'

The suspect was sitting against the wall with his knees drawn up to his chest. She sat down cross-legged in front of him.

'It's okay,' she said. 'Don't be scared, I won't hurt you.'

'Clothes,' he croaked.

'I don't have your clothes,' she said, 'but don't worry about it. I am a wrestler, I grew up watching men in langots, it means nothing to me. Here, I got you water.' She handed him a bottle.

She let him drink the water, watching him.

'You really don't know where Rajesh is?'

He shivered violently and began to cry. 'No, no, no.'

'I believe you, don't cry, I believe you.' Meera hated it when people cried.

When he stopped, she asked, 'Tell me a little about Rajesh, what kind of person is he?'

'I thought he was a good person, but now I don't know what to think. He was into animals a lot, he was always running off with a guy called Deepak—he is well known, into politics and stuff—to put medicine on injured animals. Used to waste a lot of time and money. It was an obsession with him.'

'How do you know him?'

'We used to work in a factory in Greater Noida, we lived there together as well.'

'The printing press?'

'Yes.'

'What about his girlfriend there?'

'What girlfriend?'

'There was a Muslim girl.'

'She was not his girlfriend. She used to work at the factory too, that's all. He was friendly with her. Some nights, she was scared to go home alone in a bus or auto after her shift, so he would borrow someone's bike to drop her home. People didn't like that.'

'What's her name? Where can we find her?'

'Her name … her name is Rubina. She used to live in the slum next to Regency Towers. Sector 87, not far from Pari Chowk.'

'Could he have gone there? Any other family or friends he went to visit?'

Mona thought for a moment.

'No, I don't think so. She lives with her family.'

'What else can you tell me about Rajesh?'

'He has a metal rod in one leg.'

'Really? What do you mean?'

'I don't know, you asked me if I know anything more. He has a metal rod or plate in his right leg, over here.' He pointed at his shin. 'He broke it once, but you can't tell by looking at him because he doesn't limp. Please get me out of here. Those men will kill me.'

'Don't worry, you'll live.'

Das had a thing for neatness. He was stacking the used plates and bowls on the table. Kumar asked aloud if they had enough to actually arrest Mona, keep him in custody. There was nothing obviously suspicious about him, nor could they show a definite nexus the court would approve of. Hari Singh suggested that, since he was a known dealer, they could simply plant drugs on him, have local police arrest him. Parveen thought the idea was sound. Meera entered the room. Everyone stopped talking at once.

'What were you talking about?' she asked brightly.

'Where did you go off to?' Kumar asked.

'I was talking to Mona.' Meera felt the hostility in the room spike, but disregarded it. 'We should release him, he knows nothing. We should focus on Deepak instead; I think he'll have a lot more to say.'

Meera wanted to say more, but checked herself. She waited for Kumar to think it over. To the dismay of the others, the inspector agreed. He got up to do it himself. He needed to convince the boy not to do something stupid like file a complaint against the police. He did not trust the others with a delicate job like that. A couple of thousand should do it.

'Oh, one more thing,' Meera said. 'I don't know what information you've got from him, so maybe he's told you this already, but he used to work with Rajesh at his previous workplace, the printing press, and he knows the other girl, Rubina. She and her family lived near Pari Chowk, a slum next to Regency Towers in Sector 87.'

Meera turned on her heels. The men watched her walk away. Hari Singh was the first to react.

'Madam,' he said, swiftly getting off his chair to follow. 'Madam, wait, will you tell me the address again?'

13

To Zeeshan's dismay, Kumar wanted to walk.

'Best to get fit,' Kumar said. 'I've been told fitness will be one thing they'll look at when BCG comes to fire people.'

They were going to the Srivastava house. They crossed the busy street, walked along the open drain for a few metres, took a left by the leafy park, past one of the new police barricades. The sound of traffic eased away. Zeeshan spoke.

'There's actually a big American company that goes around the world figuring out how to get rid of people?' he laughed nervously. 'Why not?' he answered his own question. 'If they can go around the world bombing and shooting people whenever and wherever they feel like …'

'Yes,' Kumar said.

'With your record, sir, who could touch you?' Zeeshan's voice held no conviction. 'If it comes to that, you'll save me, right, sir? If I lose my job, Allah knows, I'll have nothing, no one will hire me.'

Kumar felt a little out of breath. They had walked a kilometre.

'If I lose my job, I'll have to go work with my uncle in his tailoring shop. I'll throw myself in front of a train instead.'

'Stop that. What good would it do to fire you? You get paid next to nothing but work tirelessly. You know every single process, procedure and rule … which court will do what, which magistrate will help with which case, who to meet, whose palm to grease at Delhi Secretariat. You, my friend, is the last person they'll fire.'

The Srivastava house came into view, the broad gate of polished wood sweeping upwards. A guard was pacing the front of the walled compound.

'Is Mr Srivastava in?' Kumar asked the man.

'No. Do you have an appointment?'

'No. Is Mr Garg here?'

'No, sir.'

'Mrs Srivastava?'

'No.'

'Do you know when any of them will be back?'

'No.'

The family's driver, Kuldeep, poked his head out of the gate. He recognised Zeeshan and the inspector and reluctantly said hello.

'Good, you are here, will you step outside for a moment?' Kumar said.

Kuldeep took his time. He was in uniform, a slate-grey shirt, trousers of the same shade.

'Already told you everything I know,' he said.

'That's fine,' Kumar said. 'This is not an interrogation. I want to refresh my memory.'

He asked Kuldeep again about the night Jyoti died. Where he was. What time he went home. What he did that day. The answers were not new.

'Do you drive Mr Srivastava or Mrs Srivastava?'

'Mr Srivastava. Rajesh drove Madam.'

The guard stood gawping, within touching distance of Kumar. Zeeshan tugged at his sleeve, gestured for him to move away. He gave Zeeshan a spiteful look, but obeyed.

'So, do you have a daily schedule? What's it like?'

'I work from nine to nine.'

'And?'

'I take the boss wherever he wants to go.'

'There's no routine?'

'There is. We always go to the office first.'

'The one in Defence Colony?'

'Yes.'

'And?'

'It's hard to say. There are many meetings, in different locations. Sometimes we go to the factories.'

'Why are you looking for another job? You've worked here, what, fifteen years now? You must be like family.'

Kuldeep shrugged.

'Sure,' he said. 'But, you know, I feel the time has come to be my own master.'

'Does your master not treat you well?'

Kuldeep glared at Kumar.

'What happens if Mr Srivastava needs to travel at night?'

'I stay back for as long as he needs me.'

'Must be tiring.'

'I sleep in the car.'

'How many cars are there and which one do you drive?'

'There are four cars. The white BMW X1, which I drive. There's an Audi Q5, that's for Madam, Rajesh used to drive that. There's a Toyota Fortuner, but that one stays at the Defence Colony office. There was also the Alto Rajesh stole.'

'Okay. Let's talk about Rajesh.'

'Already said everything I know about him. I don't know anything more.' Kuldeep turned his head at the sound of an approaching car. The relief on his face was visible to Kumar.

Umesh Garg parked his Toyota sedan, shot out of the driver's seat.

'What's happening?' The hostility in his tone and demeanour created in Kumar a small flutter that he ignored.

'We were in the area and thought we'd stop by to double-check a few things,' Kumar said, attempting a smile.

Garg did not soften. With a jerk of his head, he commanded Kuldeep to get back inside.

'I don't think this is wise, Inspector,' he said. 'It's not a game. You finished with your questioning. For anything more, you need to go through our lawyers. That was already made clear to you. This is not a crime scene anymore that you can walk in and out of as you please.'

'I would like to speak again to you, as well as Mrs Srivastava.' Kumar's tone was ingratiating. 'You see, the last time, poor Madam was upset of course, it was difficult for her to answer our questions. I am hoping she is doing a little better now, so I would be grateful if you could arrange another session for us. Setting things up through lawyers means you'll have our legal department dancing on your head. You don't want that. Mrs Srivastava can come down to the station if she wants, or we can come here. Let me know.'

Kumar turned around without waiting for an answer and began walking back.

'What do you say we go meet the man from BCG next, he's around the corner, you know,' Kumar said to Zeeshan.

'You have some capacity for punishment, boss,' Zeeshan said. 'Do we really need to?'

Kumar laughed and shook his head.

Kumar drank a cup of tea as he carefully went through the notes in his diary. He wondered what kind of relationship Mr and Mrs Srivastava had. When he had questioned them, he had felt something missing, something that was not quite right, but he did not trust his instincts. Nothing was right about his own relationship. He thought of Garg. He admired the man's upright, confident bearing, but what did it hide? Perhaps it did not hide anything.

Kumar trawled line by line through his interview notes. Nothing jumped out. No apparent lies. No new ideas. He sighed, looked at the time. Almost nine. Not much else to do but head home. He hesitated. He closed his eyes and rested for a bit. He felt guilty. As long as he was here, Zeeshan would be in the next room, waiting.

Zeeshan came in. 'DCP sir is calling you, sir.'

Kumar opened his eyes, startled. 'He's still here?' He muttered and rose from his chair. 'You go home, Zeeshan, nothing more to do, I'll head home too after this.'

The South DCP's office was so spacious it could host a small wedding. Kumar imagined the room turned into a banquet, with long tables arranged along the rectangular perimeter on three sides, a scuffed, food-stained red carpet laid out end-to-end. The bride and groom on a small raised platform bedecked with flowers and ribbons, where DCP Ashish Singh sat behind his imposing desk, regaling his guests, Tarun Srivastava, Umesh Garg and Srivastava's lawyer, who Kumar was seeing for the first time. The man would qualify as obese. He was wearing a blue striped shirt with a tie that looked like a noose made of thin rope, tightened to the point of asphyxiation around his neck. Folds of flesh undulated above the collar before taking the shape of a nearly bald head. Small black glasses were perched on a flattish nose. Too large to fit the confines of the armrests, he sat uncomfortably on the edge of his chair, a wide smile frozen on his face.

Kumar had expected trouble, yet he was surprised to find the two central protagonists of his ongoing investigation chatting with his superior officer. He saluted and said 'Jai Hind'. DCP Singh flicked a finger dismissively at him to indicate that he should take a seat at the far end of the room.

Kumar tried harder to listen to what was being said.

'I am the tallest man in the force,' DCP Singh said. 'I'm not joking, it's official.'

Ah, Kumar thought, three tall men talking about their height. Garg must be around six foot two, Kumar guessed, which would make Srivastava a straight six. He already knew DCP Singh was six foot six. Formidable. Next, they would talk about the size of their cocks, he thought bitterly, staring at his shoes.

'Basketball?' Srivastava asked.

'No, sir, boxing,' DCP Singh said. 'When I was in the navy, but not too serious.'

'You are being modest,' Garg said. 'If only Delhi Police had more officers like you. Look at the size of your forearms, I bet you were very good at it. Doesn't he look like a champion to you?' Garg turned to Srivastava.

'You should come to the house one of these days,' Srivastava said. 'I'll introduce you to my uncle, you've never met him, but he is a big patron of sport, puts a lot of effort into developing young athletes in his district. Boxing is his favourite. Next year, I think he will contest the Boxing Federation elections. Powerful man, rules with an iron fist, you know?'

DCP Singh nodded and giggled like a schoolboy. In a loud, sharp voice, he called for Kumar. The inspector took a seat across from the DCP, keeping a five-foot gap between him and the other guests. He sat at attention.

'Mr Srivastava is saying we are not handling the case well,' DCP Singh said. 'He has come with his lawyer to discuss this. This is Mr Gaurav Kapur, of Kapur, Kapur & Ma. Mr Kapur, this is the IO of the case.'

Kumar nodded at Mr Kapur.

'I have to say, Inspector, I agree with Mr Srivastava,' DCP Singh said. 'The case needs to be handled much better. If I was investigating, I would have closed it in a week. Gaurav will remember the Saxena case, yes?'

The lawyer smiled wider. 'Yes,' he said, as if it was a private joke.

'Saxena case, a lot like this one. Closed in five days. How is Mr Saxena? Do you still represent him?'

The lawyer shrugged, bashful. 'No, but that's another story, I'll tell you when we have more time.'

DCP Singh put his elbows on the table, made a steeple with his massive hands and glared at Kumar.

'It's been, what, a month?'

Fourteen days, Kumar thought, but did not say it.

'So, where are we now with it? Have we found the driver?'

Kumar looked at Singh, opened his mouth to speak, but closed it again with a sigh.

'Yes, Inspector? Nothing? Yet, you continue questioning the family, all the people who are in Mr Srivastava's house. Still rooting around in the neighbourhood, still checking footage, what's that for?' Singh raised his voice several notches as he said the last few words and banged an open palm down on a bunch of folders. Inadvertently, his elbow hit a glass of water, which fell to the ground and shattered.

'Sorry!' DCP Singh said, looking apologetically at Srivastava, who shrugged. 'Look what you made me do!' Singh bellowed at Kumar, pressed a buzzer to call in his PA so he could get the floor cleaned.

Everyone waited silently for the cleaning to finish.

Kumar made no eye contact. DCP Singh pressed the buzzer again for his PA.

'Is ACP Ahmed in?'

'I'll check, sir.'

'Ask her to come here once the inspector leaves.'

'Sir.'

The door closed behind the PA and the boy who had come in to clean.

'Sir, we should not discuss the case here. This is a police matter, and, with due respect, they are civilians …' Kumar said softly.

'Look at what I have to deal with,' DCP Singh said, looking at Srivastava. 'You see?' He shifted his gaze to Kumar. 'Are you teaching me procedure, Inspector? Would I be sitting where I am if I did not know procedure? Do you know how many degrees I have? Do you? What's your education? Please do not forget your rank. When I speak, you say, yes sir, no sir, nothing more. Or I'll shunt you to Railways. You can spend the rest of your policing days picking up unidentified bodies from the tracks. Close the fucking case, move on. Our job is to protect these people, not harass them.'

'But, sir,' Kumar said, so softly he could barely be heard. 'Our job …'

'That's it, enough!' DCP Singh shouted. A call came on his phone. He excused himself with a smile to Srivastava and walked with the phone at his ear to the other end of the room.

Srivastava and Garg stared at Kumar, who picked up a piece of paper from the DCP's desk and read it with great interest.

'Listen, Inspector,' Srivastava said. Kumar continued reading. It was a circular issued by the Joint Commissioner of Police asking all DCPs to inform the officers in their district to not wear T-shirts and jeans when visiting PHQ. Kumar habitually wore nothing but a white shirt and blue jeans. Would he have to give it up? Or did they specifically mean the combination of T-shirt and jeans? Which would mean a collared shirt and jeans was OK?

'Motherfucker,' Srivastava hissed. 'You think you are something big, don't you?'

Kumar glanced up at the three men. The lawyer put a gentle hand on Srivastava's arm; the businessman twitched it off.

'Your DCP is a weak idiot,' Srivastava said. 'I am none of those things and I am beginning to think you have a perverted interest in dead young girls. What do you say, Umesh?'

'These days, sir, anything is possible,' Garg said.

'I am not a man who is used to being harassed, Inspector,' Srivastava said. 'My family has already gone through hell. Our house was mobbed while you motherfuckers stood around and did nothing. You have interrogated my daughter. I have not forgotten these things, Inspector, and I am not about to forgive.'

'Stop what you are doing, dragging Sir's good name through this mess,' Garg said.

'Listen, boss,' said Kapur, 'you know the lines you are crossing. You have enough experience, you know we will not stand for it …'

Srivastava held a hand up, stopped his lawyer mid-sentence.

'You have done enough. You did the whole re-enactment circus in our home. We have been very cooperative. We were nice to you. You think you can exploit our good nature? You asked for my wife to appear for questioning again at the police station. Who the fuck do you think you are? If this goes on, you will not just be shunted to Railways, you will be crushed so badly you'll wish you were dead. Do you know what one call from my uncle to the Home Ministry can do? I can call the commissioner himself, I can call on judges. I could slap you right now, you won't be able to do a thing. Don't you have a family? You don't care about them? Or is your perversion too great for such considerations?' Srivastava was livid, breathless.

Inside Kumar, the dragon stirred.

'Say something before I fucking hit you,' Srivastava said.

The lawyer began to speak, but Garg stopped him.

'Don't take this lightly, Inspector,' he said, soothingly. 'You are not as dumb as you look.'

Kumar continued to look fixedly, first at Srivastava, then at Garg, his eyes so impassive he may have been daydreaming.

'I think he is a psycho, unfit for police work,' Srivastava chuckled. 'What do you think, Umesh?'

DCP Singh came bustling up and stood in front of Srivastava with folded hands. 'Don't you worry, sir, it will be taken care of. You and your family will not be disturbed, you will not have to come here again.'

'We hope so,' Garg said smoothly as the three of them rose from their chairs. 'Or else, we won't come here. Our next stop will be the commissioner's office.'

Kapur placed a card on the table. 'If you need to contact the family for anything, please call me,' he said.

DCP Singh smiled a sickly smile, bowed. When the door closed behind the men, he sat down with a sigh. He looked deflated, small.

'You can leave now,' he said. 'Either you close the case or we take it away from you, but any which way, don't bother the family again. I'll let your ACP know too.'

Kumar left the room and stood for a moment looking at both sides of the long corridor; there was one overweight constable in uniform entering the toilet at the far end and no one else. He let out a long breath and steadied himself against the wall. You are not far from the truth, he thought to himself.

A masterful self-accuser, the thought began to creep through Kumar's mind that perhaps the DCP was right, that Srivastava had a point and perhaps he was refusing to believe the plain truth about a simple suicide, pouring into it his own muck.

He closed his eyes. Realised, with a start, that he was afraid. But there was something else too, something that brought a small, warm glow to the darkness of his anger.

He was jolted by what sounded like a pistol shot. It was the door to the ACP's office slamming shut. Sofia Ahmed strode towards the DCP's room. Their eyes met and hers shone with anger. Kumar quickly started walking away.

In his room, he locked the door from the inside. He slumped on his chair and decided there was no point going home. No point, yet again, subjecting his family to the bleak misery of his being. Anyway, he was sleeping badly at home. He decided to sleep at the office and surprise his wife by taking the next day off. It was a Saturday, so she would be off as well; they could go to the zoo. By then, he would be in a better place. His son liked animals. His wife liked the old Mughal fort next to the zoo. They had not been there in years. He would switch off his phone; he would dare to do it. A man cannot be a slave to his work. One day out of the clutches of pitiful police work wouldn't end the world.

He was surprised at how comfortable he felt sleeping on the hard bed in the tiny room attached to his office. It was perfectly dark. He thought of the zoo, of his wife, of the old fort when there was still water in the moats and people went boating, of sitting with his wife in a boat and watching the walls of the fort turn a haunting red as the sun set. It was a very, very long time ago. It was a silly thing to do, the kind of thing teenage lovers do. But they did not mind, they were so young then, the only lovers left alive.

He missed her touch, the shape of her fingers on his skin. It was not the physical act he longed for, but the textures of her body. He had thought time would make him forget, but it had been a long time and he had forgotten nothing: the smooth skin on her back, the soft, thin line of down on her belly that led to the tangle of hair between her legs, her nipples as they hardened between his fingers, the stray strands of hair around them.

He fell asleep.

Dr Kharb said, 'Too many people had touched her.'

Four fingertips contusions on the left side of the neck, one fingertip contusion on the right side of the neck. Injury is reddish in colour and recent.

He was running after his wife. He was calling her name, but she kept going, climbing the stairs, out onto a massive terrace that seemed not to end. She turned around. Her hair was short, a lock of it fell across her forehead. She tucked some of it back, behind her ear, looked at him with a frown. She smiled, but she did not know who he was.

He was scared, so scared. Finally, he said, 'It's me, don't you recognise me?' His wife stared at him. She began to cry. 'Is that really you?' she said. She touched his face, he could feel her hands and he thought, this is it, I am saved.

'Why are you crying?' he said.

'Prashant, you've grown old. How did you grow so old? You look just like your father.'

That fear again, the slither in his heart, the creeping in his stomach.

'What are you doing here?' he said.

'Pooja likes the view, she wanted me to bring her here. We called you, but you were busy.'

Kumar looked out and realised they were very high up. They were on the turret of an old Mughal fort. A terrible storm was coming. He knew the whole tower was going to fall; it was already swaying with the wind. He was paralysed. He needed to get out.

He woke up violently, like he was being smothered. The dream washed over him in waves. She was beautiful. So beautiful, kind, grown-up.

Though the stomach was ruptured …

He sat quietly with his thoughts till they were slowly replaced by familiar, faraway sounds: the faint creak of doors opening and closing, the screech of a chair pushed back, water running, boots on a stone floor, the woo-woo of sirens, always sirens.

14

Kumar drove into the police housing colony feeling well slept. He greeted the guard at the gate, squeezed his car into the usual spot. When he stepped out, his legs suddenly felt heavier. He looked up at his apartment building. It was old, the paint was peeling off, there were large splotches of scum covering the facade. A peepul had sprung from the wall, under his toilet window, watered by a leak in the pipe. He needed to get it out. Kumar wondered how long he would think about it before he got around to it. Across the first-floor stairwell balcony, clothes hung on a line. Two sets of salwar-kameez, a pair of small jeans, a red T-shirt, a football shirt with 'FC Barcelona' printed on it, a pair of black shorts, three pairs of socks. None of the clothes were his.

He started to climb the stairs, but now he was full of foreboding. Yesterday, he had not even had the courage to call and tell her he wouldn't come home at night; he had left the task to Zeeshan. He practised in his head a light, cheery tone—just the right words and just the right voice to keep his wife happy. But he could not shake off the fear that there was going to be hell to pay. The fear abruptly transformed into anger. If they did not want his company, he would sleep more, he thought. At his group, they had said, every person has a beast inside him or her, don't be afraid of it, make friends with it, get to know the beast inside of you. He knew now. But what good had that done him? He thought, 'My mother, she was a Poorvanchali rose, my father was a Paschimi brute who raped her.' He needed to get a grip on his thoughts. He was still standing at the door when it opened. His wife looked him up and down, as if asking, 'Why have you come home?'

He began to mutter an apology.

'Don't bother,' she said, her voice rising from the depths of an unlit sea. 'I actually need you for something, get inside.'

He followed her inside to find two women sitting on the sofa. One of them was howling and the other, who was the cook at their house, was holding her hands and consoling her.

Kumar was comforted by the sight. At least he and his wife were not going to fight in front of other people.

Sofia Ahmed sank into the sofa, put her legs up on the armrest. 'I think I'll sleep for a bit.'

'The job?' asked Ananya. They were in Ananya's house inside the Jawaharlal Nehru University campus. Six small steps from the front door, the ridge forest's span. Peacocks would sit not ten feet in the distance and sun themselves; nilgai would approach silently, make eye contact, pout, snort.

'It's sucking me dry, Nan, it's relentless.'

She had driven to Ananya's after her morning run.

'I hardly find the time to run anymore,' she groaned. 'You should meet these people. Daft! Regressive, illiterate, egotistic, corrupt … and the misogyny! Fuck. They are still asking women what they were doing that led to the rape, you know?'

Ananya made an irritated sound. 'Didn't you know all this?' she said. 'I know it and I've never stepped inside a police station in my life. You practically grew up inside of one.'

'Things were better in my father's time.'

'Don't be ridiculous.' Ananya, who was bent over a box of vinyls, straightened up. 'This is your mission in life, to be on the inside and make small changes, make things better. And then you'll be Delhi's first woman commissioner of police!'

Sofia made a face, turned her small frame into a foetal position.

'If you can't stand it, leave, you know, go back to literature, finish your PhD, teach.' Ananya was an assistant professor of Economics, a committed pragmatist. She shifted to the sofa, gathered Sofia's feet and placed them on her lap.

'Hey, tell me about one cool thing you've seen on the job.'

'What is this, a kiddie therapy session?' Sofia pointed her toes and poked her in the ribs. Then she remembered something and sat up.

'I have something to show you,' Sofia smiled. A short clip caught on a mobile phone of a policewoman tackling a suspect that had gone viral. She tapped play. A man came running out of a doorway, swerving hard to his right as he saw a policewoman blocking his way.

'Watch, watch.'

In a single movement, the woman sprang sideways and threw herself at him, driving her shoulder into his midriff, locking her arms behind his waist.

Ananya winced as they flew out, hit an old woman carrying her grocery, toppled a passing cyclist and rolled to the feet of the person recording it on his phone. The camera swung away.

'Wooooo …' Ananya exclaimed. 'Brutal!'

'Is she a specimen or what? She's mine, she's with me in the station!'

'Get her here immediately so we can study her closely.'

Sofia threw her head back and laughed. Her phone rang.

'Shit, a work call.'

'No!' Ananya groaned. She was looking forward to the rest of the day. She had a new record for the occasion, a Japanese pressing of Miles Davis's soundtrack for *Ascenseur pour l'échafaud*. Perfect for a slow, stoned afternoon of shutting out the world.

'I have to run,' Sofia said.

'Fuck off.'

'You fuck off.' Sofia rushed around gathering her things.

When the footage surfaced in the morning, the first thing Sofia had done was call Meera to ask whether the man was alright. He was, Meera assured her. He had been brought to the station, questioned and released.

At DCP Singh's office, Sofia came to know Meera had not told her the whole truth. The suspect had plenty of injury marks to prove it. He was showing them to DCP Singh, with his shirt pulled up, when Sofia walked in.

He was accompanied by a lawyer, a human rights activist and three reporters, seemingly led by a swaggering young man with a moustache upturned at the tips. They were all talking at once. The DCP was hunched in his seat.

He got up, raised both hands with palms outstretched and said 'please' to quieten the group. He led Sofia into the annexe and closed the door.

'Did you know?'

'No, sir, I did not,' Sofia said.

Singh sat down and began to tap on the desk rapidly. The sound annoyed her; she really could not stand being around this man.

'It's you or that insufferable Kumar,' Singh said, in a rapid murmur, as if trying to keep time with the nervous rhythm of his finger. 'You or Kumar. I'm not saying anything, but that's the choice, what can I say?'

Sofia looked Singh straight in the eye with an inscrutable expression. Tat-tat-tat-a-tat.

'I'm not saying it, but if you didn't even know about it, how are you to blame? It's your inspector gone rogue. Can't have rogue elements. Defeats the whole purpose of a uniformed force. Undermines discipline.'

There was something different about the way Singh was talking to her. Sofia felt it immediately, knew what must have happened. She did not like her father's influence creeping into her life.

'You've probably not read the Ramayana, the greatest epic ever written, but the whole saga is triggered by one rogue person. A lowly maid. Her name was Manthara. She poisoned Kaikeyi's mind. Result? Lord Ram banished into exile.'

DCP Singh shook his head as if he was personally affected by the tragedy.

'But, sir …' Sofia said, 'how else do you do custodial interrogations when you need quick results?'

Singh made a face. 'You have to do it if you have to do it, Madam ACP, but if you get caught, if you are irresponsible enough to leave marks, you have to pay for it, no? I'm not saying *you* have to pay for it, I'm not saying that, but someone has to pay.'

'Okay. Thank you, sir, I'll take it from here, you don't have to worry.'

'Worry? No, no, not at all,' Singh laughed nervously. 'I've followed procedure. I've lodged a complaint with Internal Inquiry. Your inspector is relieved from the ongoing case, maybe he will be suspended pending inquiry, we don't know, PHQ will tell us soon. Kumar is bad news. You don't know anything, so just keep yourself out of it. Move on.'

He had no right to do that, rank be damned. The team was under her direct command. Meera fucking lied to her, that dumb musclehead. And Kumar was clearly not in control. Why was she saddled with these incompetent fools? She swallowed her anger. She felt helpless, weak.

'But, sir ...'

'Look, I did it for your own good, it absolves you of everything. A rogue, low-level policeman doing bad stuff. Everyone knows that story.' That nervous laugh again. It made Sofia sick in the stomach.

'If it's okay with you, sir, I would like to speak to those people outside.'

'Of course, please do, I have nothing to do with it. Unfortunate it happened in my district, but what can you say if someone goes behind your back? There are crooks even in the police. Am I wrong?'

Sofia led the lawyer, the friend and the man with the swagger, who had been introduced as Deepak, into her office. The journalists and the activist waited outside, plied with tea and biscuits.

Sofia had not made much of an effort to convert her office into a personal space, except for a French press, a packet of expensive ground coffee and a ceramic mug the colour of the sea—a gift from her father when they had holidayed in Portugal—arranged in a neat line next to her electric kettle. The only other concession she had made to personal taste was a bright pink sofa. It stood against the wall, under the window. Men hesitated to sit on it, but Deepak had no such trouble. He leaned back and crossed his legs. It occurred to Sofia fleetingly that, despite his statement moustache, he was quite attractive.

The lawyer and Mona sat across the table on straight-backed chairs.

'Are you hurt? Anything broken?' Sofia asked Mona.

'No, ma'am,' Mona told her, halting and timid. 'Not broken, but they took my clothes, beat me, tortured me, I was telling the truth …' The lawyer nodded vigorously like he was at a heavy metal concert.

'What do you want?' Sofia said, turning to Deepak.

'We want the people responsible to be punished. We want the victim to be compensated, what else?' he said.

Sofia disliked the tone, but kept her own expression in check.

'Look, if you've seen the footage, your man here was trying to run, he dropped two of my men down the stairs, we had to catch him …'

'That's all good, but did you have to lock him in a room like a hostage?'

Sofia held Deepak's gaze, softened her voice.

'I'm sorry about that. I didn't know. I would have stopped it if I knew. I am apologising personally. The person responsible has already been removed from the case, an inquiry launched.'

'Should your apology mean something to us? Or your internal inquiry? Tell me, madam, when has an internal inquiry in Delhi Police ever found a policeman guilty?'

'I will ensure he gets compensation.'

'Are you trying to buy us off?'

A professional orator, has a future in politics, Sofia thought. One day, he will be pulling our strings.

'No, I am suggesting the best path for you. Please ask your mute lawyer what will happen if you take it out of this room and go to court …'

She stopped to look each man in the eye.

'Please consider carefully if you have the time and enough money. You won't have me but the police machinery to deal with. They know every trick in the book to drag this out forever. You will spend half your life in a courtroom. We will deny everything. It's easy to explain the bruises since he was caught on video resisting arrest. Plus, he's a drug dealer. You think those reporters outside will have any sympathy with him? Or the public? He will be forgotten in the next news cycle by everyone except us. He will be a police target for the rest of his life. He will be picked up if he so much as crosses the street wrong.'

Deepak laughed, cynical, bitter. 'You think your apology will melt us. When it doesn't, you switch to a threat. Such a simple formula.'

'No, no, Madam is right, it's the truth,' the lawyer finally spoke, interrupting Deepak.

'Let it go, bhaiyya,' Mona said meekly. 'If they give us money, let's drop it.'

Deepak got up abruptly. 'Let's go.'

'Wait,' Sofia said. 'Deepak, aren't you Rajesh's friend? Where is he? He pushed that girl off the terrace …'

Deepak slammed the door on his way out.

The journalists were easy. When Sofia revealed Mona was a peddler, their faces fell.

Kumar gathered the courage to ask his wife if their son was around. They were standing in the kitchen, watching the two women talking to each other in their living room. 'I thought we could go to the zoo,' he said, 'since it's a Saturday. Look, I've even diverted my calls to Zeeshan's phone.'

'You live in a world that exists only in your head,' she replied. Her voice was hard and she spoke under her breath. 'Why would you think we're sitting around waiting for you? Did you call to say you wouldn't be home last night? Bittu and I waited. Then we ate. At midnight, your pet idiot Zeeshan called to say you were sleeping in the office. Why?

'Bittu has gone to his uncle's house. His cousins are there today, they are going out to watch a movie, then to India Gate. I was planning to go out too, you don't need to know where, before this happened. That woman there is our cook's sister. Her son is ten years old and has been missing for almost a month. From Shahbad Dairy.'

A surge of apathy ran through Kumar. If there was a chair near him, he would have slumped into it.

'What do you want me to do?'

'You are a police officer, aren't you? What do you think I want you to do? Take the case.'

'Why has she not gone to Missing Persons? This is not my thing, it's a Missing Persons case.'

'She did. She went to her local thana as well. Don't play me for a fool. I remember very well what you told me about Missing Persons.'

His wife's voice had softened, she sounded like her old self again.

'So, you listen to what I say?' A smile crept on to Kumar's face.

'Don't. Don't smile. You've trapped me in a sham marriage. If it wasn't for our son, I would have divorced you long ago … I can neither be proud of the person you are nor of the work you do. At least do something to …'

Kumar did not wait for her to finish. He could not look at her eyes, with their haunted fire of a terrible past. He turned away and walked out of the kitchen. Everything she said was true.

Sofia could not reach Kumar on the phone. When she called the inspector, she got Zeeshan and heard that his boss had a family emergency. She could not believe it. Police didn't get to have family emergencies. She snapped. 'Get the team back to the station on the double.'

'Madam, Hari Singh has gone to his in-laws' village near Rohtak.'

'Fine.' He was exempted.

She met them separately. The problem itself had been resolved, but she was still seething that things had slipped out of her control behind her back, that she had been made to look inadequate in front of a buffoon like DCP Singh. It was time to show them who was boss.

She asked, 'So, Constable Sushil, custodial torture?'

The big man nearly broke down crying. He babbled about BCG. She could barely make out what he was saying, except, no, he would not testify against the inspector. There was nothing to say. It was routine stuff.

Parveen smiled manically.

'That crook is acting. You know the kind of people they are, looking for handouts, look at poor me, always suffering. He kept trying to run away, madam. That's why he got hurt. He dropped me and Das down a whole flight of stairs. Who would have stood up for me if I broke my neck? Would there be an inquiry then?'

Das was more pliable.

'How's the investigation going?'

'Frankly, I'm not sure what we're doing,' Das said. 'Boss seems a bit distracted most times.'

'Did he order you to beat up the suspect?'

'Yes, ma'am.'

'If there is an inquiry, will you tell them that?'

Das looked a little alarmed. After a while, he said, 'If that's what you want me to tell them, ma'am.'

'There's no need to suck up to me,' Sofia said, but it felt good.

Meera came in grinning, took a deep breath and said, 'The coffee smells so good!'

Sofia did not smile or offer her a cup.

'Were you part of the interrogation of this guy Mona?'

'No, ma'am … I mean, yes, ma'am, as in I did ask questions, but if you are asking me if I was present when he was getting beaten up, then no, ma'am, the men kept me out. I only went in afterwards.'

'What condition did you find him in?'

'Oh! Did something happen to him? He looked OK to me. A little shaken, scared, but fine.'

'I thought he was stripped to his underwear.'

'Yes.'

'How is that fine?'

Sofia let the silence hang in the air.

'I thought it's our normal way of working …' Meera mumbled.

'Show me one section in the police manual, one place anywhere, from any source, that says torture is allowed, or that humiliation is normal.' Sofia's voice took on the quality of a slap to the face. 'I thought you are a bright, good person who could be the pride of the force. I thought, hey, let's put her in one of the best units there is, instead of making her run around with files all day. This is how you choose to use the opportunity?'

Meera's silence grated on her. She looked, Sofia thought, like a guilty little schoolgirl. Sofia snapped her fingers—'Hey? Hello?'

'But I'm new, I don't have rank ...'

'You can't even get yourself to say sorry?'

Tears formed in Meera's eyes.

'You are making a mistake. You think you owe allegiance to Prashant Kumar, think he's your boss. He is not. I'm your boss. I put you in his team simply for you to get experience. I can remove you right now, make you do any work I want. You owe him nothing. You are not really part of his unit.'

'What do you want me to do?'

'I want you to do the right thing,' Sofia said. 'I am looking out for you, looking out for your best interest. I want you to trust that.'

Meera nodded, still not making eye contact.

'If the situation with the torture goes out of hand, gets into the papers, the internal inquiry gets serious, I want you to tell the truth. I want you to tell the investigators Inspector Kumar ordered the interrogation. I want you tell them what was done to the poor boy. Can you do that?'

Meera looked up at Sofia. So, this is what it came down to. She felt a sharp pang of aversion towards Sofia. Inspector Kumar was a dull, uninspiring man, the kind of inept, avuncular person Meera had known all her life, like her various wrestling coaches. But she was not about to snitch.

'No,' Meera said. 'I can't.'

'What?' Sofia almost screamed. 'Do you know what I can do to you?'

'What can you do? Suspend me? Ma'am, that's fine, suspend me. But I am not snitching.' Meera stood at attention, looking straight ahead at the wall behind Sofia.

Sofia exhaled deeply. 'Coffee?'

Meera wiped her eyes with her sleeves and nodded.

'Thank you.'

Sofia switched on the electric kettle, measured out the coffee.

'Do you know, I have never watched a wrestling match, not even on TV.'

'Not even the Olympics?'

'No.'

Meera smiled uncomfortably, waiting for the coffee to finish steeping.

Sofia pushed down on the plunger, poured the coffee and slid the cup towards Meera.

'Maybe one day you could show me a few moves.'

There was a knock on the door. For Zeeshan she had a simple instruction, issued before he could step inside: get the inspector.

15

SI Das frantically sucked on a cigarette outside the police canteen. He drank a few sips of his tea, dropped the rest in the bin. Far too sweet. His day had begun with a promising development and gone wildly downhill since. He was still trying to understand what had happened. ACP Ahmed had shut down the Jyoti Dhurwa case. The SIU was told to take the day off. Kumar, he had heard, would be suspended. Meera, on the other hand—he had seen her walk into the ACP's office smiling, and walk out smiling. It didn't make sense. She disappeared soon after, while the rest of them sat around in their room.

Distraught, shirt soaked in sweat, hair all over the place, Zeeshan got down to sorting out court dates and documents. Better to be holed up in office than go home. Hari Singh and Sushil worked impassively, organising the paperwork with Zeeshan. Das had not been in a situation like this before. He suffered silently, fearful of his fate, scared even to ask how they could be so calm. He scrolled pointlessly on his phone. He lit another cigarette.

Outside the canteen, finding Parveen standing by himself with a tea and a smoke, he ventured, 'Great deal of trouble we are in?'

'Only if the motherfucker had died on us,' Parveen said. 'Since he is alive and, if you ask me, in pretty good health, this will be done as soon as those whoring reporters lose interest in it, which will be pretty soon. But Inspector sahib's phone being unreachable? Well, I don't know. You can be shot, bleeding out on the street, but if your boss calls, you have to take the call, bhai. That's what it means to be in Delhi Police, you get what I'm saying? I think he's fucked.' Parveen downed his tea, took a drag of his cigarette, spoke through the exhaled smoke.

'It's Inspector sahib's responsibility how we detain or question a subject, get it? We are foot soldiers, carrying out orders while the officer motherfuckers flip pages in their air-conditioned rooms. Now they can eat the shit the courts throw at them, while we go enjoy the leave we never get, if you don't mind me speaking the truth, since you are a sub-inspector and I'm a lowly head constable. No one can fucking touch us.'

Das couldn't stand being at the station, but he had nowhere to go. He had no family left and no real friends. When his father died, Eastern Railways had given his mother a sympathy post, but it meant shifting to Varanasi. This was not entirely a bad thing for her, for she could count on close family in that city. For Das, the change was profound. In Kolkata, he had a rich, full life, crowded with friends in school he had known for years—and football. He began his day with training at a club ten minutes' walk from his home and ended the day bruised, muddy and happy after an energetic game at school.

In Varanasi, his earlier life vanished in a way that was beyond his comprehension. Unable to make friends, ridiculed by his new schoolmates for his poor Hindi and, worst of all, the wretched target of a group of school bullies. He preferred not to think of that time. But he couldn't help himself; in a flash, a torrent of anxiety would transport him to those days. For a few months, he had tried to push back against the loneliness by spending time on the riverbank alone with his ball, commentary running through his head as he dribbled past imaginary players and scored spectacular goals. One day, after a particularly humiliating beating at the hands of his bullies, he had gone to the river and kicked the ball high up in the air in anger, watched it rise against the backdrop of steep stone steps and temple spires on the other bank and land midstream. With tears in his eyes, he watched it bob on the fast current and sail away. He never had a football again. He worked hard on building his body, his strength. He tested his own courage by trying daredevil acts, spending nights in houses said to be haunted, climbing the ramparts of ruins or trees, standing on the tracks as a train hurtled towards him, jumping away at the last moment … yet, he always found himself lacking. Like the time he joined the boys who jumped from the ruins of the Darbhanga palace into the river. He had made it up to the spire alright, but he could not jump. Everyone laughed at him as he scrambled down the way he had come up. Over time, he had become resigned to his truth: he had been born without courage. He was always going to be lonely.

In a moment's daring, which he blamed on the nicotine overload, Das called Meera. She was in a gym near her police housing apartment.

Meera was outside the government sports compound at the mouth of Munirka village, next to a big temple, when Das parked his bike. Her wet hair stuck to her scalp, with little pointy bits poking out from behind her ears. She wore three-quarter leggings that outlined her muscular legs, a short-sleeved T-shirt that traced the contours of her shoulders. She was surrounded by dogs—he counted six—and seemed to be in happy conversation with them. She patted her stomach. A dog rose on her hind legs and gently placing her paws on Meera's thighs, stared at her eyes. Meera held the dog's face and spoke earnestly. He took a while watching her. He was a good-looking man, he reminded himself. In his fitted white shirt, dark blue jeans and aviators, his hair cropped short, women were sure to give him a second look. People who said he looked like his father were wrong. His father was a pot-bellied, heavyset man. He was neither of those things. He was strong and fit, if a little short. But so were the best footballers in the world. Maradona. Lionel Messi.

Meera was squatting down, rubbing the belly of a dog that had flipped onto her back, while fending off another, smaller dog.

'Leave your bike, I have a car, I need to get coffee,' she said loudly from ten feet away. 'I need coffee and food!'

The dogs turned to look at Das.

Meera walked up to him. '*Suthra lag raha hai aaj tu.*'

'Matlab?'

Meera laughed it away. 'Do you know PVR Priya? It's a multiplex right around the corner, there's a Starbucks there.'

'How is it you like coffee so much?' Das asked. Small talk. His nervousness had not left him. It only deepened when he saw that Meera drove a plush new sedan. She had certainly never brought this car around to the station.

'I don't know … don't you like it? I can't drink the usual chai, it has too much milk and too much sugar. Black coffee is simpler. It gives you more energy, without the sugar.'

Das was only half-listening. As she eased into the speeding traffic, Meera smelled of fresh, lemony soap and fruity shampoo. Das hoped he did not smell of smoke.

At Starbucks, Meera ordered a regular Americano and a chicken-and-egg sandwich. She wolfed down the filling, but did not eat the bread. Das asked for an Americano without knowing what it was. He regretted it as he sipped the coffee, which was bitter and watery.

'You said you found something?' Meera said.

Das opened his laptop to show her. He handed her his earphones.

'Listen to this. It's Rajesh's sister, Nilima, speaking to a friend last night, at around 2 a.m. So far, we have had nothing from her phone. Only daily calls from her mother, wailing and saying that her life is ending. She has spoken to her husband and her friends about her brother, but not anything we didn't already know. Now there's this.'

Meera put on the headphones.

A phone rang. A woman's voice, thick with sleep, answered.

'Hello?'

A shaky voice came in a rasping whisper.

'Shilpa?'

'What's happening, Nilima? Is everything okay? What time is it?'

'Something bad has happened.'

'Your husband found out? Oh god!'

'No, no, it's not that. He's fine, it's not about him.'

'Wait, I don't want to wake Chiru, let me go to the bathroom.'

Scratchy sounds, soft crying, footsteps, the clack of a closing door.

'Tell me quickly.'

'It's my brother, Rajesh.'

'Oh god. He called you, didn't he? Will you tell the police? You should tell the police. I know you love him, but you can't protect him, this is serious, you cannot destroy your life because of him.'

'He has not called me, that's the problem. Why wouldn't he call me? He used to call me twice a week. It's been almost a month since he called. I pray every day, why is this happening to us?'

'Nilu, what can you do? You have your daughter to look out for. Let's meet tomorrow, okay? What time do you finish work?'

'My brother told me.'

'Told you what?'

'He was in danger, he told me.' Nilima began to cry again.

'Don't cry, Nilu, what did he say?'

'"Didi, there is something bad going on, and I have to tell you about it," that's what he said. I said I can't talk now, I'm at work, I'll call you at night. But I didn't call him. He told me, "Didi, I can't talk to anyone else about it, I have to tell you, I have to do something about it, I don't know what to do, and I am scared." I have never heard him say "I am scared". He has not called since … Please help me, something bad has happened to him.'

Stifled sobs in the silence.

'Go back to sleep, listen to me. Everything will be alright. I'll meet you at your office tomorrow. I can get off early, I'll take the train to you. We'll talk for a long time, okay? How about seven? Is seven fine?'

'Yes.'

'Seven it is. Now don't worry, go to sleep, okay?'

'Okay. Bye.'

Meera took off her headphones, her gaze resting on her cup. Das wondered if it would be embarrassing to stand naked in front of her. He had never become quite as muscular as he would have liked to be, even if he was proud of his fitness.

He gulped his coffee in desperation and said, 'What do you think?'

'Where is the inspector?'

'His phone is diverted to Zeeshan's, no one can get in touch with him, not even Zeeshan. His wife is not taking his calls.'

'What is wrong with him?' Meera made a face. 'He always looks like he is somewhere else. Man should not be on the job if he can't handle it, no?'

Das laughed nervously. 'Such a dull person. Did I tell you about the Bawaniya raid I was on with him? On the one hand he looks too tired to get off his chair, always stooped over that stupid notebook, on the other hand he nearly killed us both during the raid, smashed his car without a thought into an SUV, while we were being shot!'

'You've been shot at?' Meera's eyes widened.

'Yes.' Das fought to control his boyish pride.

'But you are right about our boss, he is just not inspiring, you know? You can see the defeat on his face. As an athlete, I know that look. For us, it signals the end of a career. I want a boss who walks upright, talks with pride, motivates me. Anyway, he is not really my boss, ACP madam posted me to this unit for a short duration.'

She fiddled with her empty cup. 'We have to take it to her.'

'No, she took us off the case, we are in trouble, I heard you may be suspended.'

Meera laughed.

'That's sorted. At the most, I will be sent to Police Lines for a couple of months, I'll use that time to get back in shape, practise hard.'

'You mean you are not in shape?'

'You think I am?'

'I think you look absolutely fantastic. I'm sorry, I don't mean to, you know, but like, you, ah …'

'You don't think I have a terribly long nose? I don't talk too much? Or have the body of a boy? I have no breasts to speak of.

My grandfather used to say, "If there has to be a girl in the house, let her be like this one, no one can tell if it's a girl or a boy."'

Das felt simultaneously like running away and leaning over and kissing her.

'I think you are beautiful!' He looked up and held her piercing gaze. His skin felt hot, itchy. His throat was dry. Everything looked hazy. He was probably coming down with fever.

'Look, don't worry about me,' Meera said, changing course. 'I know how to handle myself. I was twelve when I left home and went into a government training centre. Do you know what that's like? No family, no one to look out for you. All these middle-aged men—like the inspector—trying to control you, dump on you their hopelessness, their sexual frustrations. I've spent almost all my life in a system where, if you don't learn quickly how to stand up for yourself, you are chewed up and spat out.'

Meera used a napkin to wrap the pieces of bread she had discarded. 'For the dogs,' she said, smiling at Das, who felt clammy with desire.

'The inspector tried something funny with you?' he said, trying to steady his voice.

'No!' Meera exclaimed. 'He would not dare. The last time a man touched me without my consent, I was fifteen and he was, like, fifty. I kicked the motherfucker in the balls like a buffalo that doesn't want to be milked. He saw the face of his great-grandmother.' Meera laughed so hard she overturned her empty cup.

'Anyway, the inspector is not that kind of man, I don't think. He's just weak. Always suffering. You can't be weak and be good at your work, can you?' Meera smiled. 'You need to be strong, look at me.'

Das said nothing. He was miserable.

'Anyway, the question is, what do we do with this?' She pointed at the laptop. 'This lady does not know what has happened to her brother, so she is not harbouring him. To my mind, it clears the mother as well. What is it she is saying about her brother being in trouble? How do we find out?'

'There is more,' Das said. 'That moustache, Deepak, he has made plenty of calls to try and find out where Rajesh is. Calls to policemen he knows. Local politicos as well. He is well connected. The way he is working the phone, he seems determined.'

'From the sound of it, he's doing more than we are. Strike him out?'

'Unless it's an elaborate ploy.'

'Seems unlikely.'

Das rubbed the side of his face. 'Yes, unlikely.'

'And I still haven't found the earlier nanny, Sangeeta. I got the warrant to get her bank details, but the bank address is of an aunt who has not heard from her since she got married a couple of years ago. She said Sangeeta may have left with her husband for Dubai. At least, that's the last she heard. Sangeeta's parents are also dead. It seems like no one cares when a woman disappears.'

Meera got up, signalled towards the toilet and left Das alone. Das felt queasy. Perhaps it was the coffee.

'I am a strong man, I can take on anyone,' he told himself. He stood up and checked his reflection in the café's glass front. A good-looking man, well-dressed, lean. 'No one can mess with me.'

He wished he had his gun on him. He would have looked even better with a gun. But the team had been made to deposit their service weapons at the malkhana by the ACP in the morning.

He saw Meera coming out of the passage to the toilets and hurriedly sat back down.

Meera said, 'ACP Madam is at PHQ, trying to figure the mess out. What do we do now? How about lunch?'

'But you just had a sandwich!'

'Yes, but I am hungry. Since you are Bengali, and I've never had Bengali food, why don't you take me somewhere?'

Das thought about it. He only knew of two places, the hole-in-the-wall in Shahpur Jat where Meera had tackled the suspect—so that was ruled out—and the Bangali para Chittaranjan Park, where there were many restaurants, but he had only ever been to one—a cheap place with plastic tables in Market No 2. Too basic, inappropriate. He looked around at the glass and wood panelling in the Starbucks she had chosen. A nice restaurant would be a good idea.

'What? Don't you know of anywhere we can get Bengali food?'

'Yes, but only locals go there.'

'Sounds good to me. Let's go!' Meera was up and moving.

Das found himself meekly following her.

'This is fun,' Meera said as she drove, her face stretched into a smile that squeezed deep dimples in her cheeks. 'I've not had a day off like this since I don't know when!'

'What do you usually do on your days off?'

'Do we even get off days? My god, once in a month maybe … I spend half the day at the gym, the rest of it eating and sleeping in my flat. I Skype with my family. I watch movies. You?'

Before Das could answer, Meera pointed ahead. 'Look at that! What's happening there?'

At the traffic stop, two dirty, dishevelled women were rushing from car to car, pleading with the drivers. They were pointing to another woman. She looked pregnant, about to deliver with her legs spread on the traffic divider. She was wearing a frayed ghagra-choli caked with dirt. The buttons of her shirt were open to expose her stretched belly. Meera rolled her window down and stuck her head out.

'Look, we've got to help!'

'We are not on duty.'

'It's not about duty.'

Das took off his aviators, gave Meera an exasperated look. I wouldn't help if I saw someone committing a murder right now, he thought.

'It's a scam, she is not pregnant, they want to rip people off,' he said.

'How can you say that? Look at that woman's belly! If they wanted money, why would they ask people to take her to the hospital?'

'Because people say no, then they say, give us money so we can take an auto.'

'Impossible! I don't believe you! We'll take her to the hospital. Now help me. Why are you men always so low on energy?'

'Sure.' Das shrugged.

Meera gave him a big smile. 'Good!' she said. 'It says in the police manual, we are always on duty.'

Das looked away and rolled his eyes. As the light turned green, Meera eased into the right lane and stopped next to the divider, hazards flashing. Das got off and rudely signalled to the honking cars behind them to go past. He was sure he was coming down with the flu.

Meera went running up to the pregnant woman.

'Hello, sister!' she said, grinning. 'Everything will be alright. I'll take you to the hospital.'

The other women looked at Meera with hostility. 'Who are you?' one of them said.

'I am a policewoman, that is my colleague,' Meera said, pointing at Das. 'We'll take you to the hospital in our car, everything will be alright.'

'Hospital?' the pregnant woman said angrily. 'Who will pay for the hospital? Do we look like we can afford a hospital?'

Meera faltered. 'But, but, you were running around trying to get people ...' She took a deep breath. 'Look, maybe you don't know, but you don't have to pay anything at a government hospital. In fact, there's a new scheme. Not only will they deliver the baby for free, you will stay at the hospital for a few days at government expense. Everything is free.'

She smiled brightly again. 'So, don't cry, come with us, we are here to help.'

The pregnant woman got speedily up on her feet. 'Fuck off. They'll steal the baby at your government hospital and rape us,' she said. Her belly suddenly did not look so big anymore. She started to run away, followed by the other two.

Meera turned to see Das watching her, leaning on the bonnet of the car, his arms crossed.

'Why didn't you warn me?' she said as she got into the car.

'I did,' Das shrugged, smiling. 'You drink fancy coffee, but you still have the village in you.'

'*Abey bavle tared! Chup ho ja!*' Meera snapped. 'If we know they are scamming people, why don't we lock them up? I made a fool of myself.'

Das had not seen Meera angry before. He did not like being screamed at, but he was going to swallow it. 'She did look pregnant,' he said.

'How do you think they do it?'

'They eat half a kilo of rice soaked overnight in milk, six eggs, two to three cups of tea sweetened with Milkmaid.'

'Really?' Meera's eyes widened. 'How do you know that?'

Das laughed. 'I'm talking nonsense.'

Meera hit him on the shoulder with a force that both thrilled and intimidated him.

'So, what, they just push their belly out?' Meera laughed. 'Look, I am going to push my belly out. Do I look pregnant?'

Das looked at her sideways. She did not look pregnant, but the curve of her belly stretched her T-shirt so he could see a bit of her stomach, the paler shade of the skin there. His eyes followed the smooth muscles of her legs sheathed by the gym tights. He could see a bit of shiny, jet-black hair on her armpit from under her short sleeves. He was suddenly aware of the smell of her sweat, mixed with the smell of soap. His head swam. His penis pushed painfully against his jeans. He placed a hand there in a casual way to hide the erection.

'I think I'm a bit emotional, my periods are coming up,' Meera said.

'Wait, what are you doing?' Das said as she took a U-turn under the flyover.

'I am feeling a little uncomfortable in these clothes,' she said, smiling at him in a way that made him even more nervous. His ears felt red hot. 'My flatmates are out on duty, they will be back late, so why don't we go to my apartment, order pizza, watch a movie? What do you think? Forget about police work and our inspector's depressing face.'

'I think you've already made the decision,' Das said meekly. 'Who all do you live with?'

'They are alright, all staff,' she said. 'There is Sarita didi, who is the oldest of us, works in the 100 Control Room, a serious woman, troubled life, but a great cook. Everyone avoids her. There's Rebecca, from Mizoram. No one can pronounce her surname. She is part of the first group of women commandos, Parikrama mobile unit. Talks a lot, like me. I like her. A proper fighter. I'm better than her, of course, stronger, but then, I was international and she did taekwondo at the state level. There is

Preeti, an ASI with the Women and Children unit. Very shy. Not sure she is cut out to be a policewoman, you know?'

SI Das heard nothing. His hands shook. His breathing was shallow. Troubling thoughts assaulted him: Did his breath smell? How could he chew gum without making it apparent? Did he even have gum? Had he used his good perfume today? What underwear did he have on? Was it a torn one? Why did he not throw away the torn ones? Fucking pig. His eyes fell on his hands and he was appalled. His nails were dirty.

'Here we are!' Meera said in a loud sing-song voice as she stopped in front of a four-storey matchbox apartment along a row of identical buildings.

'Keys, keys, keys,' she said, rooting through her gym bag. 'Are you okay? You've been so quiet.'

'I am fine … a little hungry.'

As he followed her up the stairs, he bit furiously at his fingernails. She stopped on the second-floor landing and let out a gasp.

'What's wrong?' he asked.

'I am sorry!' Meera said in a loud whisper, pointing at one of the three doors on the floor. 'No lock on the door. That means someone did not go to work today, or has a different shift … in any case, she's home, so I can't take you inside.'

Das groaned and sat down on the step.

'Oh poor man, look at your face, you look like you are going to cry!' Meera said. She sat down next to him.

'Do your balls hurt?' She tried not to laugh and snorted instead. She put a hand on her mouth and her eyes widened. 'Let's get out of here, someone must have heard me. Can you stand up or do you need help?'

He got up quickly, went down the steps two at a time. 'I'm just hungry,' he said irritably.

As they were getting into the car, two large street dogs came bounding towards them. At first, he felt jealous. Then the sight of her playing with the dogs calmed him.

'Do you get scared?' Meera asked as they got into the car. 'I grew up with dogs, cats, cows. I had a black dog, Bholi, she would snuggle up to me if I cried, stayed up with me all night if I was unhappy, went everywhere with me in the village … you know, the more I think about it … I don't believe Rajesh killed the girl. Do you? I have really good intuition. Here's a man who went around feeding strays, taking care of them, none of the people who actually know him have anything bad to say about him, he made a call to his sister saying he was scared days before Jyoti died, what does that mean? What are we missing?'

'People can do anything when they are on the edge, don't you think?' Das said coldly. He couldn't stand her talking anymore.

16

The words slammed around in his head like a bloodied animal colliding impotently against the four walls of a cage.

I can neither be proud of you nor of the work you do …

A sham of a marriage …

You trapped me …

Other words from other times swam up.

Where were you when your daughter died? In a brothel?

You are a liar, a cheat …

Which of your whores did you fuck today?

Other words from other people too, the people who made him, who put the ticking bomb inside him.

'You are not man enough to be in the army, I always knew you were going to fail …'

'Tell no one about what happens at home, okay? No one should know, that's what a family is about. If you tell people, they will think you are a monster, no one will talk to you, you will die alone …'

Inspector Kumar missed his stop. He got off the train feeling nauseated. He dragged his heavy legs up the stairs to the other side of the station. All these people at the station, he thought, are they happy? He was watching a movie playing on a screen, he was in the dark hall alone. The people … waiting, walking, riding up and down the escalators, all of them talking on their phones, texting on their phones, playing on their phones, listening to music on their phones, eyes on their phones even as they strode or ambled or tripped.

The world was burning. Everyone was on fire, but they could ignore it because they had their phones. That's why no one cared about Jyoti, Kumar thought in his delirium, not even his own people.

The train rushed into the station. Kumar got on. At the next stop, Model Town, he got off, climbed down the stairs to the road, where he was immediately set upon by autorickshaw and cycle-rickshaw drivers looking for a fare. He continued walking without acknowledging them.

He came upon a tea shop and decided to stop for tea and a cigarette. Kumar felt unable to stand, but there was nowhere to sit. The one stone slab next to the chaiwala had two rickshaw drivers sitting on it, smoking beedis and arguing.

Kumar leaned against a dirty wall and drank his tea.

He began to walk again. Before he reached the walls of Chhatrasal Stadium, he turned left, then left again a few steps later, to enter the police colony. No one would be home except Colonel. Thank god. He could not bear to meet Colonel's happy, bustling wife.

'Inspector saab! My god! You look like shit,' Colonel said as he opened the door. He was a burly man, five foot ten, with a broad salt-and-pepper moustache but without a single strand of hair on his head. He wore cheap gold-rimmed glasses, a white kurta and white pyjamas.

Kumar followed his old SI into the house.

'You still have a limp,' Kumar said. 'How are you doing?'

'My prison term is almost done,' Colonel said. 'I'll rejoin in two weeks, but I won't be in the field for at least another month. It could have been sooner, but the first knee implant had a defect, they had to operate again. Now I feel great. What about you? You don't ever pick up the phone.'

Colonel placed two chairs outside the door of his house and got busy setting up his hookah. It was hot outside, but not too bad, shaded as they were by the profusion of ficus and neem in the colony. Kumar took a long drag of the pipe. The gentle gurgling of the water calmed him. He blew the smoke out slowly.

'That encounter night, I was thinking about you, and I said to that Bengali SI of mine, I told him, if we get the motherfucker, Colonel will go around handing out sweets in his colony.'

Colonel laughed. 'I did,' he lied.

'But he, I mean my Bengali SI, he asked me a good question. Why is your name Colonel?'

Colonel laughed again, a hearty, full-bellied laugh that made Inspector Kumar smile despite himself.

'It was my nasty old father, god bless his dead soul,' he said. 'He was in the army, a lowly subedar all his life. My theory is—my brother would agree on this, his name is Captain by the way—he named us Colonel and Captain so he could come home and take it out on us. At work he is cleaning the shoes of his colonel. At home he is telling me, "You, Colonel, gandu, come here, bring me my shoe so I can teach you discipline." And bang!'

Kumar began to laugh. He choked on the hookah and coughed.

'It may be funny,' Colonel said with a smile, 'but it's a fact. People do this. There are others I know called Major, Faujdar, Zileydar, Kaptan …'

'Maybe some of these fathers want their sons to grow up to be a colonel in the army, not remain a lowly sipahi all their lives,' Kumar offered.

'Have you ever heard of a colonel in the army whose name was Colonel?'

'No, but I knew a major called Major. Major Major Singh.'

Kumar sat back and closed his eyes as Colonel refilled the hookah. He thought of his own father. A weak man who liked to take his anger out on those who could not fight back. Yet, he was in the army, he went into battle. For the next thirty years though, he did nothing but deliver files from one room to another. His father spent the pent-up energy beating up his mother. He remembered the terror of waking up in the middle of the night hearing her screams, remembered standing at the corner of their bedroom watching him sitting astride her, slapping her with both hands, left to right, right to left, till her screaming became a whimper and she looked lifeless. Then his father, the soldier, the killer, would turn on him.

He remembered his mother telling him that she lived for him. Remembered the violence that raged through him as he heard those words, the determination that he would stand up, that the next time his father beat her he would fight him. That time never came. Prashant, the little coward.

Kumar remembered his mother provoking his father, screaming, 'Hit me, hit me', and he remembered thinking to himself, yes, hit her, finish it, finish her so there's no more of this.

I was a child, Kumar thought. I was a child and I imagined the soul to be a giant dragon with many teeth. Inside the belly of the dragon, everything was red.

'You want tea? Something to eat?'

'No, that's fine,' Kumar said. 'No need.'

Colonel handed him the pipe and lit the tobacco as Kumar puffed. Then he shuffled inside anyway, reappeared a few minutes later with a tray with two small cups of tea and a plate of mithai.

'Sir, I wanted to ask you,' he said as he put the tray on the table. 'These high-ranking officers, when their children appear for the NDA exam, do they get …'

'Oh no, nothing like that happens. This is the one organisation in India that's fair.'

'Nothing?'

'No. It's people like me, who appear for exams and fail, we get bitter. We say, "Saaley, they got their own people in through the backdoor." Seven times I appeared for SSB, but I never got through. My classmates from school, they became doctors, engineers, a couple of them I coached for SSB and they are now officers. No one knows better than me what not to do. One engineer friend did a short service and is a private player in Abu Dhabi now, he makes seven crore a year. What can I say?'

'If I made seven crore in a year, I would not be sleeping at night.'

'It's destiny. In my life, I have sat seventeen recruitment exams. The seventeenth was Delhi Police. The worst of the lot.'

'You picked a tough calling. You could have chosen an easy life. People know you, they respect you.'

'I wish I had chosen an easy life, don't you?'

'No one ever gets what they wish for, that's life. Inspector, tell me about the case.'

Kumar pushed the empty cups and plate to one side, laid out the crime scene photos. The thought that was gnawing at Colonel hardened into bitter certainty the moment he saw the first photo.

'This is about your daughter,' he said. 'This is about Pooja.'

Kumar looked up, startled. No one had spoken her name for years except his wife. To hear it from another … he felt the dragon unfurl its wings inside him. He averted his gaze and gripped the pipe with great force, held it close to his chest.

Colonel kept his eyes on Kumar; he had once watched when the inspector crashed and burnt after Pooja died. He had tried to help, but his sense of decorum had stopped him from speaking out. Not anymore.

'Are you alright? Take a drag of the pipe, sir. We'll get to the bottom of this, but it won't change anything. It will not bring Pooja back. She is gone, she is with god. You have to let her be.'

The courtyard felt perfectly still. The house, the walls, there was something unspeakably sad about them. Kumar saw a golden cat sitting on a branch of the tree nearest to the courtyard, watching them.

It was early morning. Kumar was not at home. He had been drinking late. Back then, he used to do a lot of that. He was passed out in the house of a colleague. Pooja, ten years old, a happy, sprightly, sharp girl, who, despite the gloom of her home, contained in her a rare joy, a love for life immediately apparent to anyone around her, and her mother's beauty. That morning, she had missed her school bus. A neighbour who was dropping his daughter to school in his car saw Pooja standing on the street and offered to drop her. The neighbour's daughter was in the backseat, notebooks spread out, trying to finish a project before reaching school. Pooja sat in the front. The fog was dense.

At the crossing near Rohini Sector 2, where a new flyover was being built, Kumar's neighbour saw too late a slab of concrete that had fallen on the road. He tried to avoid it by swerving, but there was a truck parked by the curb, packed with rebars extending far out behind it. The car smashed into the rods at speed. A rebar went through his neighbour's shoulder.

The neighbour's daughter, at the back, was flung around, but escaped with minor injuries. Pooja was nailed to the seat by two rods that went straight through her. They had to call for cutters to bring her body out.

Kumar liked to believe she died instantly. No one had told him otherwise. It was at least three hours before he even got to know about the accident. His wife had tried calling him. Lots of people had tried calling him. His phone was thick with missed calls. When he woke up and saw the list, he was very scared.

When he finally heard the news, he felt nothing. Just a kind of dullness. At the hospital, they told him she had been brought dead. They told him they were going to do an autopsy on her. This roused him. He had plenty of experience of how autopsies were done—drunk sanitation workers forced to do what no one else wanted to do, splitting open bodies in a row, calling in family members for identification even while other bodies lay on other tables, open like burst fruit. No! No! No! He had called his police friends, got her transferred to AIIMS, got a doctor he knew and trusted—Dr Kharb—to do the autopsy.

'I was not there,' Kumar said. He began to cry. The hookah had gone off. Colonel lit a beedi.

'It's done now,' he said softly. 'You suffered enough. How long will you punish yourself?'

Yes. He had punished himself. He had punished everyone around him. He began to drink even more. He was a monster. He always knew he was one, like his father was, but now he lived it.

He became a regular at brothels. He was less and less at home, sometimes many nights in a row. When his wife tried to confront him, he let the dragon loose on her. He had promised himself, watching his father hit his mother, that he would never hit a woman. He broke the promise.

Kumar thought, squinting at the sun, only barely aware of the man next to him but watching the sleeping cat on the tree with a hunter's fixation, that their son saw all this. He had passed it on, the dragon was now inside his son, the ticking bomb.

It was Colonel who had dragged him to rehab. No alcohol in four years. On the job, then home, always.

The golden cat stood up, stretched and disappeared from view.

'Here, more tea,' Colonel said. 'The pipe is lit.' He touched Kumar's arm, helped him wrap his fingers around the mouthpiece.

'I am lonely,' Kumar said, refusing the pipe.

He started to gather the crime scene photos. He was moving slowly.

Colonel closed his eyes, took a long drag on the pipe.

'If the case happened in a house like yours or mine, like, you know, our economic status … I don't mean us as police …' Colonel stopped. He gathered his thoughts and tried again.

'Imagine the girl died in this house, and I am not a policeman but I work in the post office as a clerk, same fucking salary, what would you have done differently?'

Kumar knew already where this was going. He had asked this question of himself, but it gave him a fresh burst of energy to hear it from another.

'I would take you, my friend, put you through sustained interrogation,' he said. 'I would turn your house upside down, pick your phone and internet records apart. I would bombard your wife with questions in a dank, dark room in the belly of the police station …'

'Okay, stop, stop,' Colonel laughed. The smoke hit his throat and he began to cough. 'What a dangerous man you are. You are having fun! You can't do any of this with the Srivastava family?'

'No. The DCP is his friend. God knows who else. Family in politics. All you need is a relative who's a politician with the ruling party, isn't it? Who can touch you then? Delhi Police would rather lock me up and throw away the key than ask him a few hard questions. Even the courts will not give me a warrant without a good probable cause. Man is covered from all angles.'

'Hmm ...' Colonel had closed his eyes again. After a pause, he said, 'You don't mind if I nose around about the missing car, do you?'

His entire family was in the business—dealerships, garages. Colonel practically grew up in a workshop. It made sense.

'Yes. Have a go. Talk to Das, he was trying to track it, he'll give you the details. Should I send him to you?'

'Don't bother. I've started driving, I'll go see him if I need to. Meanwhile, find a way to jab a little at Mr Srivastava.'

'Thank you, my friend.'

'When you solve this one, we'll hand out sweets in the colony again, okay?' Colonel said.

17

It was past midnight when Zeeshan finally got the call he was waiting for. He was fitfully drifting in and out of a disturbed sleep, gnawed by a suffocating sense of failure, an impending doom that he could not quite understand. He had been woken twice by his wife's suffering, angry voice, berating him for snoring. Both times, he had vowed to himself to stay awake till she was properly asleep, but had been pulled back immediately, helplessly, into his sleeping nightmares. He had done nothing that day except try and trace Inspector Kumar. He had called Kumar's wife, who scathed at him—'If you don't know where he is, you think I would?' Kumar's listed phone was forwarded to Zeeshan's and his unlisted phone had rung off on thirty-three separate attempts. He had gone home feeling more exhausted than he had felt in a long time.

His extended family, which had gathered for tea, were surprised to see him walk in just after the Maghrib. He had straightaway gone to sleep for an hour. On waking, he had cornered his wife on her way to the toilet, kissed her. She had pushed him away. He thought she was being coy and caught her arm and pulled her towards him, only to be shocked to his senses by a hard slap on the face.

'Don't you dare touch me!' she said. It reduced him to tears of shame.

The rest of the evening had gone by in a painfully disjointed fashion. He was surrounded by his noisy family but oblivious to them. The TV had blared on for hours, but he saw nothing. All that played in his head were his wife's words: Don't. Touch. Me.

So, despite being woken from his sleep yet again, despite his wife telling him to get out of the room, Zeeshan was a happy man when he finally spoke to Kumar. He was happier still when Kumar asked him to come to the station. He had crept out of the house like a thief.

Here he was, smoking a quick cigarette while watching the 2 a.m. tableau at the Hauz Khas police station: armed constables deboarding from a long blue bus, some of them stretching, some talking in small knots; a line of PCR vans, here for a refill of drinking water before going back on patrol, led by the familiar figures of Kant and Kishore; a couple of uniformed men in animated conversation; his friend, HC Baljit, astride his bike checking his phone; a tow truck pulling up with a car with its front smashed so flat it looked like a washing machine.

Zeeshan threw away the rest of his cigarette, crossed the road. 'Survivors?' he asked the driver. The driver shook his head.

Inside the office, Kumar was bent over his notebook, Jyoti's crime scene photos laid out on the table. The room was lit only by a single overhead yellow lamp.

'What do we do?' Zeeshan asked, settling into a chair.

Kumar took off his reading glasses, leaned forward with his arms on the table and smiled at Zeeshan.

'We seize a man by the balls and hang on.'

Over the next half hour, Kumar outlined his plan to Zeeshan. It was the kind of assignment that needed a six-member team working round the clock. Zeeshan would have to do it alone. No permissions, no authorisations, no paperwork. Just the hanging on, the meticulous record-keeping of the life of another. It would keep Zeeshan busy for days.

Kumar slept at the station. By nine in the morning, when South Division Headquarters hummed with the intensity of a shift change, Kumar had taken a brisk walk around the park where he watched the dawn wash over the domed Sultanate ruins in a warm glow. He had drunk his tea and eaten his bread-omelette with joy, bathed at the station, changed into a clean white shirt, a fresh pair of blue jeans.

At 9:15 a.m., he presented himself to Madam ACP for his punishment.

Sofia Ahmed tore into him. Kumar was expecting it, of course.

'I knew I had made a mistake listening to you,' Sofia said. 'You took advantage of me, didn't you? For being new, for being a woman? You looked at me and thought, she looks like a nice, kind person, let's make a fool out of her. You fucked with the wrong person. What kind of family emergency was it that you couldn't answer your phone even once?'

Kumar made no reply. He had already said sorry, he was not going to say it again. Anyway, he wasn't sorry.

'And the girl? Have you thought about her? What happens to that case now? I gave it to you on a platter, protected you from DCP Singh. I thought I was helping you do something good, get to the bottom of a death no one else would have bothered with. I guess I have my inexperience to blame. You men are all the same. Why were you so interested in this girl's death? Was it a sense of justice or something else, huh?'

'Have you sent in the internal inquiry request?' Kumar asked.

'No, but I will today, so don't even try …'

'No, no, ma'am.' Kumar raised his palms in the air. 'I understand, I've left you with no choice. Please go ahead. I was simply going to ask if it's possible for you to not suspend me till the inquiry begins. It will take the department at least three weeks to constitute a team and start proceedings. You can send me to Police Lines till then. Or you could let me quietly work a new case that has come to light. No one will even know I'm here, that I'm working.'

Kumar outlined the missing persons case for Sofia. He knew it would appeal to her. He was right. Sofia cleared it, he kept a straight face but secretly rejoiced.

When his team began to troop in, Kumar was writing the details on the whiteboard.

Parveen was the first to speak when the briefing was done.

'Since when did we start chasing after runaway kids?' he said. 'Isn't there a whole department for that? Or have we been demoted to Missing Persons and you don't want to tell us? Also, where were you when all this shit was going down? First you chase after some stupid young girl who offed herself, then you just allow the whole thing to get dropped? You can do what you want to, why are you taking us down with you?'

Hari Singh had objections too, he quoted numbers.

'Sir-ji, last year, close to seven thousand children went missing from the National Capital Region, how many do you think were found?'

'How many?'

'Fewer than half. That too because they came back on their own or were traced to a shelter home. I don't think we recover 5 per cent with our own investigation.'

'What's your point?'

'Sir-ji, respectfully, missing children is a dead end. *Yeh khoya-paya hamara kaam nahin hai*. Already you have put us in trouble with this Jyoti case.'

Constable Sushil Kumar, who usually had little to say about these matters, objected too. He had, in fact, served in the Missing Persons unit, had hated every bit of it.

'We know that most of these children run away, disappear themselves, so there's no crime to solve really. We have ZipNet, let's post the details there, soon enough Railway Police somewhere in India will have the child in custody.'

'What do you mean they disappear themselves? The boy is ten years old,' Kumar said.

Meera came in quietly with a keffiyeh covering her face. She slid into a chair.

There was an uncomfortable silence.

'Yes, what do you mean they run away? Why are you silent?'

'Madam is sitting here,' Parveen said. 'That's why they are not telling you. The reason these children from slums run away is because these fuckers live like animals in one tiny room, ten feet by ten feet, with five, six kids. Some time or the other, the parents must get down to …' Parveen smacked his fist into his palm rhythmically. 'They fuck when they think the children are sleeping, or don't even bother with that. The kids see it, they get scarred, run away …'

Parveen leaned back in his chair and surveyed the room with a grin on his face.

The silence returned.

'No matter,' Kumar said. 'You can stop complaining. The case is ours as of now. It has already been assigned by Madam ACP. I don't care why or how or where children go missing, I simply want this one found, I want each one of you to give everything you have for the next few days.'

He looked at each of his people. A sense of weariness hung heavy in the room. Downcast eyes, indifferent postures.

'How about I order biryani for lunch?' Kumar said, the false mirth in his tone jarring even to himself.

SI Das said he had something to share too, went to the fridge and brought out a box of sweets.

'From Kolkata,' he said. 'A friend got it for me.'

'We should wait till after the meal …' Kumar said.

There was a scramble for the box. Everyone agreed that there was no sweet like Kolkata sandesh. These ones even had liquid centres—sticky, dark golden jaggery, snuggled inside the soft-yet-firm sandesh.

'How do they do it?' Parveen said. 'They inject it with a syringe or what?'

Das shrugged.

'Keep it away from Hari Singh!' Kumar said. 'He'll finish the box by himself. How many have you had?'

'Three, sir-ji.'

'See?'

Kumar smiled and looked at Meera. 'Have I ever told you the Zeeshan biryani story?'

'There he goes again,' Parveen said, laughing, 'for the three thousandth time.'

'I had to go to Kolkata for a case, worked out of a station in a place called Park Circus,' Kumar said. 'Beautiful building. Old British structure, but that's another story. The officer I was working with, Detective Mitra, he asks me one day, have you ever had Kolkata biryani? I said, no. He immediately took me by the hand. We went to a restaurant across the street. It was called … Zeeshan!' Kumar threw his head back and laughed.

'When I told Zeeshan about it, he took offence. Don't know why, it was the best biryani I'd ever had. At first, I thought, what is this? It looks like boiled rice with boiled meat and a potato in it. Then I ate some. I swear on all the gods, you would have never eaten anything like it. Fragrant, juicy, spicy, soft, moist … heaven! I thought I'll bury my head in the mound of rice and stay there. I thought, being a fool, that maybe I can make it, looks simple—I'll surprise my wife with it.'

'Your wife also eats meat?' Parveen said.

'Yes, why not?'

'Isn't she a Saraswat brahmin?'

'Anyway,' Kumar said, 'Detective Mitra, that's my friend, was well known at Zeeshan's. He told the owner I wanted the recipe. Man says, sure, why not, you have something to write on? I take out my notebook—that time I used to carry a small one in my pocket, this big'—he made a shape with his thumb and index finger—'I start writing, and then I am writing, and still writing, behenchod … sorry, excuse me!' He stole a glance at Meera. 'Thirty different steps, a hundred ingredients and two whole days of work with two people working on it.'

'You never made it for your wife?' Meera laughed.

'Madam, you must be a meat-eater too?' Parveen said.

'Yes, I eat mostly everything. When I was in Japan once for a tournament, I ate raw fish for breakfast, it was fantastic,' Meera said.

'It didn't stink?' Kumar asked.

'No, not at all. It looked so good too. Sushi.'

'Yes, yes, sushi,' Kumar said. 'Big thing in Delhi as well.'

'Is there anything you don't eat?' Parveen asked, pointing the question at Meera, his voice hoarse with contempt.

'Baingan,' Meera said brightly. 'I hate the texture.'

Parveen said, 'Madam, but in your caste, if you eat meat and fish …'

'How do you know what my caste is?' Meera snapped.

'I looked up your name …'

Meera slapped her thigh with a resounding thump. 'I entered an akhada when I was six years old, and my guru told me that day to leave my caste at the door,' she said. 'When I first entered the wrestling pit, he said, "We all look the same when we are covered in earth, so we are of pehelwani caste." *Tu ja bhai, bhadke na kare.*'

Parveen began to laugh. 'What's this shit you are saying, can you hear yourself talk, madam?'

'You worry about my caste as if I am your wife, as if you need to know if you can eat what I cook for you.'

Parveen rose abruptly, toppling his chair backward.

'What do you mean you are my wife?' he shouted, his face twisted with rage. 'I wouldn't marry someone like you at gunpoint. I don't care if you are my senior or whatever, you strut in here on a stupid sports quota, you think you can say and do whatever you want? My wife is a pure woman, a mother, she's nothing like you … *bhobra fod dunga saali* …'

Kumar took two quick steps towards Parveen and slapped him hard on the face. Parveen staggered. He looked up with bloodshot eyes, hand on his face, his anger rising, mixing with bile and blood. A force beyond him kept him from ripping into his boss. The room plunged into silence. Sushil stood up slowly and left. Hari Singh watched him go, looked at Meera, who was breathing hard, gripping the edge of the table. He looked at Parveen to check if he had a gun on him. He looked at Inspector Kumar, who stood with his legs a little apart, arms hanging loosely by his side, a blank, cold look in his eyes, as if ready to strike again.

'Meera, Das, Hari Singh, get out of this room,' Kumar said.

Das almost ran out, followed by Meera. Hari Singh looked from Kumar to Parveen and back again. He scanned the room for weapons.

'Inspector sir,' he said softly, 'I think—'

'Leave, now.' Kumar did not raise his voice. When Hari Singh had shuffled out, taking his time, Kumar sat down. He motioned to Parveen, who was still standing and glaring, to sit.

'What you did, that was not the right thing to do,' Parveen said with difficulty. 'You will pay for it.'

A long moment passed before Kumar spoke. His voice was calm, soft, almost happy.

'What would you like to do, my friend? Shoot me in the back one night when I'm walking home? Go ahead, do it. It will be a good day for me, a relief. If you have the balls to approach me from the front, I will smile and remain still, so you won't have any difficulties. How about that? Happy?'

Kumar toyed with a sheet of paper. He arranged the paperweight—shaped like a flag stand, with a tiny Indian flag attached to it—so it sat exactly in the middle of the table.

'I don't think you know much about me, Parveen, but I, I know a thing or two about you. There are two roads in front of you. Your choice which one you walk. The first, I suspend you right away, arrest you for stealing narcotics from police custody, for the possession and sale of those drugs.'

A chill ran through Parveen, though he tried his best not to show it.

'You don't believe me?'

Kumar fished his phone out of his pocket, perched his reading glasses on his nose, scrolled till he found a number. He read it aloud.

'Sounds familiar?'

It was the unregistered, pre-paid phone Parveen carried, the one he used for his narcotics activities.

'If that's the road you choose, please understand you will not leave the station. I will put you in lock-up, raid your house and guess what I will find there?'

Kumar considered telling him more. The internal report he was running through his mind featured two hand guns that had been removed from a malkhana, sold on the market, recovered by another branch of the police after a gang shootout.

He did not have to. He could see, through the anger burning on Parveen's face, a thin, ever so thin, crack of fear. Kumar glanced at his phone.

'It's forty-two minutes past twelve. From this minute on, you won't see home for a long, long time.'

Parveen sat down with a thump, looking straight at the inspector.

'The second road,' Kumar said. 'You lead the missing persons case. You solve it. I recommend you for a transfer to Missing Persons, you leave peacefully, go back to our old haunt at Kotwali. Sell drugs, do whatever the fuck you want to do. I will not interfere in any way.'

Parveen raced his bike out of the station, took a sharp right in front of a desperately braking car coming from the opposite side, ignored the red at the crossing, veered left into merging traffic with his finger firmly pressed down on the horn, straightened his bike to avoid a startled old man on a bicycle, gunned his engine into a shrieking roar and sped away. He was angry. Angry at the bunch of gutless, defeated losers he called his colleagues.

Angry at that shameful, caste-less woman wrestler who, to make matters worse, was of his own blood. Angry at that prick-less Musalman whose only skill was to suck the cocks of his superiors. Angry at that new fish-eater—whoever heard of a Bengali cop in Delhi? The puny fool fancied himself a bodybuilder. Parveen could knock him out cold with a backward swipe of his left hand if he so wished. He hated them all. Hated the treachery of the police who secretly keep him under watch even as he gave his life to the force. He ran another light.

An autorickshaw swung out of the way. A young guy in an SUV, Parveen saw in his rear-view mirror, was speeding up behind him, shouting with his head out the window.

'Catch up with me, why don't you, let's see what happens,' Parveen said under his breath. A fantasy flashed through his fevered mind in which he was smashing the guy's car with a fat wrench.

Most of all, he hated Inspector Kumar. He wanted him dead. The treachery must be his, it must have been he who put the trace on Parveen. And it couldn't have been him alone. Who else? The fat fucker at the malkhana back in Kotwali? Sure, why not? The rate at which he gave stuff away, it would take the only gentlest of pressure to make him squeal. Perhaps, Parveen thought, even my wife is involved. Even she has been turned by the inspector, is at this moment speaking to him, whispering things behind my back, getting her revenge by betraying her own husband, breaking the sacred trust placed in us by the gods.

Parveen slowed down at the Defence Colony crossing. This was a traffic light he did not want to break. CCTV cameras. He would be challaned. He did not want more official heat. When the light turned, he took the right under the flyover and raced again, swinging his bike left to right, right to left, low to the ground, past cars and bikes.

What should he do now? Now that he was compromised? He took a mental inventory of the stuff stashed in his house. The drugs had to go. But he could not just throw it away. That stuff, it was worth more than ten lakh rupees in the market. What about the bulletproof vest? He could afford to ditch that. His laptop needed to go. But first …

Parveen saw the road widening into the DND highway as he approached the Ashram crossing. Even through the fog of rage, the promise of uninterrupted speed, the wind whipping past, made an impression on him. He hit the DND at 120 kph. He felt a bit better.

Where the highway passed directly over the sludge of the Yamuna, ominous white clouds of foam rolling over the water, he stopped by the edge of the road. He took the old-fashioned phone out of his pocket. He slid the sim card out, ground it under his boot. He picked up what was left, a little golden sliver, flicked it down to the river. He repeated the action with the rest of the phone—smash underfoot, pick up the debris, drop into the river.

For an abrupt, disconcerting minute, it occurred to Parveen that he was afraid. No, he told himself. He was afraid of nothing and nobody. He was powerful. He could do anything. What he needed to do was focus on what to do next.

He started his bike again, followed the DND, this time at a reasonable speed, took the exit to Mayur Vihar. Before the Mayur Vihar-1 metro station, he took a right and came to a stop near a small park. His house was not far, but he was not going home. He sat down at the tea shop on the pavement outside the park. Apartment blocks rose around him. Across the street, there was an ATM, a golgappa-seller doing no business, a shop selling gym equipment and a petrol pump. He took a drag of his cigarette and tried to focus. No way was he throwing the drugs out—there was high-quality cocaine in his possession, plus the usual stuff—heroin, brown sugar, meth in small ziplock bags, a fucking bucket of Viagra. No, he was a fighter, it was in his blood. Nobody threatened him.

His usual contacts had to be severed, he decided. He needed a new buyer, he needed to sell everything at one go. Another thought came to him—he needed to do what Kumar had asked him to. If he could prove himself, then maybe, just maybe, Kumar, being the weak, pathetic man he was, would not want to provoke him further. In fact, he would be rewarded, his heroism recognised, he could go back to doing things his way without interference.

He put his plan into action. First, he called the barber in Shahpur Jat and made his demands. Then he got back on his bike and headed thirty-three kilometres northwest to Shahbad Dairy, the place where the boy had gone missing.

18

Colonel limped into the car workshop run by his nephew and felt an immediate spurt of joy—the smell of grease! A car stood with its bonnet yawning. He rubbed his thumb and forefinger along the external groove of the engine block and pressed his fingers together to enjoy the sensation of the sticky oil.

It did not take much to make Colonel happy. He was content with life, settled, without ambition. He found joy in his work, did it with unhurried diligence. Colonel had found solace in staying home after his injury, learning to cook from his wife, raising a terrace garden where, from one season to the next, he grew spinach, cauliflower, a pumpkin patch that threatened to take over the house, chillies, tomatoes. He loved his wife, a breast cancer survivor, his son, who had gone into the family business and opened an auto spare parts store, his daughter, who was a fitness instructor, and his three grandchildren.

He assessed the state of the car, waiting for his nephew to arrive. It had not been serviced for a long time. No coolant left in the tank. He was, out of habit, about to unscrew the container that held the engine oil when he heard the booming voice of his nephew greeting him. He turned around and held the big man in a bear hug.

'How's the leg, Uncle?'

'You see me. I'm up and about. Version 2.0, better than before.'

'You must have lunch with me.'

'Ahh ... I would love to, but today I am on a deadline, need to keep moving.'

'You are back on duty?'

'You could say that.'

'How can I help you?'

Colonel took out a photo of the missing car Das had given him earlier that day. Das had briefed him well; Colonel had made a mental note to tell Kumar he liked the new recruit. He was thorough. He had routes drawn out for every direction the car could have gone in a five-kilometre radius without getting filmed by a traffic camera—since it had not popped up on any of those cameras—and without crossing a border, where, again, it would have been captured on video. Colonel would have done the same.

'Look, there's a missing car I'm interested in, a Maruti Alto.'

He laid out the map Das had made, put his finger on the red circle that marked the area where the car may have disappeared.

'It was headed to a factory in Bawana, but did not cross the traffic camera at Samaypur Badli. In fact, it was not caught on any traffic or border or toll plaza cameras, which, more or less, gives us this area the car could have been in before something was done to it. My first question is, what could that something be? What are the likely things you would do to an Alto?'

Colonel's nephew was a tall, plump, clean-shaven man in his early thirties with long locks of shiny black hair. As recently as three years back, he was a respected car thief with special expertise in high-end cars. On his uncle's urging, he had gone straight. He laughed and swept his hair back from his forehead.

'I love how you bring me the best puzzles, Uncle, but an Alto is a shit car, I would not even have touched it. What model?'

'K10.'

'Okay, at least it had a litre engine.'

'I'm thinking it's gone to a farm in our dear Haryana to power a water pump.'

'Yes, there is demand for that …'

The nephew ran his finger around the red circle.

'Enough workshops in the area doing shit like this. Strip the car, clean and repackage whatever parts you can, sell the engine off.'

'The hull?'

'That's the hard part, because it's too unwieldy for transport. Most of these workshops can't afford tow trucks. It's risky to move it around too. A nosy, no-good person like you would stop and check …'

Colonel whacked his nephew on the head in jest.

'Best thing to do would be to dump the shell in the nearest possible place where no one would bother with it.'

Colonel stared at the map as if visualising the area.

'That's a lot of places if our theory is right. The entire zone is a sorry dumpster.'

'True. Lunch? There's a man down the road makes amazing chhole kulche.'

Colonel shook his head.

'My second question. Considering the locality, the car in question and that the Bawana gangs may be involved, do you have someone I can talk to who can narrow the search for me?'

Colonel's nephew asked him to wait and walked to the small glass-enclosed office at the back of the workshop. Colonel watched him work his laptop make a few calls.

'Here,' he said, handing Colonel the yellow leaf of a sticky pad with a number scribbled on it. 'That's Shafique.'

'I remember Shafique. Talented guy. Worked for you back in the day.'

'Oh yes, what a boy! Magic fingers, completely fearless. If you had him on your side, Delhi Police would be a better place. Call him. He knows you'll be calling. He'll try to put you in touch with a guy called Atta Satta.'

'Atta Satta? Really?'

'You thought you are the only one with a weird name? Satta is tops, knows everything going on in his area, every stolen car and bike. The finest instructor in Delhi when it comes to old-school lifting. Doesn't talk to police. May talk to my favourite uncle, though!'

The nephew beamed widely, held Colonel's hand with both his hands. 'Are you sure you won't stay for lunch?'

At ten in the morning, the sun was already high and hot when Sushil drove Meera and Das to Shahbad Dairy, honking furiously through the tangle of traffic near the last metro station on the yellow line, Samaypur Badli. On their left was a line of broken, raw-brick houses coated in grime. Between the rural bus service, the swarm of swerving e-rickshaws, the cycle rickshaws inching forward stoically, angry, revving cars and masses of people, the place trembled under a cloud of blinding dust and deafening noise.

Cursing under his breath, Sushil grabbed his siren light from the top of the dashboard, reached out of the window and stuck it to the roof of the car. He switched it on, swerved the car on to the wrong lane, jerked out of the way of an incoming e-rickshaw, sped up and immediately braked hard as an emaciated black dog ran in front of the vehicle.

The dog got away. Meera, whose heart had pounded with fear of the animal coming under the car, let out a sigh of relief. The car took the bend on the Bawana highway. The traffic eased out.

Sushil turned the siren off. Eyeing a group of stray dogs walking through a rubbish heap, he said, 'We should shoot these dogs.'

'We don't shoot dogs,' Das said.

'They shot dogs in Sitapur last month. Who stopped those villagers?' Sushil said.

'Were you ever attacked by dogs?' Meera asked, keeping her voice level.

'No,' Sushil answered. 'But my father was once bitten by a big one. Really big, like your German kind. My father jammed his hand down his throat, ripped up his stomach.' Sushil looked around the car, smiling. 'I like cats,' he offered. 'I had a cat that lived to be sixteen. One time, she clawed a dog's eye out.'

Meera considered this story, decided to erase it from her mind. She looked outside.

The car travelled down the highway, past the wasted hulls of factories and scorched plots of land piled with rubbish, before being flagged to a stop by Parveen, standing next to his bike in front of the Shahbad Dairy market.

Parveen had spent the previous day at the Dairy police station, looking over the files of the missing child. Spent the night there too, sleeping uncomfortably on a bed with no mattress in a room that reeked, like every room in every police station in Delhi, of urine. He was in an irritable mood; he did not particularly want to see the people in front of whom he had been slapped. But there was something he had found in his file-trawl that made him excited, happy even. It was not one child who was missing but many. So many, he thought maybe someone was putting together an army of kidnapped children, like he had heard they did in Africa. Must be the Musalmans.

There were two uniformed constables with him. They were from the local station; one to lead them inside the slum, the other to stand guard next to the vehicles.

Meera was unprepared for the sheer squalor of Shahbad Dairy. She had never seen poverty like this. The narrow streets were so thick with garbage she could not feel the hard asphalt under her shoes. It was a squishy, polythene carpet over rotten fruit, piss and shit. The houses were built of bare bricks stacked on top of each other, stayed by a dab of cement, each house pushing into the next without an inch of space in between. They passed a public toilet complex broken and overflowing with garbage. Ghostly men leaned against the shattered walls, drugged, oblivious. Snaking past them, past enormous black pigs tramping about, was a line of women and children, carrying gallon jars to collect water. At the end of the queue stood a water tanker with three men standing atop and shouting instructions, trying to control the distribution. The tanker clearly did not have enough water to meet the demands of half the people standing in line.

Why do people come here? Meera thought. What could be so bad in their villages, their towns, wherever they come from, that they come live here?

The uniformed constable stopped in front of a shanty whose walls and roof were black and sticky with soot. At his call, a thin young woman stepped out. She looked at Meera and her eyes shone with hope. She took the policewoman gently by the hand and led her inside.

'Madam Inspector has come!' she announced with enthusiasm to her husband, a gaunt man who sat in one corner of the room, resting his back against the soot-stained wall. The house—one brick room with no furniture—had mattresses on one side, a couple of steel trunks in one corner, a small stove and a stack of steel utensils in another corner. It smelled heavily of stale smoke. From one wall hung the mangled remains of electrical wires, the rubber melted and fused into a black mass.

The husband rose with folded hands. He bent down, opened one of the steel trunks and took out a sheaf of papers wrapped in plastic. Carefully, he brought out a photograph and held it up to Meera.

'This is Kalicharan, our son,' he said quietly. 'Here is the FIR. We saved it from the fire.'

'It came out of a computer,' the woman said, smiling cheerfully.

Meera took the FIR, which was burnt at the edges, glanced through it. She had already read the file, dated 7 April. Kalicharan, son of Ramprakash, missing since 5 April. Left home for school at 9 a.m. Both parents in the house at the time. No one at school saw him. Ten years old, wearing khaki shorts, white shirt, black chappals. Identifying mark, none. Build, slight. Colour, wheatish. Eye colour, black. Hair, short. Birth mark, on right buttock.

'How did the house catch fire? When?' Meera asked.

'That was six days ago,' the woman said, in a tone that suggested something exciting and adventurous had happened. Her vitality, in contrast to her husband's silent, weary presence, began to lighten Meera's load.

'What's your name?' Meera asked the woman, whose name did not appear on any of the police paperwork.

'Maya.'

'Maya, I know you've spoken about it before to the police, but will you tell us again how Kalicharan went missing? Tell us everything you can remember.'

'It was like any other day, the fifth of last month,' Maya said. 'Our boy was simply going to school. He is a good boy, a studious boy. He goes to the government senior secondary school five kilometres away, near market number three, at Barwala crossing, have you seen it?'

Meera nodded, though she had not.

'Everyone goes there. There used to be a school in Dairy, but last year one boy died after the ceiling in a classroom collapsed, so they shut it down, shifted everyone to this one,' Maya said.

'How does he get to school? School van?'

'No,' Maya said. 'There are very few vans. Sometimes he is lucky and he gets one, but mostly he takes a bus.'

'There are only a few vans, the boys are always scrambling to get into one,' Kalicharan's father said feebly.

'He left at the usual time, around nine,' Maya continued. 'School starts at quarter to ten. But he did not reach school that day. People saw him walking with his bag on his back. There's a small shop on the way, five minutes from here. He stopped there to buy a pencil. The shopkeeper told us.'

'Was he with anyone else at the time? Does he usually walk alone or with friends?' Parveen asked.

'He was alone, but there's no fixed thing, sometimes he walked with his friends from here, sometimes alone, it's a short walk,' Maya said. Her husband nodded periodically, keeping his eyes to the ground. 'We spoke to all his friends. One of them had seen him at the shop and said hello. But the others said they had not seen him that day.'

'Lots of children from here go to that school, right?' Meera asked. 'Isn't it strange none of the other boys saw him on the way? The streets are so narrow, you can't pass without bumping into people.'

'Yes, yes, absolutely!' Maya said, her eyes wide. 'That's what I told the police. So many times, I told them, "Speak to my son's friends, maybe they know something but are scared to tell us … they'll tell you because you are in uniform!" They did not speak to anyone. No police has come or asked questions or done anything at all … you are the first.'

Maya looked down at her feet and fidgeted.

'I don't mean to say the police are bad, you are a good inspector, madam, I can feel it. So many of you have come, I'm very grateful, I'm feeling hopeful something good will happen, but the police did nothing. They said we've done the FIR, we've put it in the papers, we will wait. They said, your son ran away, he will come back when he gets hungry. When we go to the station, they tell us to go ask around, they say, if you hear anything, come tell us.'

Maya began to cry. Her husband continued to look down at his toes. Parveen was about to speak, but Meera signalled for him to stay silent.

'We've asked and asked and asked,' Maya began again, between sobs. 'On that day … we came home early that evening actually.'

'Came back from where? What do you do?' Das asked.

'He works as a mason,' Maya said, pointing to her husband. 'I help him. I carry the bricks. We were working on a house about three or four kilometres from here, inside Dairy. We finished work at four in the evening, came home by half past four. At first, we thought he was with friends and would come back any moment. He did not. We panicked. We asked his friends and classmates. No one had seen him. We searched everywhere till one or two at night. I didn't know what to do. I was crying, I could not breathe. I stayed home till half past four in the morning. Then I left for the mandi. His father went to the school, and they told him he had not come the previous day. I had a feeling maybe he went to the mandi—it's a place he really likes—so I went there with his photo.'

'Which mandi?' Meera asked. She was beginning to warm up to her role. Inspector Kumar's absence made her feel more liberated, more assured.

'Azadpur. When I came back, my husband and I went to the police station and filed the FIR. I went back to the mandi. I stayed there for two days, walking around like a madwoman, asking everyone, showing everyone the photo. No one had seen him.'

She stopped when there was a commotion outside the house, a woman was arguing with the uniformed constable at the door.

The policeman peeped in, said, 'Madam, there's a ...' A stout woman in a tightly fitted salwar-kameez shoved him aside and entered the house.

'Madam Inspector,' she said with folded hands, 'My name is Anita, I live in this area too. Maya knows me. Please help me, both my sons are missing.'

Meera was shaken by how quickly their search for one missing child had spiralled into a chaotic epidemic of missing children. Soon after Maya's friend Anita pushed her way in, Meera and Das had decided to spread the word in the area—families with missing children complaints, please come to the burnt house in gali number six. The local constable went out with Parveen.

The information travelled from one house to the next, from shopkeepers to customers, through a local NGO and over phone calls made from concerned parents to other concerned parents. Parveen was smiling—he already knew the scale of it from his exertions the previous day at the Dairy station. He was enjoying the reactions of his fellow cops as it dawned on them that they were treading deeper and deeper waters.

I hope they drown, he thought.

Anita had recounted the story of her missing children in one breathless monologue.

They went to the same school as Kalicharan, took the same route, went missing the same way. Left for school on 13 February, did not come back. Aged twelve and ten. The younger one a close friend and classmate of Maya's son.

'The first time I went to the police station, they turned me away saying you've come three days after your sons disappeared, get out, you are not serious,' Anita fumed. They told my husband, "What were you doing, you piece of junk? You must be a junkie. *You* must have done something to the boys."

'The next day, I went back with the NGO people and they wrote the complaint. I took my eldest son, who is fifteen, went searching for days. We went to all the railway stations. We went to Old Delhi. My husband went to other places. He drives a cart. He would work two days, make three or four hundred rupees, take a day off to search. No one had seen them, not my neighbours, not anyone. People would say, maybe you should go there, and I'd go there. When Maya's son also went missing, we decided to write a letter to the chief minister.'

Anita produced a copy the letter, which was tucked into her bra.

'The IO in the case changed thrice in the last three months. The first one, Dayanand, was transferred within a week. The next one went a month later. Not a single policeman has come to my house. I have been to the station ten or eleven times. Maybe the children went together to the canal and my boys got taken by the current and the other kids are not telling? Who knows? I have gone walking along the canal so many times. Once, I saw a corpse float up and thought it was my son … it turned out to be a fully grown man. I was …' Anita paused to consider what she was saying. 'I was relieved.'

'How old are you? Maya asked.

'Thirty …' Anita counted on her fingers, 'plus seven.'

'Where are you from?'

'We come from a village on the outskirts of Aligarh. Got married and came here. My man comes from Saigad Nagariya, which is near Aligarh. My husband's brother used to work in a factory here, he got us land, told us, why don't you build a house? That was thirteen years back. We had no money or land in the village, so we came. We are illiterate, low-caste. If we stayed in the village, we would have been farm labourers and our children would have been farm labourers, so we came here to give them an education.'

Anita paused for breath, and broke down.

'Now they are gone!'

Over the next three hours, sixteen families arrived at Maya's house with their complaints, photographs and papers. Among them was one woman whose daughter had gone missing eight years ago. But the rest had children who had disappeared within a tight timeline—seven months.

19

Meera quietly turned the key in the lock. As silently as possible, she entered the house, closed the door behind her. She switched on the screen of her phone, tiptoed in its faint glow to her room. She closed the door, switched on the light and sat on the edge of her bed for a few minutes. She undressed down to her bra and briefs, did a few push-ups and squats on the floor. She picked up a T-shirt and boxer shorts, headed to the bathroom she shared with the three other women. For the first time since she had joined the police, she felt something close to hope—the thrill of a hunt.

Lying in bed with the lights off, her mind wandered to Paris, where, eight years ago, as an up-and-coming wrestler, she had gone for an international tournament. Her thoughts were of a boy she had met there, a French wrestler, shy and silent, called Thierry. His skin was black, his eyes grey-green. She thought he had the lips of a voluptuous woman. His hair was shorn close to his scalp. She could still feel how it felt to run her hand over the thick, warm fuzz of his head. There was a ghostly tingle on her palms.

She had been abandoned before a bout. The team coach, the support staff, the other girls, they had all gone to watch a teammate—the most celebrated fighter in the team—compete in her gold-medal match. Meera's bronze-medal fight was to follow, so she had remained in the holding area, going through her warm-up routine alone. Thierry was passing by, said hello, signalled to her a question—did she need a partner for her warm-up?

Meera said yes. Her focus had been on the upcoming bout, so she had not noticed anything about Thierry at the time—the two had simply gone through the well-established pre-fight routine.

Crouched postures. Hands on each other's shoulders. Gentle pulls and pushes, clockwise and anticlockwise shuffles. Disengage. Crouch, re-engage.

After she had won the bout, she had searched for him in the crowd of athletes, given him a hug to acknowledge his help. No one had said anything to her then. Later, in the dining hall, the two met again, introduced themselves, fell into a conversation carried on in broken English, laughter and energetic mimicry (they had common experiences, both had grown up in dairy farms, and the time had passed quickly talking about cows, buffaloes, farm animals and their antics). It had not gone down well with the team management. She was told by her coach, a couple of the support staff and a few of the girls not to go whoring with black-skinned beef-eaters—in exactly those words, in a tone so vicious it made her feel like throwing up.

Meera had never felt humiliation like that.

The next day, the final day of the tournament, was a day off for both Thierry and her. She had deliberately sought him out at breakfast. They left the stadium together in plain view.

The day turned out to be an enchantment. Thierry lived in Paris, and he had taken her on a jaunt of his locality—11th arrondissement—a word Meera had not even tried to pronounce. She had marvelled at the buildings, at the steps of the opera house, the buzz of the local market where he had bought her flowers and treated her to crêpes filled with chocolate, the endless row of shops with their gleaming displays, all those happy people sitting and drinking on the sidewalks, absorbed in their raucous conversations, the street musicians playing melodious, upbeat music—paradise!

They had walked along a canal and, on a whim, raced down it (he thought he would let her win, but she was faster than him), cheered by onlookers.

He taught her how to take a bow. At the end of the canal, they found themselves at a public gym where a group of bare-chested, heavily muscled men were engaged in calisthenics. Their well-honed competitive spirit, that youthful surge in their muscles, was unquenched by the race, so they had competed again, this time to see who could do more pull-ups. He had beaten her handily, but again, she was the one who got the applause. She took a bow.

He had taken her to the bakery where he worked (she was surprised—in India, being an elite sportsperson was a full-time job). Of all the new wonders she had experienced that day, she loved this the most. The smell of butter, burnt sugar, freshly baked breads; pureed fruit bubbling in shiny copper vats and giving off sweet, intoxicating fumes; long ropes of dough being slapped and kneaded, sending up clouds of flour. The heat from wall-to-wall ovens as bakers deftly brought out finished breads. She had admired the tattooed forearms of the bread makers, told him with a wink, 'Now I know why your arms are so strong!' He had gone red in the face, all the way up to his cauliflower ears. The assembled bakers had treated her like royalty, bringing out little treats for her, saying many things to her in their rapid, incomprehensible language. She replied in rapid Haryanvi, everyone laughing like it was an insane asylum.

Outside the bakery, he had stooped to kiss her. She had not felt awkward—in fact, it felt like the most natural thing in the world. When he had whispered to her a proposition, she had not hesitated, nodding at him with shining eyes. She did not understand the words, but there was no mistaking the intention. The metro ride to his apartment lasted ten minutes—the longest, most excruciatingly delicious ten minutes of her life.

It was not her first time, but it was the first time she had felt so good, so free and uninhibited.

It was the last time they met.

When she returned home, it was to find that her dog Bholi had died. Her world crumbled at the news. It had happened the day she left for France. She had spoken to her parents every single day she was away, yet no one had informed her about the death.

Why? Why? Why? She had never felt anger like this eating through her, burning in her mind.

'You would have been sad,' her father told her. 'How would you give your best on the mat? I would not have told you if your mother had died.'

There was a sick, clenched feeling in her stomach. A rage that made her cry, alone, helplessly, for hours. Her family behaved like nothing had happened, like they did not even understand why she would be so sad, so angry. They spoke the same language, shared the same life, and yet … no one could say where her dog was buried. Was she not buried then, but thrown away like garbage? The thought was too much for her to bear.

She had sought relief from her grandmother, whom she relied on for all manner of kindness and tenderness. She needed to know, who had buried her Bholi and where?

'I don't know,' her grandmother said.

Who knew? Who? Who?

Meera sat up on her bed, feeling uncomfortably hot. She took her pillow and lay on the cool floor instead. Inspector Kumar intruded into her sleep-drenched brain. Did all men become like him when they aged? Indifferent, defeated? She thought of ACP Ahmed and felt a jolt of anger. She had tried to manipulate her. The fancy city woman and the rural idiot she could boss around. She could see it from a mile away.

Meera thought of the dead girl. There was something so pure about her face, youth unsullied by the numbing pain of life. And then a grotesque death. Where was Sangeeta, the nanny who had worked there earlier? Her aunt and their family had forgotten her, no phone number, no address. She could be dead too. Lying next to a broken toilet, like the addicts from the morning. Meera fell into a fitful sleep.

Parveen parked his bike well short of the address, and walked through the thin, silent lanes, the feeble streetlights only deepening the darkness. A dog began to silently follow him. He stopped, turned around, pretended to pick up a stone. The dog vanished into the shadows. He checked his watch, 2 a.m. Still the heat rose in waves around him. He walked on, past a children's park, past the darkened signs of shops, through a slim passage between two hulking buildings. This was where the big guys played, according to Anwar the barber, the ones who would take his stash off him. The first meeting had to happen face to face, not on the phone. So here he was.

Parveen tried to make out the house numbers in the near complete darkness. He had taken a few steps with his hand feeling the wall when he was yanked off his feet without warning, dragged backwards and slammed to the street. Before he could regain his breath, he had been pinned down, his hands splayed, held down on each side by different men, while two more knelt down, painfully pushing their knees into each thigh. Rage spluttered through Parveen.

'Motherfuckers, you know who I am ...'

The words were kicked out of him before he could finish by a foot that slammed into his ribs. Parveen stopped breathing as a jagged bolt of pain ripped through him.

'Of course we know who you are, madarchod,' said one of the men, hovering above him with his face covered. 'Do you think we hand out such VIP treatment to just anyone? The question is, do you know who you are? Or do you think you are the prime minister of our great country?'

This was followed by another kick, delivered to his neck.

'Careful, don't leave marks,' someone said.

'See? That's the kind of stuff we learn from you,' said the masked man, and stepped on Parveen's crotch.

The policeman gagged.

'Ashu bhai says hello,' the masked man said. 'He was wondering why you would want to stop working with him, try and make a deal with someone else. Did you get caught? Your phone is unreachable. Have you destroyed it? Is it with the police? Is Ashu bhai in trouble? He wondered if you needed to be killed. Do you need to be killed?'

'No, no,' Parveen said weakly. 'Yes, I have been caught, they know about the phone. I've destroyed the phone, but no one is coming after Ashu bhai, they don't know about him. Also, he has friends in high places.'

The man stepped on his groin again, sending spasms of pain down his thighs.

'Please,' Parveen said.

'Fucking coward, you are like a mangy dog, you know how to bite people, but when you get the stick, you've got your tail between your legs. Let's see your tail, let's see it wagging.'

The man unzipped Parveen's pants and exposed his penis.

'My boy says don't leave a mark, but my feeling is, if I cut your dick off, that's a mark you'll keep hidden from everyone.'

Parveen felt something cold and sharp, like a knife, on his penis. He wanted to cry.

'Please,' he said.

'We think you underestimate Ashu bhai, you think you are better than him, more powerful. You think you can get away with doing whatever you want. Just because bhai was nice to you. Now maybe you know better. Do you?'

'Yes.'

'Here's what you will do. You will pretend like you do not know who bhai is. You will stop doing your narcotics business, with us or anyone else. Whatever stuff you've got on you, throw it away when you get back home. If you try anything else, we will come not just for you but for your sexy wife and that disgusting, spoiled kid you've spawned. It's the end of the road, understand? If we get a whiff from the police that they are trying to come after bhai, we come after you first. So, you do what you need to to make this go away.'

'Yes,' Parveen said weakly, and was rewarded with a final kick to the ribs.

He felt the hands and knees holding him down release the pressure. He turned around and vomited.

Parveen zipped his pants, lay flat on his back for some time and cried. When he coughed, the pain jolted through his ribs, groin, neck and stomach. He gasped for breath again. Slowly, painfully, he pushed himself up and sat leaning against a wall.

By the time he sneaked into his house, it was almost dawn. Everyone was asleep. Parveen slumped down on the floor. He could hear the couple next door arguing. A white ball of rage punched through the fog of his disgrace.

I'll kill that man and fuck his wife with his body lying next to us, he thought.

He crawled on all fours towards the bedroom. He wished he was alone. If his wife woke up and saw him like this, he would smash her face in. He got to his feet when he reached the door to the room, peered in silently. His wife was asleep, mouth open, drooling into the pillow. In another bed, on the side of the room, his son was sleeping on his stomach. He slipped in next to his wife with his back to her. If it wasn't for her, he would have shot those men today.

As he drifted to sleep, he thought of a world without women. Only men. Men fighting, men doing whatever they wanted. Men without desire. Men without children. Men without guilt or confusion or fear. Men who worked all day and slept without dreaming. It would be a perfect world, refreshing, clean, like riding his bike on a highway.

At 10 a.m. on Tuesday, 8 May, Inspector Kumar, Das, Meera, Hari Singh and Sushil met in ACP Sofia's room. Parveen was missing. His phone was off. Kumar worried about it, but he was relieved too. He knew why Zeeshan was not at the meeting, but no one else did.

Meera did her presentation on the missing children's case.

Sofia's lips turned downwards in disgust as Meera elaborated. If she had any doubts about having made a poor decision in joining Delhi Police, those doubts were dispelled anew.

'Good work,' she nodded at Meera. She looked at Kumar. 'Why do we even have a Missing Persons unit? Why not close it down, transfer everyone to Traffic where they can stand around all night asking people to blow into breathalysers?' She made a clucking, irritable sound. These days, she was always irritable.

'Look at the bright side,' Kumar said. 'Local police made no effort. We've got so many children missing there, my feeling is, if we do even the bare minimum, we'll have a result.'

Sofia nodded.

'They didn't look at any footage, didn't speak to anyone. Isn't that right, Meera?'

'Sir, yes, sir. Most of the families I spoke to said police did not question anyone or make any visits.'

'They uploaded details on ZipNet and their job was done,' Kumar smirked. 'Even this they did not do properly. Tell me, Meera, when you went to the missing kid's house, what's the first thing the mother did?'

Meera pulled out an A4 sheet printed with a black-and-white photograph of a young boy.

'She gave me his photograph.' Meera handed it over to Sofia. 'Kalicharan, age ten, missing since 7 April. Left for school in the morning as usual, never came back.'

'I called the SHO at Dairy, said, hey, how come there's no photo of the boy on ZipNet?' Kumar said. 'He says, the family has none, am I to produce a photo from my ass? Pardon my coarse language, ma'am.'

Kumar leaned forward and said in quiet voice, 'Imagine what we can do with just basic police work.'

He was overselling it, but it was not untrue.

'You need me to get you permission to work in Outer, right?' Sofia said.

'Yes, ma'am.'

'Any of these children have any connections to our district?'

'It's unlikely.'

'How about we say we have a solid lead in the case that's come from one of your informers, that the informer will speak only to you?'

Kumar nodded in agreement.

'If PHQ thinks there is a chance we can find a few missing children, they won't say no,' Sofia said. 'It's great PR for them.'

'I think that's exactly right.'

'We have the full team on it, right?'

'Yes madam,' Kumar lied.

'So, where are Zeeshan and Parveen?'

'Court appearance, madam.'

'We'll have to do a lot of running around today to get the clearances for this case.'

'Absolutely, madam, I am ready.'

Kumar checked in with Zeeshan, drove the kilometre and a half from the station to Panchsheel, parked well before the house. The city had turned into an oven. If any illiterate fuck had any doubt about the sun being a giant ball of fire burning in the sky, let him be out and about in Delhi in May, Kumar thought. It was nearly unbearable, but at least he had shade.

He was in a quiet, tree-lined lane, with imposing houses on both sides. Rows of amaltas in bloom, drooping under the weight of their dazzling yellow flowers. In patches, they turned the sun's violent blaze into a benevolent, beautiful glow. It was miraculous. Someone had once told Kumar that the amaltas was the tree that defined Delhi. Not true, he thought, but if you lived in a place like this, you would believe it.

He began to walk, studying each house he passed, reading the nameplate wherever there was one—Mathur, Singh, Gehlot,

Dubey, Singh-Varma—hefty names. He stopped briefly at a house where he recognised the name, a famous newscaster with a primetime show. The guard outside the house uprooted himself from his booth when he saw Kumar lingering, but seeing him, Kumar began to walk again. The guard sat back down. Every house here had a guardroom. Some outside, some inside the gates—identical structures, the shape and size of the telephone booths of earlier days.

As he approached the house, he began to do a mental check of the CCTVs in the area. He passed the house—gates closed—crossed the lane emerging from Shahpur Jat, entered a cul-de-sac. The houses in this lane seemed even more impressive. White, spotless facades. The glass on broad windows gleaming and squeaky. No damp spots or cracks in sight, no trees growing out of cracks or flaking paint. Even the plants hanging from balconies or sprouting like fountains out of huge pots framing the gates had shiny leaves freshly washed every day. But all this was background noise in Kumar's head, which was focused only on one thing—CCTVs. He wanted to ensure they had not missed a camera. Red-brick house, two cameras, check, check. White two-storeyed house, four cameras. Check. The bungalow-type house with a wraparound balcony: one camera, not functioning. This one, a fake. That one, wrong angle, no visuals. The house with three layers of barbed wires, six dogs and eight cameras, check, check, check.

There was a time once, not too far back, when there was no footage of anything. How did the police get any work done? They spoke to people, they spent time in their communities, they knew whom to trust, they asked the right questions, they had better instincts.

Pure nostalgia, fucking lies. If he had his way, he would cover the entire city with these cameras. Before CCTV, people got away with their crimes and the police doctored the crime data. That old trick—if you don't register an FIR, there is no crime. When a case gets too hot to ignore, frame someone. Harder to do now. If it wasn't on CCTV, it was on a mobile phone.

Fucking mobile phones. How did anyone get anything done without one? I can't figure it out anymore, Kumar thought, even though I've spent most of my life without one. He tried to remember what it felt like to dial on a rotary phone, but his memory failed him.

The street ended in an unusual looking primary school building set amongst a dense foliage of trees and the entrance to a long sliver of a park that, on a previous visit, Kumar had deemed the prettiest park in Delhi. The ruins of a thirteenth-century wall ran through the middle, trees and bushes thick with flowers of all kinds sprouting wildly. The park ran parallel to the lane he was on.

Satisfied that no CCTV had been missed, Kumar retraced his steps. When he got to the crossing again, he took a left and walked out on to the main road. The sun was blinding and the noise of the traffic hit him like a shriek. He got into his car, switched on the faulty AC and breathed a sigh of relief. He was prevaricating. He took a moment to adjust to the new reality, looked at the foot overbridge in front of him. Hmm. It was no more than seventy metres from the Srivastava house. Probably less.

'*Mujhe chalte jana hai, bas, chalte jana* ...' he sang under his breath, easing the car into the traffic. Meera had briefed him about Sangeeta, in passing, a few days back. No address, no whereabouts, no phone, no photos, just plain vanished. He had thought about little else since then. Meera had managed an Aadhar number for her from a dormant bank account. Kumar had fed the number into the system and found that it had been surrendered two years back. He could not officially request for more details without the backing of his superiors, so he had gone to DCP Khandekar and made a personal appeal. Khandekar's probe unearthed that the Aadhar had been used by Sangeeta to make a passport a few months before it was surrendered. Zeeshan knew an officer in Delhi Police's passport cell at Asaf Ali Marg and made the introductions. That's where Kumar was headed.

20

Zeeshan unlocked the bonnet of his car at the security barrier, keeping his eyes on the white BMW ahead of him as it swept up the curving driveway to the doors of the five-star hotel. He hoped he was not too shabbily dressed to enter the hotel. White shirt, blue jeans. It was okay. He looked down at his jeans to see if they were stained and heard his bonnet clicking shut. He looked up to see the guard motioning him to enter. He was conscious of how cheap and dirty his car was compared to every other car he could see in the driveway. He considered taking it down to the basement parking. Fuck that, he said to himself and pulled up at the entrance. A valet opened the door for him. He got out with more of a swagger than was necessary, signed the parking slip, pocketed his half. He took a deep breath and entered the dazzlingly lit foyer, adorned with towering flower arrangements on a marble-topped table in the middle.

He walked around the lobby, scanning for his target. He found a loo and went in, saw that he was alone, picked up one of the tightly rolled towels stacked next to the basins, wet it a bit and tried to rub out the yellow stain on his jeans. It made matters worse—now there was a damp patch highlighting the stain. Irritated, Zeeshan left the loo and took another round of the lobby. Still no sign of his mark. In the last eight days, he had learnt enough about the habits of the man he was following to fill a fat dossier. Like the tortoise, he had followed behind the hare, noting places, faces, meetings, words, hotels, restaurants, malls, clothes, salons, spas, minuting the hours. Only on four of those nights had the man returned to Panchsheel for the night. On the other four, he partied, got drunk, slept in different hotels, at least once accompanied by a professional, or so Zeeshan had concluded from her look, clothes, youth and air of detached severity. He had photographs, dates, times.

Only twice in those eight days had the man visited his factories—one day in Bawana, the other day in Meerut. On the Meerut visit, Zeeshan could not get close to him; the factory was deep inside an expansive gated industrial complex. He could not even park close to the entrance without arousing the suspicion of the armed guards and bike patrols. He had spent four patient hours in his car, parked six highway lanes away from the complex, watching the gates of the factory compound through a pair of cheap binoculars, expecting at any time to be caught by UP Police patrol and questioned. He had been unable to identify most of the people, except the man's politician uncle, who came and went in a cavalcade of five vehicles.

The closest Zeeshan had got to him was the rare day the man did not eat lunch at a five-star hotel or in his office but walked—another rarity—to a shabby, crowded restaurant called Sagar Ratna in the Defence Colony market with two colleagues. It took Zeeshan by surprise. He hesitated before following them into the narrow, small room with eight tables. He spotted them as soon as he entered, and was relieved that only the overweight lawyer was facing him. Srivastava or Garg would recognise him, but the lawyer won't. Zeeshan took a seat at the table immediately behind Srivastava and Garg. He was inches from them. He pointed at a masala dosa on the menu and nodded at the waiter, then he sat stock still and listened.

The conversation was almost entirely dominated by Tarun Srivastava. It was about taxes. It moved on to buying property in UP and Jharkhand, a complicated scheme to cheaply buy off forest land illegally encroached on by mining companies and tangled in disputes. Zeeshan's dosa arrived. It was delicious. Then he heard something that made him swallow what was in his mouth and stop chewing.

'The Jharkand thing reminds me. I think it's a good idea to suggest to your uncle that he get rid of Shilpi,' Garg said.

'Why, boss?' Srivastava said.

'I don't have a good feeling about it. If the police get it into their heads to start poking their nose over there, your uncle will have another headache to fix.'

'Umesh, what are you talking about? Why are we still bothering with this? There is no fucking investigation anymore. Where's the investigation? What's happening that I don't know about?'

'No, no, sir, nothing else is happening,' the lawyer said. 'They are closing the file, it takes a bit of time to make a closure report and get it through the DM's office.'

'I still think we should distance ourselves from any Jharkhand connections for a while,' Garg said. 'Why would you keep that woman around after what has happened? Best to tie up loose threads. I think you should go for a family holiday for a few weeks.'

'Fuck all that,' Srivastava said. 'I'm not going anywhere. You think I'll survive the missus on holiday for a few weeks? I'll tell my uncle about the woman.' Soon, Srivastava was joking and laughing about his wife. Zeeshan went back to eating but did not taste anything anymore.

When they got up to leave, Zeeshan bent down and pretended to tie his shoelaces under the table. The men spent a bit of time at the cashier's by the door, picking up sweet paan. Zeeshan's back spasmed.

Two days had passed since then, but Zeeshan's back was still sore. He rubbed his lower back, watching as a flight crew made its way across the lobby—two middle-aged, bearded white men in pilot's uniform and six white stewardesses waddling awkwardly in their tight dresses and bleached make-up. Zeeshan took three steps down from the lobby towards a passageway leading to a restaurant on the right and a coffee shop on the left. In front of him, there was a bakery display piled with breads along the wall and a neat line of colourful pastries in a glass cabinet. Zeeshan turned right, took a few steps, mulling over whether he should enter the restaurant, when he became aware of people exiting the coffee shop behind him. He turned to look and saw his target laughing with a young woman. There was another couple with them—the man was familiar to Zeeshan as one of his target's business partners. The companion, he noted, was yet another woman in a short, tight dress, teetering on pointed heels.

Zeeshan turned away, pretending to look out of the glass wall lining the passageway. With a start, he realised he had a view of the swimming pool. A line of beach umbrellas shaded the women in bikinis, who lay sprawled out on lounge chairs around the water.

He could still hear his target talking, laughing. Zeeshan dared not shift, but this was terrible—if anyone saw him staring at the pool, what would they think? Why would anyone put a fucking glass wall overlooking the fucking pool?

A man came up behind him. 'Sir, excuse me.'

Zeeshan turned around feeling guilty. He knew that, to the burly security person, he looked like he had been caught red-handed doing something shameful.

'Can I help you?' The security man spoke in English, in case this man was a guest of the hotel, but he highly doubted it—more likely a pervert driver who sneaked his way in to look at ladies.

Zeeshan stole a glance at his target, only to see him walking away.

He sighed. There was no way out of this. He said, 'police', reached for his wallet, dug out his ID. He watched as his target and his friend and the two women strode towards the lobby and turned right.

Zeeshan showed the security man a palm, quickly took a few steps to keep his target in sight. He watched the man entering a lift that could only be operated if you had a key-card to a room. He felt the security man grip his left wrist painfully.

'What are you, a former pehelwan?' Zeeshan spat the words at the man, who stood half a foot taller than him.

'What are you doing here?' The man was unfazed. 'Do you have permission? Does the GM know?'

'Of course I have permission. Let go of my hand, bhaijaan, I am not running away.'

'I don't think you have permission. You come with me.'

Zeeshan did not want to make a scene.

'I'll come with you, but let go of my hand. I'm a policeman, you can't touch me.'

The security man ignored him, led him down a spiral staircase to the basement room that was clearly the security hub. A bank of screens at one end of the wall showed closed-circuit footage while a pair of uninterested security men, dressed like his captor in black bush shirts and black pants, idled in front of the control panel. A familiar sight for Zeeshan. Every district HQ had one like it, the only difference being that this one was less rundown.

A short, bald man with thick muscles bristled in through the door.

'Who the fuck are you?' he said to Zeeshan, who guessed this must be the head of security.

'Head Constable Zeeshan, sir, Crime Branch.'

'Why are you here without informing us? What are you doing? A drug deal? Blackmail? Delhi Police, you guys are the worst, cannot be trusted on anything.'

'I'm guessing you are not ex-police. Army?'

Before the man could answer, the door opened again and another man walked in. He was bald too, but tall, slim, dressed in a black suit, about ten years younger than the head of security.

'Who is this man?' he said.

'Delhi Police, sir, up to no good.'

'March him to the station, file a complaint,' the general manager said. 'What was he doing?'

His captor spoke up. 'I saw him staring at the women by the pool, sir, but I think he was following one of our guests.'

'Is that true?'

'Yes.' Zeeshan was almost relieved to get a chance to speak. 'Listen, I'm sorry I did not inform you, but I did not have the time. I am not here to blackmail or do anything illegal. It's a big, big case … national security.'

'Why should we believe you? It's illegal for you to come in here without informing us. Or are you too illiterate to know the law? Call your boss,' the head of security said.

Zeeshan called Kumar. No answer.

'Not again,' he thought.

The few minutes he asked for stretched into an hour as he sat helplessly in the basement, dialling Kumar's number every ten minutes. He started to banter with the two men scanning the cameras. At one point, he saw his target enter a lift alone, emerge into the lobby, walk out of the hotel. He duly noted the time.

Inspector Kumar was served tea and biscuits by Inspector Gurmeet Singh in a dusty, file-swamped room that made him nostalgic for the old days. The faintly sweet smell of damp cardboard filled the air.

'Zeeshan speaks so highly of you, Kumar saab,' Inspector Singh said. 'He is most devoted to you.'

Kumar managed a weak smile.

'He is a fine man, Zeeshan,' Inspector Singh continued, keeping his eyes on his laptop. 'We were struggling to get our daughter admitted to school … I don't want to lie to you, she is a little different. Zeeshan knew a madam who runs an inclusive school. Do you know what that is?'

'No,' Inspector Kumar said.

'It's a school where children like my daughter, children with … nowadays they say "special abilities" … it's a good thing, no? In our days we used such ugly words—loola, langda, pagal.' Inspector Singh stopped to stare at something on his screen, clicked his mouse rapidly a few times, raising Kumar's pulse.

'A school where my daughter can get the attention she needs, learn at her pace, in her time, but still attend classes with other children, whether they have autism or not,' Singh said. 'Zeeshan took me to meet the lady who runs the school. My missus would have left me for Zeeshan, she was so happy!' Singh guffawed at his joke.

'Got it!' he said triumphantly.

Kumar sat up, leaned forward.

'Here's the passport form. You are lucky it was digitised. If this application had been made three months before, you and I would have been here all day and night, rooting through these files.' Singh gestured at the cabinets surrounding him.

'This phone number is not working, you said?'

'Yes,' Kumar said breathlessly.

'I can give you another number. She has registered a foreign national as her husband, she attached her marriage certificate. He lives in Dubai. Imtiaz Hussein. Here is the number she put on the form for him. By the way, her passport was surrendered too, just a year or so back. I think she is now a UAE citizen.'

Inspector Kumar got back into the car and realised he had left his phone behind. A string of missed calls from Zeeshan. He called back. A most cordial man told him, 'Inspector? Nothing against you, sir, but we would need to speak to a higher authority.'

Then he called the UAE number. A deep-voiced man picked up after three tries.

'Yes?'

'Mr Imtiaz Hussein?'

'Yes? Who is this?'

'My name is Inspector Prashant Kumar, I am an officer of Delhi Police's Crime Branch. I am calling about Sangeeta.'

The phone was cut. Kumar tried again. No response.

He drove. Who will reimburse me my knees, he thought, in the slow southbound traffic. When he reached the spot again, he parked. He climbed the stairs, stood on top of the bridge and turned back to look. Ah! He could make out the Srivastava terrace. There it was, the servants' quarter. The big spaceship-like solar water tanks. He could see a little of the spiral staircase used by the servants. The potted plants. The next house with its abandoned terrace. The house to the right with the pretty rooftop garden. And. Yes. He could see the part of the terrace from where the girl fell.

Kumar looked around for the cameras. That was what he had been after. He found two, both attached to the bridge, neither pointing anywhere in the direction of the house. Below him, the traffic had become even more frenetic. The horns ripped through the air in a continuous assault.

Kumar became aware of a man who had emerged from the stairs on the other side. The man stood there staring at him. He had long, dirty hair and a beard, and was wrapped in a grey shawl. He carried a plastic bag so stuffed it was fit to burst. Kumar took a step towards him. The man, who had spent so many years surviving on the streets that he could spot a policeman from a mile away, uniformed or not, turned with unexpected speed and disappeared back down the stairs. Kumar broke into a run.

'Wait!' he shouted. 'What's the point? You can't run away. I just need to talk to you.'

The old man quickened his pace. Kumar took the steps two at a time.

'I don't want trouble, I'm poor and old,' the man said when Kumar caught up with him.

'No trouble, tau,' Kumar said. 'No trouble. Just want to ask you about something, then you can go. Do you want tea? Something to eat?'

The man refused to sit at the tea shop, so Kumar went to get the tea.

'Don't start running again, old man,' he said. He walked the few steps to the shop, picked up two cups of tea and a packet of biscuits. They sat on two pieces of fallen concrete by the side of the service road.

'What's your name?'

The man stared defiantly at Kumar.

'Fine, no name. Do you have family or do you live alone?'

The man looked down at his feet, swung his head slowly, left to right.

'No family?'

The man nodded.

'I am guessing you sleep up on the overpass there?' Kumar said, pointing to the bridge, which was a few metres behind them.

The man nodded.

'Good place in the summer, must be cooler up there than down at the street level, and cleaner too.' Kumar tore open the packet of biscuits and held it out to him.

The man took a couple and dunked them in his tea. Kumar did the same.

'All I need to know, old man,' Kumar said softly, as the noise of the traffic receded in his head, 'is if you saw something strange, late at night, about a month ago.'

The old man continued to look at his feet.

'You could have seen it from up there if you were awake. If you saw it happen, you know what I'm talking about.'

The man finished his tea in a gulp and threw the paper cup away.

'It's only me, I need to know. Nothing else will happen, no one else will question you, you will not have to go to a police station or anything. No statements, nothing written, no courts. No one would believe you in a court anyway …

'I can see you know a lot about life, you have wisdom, so you know none of these things will happen, because your word means nothing to most people in this world, right? Except to me. If you tell me what you saw, maybe I can do something about it. Maybe there will be justice.'

Kumar watched the old man. He waited. He practised his breathing. In, out. In, out.

'I saw it,' the old man said. 'The girl.'

Kumar breathed. In, out. In, out. Even though they were sitting next to the main road, a strange silence had descended, an invisible wall between them and the traffic flowing past.

'She was fighting with someone on the terrace. I saw her running. Saw him catch her, hit her. It was difficult because it was dark, but I have very strong eyes.'

Kumar's mind raced back to the autopsy report.

Restrain mark on left shoulder. Restrain mark on right upper arm.

4 fingertips contusions on the left side of the neck, 1 fingertip contusion on the right side of the neck. Injury is reddish in colour and recent.

3 crescenting abrasions in the antero-medial aspect of right arm around 6 cm above elbow joint. Injury is recent and reddish in colour.

Contusion measuring 4 cm by 2 cm on the left side of the face on the cheekbone, reddish in colour. Petechial haemorrhages in the left eye. Injury is recent.

His own voice echoed back inside his head—*'Held her by the throat, scratched her, slapped or punched her in the face.'*

The old man looked at Kumar and smiled.

'No one knows this,' he said, 'but I have very strong eyes. It was all shadows, but I saw it.'

'And then?' Kumar whispered.

'He hit her again, she fell. Fell off the terrace, fell down below, there was no noise, no screaming, nothing.'

'Did you see what the man looked like? Can you describe him? Anything about him? Height, clothes? Thin, fat?'

'Well, it was dark, they were moving around in the shadows, so I don't know … the man looked big compared to the girl.

Like your size, but not fat like you, perhaps, I'm not sure. I don't know what he was wearing.'

'Was there anyone else there?'

'No.'

'Then?'

'What do you mean?'

'What happened then, after the girl fell?'

'I went back to sleep.'

'After the girl fell and before you went back to sleep, did you see anything more?'

'The man was there for a time, on the terrace, looked like he was cleaning up. Then he went down.'

'By the spiral staircase at the back?'

'No, the other one.'

Squaring his shoulders, Kumar went into the station to confess to ACP Ahmed. He let her combust before he started telling her. When he finished, there was no sound to be heard except the hum of the air conditioner in the room. To his surprise, he had tears in his eyes. He was caught in two minds—should he wipe them? Then she would know for certain he was crying, perhaps even think that he was putting on a show. Or should he endure the discomfort, hope the tears would dry up quickly? He took out his reading glasses, wore them to read out the number for the hotel's head of security. Sofia made the call.

'Now *I* will speak to Sangeeta,' Sofia said, typing out a request on her laptop. She pointed at the printer. Kumar fetched the letterhead printout. Sofia stamped it.

'Send a photo of this to that man. When he sees it, call him and let me speak.'

Kumar anxiously waited for the two blue ticks. He made a video call the instant it appeared.

'What is this harassment?'

'Sir, please speak to my boss, Assistant Commissioner of Police Sofia Ahmed.'

Sofia gestured for Kumar to leave the room.

'Mr Hussein, pardon our intrusion. The house Sangeeta worked in as a nanny, the girl who replaced her has died in that house under unclear circumstances. We just need to speak to Sangeeta on the phone once, we mean no harm.'

There was silence, the kind of pause that nourishes any police anywhere in the world.

'Can I ask you, janab, if you know, did something happen to Sangeeta in that house?' she said, softly, clearly.

'Her name is Amina now,' the man said. 'There is no Sangeeta. I will ask Amina if she wants to speak to you. She does not want to remember that time or talk about it. But a girl is dead, you said. Well. Let me ask her.'

Sofia said, '*Allah ki rehmat ho aapke saath*,' but he had clicked off. A few minutes passed, then he called back.

'Madam, this is what I can tell you. Tarun Srivastava is guilty of raping Sangeeta over the years, making her work, giving her no money. He showed her photos of dead bodies, claiming that he ordered the deaths, the police worked on his command. That Sangeeta who had no parents, who was alone in the world, she is no more. Madam, how does this bastard, pardon me for saying, find another girl to harm? Amina ran away one day. She hid on a train to Mumbai, restarted life there under a different name, working at an orphanage as a teacher. I met her through my philanthropy. She has agreed to give a video statement, but only if you and a lady magistrate are present, no one else.'

ACP Ahmed leaned back, pinched the bridge of her nose. She summoned Kumar and handed over his phone.

'It's what we thought. How does this happen again and again?' She filled him in on her conversation. 'On the basis of her statement, can we get him? Is that enough?'

'No, ma'am, not nearly enough. Does not prove anything in relation to Jyoti's murder. The old man's testimony will be laughed out of court. Amina's will become her word against Tarun Srivastava's.'

'Okay. Keep the case going, from a-f-a-r, everything tightly under wraps. Let me get Amina's video testimony. We will take this chutiya down. You understand?

'Also, the next time we get a situation like this one with Zeeshan, I will suspend you, Inspector Kumar, and your team, gladly, without hesitation.'

Kumar thanked her stiffly, took off his glasses, wiped his face with a handkerchief, saluted.

In his room, he waited for Zeeshan to arrive. At some point, he slid into a soothing sleep sitting in his chair. Later, over the course of an hour, and a dinner of dal-roti, Kumar heard the things Zeeshan had to say about the target.

'So, I dug a little into this woman Shilpi,' Zeeshan said, producing a piece of paper. 'Shilpi Soren.'

Kumar nodded. He had spoken to her on the phone.

'Look. It's from ten years ago. FIR with Ranchi Police.'

Kumar read it. A child trafficking case. A woman named Shilpi Soren was implicated.

'Jyoti's so-called aunt,' Kumar said.

'Yes,' Zeeshan said. 'The one who got Jyoti to this house, the one who the Srivastavas say works for their family in Lucknow.'

'Can we be sure?'

'Case was dropped within a month after the FIR was filed. You won't find it mentioned anywhere, no online trace. I have a friend who has a friend in Ranchi who dug through the old records.'

'May your friends and their friends live a hundred years.' Kumar closed his eyes and rubbed his chin. 'Is there a way to dig deeper into it without anyone finding out?'

'No way to do it without local police. No way of controlling who leaks what information to whom. We can't touch Srivastava … how will we start something where the uncle is directly involved?'

Kumar put his head in his hands. 'Are we going to go round and round in this hell?'

'So, this madarchod was raping the poor girl? Things got out of hand and he killed her?' Zeeshan said.

'That's it, that's what it is,' Kumar said. 'And the driver?'

'He was either in love with, or at least friendly with the girl according to all accounts. Perhaps she confided in him? She was lonely, scared, had no one to speak to, no one to call. So she told Rajesh.'

'Yes. Remember the phone call Das stumbled on? Is that what he was trying to tell his sister? Maybe he confronted Srivastava or blackmailed him.'

'It would make sense to get him killed.'

'Do we know which gang collects taxes at Srivastava's factories?'

'Bawaniya.'

'Of course.' Kumar picked his nose carefully. 'Of course. He would use them for a killing surely. But with Vijay in jail, who's running the show?'

Turning the question over and over in his head, Kumar drove back home at 2 a.m.

When he reached home, it occurred to him that he was late. Now the guilt. Yet again, furtively entering his own home, heart pounding, mind exhausted, hoping his wife was not awake. He would sleep badly. The next day, avoiding his wife, barely speaking to his son, he would go back to work.

But what good would it have done if he had come home early, Kumar thought angrily. Would anyone be happier? His wife would be watching television and texting on her phone at the same time and would barely acknowledge him, unless she needed something done, that is. His son would be absorbed in a violent game on his phone, full of the sound of gunfire and military-style radio crackle. Why did he feel guilty? Why was he slipping into his own home like a thief?

He sat on the sofa in the darkness, trying to find the courage to get up and use the bathroom, change his clothes, get into bed.

'Prashant?'

He thought his heart had been kicked out of his chest. It was his wife.

'Prashant, did you find anything?' She meant the missing child.

'No.'

In the darkness, he could hear his own voice, he could feel the hardness in it. He knew he was preparing for a fight. He was tired. This was no time for a conversation.

Silence.

'And the other case? The suicide? Why are you working on a suicide?'

Kumar wondered if his wife had made the same connection he had—*this is our daughter, he wanted to say, our daughter, all over again, don't you see?*

'It was not a suicide. She was killed. I got to know today.' His voice was soft. If he'd had the courage, he would have said, come, sit, let's switch on a light, let's make tea. We share the same pain, you and I. Instead, he said, 'She was just a little child.

We think she was being raped. Then she was killed. We found another woman who was raped by the same man, she lives in Dubai now.'

'Prashant,' she said, and there was something different about her voice. It sent a chill down his body. 'A lot of bad things have happened. We have suffered a lot. Both of us have suffered, I know, it was not just me, you suffered too. You have not been good to me. I know I have not been good to you. But you are still here. I am still here. You have a lot of strength in you, perhaps you don't even know it. The cases will work out, you will see. I believe in you.'

He said nothing.

He heard her shuffling back to her room.

21

The team commandeered a dimly lit room at the back of the Dairy station, sparsely furnished with a table, three chairs and a cheap bed made of plywood, which had no mattress. It was the tenth of May.

Sushil laid out copies of the FIRs of the missing children, with a photograph of the child on top of each. Parveen was in a chair, hunched over the edge of the bed, sorting through the investigation reports, cross-checking them with the FIRs. He may as well not have bothered, he thought, considering how little the reports contained.

'No information can be found', one read simply, signed by the IO.

SI Das had gone around soliciting, unsuccessfully, for a whiteboard. He returned with discarded A4 printouts, unprinted side up, pasted them directly on the wall to form a white rectangle of a good size. With a marker pen, he jotted the names and dates of the missing children, along with the name and phone number of the IO in each case. There were seventeen. The first, a twelve-year-old boy called Shailesh, date 11 August 2017. The last, Kalicharan, age ten, date 7 April. In all, twenty-four different IOs had been assigned to these cases, for periods ranging from a few weeks to a couple of months. Most IOs had been assigned multiple cases. They had spoken to eleven of the investigators. None of them had done anything beyond asking around at the school.

Meera and her team had visited the school too, but found no information worth pursuing. Instead, they had faced a barrage of complaints. After the Dairy school was shut down in September, the students, seven hundred and eighty eight of them, had been shifted to the Barwala school. Except, the school at Barwala already housed a thousand three hundred and twenty-one students. There was simply no space. The new students could not be fitted into the existing classrooms. No one kept track of them. No one attempted to hide the fact that attendance was marked for the Dairy children automatically, whether they were at the school or not. The seventeen children on their list had perfect attendance.

Some of the drivers of the school vans and buses knew the children vaguely. Eight vans—four that had serviced the Dairy school earlier (because the school was meant for people living in the area, most students simply walked there, so even those four were a luxury) and four that had been diverted from the Barwala school in the face of pitched resistance from parents. Together, they could carry around ninety children, leaving nearly seven hundred to fend for themselves. A few private vans also operated, the drivers told Meera, but the majority of the students either walked or used public buses.

A boy came into the room with tea and biscuits. Das took the stack of paper cups and the plate of biscuits off the boy and laid them out on a chair, watched the boy pour the tea. Sushil picked up three biscuits, piled them one on top of the other, and put the whole thing in his mouth. Unselfconsciously, Meera bent down from the waist and wrapped her hands around her ankles to stretch her back. Parveen sat back on his chair and watched her without qualm.

The team had finished putting up their framework. It was already past 9 p.m.

'It cannot be a coincidence that all these children started disappearing when the Dairy school closed down,' Meera said, straightening up. She took a sip of her tea and was jolted by its extreme sweetness. 'Every one of them left for school and did not come back home.'

'Except one,' Parveen said, searching for the case in the line-up. 'This one.' He picked up a sheet and the corresponding photograph with a thumb and index finger. Das peered at it in the yellow gloom of the room, turned back to his board on the wall.

'Yes, Jagan, fifteen, the oldest of the lot, 3 November.'

'Let's look at him separately,' Meera said. 'Sushil, you take Jagan.' She felt invigorated. 'Is it normal?'

The policemen gave her a quizzical look.

'Is it normal that we are missing boys? Is it not more common that girls are kidnapped?'

'Boys are kidnapped mainly for labour, girls mainly for prostitution,' Parveen said. He scratched his chin. 'You could be right. It is odd that it's only boys.'

'But we made the pattern happen,' Das said.

'What do you mean?'

'I mean, we went to Maya's house, and her friend, whose sons go to the same school as Maya's son, heard about it and came. We asked them to contact whoever else they knew and ask about missing children. They called other parents whose children went to the same school. We set the pattern up. But if we look at ...' Das pointed at the fat register next to Parveen, which had all the missing persons cases filed at Dairy station. Parveen reached out and handed him the register. Das flipped through it.

'Yes, see, there are a lot more cases …'

'No doubt,' Meera interrupted. 'But we have sixteen boys, all of whom left for school and did not come back, all from the same school, all missing in the last seven months, after their old school was closed down. It's a pattern.'

It dawned on Parveen what Meera was thinking. He smiled. He liked it.

'You are saying someone is systematically picking up these kids in a car or a van … driving off with them?' Parveen said. 'That's good, that's a good one.'

'Yes, that's what I'm saying. What do we do next, if we want to follow this thought?'

'CCTV,' Das said.

'Hardly any in Dairy.'

'There is one outside the old school, if it's still working, that is,' Parveen said.

'And one traffic camera at the mouth of the market, near the bus stand,' Sushil said.

'Imagine if you had to do this,' Parveen said, his smile widening to a leer. 'The kidnappings, I mean. One person, or the same group of people, doing it repeatedly, picking up school-going boys. What kind of vehicle would you use?'

Meera's eyes shone. 'A white van,' she said. 'Like the other eight that are ferrying the kids.'

'Madam's brains are as big as her muscles,' Parveen said. '*Kasutta pench maarey tanne!*'

Das turned red. Meera could not help it, she laughed, slapped her right thigh hard with the palm of her hand.

'*Ghana bhadke hain tu*,' she said.

Hari Singh was glad not to have to search for missing children. This was much more his thing. Driving around with his old friend Colonel, the police-issue Toyoto Innova rolling on second gear, his foot not even on the pedal, he felt both the gentle ease of being with someone with whom he could share long periods of comfortable silence, and the slightly heightened awareness that comes with searching for something carefully and patiently.

They were in a lane down the road from Azadpur Mandi.

'There used to be an akhada here, next to that petrol pump we crossed,' Colonel said. 'Did you see the broken boundary wall? With the big bougainvillea? Used to be a famous guru there. His student was the first world championship medallist from India.'

'What happened? The akhada is gone?'

'Last year, the guru died, I can't recall his name. Within days, the akhada was abandoned. Right, here we are.'

Hari Singh parked near a plot of land overgrown with weed. Must have been at least twenty cars there, in various states of ruin: rusting shells, the skeletons of cars, yawning gaps where the doors and windows should have been. Some bore the signs of accidents; smashed from the front, crushed from the side, crumpled from the rear.

'What do you think happened to this one?' Hari Singh said, pointing to a car with a collapsed roof.

'A tree fell on it?' Colonel said. He limped around the graveyard, carefully avoiding craters of mud, rusting shards of metal, fat springs, half-burnt tires.

'Watch out!' Hari Singh cried.

A thick, striped snake darted out from under a heap of twisted metal. Colonel watched it impassively.

'It's a rat snake, not poisonous. I have one living near my house.'

'You sound like you take it milk in the morning and scratch its belly.'

Colonel laughed. 'Not quite, not yet.' He pointed to a car a few feet away. 'I won't be able to get there, will you have a look?'

It was a shell too, but still had its paint on it—red, though it was not easy to discern the colour under the grime that covered everything. Hari Singh struggled over the dirty bonnet of a hatchback.

'No,' he said. 'It's a Zen.'

The two men finished their search and went back to their car. Hari Singh opened a packet of pan masala, tapped a bit directly into his mouth. He offered the packet to Colonel, who followed suit.

They sat for a while in the heat, chewing silently.

'Let's take a break,' Hari Singh said, reclining his seat almost to the full extent. He clasped his hands behind his head and closed his eyes.

'This is too much,' he said. 'It's like searching for a grain of mustard in a haystack.'

'That's from a song, isn't it?'

'You are a sharp motherfucker,' Colonel laughed. 'It's from that gangster film.'

'*Gangs of Wasseypur*.'

'Yes, that one,' Colonel nodded. 'But tell me, isn't that our job?'

'Sure, but you need one hundred men for this, not the two of us driving around for … what's it been? Five days? We must have checked two hundred cars and clocked a couple of hundred kilometres in this vehicle. Who is paying for the fuel by the way? Considering the case is not with us anymore, we can't bill the department.'

'We'll do some creative accounting, we'll find a way.'

'But it's desperate, like everything about this case. An absurd way of doing it.'

'I agree, brother. We need a lot more people. But it's not so outlandish. If the car had been missing for longer, if I thought it had turned to rust, there would be no point. But we are looking for a red Alto, something we can scan easily in these graveyards, right?'

Hari Singh remained quiet for a time. He clapped his hands together and straightened his seat, started the car.

'You would think a red Alto would be common, yet we have not seen a single abandoned one since we started the search,' he said. 'Where to?'

'Keep going straight, take the third left.'

'Yesterday, the black BMW that was left rotting under a cover, I have my mind on it,' Hari Singh said. 'I took photos, we should run the numbers. If someone leaves a car that expensive to crumble, that person has something to hide.'

'A hit-and-run?'

'Could be.'

'Good idea to run the numbers,' Colonel said.

Hari Singh took the left.

'First right, then left again.'

They passed a small market—vegetables on carts, squat buildings with their facades thickly covered with hoardings and fat jumbles of wire, an overflowing vat of garbage with scavenging cows, a man selling pressure cookers in a big, shiny pile on the pavement—before Colonel told Hari Singh to take another right. They emerged at one end of what had once been a park. It was now a wasteland of black mud, plastic and thorny bush dripping with grease. Around its rim were salvage shacks set between heaps of scrap metal and other detritus. A line of abandoned cars. The two policemen needed only a glance to see that there wasn't a red Alto among them.

'Let's continue with our Dilli Darshan,' Hari Singh said with a smirk.

'I am waiting,' Colonel said, 'to meet a man I'm told knows everything about the movement of stolen cars in the area. It's taking time. He does not like to meet the police. I thought, instead of sitting at home waiting, we should cover some ground on our own.'

'You know, you are like the inspector in some ways,' Hari Singh said. 'Stubborn and without a sense of proportion.'

Hari Singh made the car crawl again, alongside a wide, open sewer line.

'I'll tell you one thing,' he said. 'The inspector thinks no one notices, but his mood is all over the place. He has a pretty bad case of depression. His wife and he don't talk to each other. Again, he thinks no one knows, he's always lying about his wife doing this or that …' Hari Singh snickered, not out of malice, but discomfort. 'Yet, he is always in the office. Sleeps there at least twice a week. Never brings food from home.'

'Why is it a concern?'

Hari Singh took both hands off the wheel to gesticulate. 'Because the unit gets fucked! Look at us, chasing something we should not be chasing … what are these cases? Some random young girl's death, some missing children from a slum … we've had nothing good to show since the Bawaniya arrest. Did I tell you about the day he slapped Parveen in front of everyone else? Who does that? I've got to give it to the inspector that he is strong, rocked the big bhaunsrikey to his knees.'

'Yes, you told me.'

'I don't know what I'm supposed to be doing most of the time. We have a woman on our team and we have to watch how we speak, not one but two rookie SIs, including her, one dumb musclehead, one out-of-action cripple—that's you, by the way—and one certified bad character. That's a pretty terrible scene.'

'And how, my friend, would you describe yourself?'

'The good cop.'

The two friends laughed as the car headed towards the Ring Road.

On 11 May, Kumar, Meera and Zeeshan were squeezed together on Sofia's pink sofa, when, to Meera's complete shock, the ACP began to discuss the Jyoti Dhurwa case. Meera tried to keep a frank and open face, but her right foot tapped the ground in an involuntary rhythm. All this time she thought the unit was off the case. What was going on?

'Okay. Begin,' Sofia said. 'Rajesh Mondal. Let's assume he was killed. At the moment, seems most likely. If he was, where did the killing happen? Who could have done it? We have a final location of the car he was driving that night, near Bawana road, heading towards Srivastava's plastic factory. Then the car disappears. None of the border CCTVs picked it up. Can we assume this is where he was intercepted? Makes sense, since Srivastava had dealings with the Vijay Bawaniya gang, whose turf this is. If the Bawaniya gang was given the hit for Rajesh, what's the most likely thing they would do?

'The car would go to a dismantler at one of the auto-repair shops in the area, the body into the canal,' Zeeshan said.

'Which one?' Sofia asked, betraying her inexperience.

'Munak canal,' Zeeshan shrugged. 'If it was weighted down, then in about five days after it was dropped into the water, it would bloat and float, hit Haiderpur Gate.'

'Right,' Kumar said. 'Which means Ambedkar Hospital.'

'There are a few other morgues in the area too,' Zeeshan said.

'Go on, get moving,' Kumar told him. 'Check their records for autopsies done on unclaimed bodies around those dates.'

'But what am I looking for? By our calculations, they would have got a decomposed body. They are hardly likely to do a proper check on an unclaimed, wasted corpse. How would I identify anything?'

A memory tugged at Meera. She frowned in concentration.

'Wait, before we go further, where's my case-on-a-plate? What's happening with the missing children?' Sofia directed her question at Meera. Startled, she began to stammer.

'We've put Sushil, Parveen and Das with SI Meera,' Kumar took over. 'We have promising leads. The children are probably getting picked up in a vehicle that looks like a school van. Meera and Das are heading to C4I right after this, to access Traffic CCTVs. Only two cameras there—one outside the old school, one near the bus stand outside the market. We'll check if there are any white vans that look like the school vans but are not one of the eight official ones.'

Sofia gently rolled the paperweight on her desk.

'It's only a matter of time,' Kumar said.

They could hear the DCP South walking past, talking loudly.

There was something relevant, important. Meera thwacked her thigh, startling everyone.

'A metal plate!' she said.

'What?' Sofia squinted at Meera.

'That friend of Rajesh's whom we picked up and interrogated, he told me Rajesh had a metal rod or plate in his right leg, in the shin.'

Kumar looked at Meera, then at Sofia, and smiled.

'There,' he told Zeeshan. 'A body with a metal plate in the right leg.'

The day turned to night. Meera and Das sat in the brightly lit but cramped police canteen and ate their dinner in a desultory way. Meera was not enjoying it—dry idlis, thin, over-spiced sambar, chalky coconut chutney. Das was not even hungry.

They had gone through a few hours of footage for five of the more recent kidnapping dates, but found no white van except the ones they already knew of. Each day, around the same time, they saw the eight vans pull up outside the old school, get crammed in a matter of seconds as children pushed and pulled and squeezed in. They left in a haphazard manner, jostling amongst themselves for no apparent reason on the crowded, narrow street, chased by a gang of children in white uniforms who had not managed to get space in the vehicles. The vans were picked up turning onto the highway by the second CCTV. On one occasion, one of them narrowly avoided being hit by a speeding bus.

They played and replayed the scenes over and over again. They went frame by frame. So many children in uniform. Not all of them walking towards the highway. Some, presumably, had used the excuse of school to get out of the house, were headed elsewhere. Other children were on cycles, or riding pillion on bikes.

The only other white van they found came and parked next to a makeshift garage near the school, stayed there for hours, got work done on the engine and left.

At one point, Meera and Das had taken a break to join the staff at C4I, who were immersed in the drama of a public fight between a young man and a woman in a short dress outside a mall, streaming live on CCTV. The men had whispered lascivious things about the woman, trying to avoid being heard by the lady SI. The two guests had been plied with many cups of sweet tea. Meera had not touch hers. The tiny paper cups—six of them—stayed in two neat rows on her table.

Now here they were, feeling deflated, a little defeated and enormously tired. Their eyes hurt. Das's lower back and shoulders had become bands of iron. They chewed silently.

'Let's come back tomorrow,' Das said. He was beginning to feel uncomfortable around Meera. He desperately wanted her to bring up that day, make a move again, show some emotion, even desire. He believed if she did that, he would react better, he was prepared, he wouldn't let the opportunity go to waste. Why had she offered to have sex with him that day anyway? She had said, '*Suthra lag raha hai aaj tu*.' He had found out later that it meant he was looking handsome. Then he had gone and spewed that rubbish about her being a villager. Stupid, stupid, big mouth. She had gone cold to him since then. He suffered silently, the rejection eating away at him.

Meera made no reply to Das's suggestion. She was planning an all-nighter, wondering if there was a private corner in this humongous building where she could get in a quick workout to refresh herself.

Colonel had arranged everything. The ambulance inside which Kumar sat was old, smelly and rickety. It was claustrophobic, hot and sticky everywhere. The cabin light was feeble and served only to deepen the sense of gloom.

Put me in this thing and I will never reach a hospital alive, Kumar thought. He was in a paramedic's uniform. That too was smelly and sticky. He hoped it was not blood, then, thinking of other bodily fluids that could be responsible for the stains, he muttered, 'Let it be blood.' At least the surgical mask hanging around his neck was new. He had bought it himself.

Kumar looked at his watch. There was time. He decided to get some fresh air. He opened the door, told the ambulance driver he was going to the toilet, walked instead to the nearest exit. It was a gate that opened on to a side street, relatively traffic-free. He looked up and down to see if there was a tea shop. He cracked his fingers, stretched his arms, massaged the sore muscle in his shoulder.

A bike came screeching from Kumar's right. It was being ridden by a young man in a red T-shirt and black trousers. Behind him sat a boy in a school uniform, clutching on to the man and squealing in delight. The man took a daredevil turn at the end of the lane, came zooming back. The boy had his arms stretched out, feeling the wind. Kumar wished they at least wore helmets. And anyway, what was a boy doing in a school uniform at this time of the night?

Another thought followed. He fumbled for his phone.

'Meera,' he said when she picked up, and realised how loud he sounded. He dropped his voice a notch. 'Meera, look for a bike, not a van.'

'What do you mean?'

'Think about it, our boys went missing one by one. Would you use a van to drive around one boy?'

'No,' Meera said. 'That would look suspicious.' She felt the down on her arms rising.

'Yes, one boy in a van would immediately draw attention, someone would have seen it, filed it away as suspicious, told you when you were canvassing. But one boy on a bike, that's perfectly normal. Right? Imagine, put yourself in the shoes of the kidnapper. If you had to lure a boy, go off route without alarming him, what better way than to entice him with the promise of a thrilling bike ride? Not too many boys would refuse that. I think our kidnapper is a known face in the area, the boys feel at ease with him. He would say, "Forget school, let's go racing down the highway," that's it, you get it? They would be out of there, out of reach.'

'Yes, sir!' Meera screamed down the phone.

Kumar cut the call and looked at the time. Shit, he was late. He broke into a run.

Meera took the stairs back up towards C4I at explosive speed. Das tried gamely to stay at her heels, ignoring the pain in his back.

'The enthusiasm of newbies, so nice to see,' said the policeman in charge of the C4I roster, smiling at Meera. She gave him a quick flash of a smile, made her entry, went back to her terminal.

On Day 1, they found thirteen bikes on the CCTV at the old school, carrying uniformed boys. One of them was being driven very slowly, had three boys of various ages stuck to each other, riding pillion. They discounted that one. For the rest, Meera jotted down licence plate numbers. Das did the same with Day Two. He found seventeen examples. It was two in the morning by the time they had gone through five days of footage. They had twenty-three different bikes in all, most of them had ferried children on all five dates.

As the ambulance left the hospital compound, Kumar took off his mask with relief.

'This is a very special visit,' said the man on the gurney, sitting up.

'I don't want you dead,' Kumar said. 'You never know who is watching. Imagine if a gang member saw me coming into the hospital, meeting you. What are you still doing in a hospital anyway, thought you'd be long gone?'

'So did I, Uncle,' said the man, Kumar's nephew and informer, the man Das had shot when they caught Vijay Bawaniya. 'So did I. They put something in my hip that gave me a horrible infection. I had to come back to this hellhole to get it fixed. Can't trust doctors. I wonder if I'll leave here alive once they are done with me.'

'Where's your wife?'

'Far away, safe,' the man said, smiling. 'Gone, vanished, out of reach. If these doctors will leave me be, I'll do the same.'

'How come you are still alive?'

'I have a brain the size of a computer,' he said, cackling. 'No, seriously, no one suspected me because I am a nobody in the gang. All I did was transport local alcohol. No drugs, no guns. I was not part of their system really, just a driver. Never went on an extortion call, never sat in a meeting.'

'But that day, you were driving him.' Kumar was careful not to say the name. The ambulance driver had ears, even though he was a cop too, related to Colonel, and could presumably be trusted.

'Very unusual. I had never driven him before. But after that incident at the court, he had sent most of his men out of station. Half his crew were in hiding in Haridwar, a bunch of them hiding out in Khatauli. There were a few of us, insignificant ones, sitting around in Delhi.'

'I need your help again,' Kumar said. He explained what he was looking for without going into much detail.

'It's not the hitman I am after, I need to know who ordered the hit. With our man behind bars, who is running the show?'

The young man thought about it. He winced in pain and shifted his weight. 'The father,' he said eventually.

'That old nutcase?' Kumar was incredulous. 'We've spoken to him. He is senile.'

'Actually, he runs the show,' the informer said. 'Our man is a babbling baby in front of him. The old man is good, he fooled you guys pretty well, huh? *Ek number ka haarami hai!*' He chuckled, winced again in pain.

Kumar knocked on the panel separating the driver from the rest of the van and said, 'Take us back.'

'Will you walk again?' he asked his nephew.

'Think so, the doctor told me there's a good chance. You are a bad shot. Missed my vitals.'

It wasn't me, Kumar thought, but did not say it.

'I am sorry,' he said instead, and put a hand on his nephew's shoulder.

'Don't be, I should have got out of it a long time ago, back when you first saved me. What I was doing, I was bound to get shot sooner or later, or worse. Strung up, tortured, skinned alive, dumped in the canal … think of it as you saving me, yet again.'

'What will you do? Can't you do something normal for a change?'

'Yes, I will, I'll go to …' His voice dropped to a whisper, 'Bangalore. That's where Manju is, she has an uncle there who runs a swank car repair shop, Mercedes and stuff. I'll join him.'

'Take good care of her,' Kumar said. 'She is beautiful. If she had not met a loser like you, maybe she would have been a movie star.'

The informer laughed. 'I will.'

'You don't beat her, do you? If you do, I'll take better aim at you next time we meet.'

'For that, you should practise a lot. Better still, get a personal coach.'

22

Gulabo Mahal, or the Pink Palace, had lost its blush to time and neglect. Its paint had stripped away, leaving only patches of pink. The only exception was the ornate faux-arch spanning the wide entrance: pale pink, clean. Under it hung a massive poster for the movie on show, a horror flick called *706*.

'What do you think, bhaisaab, shall we relive our youth?' Hari Singh said.

Colonel was amused too. It had been a long time since he saw a movie in a cinema hall, even longer since he had entered one that was not in a multiplex. It truly was a throwback to childhood.

'Only if it halves my age and cures my limp,' he said.

At the entrance, they were stopped by the gateman. When they explained they were policemen on assignment, the man became indignant. They needed to have a warrant, or they needed to buy tickets. They argued for a few minutes politely, which was Colonel's way, but the gateman refused to budge.

'What is this? Are you running a prostitution racket inside? How else does a single-screen hall survive in the city? Is that why you don't want us to go inside?' Hari Singh said, beginning to lose his temper.

A call came on Colonel's phone. It was Shafique, the car thief.

'Uncle, you don't need to enter the hall, get back in your car. Meet us at the Shiv Mandir behind the Karala Government Hospital, it's only two kilometres from here, got it?'

'Okay.'

Colonel dragged Hari Singh away by the arm. 'Let's go, they've changed the meeting point, must have been watching us, making sure we are not trying to trick them.'

'Paranoid behenchod,' Hari Singh spat.

As they approached the temple, Colonel spotted Shafique sitting atop his bike.

'There,' he said, pointing him out to Hari Singh.

The thin, tall man with oiled hair tied in a ponytail signalled for them to follow before speeding away. He did a wheelie and looked back at the policemen, flashed them a grin.

Colonel shook his head and grunted.

Shafique took a turn into a muddy lane ahead of them and came to a stop outside a ramshackle shop that repaired car and bike tires. He walked up to Colonel.

'Uncle, namaste!' he said with a wide grin. 'Been a long time. How are you? Sorry for the detour. Satta bhai is very careful, in fact, he never meets with the police. He only agreed because your nephew and I, we persuaded him. Come.'

Atta Satta was sitting on a plastic chair outside the shop, his face covered with a keffiyeh. He stood up and shook hands with the two policemen.

'I really don't like police, let's make it quick,' he said, in a thick, muffled voice. 'First, what is this information worth to you?'

'It's important,' Colonel said, 'because it's part of a case we think is murder. But as for value, this is just us, not the department … the department does not care a fuck. The dead girl is an orphan, worked as a servant in a rich house. You know how that goes? You'll have our debt if you give us the information. Any time you are in trouble, you only have to call me, or Hari Singh here. As for money, we have only five thousand rupees to give.'

Atta Satta uttered a short, bitter laugh.

'Your debt? Brother, there is no one with less honour than Delhi Police,' he said. 'I would rather have a pimp give me his word than you people. And five thousand is shit money. Talk sense.'

'Brother, we can all agree Delhi Police has no honour,' interjected Shafique. 'But this man I can personally vouch for. His inspector too. They are good friends to have when you are in need.'

'I don't need anyone,' Satta said.

'How about 10,000?' Colonel said.

Hari Singh looked at him in alarm.

Satta considered for a moment without taking his eyes off Colonel.

'Okay, money first.'

Colonel took out his wallet, counted out five two-thousand rupee notes.

'Show me,' Satta said.

Colonel showed him the photograph of the car.

'Yes, I know this one.'

Hari Singh had not expected this. He took a step towards Satta, spun around so he was shoulder to shoulder with the man, peering at the photo.

'Are you sure?'

'Absolutely.'

'Where is it? Can we get it?' Colonel's demeanour had not changed.

Hari Singh studied the man with new interest. He took in his height (around five foot eight), weight (perhaps fifty or fifty-five kilos), broad shoulders, long fingers, black hair, black eyes, blue mechanic's pants with extra pockets and grease stains, black sneakers, grey shirt with black stripes.

'Yes,' Satta said. 'It's at the Kanjhawla police station.'

'What?' Hari Singh said, his face scrunched into a disbelieving scowl.

'What?' Colonel laughed and nodded. It made perfect sense to him.

'Those guys picked it up and did not tell us?' Hari Singh shouted. 'But we had specifically informed the Kanjhawla SHO when the car went missing!'

'They did not pick it up,' Satta said. Colonel had the distinct feeling he too was smiling behind his keffiyeh. 'It was put there. Because they have an excellent car graveyard. So many rotting cars. No one will notice another one. Which policeman goes searching inside police stations?'

Shafique was grinning like a maniac, standing behind Hari Singh. He looked at Colonel, put a finger on his lips. He produced Hari Singh's wallet, holding it up behind the policeman's head to show it to Colonel. He pointed to Hari Singh's phone, which was in the policeman's breast pocket. Colonel watched the scene unfold without changing his expression. Shafique was such a show-off. He should have been a performer, doing magic tricks.

'Let's go right away, Hari Singh, before the sun goes down,' Colonel said. 'Thank you, Satta-ji, I am grateful. You'll see, when you need me, I'll be there.'

Shafique put an arm around Hari Singh and said, 'It was nice to meet you, sir, any friend of Uncle's is a friend of mine.'

'I think both your phone and your wallet have been taken, Hari Singh,' Colonel said impassively.

'What? What are you talking about …' Hari Singh fumbled with his pockets, realised he was indeed missing both. 'Behenchod!'

'Hand them back,' Colonel said.

Still smiling like a lunatic, Shafique extended his hand, Hari Singh's wallet and phone in his palm.

'How …?' said a bewildered Hari Singh.

From Kanjhawla station, Colonel made the call to Kumar. Found the car, requesting forensics.

A few hours later, Kumar, Colonel and Hari Singh were standing under a black tent erected around the red car, which had been stripped of its engine and other useful parts before being dumped. The forensic team were spraying luminol. In the darkness, Kumar and his men held their breath every time a part of the car lit up in blue where the spray landed.

It was the promise of blood.

'We're done, let's open it up,' said the head of the team.

A policeman holding up one side of the black tent let it fall. Light flooded in.

'And?' Kumar asked the lady, blinking in the sudden light.

She shook her head.

'We'll take swabs, but there seems to be no blood anywhere. Looks like the inside of the car was cleaned with bleach,' she said. 'Luminol reacts with bleach too.'

'Yes, I know,' Kumar said irritably. 'No fingerprints either?'

She shook her head again. 'No.'

'Madam, let's open up the seats and do a quick check, it's the only thing left to do,' Colonel said.

Kumar borrowed a pair of gloves. One tore at the palm before he could pull it all the way up.

'Don't worry,' said the lady. 'It won't matter, use your fingers.' She held up her own hand to show a tear in the glove. 'They are pretty old, the rubber's not in good shape, what can we do?' she shrugged.

They got down to it, carefully tracing the seams running through the seats, the cracks and gaps, where they inserted their fingers and poked and prodded. Two men ripped through the fabric of the seats with blades.

'What's this?' said one of the searchers, a young man with long sideburns, pointing at the ruptured driver's seat. 'Look here!'

The team congregated around him as he held up his find.

'A SIM card?' Kumar said.

'No,' said the man. 'A storage card, for phones.'

'Jai ho, jai ho,' Kumar said under his breath, then loudly—'let's take it in right away, get it into a computer.'

'Wait, prints first,' said the lady.

Kumar nodded and stepped back. He fidgeted. His mind raced with thoughts. He rocked on his heels. He walked over to check the seat from where the object had been retrieved. He knelt and carefully probed the area with a finger. The card must have been hidden quickly by the driver, in the face of danger. The man realised something was wrong—perhaps the timing of the drop set off alarm bells in his head. He tried to protect something valuable; slid his phone open, pinched the memory card out, but did not have time to find a proper hiding place. He dug his fingers under the seat, trying to find a crack, found one, slipped the card in. That must be it.

Kumar got to his feet and walked up to one of the station's uniformed police. 'Do you have a computer lab here?'

'No, sir.'

'Madam, are you done?'

'Yes.' She handed the card to Kumar in a small plastic sleeve.

'Hari Singh, Colonel, stay here and finish the search. I'm off to the station.'

Kumar sat shivering inside the overly cold computer lab at Hauz Khas. Shaken, yet highly aroused by the smell of prey, he was finding it difficult to stay in control.

'Let it be, stay with the feeling, don't fight it,' he said to himself. 'I know when I'm breathing in, I know when I'm breathing out. In, out.'

He closed his eyes.

He opened them when he heard the door.

ACP Ahmed came in.

'Yes?'

'I have something to show you,' Kumar said. 'You should sit.' He pulled out a chair for her, clicked the mouse to set the video up. Jyoti Dhurwa's face came up on the video player. Centre of frame, handheld phone, trees behind her, thick shrubbery, an old stone wall.

'It's her!' Sofia exclaimed, and looked up at Kumar with wide eyes.

'Yes, my guess, shot by her friend Rajesh, in a park close to the Srivastava house. Hari Singh and Colonel found the car, this was hidden inside the driver's seat.'

He played it.

Jyoti Dhurwah looked at the camera. In a barely audible voice, she said, 'My name is Jyoti, I am fifteen years old.'

She looked away.

'I am recording this on 28 February, which is my birthday, I think.'

She stopped. The call of birds. Someone else talking, passing by off-camera, Jyoti's eyes following the person.

How hard it is, Kumar thought, to see her alive, harder than looking at her lifeless body in the crime scene photos, how strange. What was it his wife had told him? He cared more for the dead than the living.

'I need you to know that I work in house number C327 in Panchsheel Park, Phase 2. I am molested there. The owner of the house, Mr Srivastava, he makes me do things to him. Sexual things. He forces me. He threatens me, beats me. I have no one. I am an orphan. I am afraid I will be killed if I say anything. He tells me he will kill me and bury me in their garden and no one will know. Please help me.'

She said it without faltering, without tears, but without looking at the camera. The video ended.

'Fuck!' Sofia said. She leapt up from the chair, sent it rolling backwards into the wall. 'Fuck!' She turned to face Kumar, her face twisted. 'Can we get him now?'

Kumar shook his head. He took a few steps towards the door of the computer lab and locked it. He drew up a chair, gestured for Sofia to sit. 'The prosecution will question the authenticity of the video. They will say it was coerced, that there was a conspiracy to blackmail Mr Srivastava, etc., etc. They will say this is not direct evidence that there was murder.'

'We can leak it to the press, destroy his life.'

'We could do that, I don't know if it will destroy his life. Everything passes, people forget … though maybe we will have to leak it at some point, anyway. If we do it now, then whatever value the evidence has will get tainted. We need to have something better, something that, when we add it to the video, will make for such solid proof that the prosecution will not be able to budge us. We have an incredible opening in our hands. We need to be patient and careful and build on it.'

'I was thinking I should speak to Neha Srivastava,' Sofia said.

'Why?'

'The way her husband is, she can't be a happy woman. I bet she knows about this too. Maybe she is suffering. You said that you feel there is domestic violence. She must have a lot of anger inside her towards him, maybe we can push her, see if she will turn? We can't tap Srivastava's phone, we won't get clearance. Can't interrogate him the way you want to. I don't know what else we can do.'

'That's a good idea, but even if she turns, do you think you will get her to talk in front of a magistrate? If she confesses to us, by the time the case comes up, she will simply claim police harassment, retract her statement and turn hostile.'

Sofia screwed up her nose and chewed her lip.

'Her anger won't last the course of a trial,' Kumar said. 'That leaves us with her conscience.'

A bitter laugh escaped Sofia. 'What about the manager, Garg?'

'I have no doubt he knows everything that goes on in that house. I know people like him. Men devoted to duty. There's a better chance of Srivastava confessing than this guy opening his mouth. Again, we have no legal way of getting to him.'

'So, we wait? Keep digging secretly?'

'Yes. Wait. A little more. At some point, we'll have to do all the things you are suggesting—leak the video, get the wife to turn, perhaps Garg too. Grab this aunt of Jyoti's, who may be running a child-trafficking ring.' Kumar smiled. It was so odd that Sofia felt a bit scared.

'Look at me daydreaming,' he said. 'First …'

'You have a plan?'

'Yes.'

III

SHAHBAD DAIRY

23

Sumit held out his hands in front of him and stared at them. They were still trembling. He buried his head in his quivering hands and sat cowering and rocking gently. He was alone, which was good, sitting here, next to the canal.

He began to laugh, a rattling, sniggering sound through clenched teeth, interspersed with coughing, mingled with tears and snot. Threw up. He wiped his mouth with his shirt and jumped up. Something was bobbing up in the water a little ahead of him. He ran towards it, tripping on a piece of scrap metal that cut his shin. He hurtled to the ground and lay there writhing and crying. Even though pain shot through him, he was careful not to make any noise. He closed his eyes, curled up on the ground in a foetal position. When he got up to look again, whatever was in the water was gone. A relief.

Half an hour had passed since he had killed the boy. Thrown the body into the canal. He was tormented with the thought that the body would float up again. He had travelled downstream, about two kilometres, to this spot before he had to make a stop because his hands shook so badly.

Sumit had never killed before. He was cold as ice, soaked in sweat, even though it was almost forty degrees. He shivered like he was going to die. What he needed was a drink, but he could not risk going into one of his watering holes looking like this. Everyone knew him, they would start asking questions.

He needed to tell someone what had happened, but whom? He had thought of and discarded a dozen names in his head. There was no one he could tell.

In the morning, he was looking for a straggler, as he did on auspicious days, about once or twice a month. He had rules for the work. He checked his religious calendar to ensure the day was well-aligned and would bring him luck. And he picked up only boys between seven and twelve years of age. They had to be small, thin. They had to be in their school uniform. They had to be alone. They had to readily agree to get on the bike with him. He had become good at gauging their attitude as he spoke to them.

If he saw hesitation, fear, he immediately dropped the project.

When he first started doing it, about a year back, he had hated the idea. He had felt like he was going to die, like he was feeling right now, the day he had picked up his first boy, delivered him to the warehouse beyond the border. For the next two months, he had lain low.

But … the money was excellent and he needed it so badly. There was no heat either. No police. No one asking questions.

The money. He was nothing without it. His father had died a long time back, crushed by a truck. His older sister, who had worked tirelessly to support his mother and him, died in childbirth. Her husband had refused to take her to the hospital. The neighbours called the police, she was in so much pain. The police called the government ambulance service, which duly arrived, but the husband would still not let her go. Finally, the police came. They slapped the husband around and carried his sister to the ambulance. It was too late. The child died too.

Now his mother was dying. She had been ill for as long as he could remember. When he was a child, he had no idea what it was. Now he did. Cancer of the stomach. She could barely keep any food down. He had already arranged money for a surgery for her, radiation sessions as well. He had found a job as soon as he quit school, running country liquor across the border. The demand was so high, it was impossible to keep up. Every lane in the JJ colonies had at least one, if not two or three, hole-in-the-wall drinking places—small rooms behind tattered curtains—open round the clock. At first, he was an assistant to another man with a car, helping him load and unload. Soon, he had enough money to buy a bike and carry crates himself. That's when he made enough money to start his mother's treatment. He was proud of himself. Sumit began to wear nice clothes. He bought sunglasses. He treated his friends. He began going to a gym. When the friend he had first started bootlegging with fell ill with dengue, he took over the task of driving the van. He made five times the money he made delivering on a bike. This went on for a couple of weeks—four hundred quarter bottles, that's eight crates, each crate sold for three times the price in Delhi. Eight thousand rupees per run, three runs a day. Made him heady just to think about it.

One night, before crossing the border, he saw a broken-down car blocking the road. It did not feel right. He had no option but to slow to a stop. It happened without fuss or violence. There were about ten men, bandanas tied around their mouth and nose, some with country guns, some with stout sticks, and one, he saw with terror, with a sword. They surrounded the van and tapped on his window. He held his hands up, as did his helper, and stepped out.

'It's just alcohol, not beef,' he shouted, the only words he spoke. The masked men nodded in acknowledgement. They got into the van and drove away. A couple of men picked up the rear fender of the car blocking the road, slammed it back in place, drove off. He and his helper were left alone on the road in the eerie darkness.

The aftermath, on the other hand, was all noise, pain and chaos. He was hung from the scaffolding of a factory roof by his wrists, beaten with sticks till he pissed his pants and bawled in pain. His screams mixed with the loud clanking of hammer on iron and steel and the hiss and spark of welding machines. The Bawaniya men believed he was lying to them, that he was working with another gang, pulling a fast one. When they had beaten him enough, were satisfied he was not lying, they demanded that he repay them for the value of the goods he had lost, as well as for the van. That came to a few lakhs. Money he did not have. They said they would kill his mother. They were ready to send a couple of men down to his house, get her picked up, brought here. They said they would kill her by hitting her with hammers. In his confusion and terror, he begged for a way out. He pleaded with them to give him any work, anything at all, so he could earn the money back for them. He would kill if necessary. When they brought him down, he fainted.

Later, they outlined the plan for him. How he needed to pick up the boys, where he needed to drop them. He would be paid ten thousand rupees per boy. He would be able to repay his debt with about twenty boys. No one cared for these boys. They were unwanted. No one would miss them. He did not dare ask what would become of the children, though once he became quite good at it, he got deeper into the system, learnt a little more. He got to know about the various safe houses where the boys were kept while they were being moved around. Most of them ended up as slave labour in brick kilns, leather factories, large farms, even highway dhabas.

He found the work was not hard. His early nerves gave way to a quiet confidence when he realised how readily the boys agreed to get on his bike, how desperate they were for thrills, something new and shiny. How susceptible they were to offers of a lift when walking down the long highway to the far-off school.

This morning had promised nothing different. He was, as usual, ambling along one of his routes by the canal, away from habitation, hoping to get lucky, find a lone straggler. He found one. He followed the boy for a bit, keeping his distance, rolling the bike along as silently as he could. When he was happy with his spot, he roared past and screeched to a halt a few feet ahead, turned the bike around with style. He did a wheelie as he came back towards the boy.

'I know you, don't I?' he said.

'Maybe,' said the boy.

'Are you bunking school?' he said, trying to sound nonchalant.

The boy looked at him closely, eyebrows knitted together.

'What class are you in?'

'Class 5,' he said, then, 'I know you.'

'Of course you know me,' said the man. 'I work at the tea shop outside the old school building, remember? I do stunts on this beautiful bike, you must have seen me do it. Have you ever been on a bike like this?'

'No. I know you because I saw you pick up my friend.'

A chill went through his body. He stopped smiling and looked at the boy more carefully. The boy was staring at him, eyes narrowed, lips puckered, schoolbag held tightly by the straps.

'My friend Akbar. You stopped next to him, near here, many months back. I was running towards Akbar, trying to catch up, but I was too far away, I saw him going with you.'

His head was spinning. He wanted to get away, but something made him stay.

'My friend never came back,' the boy said. 'I told my parents the man on the bike took him, but they did not believe me, they said I should forget about Akbar. But you took him!' The boy screamed and began to run.

He dropped his bike where he stood and sprinted after the boy. When he caught up with him, the boy struggled and screamed. He held on, trying to speak to him in a soothing tone, asking him to calm down, telling him he would explain everything. But his sense of time and place was getting warped. He was not sure the words coming out of his mouth were his own. The boy bit him. He clutched his hand and screamed. The boy started running again. He picked up a stone and gave chase. In eight, nine, ten, eleven steps, he was upon the boy. He tackled him to the ground. He smashed the stone down on the child's head. Again. Then again. Bloodied, frenzied, eyes bulging, drooling, he looked around him like a hunted animal. He saw no one. Just the blackened, dirty reeds, the canal water swirling, sleek like oil, a polythene bag being lifted and carried away by the hot wind. He dropped the stone. He tried not to look at the boy's face. He ran back to his bike and got a piece of rope. He found a heavy, flattish stone that he dragged with difficulty towards the edge of the canal. He dragged the boy to the same place. He took the clothes off the boy. He tied one end of the rope to the boy's ankle, the other end to the stone. Gently, he pushed the boy into the canal. He watched as the body made a splash and got sucked in.

He collected the clothes and the school bag and went towards the reeds. Dumped them in a pile, ran back to his bike. He was breathing hard and with great difficulty. From the bike's storage, he took out a one-litre water bottle in which he kept emergency fuel. He walked back to the pile of clothes and emptied the bottle on it, lit the pile, watched it burn for a bit. He looked around. No one had seen him.

He went back to his bike and drove along the canal.

It was Parveen who made the breakthrough.

It began with Das spending a restless day at the tech room adjoining C4I, waiting impatiently for the engineers to finish their enhancements so they could read the licence plates that were hazy or partially visible at first attempt. By the end of the day, he had gone through at least ten cups of awful tea and sixteen cigarettes. He felt ill, but he had the list—all but one of the bikes on his list had been identified, thirty-nine of them.

Two more days passed as the team cross-checked registrations to addresses and knocked on doors: 'Is there a child in the house who goes to the government senior secondary in Barwala?'

At one house, a typical unfinished brick hovel with no windows, a broken handpump and a stinking open sewer outside, Parveen had had enough. There was no one in the house except a sickly, frail woman with a strangely bloated stomach. One of the bikes was registered to this address.

'Does your son go to the school in Barwala?' Parveen asked the lady.

'Do I look like I have a son of schoolgoing age?' The woman was combative but spoke with difficulty.

'Hard to say. You look like you are sick, who can say if you are thirty or sixty, or what age you gave birth,' Parveen said. 'Answer the fucking question and I'll leave.'

'Yes, I am sick, I have cancer of the stomach, I am very sick, I've been sick a long time,' the woman said. 'What will you do? Cure me?'

'So, who else lives here? There is someone in this house who owns a bike.'

'Why? Why do you ask? Has the bike been stolen?'

'Just answer the fucking question. You have too much energy for a sick person.'

'My son has a bike, he is the only family I have left, he's my everything, I'm alive because of him. But he doesn't live here anymore.'

'Is he married?'

'No.'

'What does your son do?'

'He does exercise, you know, teaches it, fancy job at a fancy place.'

'A gym trainer?'

'Yes, whatever you said.'

'Does he drop someone to the school in Barwala?'

'Maybe.'

'What do you mean, maybe?'

'Like I told you, he doesn't live here. I don't know if he's taking someone to school or what he is doing. How would I know? I am an old, diseased woman.'

After that, Parveen had abandoned his task, gone off to clear his head. Riding fast down the wide highway, he was in Barwala in minutes. He slowed down as he saw the government school, came to a stop, looked left and right, slowly began to roll again, came upon a four-way crossing, stopped abruptly, forcing cars and bikes behind him to swerve, their drivers letting out a stream of abuse. Unfazed, Parveen waited for his instinct to tell him which way to turn. I have a child riding pillion, a child I am kidnapping … not left, not towards the city … not straight, not into the heart of the village. Even if the Bawana gang is involved, they won't move the children through their own village …

Parveen turned right. His instincts approved—the road opened up: farmland, a large pond, fallow land piled with garbage, a grid of under-construction high-rises. He felt good. He picked up speed.

A few metres before he hit the big crossing at the Western Yamuna Canal Road, Parveen screeched to a halt in front of a petrol pump. A narrow dirt road went past the pump, running parallel to the canal road, going towards the Bawana Industrial Area, Delhi's border with Haryana. All around him was wasteland and garbage. He rode into the pump, stopped in front of an emaciated-looking attendant.

'Do you have CCTV at the entry?' Parveen said.

'Why? Who is asking?'

'Police, motherfucker, who else?'

The old man pointed at the small 24/7 shop at the back of the pump and looked away. He was not in the mood to be insulted by cops.

Parveen entered the shop, flashed his ID.

'How long do you keep your CCTV files?'

'I am not sure, sir,' said the young attendant, with a fidgety mix of fear and awe at having to speak to the police.

'Well, how about …' Parveen took out his diary, checked the dates. '7 April.'

It took the attendant less than a minute to find the file.

'Here you go, sir.'

Parveen strode over to the attendant's side of the counter and took charge of the mouse. He speeded through the timeline and stopped at 9 a.m. He scrolled carefully from there on. The camera showed the entry to the pump. It was of poor quality. Every time a car entered, the glint of the sun reflecting off its windshield blinded the camera. Parveen watched. He hit pause. He looked around and found the refrigerator and got himself a Coke. He hit play. There weren't too many vehicles coming into the pump. When the time stamp read 9:39 a.m., a truck rolled in slowly.

'C'mon, behenchod, move, keep moving,' Parveen muttered under his breath. Then he saw it. A man on a bike appeared behind the truck as it turned into one of the filling lanes. A boy in a school uniform sat behind the man. Parveen felt light-headed. He clicked pause. His face broke into a wolfish grin. He imagined the pleasure of interrogating this man when they caught him. A feeling of pure delight surged through him as he reached into his pocket and retrieved his phone.

Inspector Kumar's path may or may not have crossed SI Parveen's at the intersection of Bawana road and the massive unfinished highway known as UER II, or locally as the canal road. But, at around the same time that Parveen took a right after Barwala towards the canal, Kumar went straight down the crossing towards Bawana village, past the factory sheds, past Bhagirathi Motors, Lucky Car Accessories and countless other workshops, many of which served as hubs for the immense network of car thieves in Delhi.

Kumar was driving. Next to him sat Colonel, happy to be in the badlands. In the back seat, Meera sat alone, secretly nursing a grudge. Kumar turned his head and smiled at her.

'Not scared, are you?'

'Why? Should I be?'

'No, no, we are safe, but still, this is the lion's den.'

'More like a snake pit,' Colonel muttered.

Kumar and Colonel had concurred it would be good to have Meera around. For one, she seemed like the brightest prospect, since, well, ever. It would be great training for her, a meeting with the head of one of Delhi's most notorious gangs. Kumar felt proud, paternal—showing the talented young kid the ropes—what could be bigger than this? He didn't notice or care that Meera was not happy to be pulled out of her missing children case on a day when she believed she was getting closer than ever to tightening the net around it.

Second, having a woman around for a meeting like this was to offer a bit of distraction, a bit of softening of the situation … or so Kumar hoped.

Of course, Colonel was still walking with crutches, so that was vulnerable too.

Kumar was scared. He could feel it in his body, in the way his hands trembled slightly, in how forced his smile felt, the effort it took for him to speak, to keep up the banter. No one else is scared but me, he thought.

'There,' said Colonel, pointing at a narrow lane on the right, past a two-storey building which said 'Manoj Primary School'.

Kumar took the turn.

Empty plots of land on both sides of the lane, then the high walls of a big house. Soon, an imposing, ornate but commonplace wrought-iron gate loomed into view. Kumar went past the gate and stopped the car along the wall. He took a deep breath. He turned around to face Meera again and forced a smile.

'Let's go.'

The gate was already ajar. Kumar automatically made a note of the cameras, was impressed at how many there were. The man holding the gate was more than six feet tall, long hair streaked golden brown, biceps and belly bulging out of a tight black

T-shirt. He let them in without a word, signalled to them to remain standing, and shut the gate.

They were in a wide, cemented driveway.

'A woman has also come,' the big man said aloud in the direction of the house.

Kumar, Meera and Colonel waited. Kumar stood still with his head bowed, hands clasped behind his back. Colonel leaned on his walking aid, picking his teeth with a fingernail, looking around. Meera stood at attention and bit her lips self-consciously.

Two more men came out from the house. One of them was rubbing his head with a towel. They stared at the three cops.

'Which one is the inspector?' said the man with the towel.

Kumar looked like he was coming out of a reverie.

'Me,' he said, smiling sheepishly under his moustache.

'Why did you bring a woman? How will we frisk her?'

'Why do you need to frisk us?' Kumar asked mildly. 'We have come to talk, we need something, we mean no harm.'

The man with the towel spat on the ground.

'You really think we trust you? Trust the police? Not in this village, you are not welcome. You'll be lucky to leave here alive.'

He went back inside. The cops remained standing, this time flanked by two men staring at them instead of one. Meera was starting to feel uncomfortable. Were those two staring only at her? They had left their phones in the car so she could not even use her usual distraction—pretending to stare at a screen. She looked at Kumar, who had resumed gazing at his feet. Colonel was leaning against the gate for support; it had been a while since he had stood for this long. Meera decided to stare back. She looked from one man to another, with, she hoped, an inscrutable expression.

To her relief, a woman came out of the house. She looked young and strongly built. Her face was covered by her dupatta, revealing only her eyes. She walked briskly towards Meera, started frisking without a word. When she was done, she went back in as abruptly as she had come out, still without a word. The man with the towel said, 'Girl is okay, do those two,' pointing at Kumar and Colonel.

When they were led inside eventually, Kumar realised the building they were facing was one arm of an L-shaped structure with a courtyard. In the centre of the courtyard stood a resplendent peepul tree. Under the tree, a slim old man sat on a red plastic chair. He had closely cropped silver hair partly stained with henna. He was smoking a hookah.

Bawaniya, senior.

Kumar scanned the scene. Eight doors, four along each arm of the L. In front of one stood a large figure, partially hidden in the shadows. Two colossal black buffaloes stood tethered in a corner of the courtyard, under a neem tree, eating from a trough. Next to the buffaloes there was an empty shed with a tin roof. At another end of the courtyard were a mango tree, a neem tree and a structure that looked like a storage room or a garage.

While Kumar took it all in, Meera's gaze did not move from the raised earthen platform next to the mango and the neem. It was a wrestling pit, an akhada.

Three red plastic chairs were set out for the cops.

'See here, Inspector, see what you have done,' the old man said in a thin, nasal voice. 'This here is an akhada, a sacred space, we don't allow girls!'

Kumar broke into a big smile.

'Tau!' he said loudly, as if talking to a person hard of hearing. 'She is no ordinary girl, she is a champion wrestler herself, international medallist, a pride of India!'

Meera folded her hands and said a demure namaste.

Bawaniya Sr looked her up and down.

'Is that a good thing?' he said. 'It's worse. In our Indian culture girls don't wrestle. It's obscene. No girl should enter an akhada. How do I know she is not bleeding right now? It's shameful. But, what can I say, these are bad times, bad times. Sit. Tell me why you are here. Since you have contaminated my akhada, will you get me Gangajal to purify it? No? I don't think so.'

The old man stopped to draw breath. The three cops took their seats with relief.

'What happened to this one?' the old man asked, pointing a finger at Colonel.

'Oh, he, you know, he got shot when your son went on a shooting spree outside the court. Remember?'

'Lies, lies, lies,' the old man said. 'My son never did anything like that. He is a simple boy, a good boy, you police are always making things up, you lie about everything. You kidnapped my son, right?' Bawaniya Sr said, pointing another long, bony finger at Kumar.

'I caught him, yes,' Kumar said.

'How dare you show your face here?'

'I'll tell you who gave me the location of your son,' Kumar said. 'I'll give you your rat.'

Kumar kept his eyes on the old man but said nothing more. Under the peepul tree, the shade was cool and deep, the silence drowsy. It was difficult to believe that a few metres away, there was the chaos of a tangled city street, the deafening noise of traffic.

Bawaniya's face had changed, Kumar thought. He looked sharper, less old. Kumar smiled in an idiotic fashion. For Colonel, it was an unspoken signal he had acted on hundreds of times.

'The problem is, your son's case went to a madam judge,' Colonel said.

Bawaniya jerked his head, looked piercingly at Colonel, as if he had forgotten his existence.

'What can I say?' Colonel continued. 'It's the Kal Yug. Her father is a retired judge. Nepotism. That too, a woman. I told your lawyer, I said to him, Vineet, don't even talk to her, don't go to her chamber. Vineet is young, he doesn't know the ways of the world. He went to make his appeal, it only made things worse. Your son could have been out on bail. You were there at Vineet's wedding? I know him through Sachin … Sachin's uncle is related to me, we go back a long way. But Vineet really chose his honeymoon well. Was it your idea?'

Colonel stopped and waited for a reaction.

The old man nodded reluctantly.

'I knew it. Shesh Nag! What a place! Heaven on Earth. Everything is there. Mountains, rivers, lakes, Lord Ram's story laid out on in front of your eyes. It makes you pure! Automatic.'

Colonel closed his eyes and chuckled, as if revisiting the pilgrimage in his mind's eye.

'The rivers there carve the rocks in the image of Ram Bhagwan. Isn't that right, Inspector saab?' Colonel turned to Kumar, who kept his dopey grin plastered on his face. 'You remember the time we went there together? In our big Scorpio? Then on the ponies? At Shesh Nag, we went in to bathe?'

'You can bathe there?' the old man said.

'Oh yes!'

'Water's clean?'

'What are you saying, tau, it's the cleanest water you've ever seen,' Colonel said, enjoying himself, reeling it in. 'Around you, mountains, forests, pure air, pure water, giant trees.'

Kumar's smile constricted into a grim, tight line. He leaned forward in his chair.

'I will give you the informer in your organisation,' he said. 'He didn't just give up your son. Remember, last month, when your big consignment of guns was captured? The ones hidden under grain in a truck? That was him too. How else do you think we knew where to look?'

Kumar's plan needed a pawn. He had chosen one with care. The man, a known killer—what the police call a 'sharpshooter'—really was a snitch and had given the police the gun haul, but he certainly had no hand in getting Vijay Bawaniya caught. Mix a truth and a lie and the lie becomes the truth. Of absolute importance for Kumar was that the snitch's phone was already in the system as a known member of the Bawaniya gang. It was under constant surveillance, including a bug that gave them access to the encrypted apps.

Yet, Kumar's conscience nagged at him. These days, he thought, he could not take a step without feeling like he was doing something wrong, something that would come back to haunt him.

'Plus,' he said, 'I offer my help and influence in keeping your son safe in jail and in court. I can ask my network to tell me if there is ever a threat to his life. I have, as you know by now, a very informed network.'

Kumar paused to see if the old man was following.

'I need something in return. I have a plan that will make you happy. Do you want to hear it?'

Kumar pulled out the crime scene photo of Jyoti Dhurwa and held it up.

'The girl was killed in March,' he said. 'She is poor, an orphan, she had no one. She worked in the house of a businessman you know well. She was being raped by him. He killed her. Threw her down from the top of his house. Then he asked you to kill the only person who knew anything about the matter. His driver.'

'What is all this?' the old man said. 'Why are you saying kill, kill, kill? I am a poor old man, I know nothing about killing.'

'What word would you prefer, tau?' Colonel interjected. 'Sent heavenwards? Gone to Kailash? Fuck that. You are a killer. I am a person who chases killers. Why be shy? But let me tell you about one person who was not killed. Your son. Do you know why? Because this man you are talking to right here? This inspector? He is not the kind of police you know. He is an honourable man. That night, it would have taken nothing for any of us to put an end to your son. You know that, right? But not a single bullet touched him. Because of this man. When he tells you he will protect your son, I suggest you listen to him.'

Kumar laid out the plan.

'Sounds good?' he said. 'You get to do what you want with your snitch, but only after the call goes through and the conversation is on tape. Once we give you the signal that we've got our target, you can grab your snitch.'

The old man's eyes were closed. He leaned back in his chair. Meera thought he had fallen asleep, but his fingers were tapping a slow beat on the armrest. She felt suffocated by the silence, drowsy from the heat. Colonel lit a beedi, and the sound of the match striking the box made the old man open his eyes.

The sharp smell of sulphur stung through Meera's listlessness. She looked at Bawaniya, who was staring at Colonel, murder in his eyes. Colonel took a drag, looking for all the world like he was sitting in a beautiful garden to pass the time listening to birdsong. Kumar had not taken his eyes off Bawaniya.

'Yes,' the old man nodded. 'Yes, it is agreed.'

As they were leaving, the old man spoke again.

'Inspector,' he said, his voice suddenly clear and steady.

Kumar stopped and turned to look at him.

'Did you ever hear the story of the man who fell from a tall building, and as he passed each floor, he said to himself, well, so far so good ...'

'Then he smashed into the ground and became a bloody pulp?' Kumar finished the sentence and smiled. 'Yes, I have. It's a good one.'

Back on the highway, Colonel said, 'We should take the old man out.'

Kumar glanced at Meera, laughed and said, 'The things this man says.'

Colonel laughed too, and lit another beedi.

'Imagine,' Kumar said, 'if you were in the US Army, posted in Iraq or Afghanistan or wherever it is the US are at war, and you came upon an enemy house like that one. All you need to do is fix the location on your GPS, call in an airstrike. Next thing you know, a drone comes, a flash in the sky, and boom! The whole compound is up in flames.'

'What's this? You saw it in a movie last night?' Colonel said.

'No, boss, it's how they do it, I saw it on a news clip.' Kumar turned to Meera.

'At your training, did you fly drones?'

'No, sir,' Meera said. 'I have never even seen one.'

'Look at this now,' Kumar said, 'We are using drones in every district, but they still haven't included it in the training module.'

For a while, they drove silently. Colonel dozed off. As they passed Azadpur Mandi, navigating past the carts piled high with mausambi, melons, bananas and mangoes, Meera said, 'What now?'

'What?' Kumar said.

Colonel opened his eyes.

'What now? With all this, the man, the murder, the gangster, what now?' Meera said.

Kumar offered no reply.

Akhilesh poured himself a drink.

A part of him said, no, stop.

Another part of him said, fuck that, you deserve it.

He had gone through eight bodies. The first one, ah, he had made such a fine incision, a carefully drawn straight line, the slightest deviation to bypass the navel, the upper layer of the skin split like a jacket being unzipped. It was a fine body too. Young, athletic man with good muscles, clean fingernails, shaved chest sprouting a stubble. If you didn't see the left side of his skull, you would not know he was dead.

He tackled the man's wife next. That was okay too. The baby he did not want to touch. He had done his share of babies. There was no reason to do an autopsy on this one, the beautiful, innocent one-year-old with skin like polished metal. All three were on that bike, none wearing a helmet.

The law is cruel, he thought, to insist on cutting up babies when there was no need. He had made the first incision, then sewed it up to look like an autopsy had been done. He had patted the good side of the girl's head, murmured, 'Sorry, little girl.'

By the sixth body, he was aching all over. He felt pity for himself—I'm a small old man, how long can I do this? His gloves were torn but he did not notice. The seventh body was bloated and decomposed. A gift from hell. Or a punishment for self-pity. He barely paid attention, hacked right through it.

People think if you wound yourself long enough, you get immune to it. Akhilesh had been told this theory many times, by many different people, including his father, who was also a sweeper at the morgue, and who had taught him the vocation. It was true in many ways, but the smell of a decomposed body never really loosened its grip on you.

He had resolved not to drink today, but once the smell drilled its way down his nostrils, he knew he had to. His father had died of cirrhosis of the liver. He was a drunkard, the fool, god rest his soul. His son, whom he had inducted into this netherworld trade, so steady with the knife, who had helped carry his first body when he was fourteen, done his first autopsy when he was seventeen, gone too! He could not really understand what the doctors told him, but he did understand that one reason his son did not survive was that the liver was not in good condition. He was just thirty-four. Today was the day he passed. That is why Akhilesh had promised himself he would not drink.

Ah, what the hell, he thought, swallowing a peg of cheap, warm whisky in one gulp. He lit a beedi. He squinted from the smoke, saw a man open the gates of the mortuary and walk in. He knew it was police at first glance. White shirt soaked with sweat, blue jeans, black boots. He spat. He did not want to talk to the police. As the policeman walked deeper inside the compound, looking around to find his bearings, Akhilesh saw something else. He saw a man who looked like his son. Small-built, thin, hair slightly long and swept back, long, thin nose, kind eyes—a beautiful boy. He took a long drag of the beedi, threw the stub on the floor and walked to the door of his room. He called out to Constable Zeeshan.

When the boyish policeman asked him about the body with the metal plate, Akhilesh had no trouble remembering. He even refused the bottle of whisky, at first. They went inside the morgue. The familiar smell of incense, rotting flesh, bleach. The light reflecting in odd waves off the steel refrigerators and beds.

Akhilesh scanned the register—3, 4, 5, 6, 7, 8 April. On 9 April, he stopped. He put a stubby finger, nails long decayed and fused with the flesh, on a barely legible entry. Zeeshan, his heart jumping with adrenaline, took the register close to a light. Barely managing to hold on to his phone with the other hand, he took a series of photographs. He took out his notebook, jotted down the MLC number. He would use it to pull the autopsy report from the state records.

It had taken him a couple of days, going from morgue to morgue in the atrocious heat, but Zeeshan had found Rajesh. Or the trace that remained of the man who was once Rajesh. In his excitement, he squeezed the hand of the morgue sweeper and said thank you.

To Zeeshan's alarm, the man began to cry.

24

Kumar was so overjoyed to see the CCTV grab of the kidnapper, he almost hugged Parveen. Good hormones flooded through him. He could feel it. He was on top of the world. He strode towards the ACP's office, took the steps two at a time.

Sofia studied the photograph.

'You have a team ready? Do you need more people? Is there a jurisdiction issue?'

'If you clear it, madam, no issue. I have a friend at the Crime Branch in Outer, we can always do a joint op, everyone will be happy.'

'Except Missing Persons, that is.'

'Yes, they deserve it.'

'Yes, they really do. You will have to prioritise the child snatcher. He is on the field, he is active, we can't wait. When we finish with this, we move on to our killer.'

'Yes, ma'am.'

They would stay put at the station, he thought. As he took the stairs, he bumped into Zeeshan, who was racing up.

'I was looking for you, you haven't been taking my calls. Again!'

'What's the matter?'

'I found the body! Rajesh, the driver, you are right, he is dead, his body washed up as an unidentified, the morgue at GTB did the autopsy, here's the report, see? Unidentified. Metal plate in the shin bone, age, height, weight, everything matches.'

'May Allah shine his light on you, my brother,' Kumar said.

On 22 May, a ragingly hot day, SI Meera made her way through the weary, restless crowds at the main market in Shahbad Dairy. It was 8:45 a.m..

She wore an ill-fitted salwar-kameez that hid the shape of her body. A dupatta covered her head. She had turned into her mother! She passed Parveen, drinking tea at a pavement shop. He winked at her, sweating profusely.

She clutched her phone in a sticky palm. Already she could feel a hundred pairs of eyes, all male, scanning her. Or perhaps she was only imagining it. This was no place to be still. The crowd jostled, pushed and shoved. The street was choked with garbage and excavated mud. Feral pigs sat in the sludge. Cows nudged past them. The air was thick with flies. At least it was not mosquito season. No dengue or chikungunya. When the school came into view, with its high walls and barbed wire fencing, Meera stopped next to a cart piled high with bananas and pretended to talk on her phone.

Inspector Kumar drove himself into the alley with difficulty. He parked near the school but stayed in the car. He took a sip of cold water from a flask and dabbed some on his face and neck. The information they got from Dairy station, where their target was already known as an alcohol smuggler, was that his regular business haunt was a storage unit a lane away from the school building. With the summer holidays on, his presence in the area, the police guessed, was not because he wanted to pick up children but to attend to his other occupation.

About twenty metres down the road from Kumar, Sushil waited astride his motorbike, phone to his ear. Perhaps he too was pretending, Meera thought.

Das was on the terrace of a narrow three-storey house facing the school. The building housed the NGO that had helped the police put together the list of missing persons in the area. They were the only civilians who knew what was going on, knew the street below them was full of police in plainclothes, waiting for a tall, muscular young man with clean-shaven, short-cropped hair with fades on the sides like you get in the military, probably with shiny aviator-type sunglasses, riding a bike with the number DL1C4837.

The man was in the area, this much was certain.

His vehicle had crossed a border nakabandi at 7:43 a.m. Outer district Crime Branch had immediately deployed two men to the school area and two to his mother's house, the old woman suffering from stomach cancer.

Fourteen more policemen and women had reached the location in ones and twos, but the bike was yet to make an appearance.

Meera prayed he would come. She wanted it badly. It was a familiar feeling to her, the pre-competition knot in the stomach, the winning tunnel in the brain that blanked out images, memories, thoughts, people, sights and sounds, till it was wholly consumed by only those stimuli necessary to the task at hand. If that child-lifter appeared, she knew she would see him through the crowd like a hawk sees its prey from high up in the sky.

There was a great swirl of people, walking, buying, selling, smoking, staring. She saw a woman exit a house, crying. A drunk man was being dragged by another drunk into the mouth of a bylane when yet another man, a burly one, pushed them out of the way. The two drunkards fell on the street laughing.

Two young boys started a savage fist fight. Sushil got off his bike, his eyes on the boys, hesitating between his instinct to intervene and his training, which said to stay put.

Meera looked away, towards her left. He was on his bike, stationary, staring straight ahead. Even from thirty metres away, through the crowd, she had no doubt.

What was he waiting for?

With a start, Meera realised he was looking straight at her. She froze. Shit, shit, shit. Was there a policeman behind him? With great effort, she forced herself to look away.

'What are you doing, lady, are you buying?' shouted the banana-seller, gesticulating at her. With trembling fingers she made the call to Das.

'He's here, to my left, where the road bends. Maybe he's seen me, I don't know, who's behind him? If he's seen me, he'll turn back …' Even as the first words came out of Meera's mouth, Das pressed the button on the police app that sent out an alert to the phones of every member of the team that the target had been spotted.

Sushil rolled his bike out on the street, smooth and steady. Kumar stepped out of his car. The man went past on his bike, threading his way through the crowded street.

Meera felt the blood return to her hands and legs. She took quick strides, keeping the target in view. Ahead, Sushil was manoeuvring his bike towards them. One, two, three, four, five, six steps … Sushil had blocked the way.

The man on the bike spat out a curse. Then he took a proper look at the plainclothes policeman blocking his way. The truth hit him. He dropped his bike and sprang away to make a run for it. Neither Meera nor he saw Kumar's big fist coming. The punch got him on the collarbone. The man spun in surprise, tried to pivot on his heel, faltered, tripped and hurtled straight into Parveen, who had come running up from his location, following Das's bird's-eye view. He grabbed the man classically, one hand on his arm, one gripping his neck, using all his strength. The man squealed in pain.

'You motherfucker, you steal kids? We are going to shred you to pieces,' Parveen hissed.

Kumar grabbed the other arm.

A young boy, who had been watching intently, started running down the street in glee, shouting, 'Thief, thief, they've caught a thief, he steals kids!'

Kumar heard the voice trail off. Even in the heat of the moment, alarm bells tolled in his head. 'Move him to the car fast, get out of here,' he said.

The crowd began to fuse into one around them. Shouts went up: Thief! Child stealer! Hit him! Don't let him get away! Kill him!

A young man broke away from the pulsating mob, leaped at them, landed a glancing blow on the apprehended man. Parveen reached for his gun.

'No, no,' Kumar whispered urgently, 'don't do that, keep moving.'

The crowd was inching closer.

On his perch on the balcony, Das recognised a strange sensation, something he vaguely remembered feeling before but could not quite place. His mind was working at a frenetic pace, but he found it difficult to hang on to a thought or to make his body listen to his mind. He would have liked to make a call to 100 about the mob build-up, followed by another call to the Outer District HQ. He thought of Meera. An image unspooled in his head of his own heroic act, how he would jump into the throng and protect Meera, if not the whole team. Maybe he would fire shots in the air and command the mob to disperse and they would. Except, his legs refused to cooperate. He watched as the mob swallowed the team. His hands seemed weighted down by boulders.

Meera felt a man's hand jab her hard in the crotch. Another hand furiously groped her left breast. She propelled herself backwards, stamping her heels hard, hoping to crush a few toes, driving her left elbow behind her. The hand on her breast went away. Someone was pulling at her hair, her dupatta. She wanted to scream till her throat burst. Instead, she held on tight to the child-lifter, trying to shield him with her body, inching, inching, towards where or what she did not know, even though Kumar's car must have been less than thirty feet away. They were behind a wall of sound, people baying for blood, the inspector saying, 'It will be alright, it will be alright, hold on.' A blow landed on Meera's neck. Another on her head.

Gunshots rang out. The sound of sirens, a madly honking car. Meera felt the weight of the mob lift away from her. She blinked away the stinging sweat in her eyes to look in the direction of the noise. Das. Using the spare set of keys the inspector had left with him for exactly this kind of an emergency, he had managed to bring Kumar's car through the crowd. He had his gun out.

Kumar grabbed the door. 'In, in, in, in,' he urged his team. Meera went first, pulling the kidnapper in with her, followed by Parveen. Kumar slammed their door and got into the front. The mob surged back. Meera turned to the kidnapper, who was sobbing uncontrollably, and smashed his head into his knees.

'No, no,' Kumar said, 'Madam, no revenge.'

She disregarded him. Through the bloody fog of violence, she had been struck by an idea. She grabbed the kidnapper by the nape.

'Listen to me,' she snarled. 'Listen to me. These men, they don't really get the evil you are. But I am a mother, I have three children, and I am right now not a policewoman, I am an animal who wants to save her babies, do you understand? What I want to do more than anything else is throw you out of the car and let those people rip you apart.' She yanked his head up.

The man stared, eyes wide in terror.

'Do you understand?'

He nodded, mouth open, tears streaming down his face.

'Who do you work for? Names, numbers. Where do you take the children? Tell us now, now, now …' Meera slapped him. 'Or I shove you out and your head gets pounded into the street. They will have to scrape off parts of your brain.'

'I'll tell you, please, please drive.'

A tangle of hands thumped and slapped the sides and windows of the car. The man began to speak. Kumar whispered to Das, 'Move, now.' Das eased forward, one foot on the clutch, one foot on the accelerator, one lurch at a time.

They heard the sirens, the metallic boom of a voice speaking through a megaphone, saw people start to run away.

The man finished talking as Das drove past the gates of Delhi Technological University. Kumar stopped recording. Meera loosened her grip on his hair.

'Water …' he croaked. Parveen, still breathing raggedly, eyes bulging and sweat dripping from his face, punched him in the ribs with a sickening crunch.

'Enough!' Kumar barked.

He called Sofia.

'We have the child-lifter,' he said. 'I've sent you a recording of his confession. He has given us names and multiple holding locations. Delhi, Haryana, UP.' Kumar imagined that he could hear ACP Ahmed's joy over the line. This was going to be big. A multi-agency crackdown. Her career was about to soar even before it had properly begun. Kumar looked at the man, who was bent over and sobbing uncontrollably, Parveen's hand gripping his neck.

'Ma'am, you have this guy's mother's address in Dairy. Have her sent to holding or else she might get killed in retaliation.'

Kumar felt suffocated. The AC in his car was struggling against the unbearable heat. He rolled his window halfway down and a blast of hot air hit his face. At least he could breathe now.

'Is everyone okay?'

He got no reply. He dialled Sushil. He remembered losing him in the crowd. He got through on the second try. Sushil was being driven to GTB Hospital, minor injuries. He wailed that his bike was badly damaged. The call was abruptly interrupted when Das braked hard, stopping millimeters from the bus ahead of him. Kumar's phone slid out of his hand.

'Behenchod!' Meera screamed. She punched the headrest behind Das. 'Can't you at least drive properly?'

They had stopped at the red light near the long saffron-and-white complex of Rohini Prisons. Kumar asked the shell-shocked Das to move over and took the wheel. They had a long way to go, at least an hour more through this volcanic weather. Kumar passed his cold flask of water around. Das took a long drink and passed it to Meera, who took a disciplined sip, passed it to Parveen. The big cop glugged from the flask, maintaining his crushing grip on the kidnapper's hand, their squelchy, slippery fingers interlocked. He offered the man the flask, grinned and upturned what little was left in the flask on his own head.

At Hauz Khas, they made quite the entry. Kumar, Meera and Parveen, red eyes puffy, clothes torn, dripping sweat, hair standing in unruly clumps. A tall, brawny man with a white hood over his head, his fingers interlocked with Kumar's fingers on one side and Parveen's on the other. ACP Sofia was waiting for them.

Two constables hurried up to Kumar and Parveen, took the arrested man off their hands, led him to the lock-up. Sofia and the other cops burst into applause.

Kumar saluted Sofia.

'At ease,' Sofia said. 'Congratulations on a brilliant arrest, Inspector. Today all of you have done truly heroic acts, truly good. I am very, very, proud of you.' Sofia was grinning. 'All of you need to visit the hospital immediately.'

She took Kumar aside, trying not to flinch at the stink.

'Massive op underway. Twelve locations. Even the commissioner called. We got news from one location already, recovered six boys.'

Kumar nodded. He leaned closer to her ears and said softly, 'Ma'am, when I am back, make the call.'

25

Kumar checked his watch. 8:35 p.m. He wondered whether he would get home tonight. He had been living at the station for the past three days, sleeping in the room behind his office. Zeeshan was sleeping inside the office. Parveen, Das, Sushil and Hari Singh were resting in their shared room at the guest house in the police colony attached to the South District headquarters. Meera was on her own in a room in the women-only section. Kumar made a call to Hari Singh and entered the technical surveillance room. There was no one there. Computers hummed. Audio graphs ebbed and spiked on the screens. Large black headphones lay scattered on the tables. What was this? A team dinner? They could have left one person in here, Kumar thought, and dialled Zeeshan. He took a seat. The AC in the room had been cranked up high. In ten minutes, Zeeshan entered the room, accompanied by a guilty-looking technician.

'No crimes happen between 8:35 and 9 p.m., is it?' Kumar asked the man, smiling. The man laughed uncomfortably.

'No, yes, I mean, what it is, there's a birthday …' he started to say.

'Don't worry, no harm done. This number is on your Red List.' Kumar held up his phone to show the number. 'Known gang member. Let's look at its activity, put it up on the screen. I am expecting a call.'

'Sir,' said the technician, and got to work.

'These recordings don't fail, do they? Kumar asked. 'Ever have malfunctions?'

He was nervous.

'No, sir, I can't remember any since I began doing this. It's pretty solid. If there's a problem, it automatically switches to backup.'

'How long have you been working here?'

'Three years.'

'That's a long time. I've never seen you before.'

The technician laughed. 'You are a busy man, sir. I was there in the morning when you came back with that bastard kidnapper. Congratulations, sir. You are a brave man, sir.'

Kumar grunted and fell silent. The technician did not know it, but the most effective way to end a conversation with Kumar was to praise him.

Kumar sat and touched his nose. It hurt too much. His neck was in a brace. He watched as the number came up on the screen. It was idle. The location was triangulated to Karkardooma.

Tarun Srivastava had guests over. More precisely, they were his wife Neha's friends. He could not stand them. One was a doctor-couple—neighbours—who were monopolising the conversation, protesting about how the essentials in an Indian hospital were made in China. The man was explaining to Neha what a canula was, how many different varieties there were and how, of course, they were all made in China.

Soon they would turn to him, ask him why he didn't start making things like that, since he was into plastic manufacturing. He had a good mind to tell them to shove their canulas up their holes. Tarun Srivastava was bored. He chewed on a piece of paneer tikka but did not taste a thing. He wished he could go to his room, quietly watch a movie. The warm glow of a good whisky was being wasted sitting here.

'Why don't you make canulas, Tarun?' His wife's nasal drawl put him on edge.

His phone rang. A voice identified herself as ACP Sofia. He remembered her of course. Petite, thick lips, high cheekbones. He felt horny for her. He smiled to himself. Anything to be able to excuse himself from the gathering, even better if it was a pretty woman calling. He gestured to his guests, left the living room and went into his office.

'Yes, ACP Sofia, you have such a nice name. Has anyone told you that? And how come you are calling me at this hour?'

'I have really good news for you,' Sofia said.

'Good news? Tell me?' Suddenly, Tarun Srivastava was not feeling so sure.

'We've managed to track Rajesh, your old driver,' Sofia said, her voice calm but cheerful. 'It took an incredible amount of work, but we did it.'

There was a pause.

'How?' Srivastava said.

Sofia thought she could hear him faltering.

'I mean, how did you catch him?'

'Oh, that's a long story,' Sofia said. 'So many teams were out looking for him, it was only a matter of time. I know you were upset with us, but we took the case seriously. How long can a man run? But, anyway, we can tell you about it in person soon. They'll reach Hauz Khas station by early tomorrow morning.

We would be most obliged if you could come in around 9 a.m., so we know to ask the right questions.'

'Yes, sure, alright, I'll do that.'

'You don't sound too happy!' Sofia tinged her voice with a playful girlishness.

Tarun Srivastava softened.

'I am happy you've caught the killer,' he said, ' just that you've reminded me of the tragedy, reminded me of the horrible death of a girl who was like our daughter.'

As Sofia ended the call, a line from Shakespeare came to her:

Would he not stumble? Would he not fall down,
Since pride must have a fall …

She wondered which play it was from. She felt heady with anticipation. He would stumble, of this she was sure.

Umesh Garg loved nothing more than discipline. His stint in the army had been short, only six years before he had been discharged because of an injury, but it had left an indelible impression on him, and his life.

He woke up at six. It took only two rings of the alarm on his phone before he was up; he never hit the snooze button, which recourse, to him, was a sign of weakness. He started his mornings with a hundred surya namaskars, followed by a few minutes of yogic breathing, chanting and meditation. He ate two slices of toast without butter, a banana, half a cup of oats mixed with warm milk and eight soaked almonds every single day for breakfast. He almost never ate outside if he had a choice; his wife packed him lunch and a snack for the day. At night, dinner was at home, no matter how late he got. His wardrobe was strictly limited to solid or striped formal shirts, blue or black formal trousers, or stiffly ironed kurta-pajamas. He was never late for an appointment.

It did not bother him that Tarun Srivastava was his exact opposite, always late, always eating out, disorganised, lazy, louche. He simply accepted that it was his duty to streamline Mr Srivastava's life. A duty, he could proudly say, he fulfilled with great precision and skill.

He closed the main door of the house softly, cutting off the warm sound of laughter and people talking at once. He checked his watch and smiled. It was eight o'clock. He would be home earlier than usual today, maybe even in time to join his wife and children for dinner. Garg eased his car out of the grounds but did not drive away immediately. He parked it by the side of the road, watched the gates being drawn back together by the guard and lit a cigarette. This too was part of his daily routine. A single cigarette at the end of the work day, no more.

About forty-five minutes later, less than fifteen minutes from home, he was humming along to a devotional song, wondering what was for dinner. As he approached the brief chaos that always surrounded Shakurpur metro station—autorickshaws, buses, cars, cycles, bikes, all jostling for space—he began to slow down.

His eyes caught a flash of it in the side mirror on his left before the bike crashed into his car with a rude jolt and skittered onto the street before him. He braked hard. Furious, he stepped out of the car to see what had happened. A thin, tall man with a ponytail lay writhing on the street, next to an older, balding man with a walking stick. The tires of the fallen bike were still in spin. A crowd was gathering.

It did not bother Garg. He knew how to take care of situations. The thin man jumped up and began to wail. 'That guy almost killed us! He probably killed my old uncle!' He pointed at the old man lying next to the bike. Two men were kneeling next to him. A woman said, 'Let me take a look, I'm a doctor.'

Garg looked at the old man and took out his phone.

'I'm going to call the police,' he said. He gestured at the younger man. 'You are drunk, you came and crashed into my car. You are not going anywhere.'

Garg dialled 100, gave his location and filed his complaint.

'He's okay, a little shaken,' said the woman kneeling next to the old man in a loud voice.

'Yes, call the police, call the police, you with your fancy car. You would have killed us.' The thin man turned to someone in the crowd and said, 'Didn't you see it? Didn't you see how he was driving? Did you see what speed he came at? With so many pedestrians around?'

A man in the crowd nodded. 'Yes, it's true, I saw it, he was speeding.'

Garg looked at the thin man calmly. 'You can say what you have to say when the police come.'

'He's going to run away!' the man said hysterically. He leaped towards Garg, grabbed him by his shirt.

Garg felt his composure slipping a little. 'Let me go, behenchod!' he hissed, 'Do you know who I am?'

'He's going to make a run for it! Don't let him get into the car!' the man said.

Garg slapped the pony-tailed man hard in the face. He fell back on the ground, howling.

The older man got up. He walked with a limp. He said, 'First you hit us with your car, now you are raising your hand? Are you seeing this?' he appealed to the crowd. Cars honked furiously around them. A man in the crowd shouted, 'Take his keys away from him!'

Garg gripped his keys tightly with one hand and searched for his phone with the other, but could not find it.

'I'm going nowhere,' he said. 'I'm going nowhere. Stay away from me. Let the police come, it's no one else's business, I've called the police myself.'

A murmur went through the crowd, but Garg could not decipher what was being said. 'Look, no one is hurt,' he said loudly, spreading his arms as if to keep people away from him. 'Let's not do anything foolish, there's no need for a crowd.'

A single policeman on a bike arrived with his siren going. Garg was relieved.

'What's happening here?' the constable said, speaking into his radio to give his location and ask for backup.

The old man came limping forward, leaning on his walking stick. 'Janab, I am staff, Crime Branch.' He held out his ID. 'SI Colonel Singh.'

'Sir,' said the constable. 'Everything alright?'

Garg was a little surprised at this. He came forward to speak, but was shushed by the constable.

'Let him speak first.'

'Me and my nephew, we were passing by on his bike. This man came speeding out of nowhere and hit us from the side. We fell badly, but by god's grace we got saved, my nephew has great control over the bike,' said Colonel. 'This man could have killed us.'

'Wait,' thundered Garg, 'what is this shit? You are lying! What do you want? Money?'

'You wait, sir,' shouted the constable. 'You'll get your chance to speak.' He turned back towards the policeman. 'Are you okay?'

'Yes, by god's grace. He slapped my nephew. He was going to hit me as well. We need to file an FIR for assault.'

Another police vehicle drew up. Garg began to walk back towards his car, but the constable held up a hand and stopped him. 'Give me your keys.'

'Why? Why should I give you the keys? What right do you have? I think some sisterfucker stole my fucking phone while these bastards were trying to get me killed. I have another phone in the car, I need it.'

Two policemen emerged from their car, walked straight up to Garg and grabbed his hands.

'You are going nowhere, brother,' one of them said, 'you are coming with us.'

'Fuck you,' Garg said. 'You don't know who I am. I'll get each one of you suspended. I know every DCP in Delhi. Get me my phone, you'll see.'

'Sure,' said one of the policemen, 'you can tell us about it at the station, but first we need to file the FIR. You assaulted someone. Everyone here is saying so. You almost killed someone with your car. We can't let you get into the car again. My colleague will bring it.'

Garg took a deep breath. 'Okay, fine, but let me get my phone, call my lawyer. Here, you can have the keys. Which station are we going to?'

'Punjabi Bagh, but hold on, you stay here with my colleague, I'll get your phone. We can't take a chance. What if you have a gun in the car? Do you have a gun in the car?'

'Yes, I do, it's licensed.'

'There, see? You understand? Let me get your phone. Where is it?'

'The small storage box between the front seats, behind the gearbox.'

The policeman walked to Garg's car, found the phone, switched it off, pocketed it. He walked back.

'There's no phone there, sir.'

'But that's impossible!'

'There's no phone. We can't waste any more time. The sooner we get to the police station, the better for all of us. You can look for your phone there once we have processed you, once our inspector clears it. Let's go.'

Colonel looked at the time. Almost an hour had passed since they hit Garg's car with their bike. They would be able to tie him up for at least four more hours without a phone. Put him in a processing cell at the back of the station, forget about him for a few hours. It would buy them enough time.

It was 10:08 p.m. The phone had been idle the whole time. No calls made or received. No messages. Even WhatsApp was idle. Whenever the call came through, Kumar was sure that it would be via an encrypted system. Everyone knew it was child's play to listen in on normal calls. No one would risk it on this number.

Kumar expected Tarun Srivastava to panic after ACP Sofia's call. He would call Umesh Garg, but the manager had been removed from the playing board. Kumar had studied Srivastava closely. He would wager any amount of money that with Garg unreachable, Srivastava would not do the intelligent thing. He would not call his lawyer, whom he had no regard for. He would not call his politician uncle about a criminal mess, the uncle must have drilled that much sense into him. Tarun Srivastava had nothing but contempt for everyone around him, everyone except Garg. He walked on air, believed he was untouchable. Now he had a ghost tapping him on his shoulder, mocking his plans. The man would not know how to navigate such a nasty surprise. He would react with rage.

He would, Kumar hoped, call whatever number he usually called to get in touch with the Bawaniya gang. If he did that, he would be given a different number and told that it was a secure line to the head of the organisation. He would be told Bawaniya

Sr wanted to speak only to him, leader to leader. The number given to Srivastava would be the same one that was up on the screen in the surveillance room in Hauz Khas.

The informant who carried the phone had already been briefed by Bawaniya Sr, lured to his own downfall—that is, if that mad old man had kept his word; how could he be trusted?

It was a lot of assumptions. A plan that hinged on the word of a half-crazy, half-senile leader of a chaotic, self-detonating criminal group. Suddenly it seemed absurd to Kumar, doomed to fail, a horribly flawed scheme from his fevered and limited imagination. He would have to face the embarrassment, meet his fate head on, live out the rest of his days as a clerk at PHQ at best.

Sofia had slipped into the surveillance room soon after making her call. The room was stuffed with people.

At 10:14 p.m., the informant's phone rang. A WhatsApp call. The oxygen was sucked out of the room. Fifteen pairs of eyes stared at the screen like a pride of lionesses looking at a baby deer. Sofia gritted her teeth so hard it hurt. Only Kumar felt freed from all his burdens. The chatter in his mind had ceased. There was the hint of a smile at the corners of his mouth. On the fourth ring, the informant answered.

'Hello? Who is this?'

There was a long pause.

'I need to speak to the chief.'

It was Tarun Srivastava.

'Yes? Who is this?'

'He is expecting my call.'

'My dear sir, you will have to tell me who you are. The chief gets many calls, I can't hand him the phone unless I know who it is.'

The call got disconnected.

'Teri ma ki!' Parveen screamed in the surveillance room.

There was a collective sigh of disappointment.

Kumar was standing with his eyes closed.

Three minutes passed. The phone rang again. Same number. Tarun Srivastava. The techies had already triangulated it, it came from Hauz Khas, the location radius neatly encompassing the Srivastava house. The number was not known to the police. But there was a plainclothes raiding team outside the Srivastava house, ready to burst in when given the signal and grab every electronic device in the house.

'This is Tarun Srivastava,' said the voice on the phone.

'Yes, yes, the chief said you would call. A minute, sir,' the voice said.

Another voice came on the phone, identified himself to Tarun Srivastava simply as the 'Pradhan'. It was not the voice of Bawaniya Sr.

'You know why I am calling,' Srivastava said.

'It's that driver you asked us to take care of. Rajesh, right?'

'Yes,' Srivastava said. 'You are sure this line is okay to talk on?'

'Of course it is,' snapped the voice from the other end. 'I would not be on it otherwise.'

'Then what the fuck happened?' Tarun Srivastava's voice flared up in rage. 'I told you to get rid of him. Why the fuck is that bhausadikey still fucking alive? Do I not pay you enough? Did I not send you the boy on a fucking platter?'

Kumar could hear the fear in the voice. A sense of deep relaxation flooded through him.

'Talk with respect, brother,' the voice at the other end said. The phone was disconnected. A few seconds later, the number on the screen went offline.

The surveillance room erupted with voices, with the sound of people getting to their feet, of Meera clapping and laughing loudly. Sushil thumped Parveen with a wild, celebratory swing of the arm. Parveen bit his lower lip and glowered at him.

'We got him,' Hari Singh said, almost in disbelief. 'We got him!'

Kumar opened his eyes, took the scene in.

Sofia smiled at him and nodded. She made the call for the raid on the Srivastava house to go ahead.

They had their man. The fool had implicated himself on record, talking to a known assassin under surveillance, admitted to ordering the hit on Rajesh Mondal. They could throw every weapon in their arsenal at Tarun Srivastava and the magistrate would sign off on it. The first thing would be to take his unlisted number and disembowel its history. A thorough search of the house. The family under interrogation. They could even go after Jyoti's aunt and Garg and his family. They would request IT to go through Srivastava's taxes, raid his factories. They already had Sangeeta/Amina's testimony recorded in the presence of a magistrate. Somewhere along the line, Sofia knew, she would leak Jyoti's video to a friend who was the city editor at a major newspaper. For a brief moment, Sofia thought of Srivastava's daughter and felt a tinge of empathy.

It was past midnight when Kumar eased his car into his parking spot. There was something old and familiar, something of childhood and forgotten places in the way the yellow glow of the streetlights lit up parts of the building and cast deep shadows around it. The peepul growing from the wall looked like an otherworldly creature.

Kumar was weary. His mind was playing tricks on him. His body ached. He wanted, more than anything else, to touch his wife, to be touched by her. He wanted to hold her. He had driven home after three nights, technically four, his mind dancing with energy, racing with thoughts of all the things he would tell her, all the successes, how he had worked towards them, how clever and strong and worthy he was, how he had got the children back—forty-three had been rescued on a single day, including Kalicharan, the son of the woman who had come asking for help—how he had caught the vile man who had raped and killed an innocent girl. He thought, it will be like the old days!

His spirits fell. What old days? Whose old days? There were no old days. The old days were lies, he told himself, a tangle of deceit into which he had sucked his wife. There was just this day, and this day was what he had made it.

What had Meera said to the child-lifter in the car? 'They will scrape your brains off the road.'

How did she know? In the first week of his job, Kumar had to help in doing just that, after being called up to the site of a terrible road accident. He had almost quit the force that day.

That's what his relationship with his wife felt like to him. The remains of a bad collision. A collision he had engineered.

He walked up the stairs softly, pulling one knee behind the other with effort, stepping heel to toe with deliberation. He did not want to wake up his wife or son. At the door, he stopped and caught his breath. He listened for any sounds coming from inside the house. Slowly, with one hand braced against the handle in a gentle pull, he turned the key with the other hand. Once inside, he took off his shoes in the dark. By the light of his phone, he made his way silently towards the bedroom. He leaned on the door frame and looked at his wife and his son, sleeping. He stood there for what seemed like a long time.

His wife, her eyes still closed, her voice heavy with sleep, said, 'Prashant? Is it over?'

'Yes,' he said. 'It's over.'

ACKNOWLEDGEMENTS

I am deeply grateful to my wonderful editors Karthika V.K. and Ajitha G.S. for their careful work on this book; Shruti Debi, for her meticulous, generous and insightful guidance from the first draft to the last; Sukumar Ranganathan for allowing me the time and space to follow odd stories in a setting that rarely encourages it; Dr Sudhir Gupta and Dr Indrajit Khandekar for being my guide through the world of autopsies (the 'autopsy report' in this book is Dr Khandekar's professional response to the scenario I presented him with); the many policemen and women who kindly suffered me so I could get a glimpse into their lives, including officers Devender Arya, H.S. Dhaliwal, Suman Nalwa and Ashish Dube; Prawesh Lama for keeping the 'procedure' in 'police procedural' in check; Sujoy Chakravarty and Devalina Mookerjee for always keeping the door to their home open for me (much of this book was written there); Aparajita Bhattacharya for kindly reading the shambolic first draft and giving me just the right words of encouragement to keep at it; and finally, Mandakini Gupta for her deep support through good times and bad, insights, conversations, and sharing with me her immense love and empathy for animals, some of which permeates this book.